"Very rarely does one encounter a novel from contemporary China that transcends the mere story, however spectacular or unheard of, and wrestles so deeply and intimately with the structural truth and secrecy of the way things are. A stunning display of the mimetic power of language and narrative, and through masterful arrangement of sentences seeking and connecting with each other, *Someone to Talk To* invites all of us to rethink the meaning of realism and, for that matter, of literature as such."— XUDONG ZHANG, author of *Postsocialism and Cultural Politics: China in the Last Decade of the Twentieth Century*

Praise for
LIU ZHENYUN

PRAISE FOR *The Cook, the Crook, and the Real Estate Tycoon*

"Liu's fiction is a romp through modern Beijing that pits migrant workers from the provinces against billionaires and officials, making a wry statement about modern China and a thoroughly entertaining book."
—*Kirkus Reviews*

"[An] intricate, dark-hearted crime tale . . . The web of deceptions, double crosses, and betrayals Zhenyun builds into his ambitious, complex novel result in a rich depiction of the criminal underworld."—*Publishers Weekly*

"Those who enjoy Chinese literature will appreciate how the novel openly provides commentary on the disparity between the economic social classes and unscrupulous corruption found in almost any society."
—*Library Journal*

PRAISE FOR *Remembering 1942: And Other Chinese Stories*

"Liu rigorously confronts major facets of contemporary Chinese society with judicious insight and shrewd indictments."—*Booklist*

SOMEONE

TO

TALK

TO

SINOTHEORY

A series edited by Carlos Rojas

and Eileen Cheng-yin Chow

SOMEONE

TO

TALK

TO

A NOVEL

LIU ZHENYUN

Translated by Howard Goldblatt
and Sylvia Li-chun Lin

DUKE UNIVERSITY PRESS
Durham and London
2018

Library of Congress Cataloging-in-Publication Data
Names: Liu, Zhenyun, author. | Goldblatt, Howard, 1939-
translator. | Lin, Sylvia Li-chun. translator.
Title: Someone to talk to: A novel / Liu Zhenyun ; trans-
lated by Howard Goldblatt and Sylvia Li-chun Lin. Other
titles: 880-01 Yi ju ding yi wan ju. English Description:
Durham : Duke University Press, 2018. | Series: Sino-
theory | Includes bibliographical references and index.
Identifiers: LCCN 2017039417 (print)
LCCN 2018000175 (ebook)
ISBN 9780822371885 (ebook)
ISBN 9780822370680 (hardcover : alk. paper)
ISBN 9780822370833 (pbk. : alk. paper)
Classification: LCC PL2879.C376 (ebook)
LCC PL2879.C376 Y52513 2018 (print)
DDC 895.13/52—dc23
LC record available at https://lccn.loc.gov/2017039417

*The English-language publication of this book was
proposed and supported by Changjiang New Century
Culture and Media Ltd. Beijing. Duke University Press
gratefully acknowledges this collaborative support.*

CONTENTS

Carlos Rojas

Anytime you ask me something
I'll still give you a straight answer.
—Yang Baishun, in *Someone to Talk To*

Yang Baishun (a.k.a. Moses Yang, a.k.a. Moses Wu, a.k.a. Luo Changli) is a man of few words, which is to say he is not particularly good at "shooting the breeze"—to borrow Howard Goldblatt and Sylvia Li-chun Lin's translation of a local Henan expression that Liu Zhenyun uses repeatedly in his 2009 novel *Someone to Talk To*.[1] Yang's life, however, is characterized by a series of twists and turns that lend themselves perfectly to Liu Zhenyun's elliptically prolix narrative style, which delights in tracing the complex interrelations of seemingly independent plotlines.

The winner of China's prestigious Mao Dun Prize, *Someone to Talk To* is divided into two halves. The first half follows a tofu peddler named Yang Baishun, who repeatedly changes his name and occupation as the narrative unfolds. He eventually marries a widow, who subsequently leaves him to run off with another man (leaving her five-year-old stepdaughter with Baishun). While Baishun is half-heartedly looking for his estranged wife, his stepdaughter Qiaoling is kidnapped, whereupon Baishun immediately shifts his attention to a desperate search for the girl. The second half of the novel, meanwhile, is set seventy years later and revolves around a thirty-five-year-old man by the name of Niu Aiguo and his attempts to learn about his mother's past. The two halves of Liu's novel have a number of parallels, including the fact that they both feature a "fake" search that subsequently evolves into a real one. Wedged between the male protagonists of each half is the figure of Qiaoling, meanwhile, whom we barely see in person but whose disappearance ends up haunting the remainder of the story.

The narrative style of *Someone to Talk To* and other works by Liu Zhenyun may be viewed as a postmodern twist on Chinese "linked-chapter" novels like the Ming dynasty classics *Water Margin* and *Romance of the Three Kingdoms.* These linked-chapter novels tend to have a distinctive narrative structure that may be likened to a billiards game, in the sense that the main narrative typically follows one character through several episodes until he or she has an encounter with a second character (like a billiard ball colliding with another), whereupon the narrative line then veers off and follows this second character through several more episodes until the second character has an encounter with a third, who then becomes the new object of narrative focus.

In macrostructural terms, Liu Zhenyun's *Someone to Talk To* adopts a version of this billiard-ball structure, in that the first half of the novel follows one character, while the second half follows a different one—who, it turns out, is related to the first in a somewhat mediated manner. In microstructural terms, meanwhile, Liu's novel implodes this traditional narrative structure—and rather than following one figurative billiard ball until it bumps into another, the work instead features many passages that gesture elliptically to the complex chains of reaction produced when various narrative strands simultaneously ricochet off one another. The result is a work that closely tracks individual characters, while at the same time offering a wide-angled panoramic view of the network of the complex chain reactions that end up determining their fate.

Someone to Talk To is the first volume in our Sinotheory series, which will include theoretically informed analyses of Chinese cultural phenomena as well as translations of Chinese literary works that make theoretical interventions in their own right. In this novel, Liu Zhenyun explores the way in which social reality is shaped by the interwoven narrative threads by which we attempt to make sense of our surroundings. At the same time, however, the work also examines the role of dialogue in structuring people's lives, together with the remarkable efforts people often make to find someone in whom they may confide.

Liu Zhenyun, who teaches literature and creative writing at Beijing's Renmin University, is notable not only for a focus on the role of narrative within his works but also for the way in which his works have frequently played a critical role generating social narratives in their own right. Liu's 2007 *I Am Liu Yuejin*, for instance, helped bring attention to the fate of the migrant laborers who increasingly pour into China's cities seeking work. His 2003 novel *Cell Phone*, meanwhile, sparked a national dialogue about confidential (and potentially explosive) private information that is frequently stored on people's cell phones and other digital devices.

Liu began writing fiction in the early 1980s, but his career really began to take off when the director Feng Xiaogang adapted two of Liu's stories (*Working Unit* and *Chicken Feathers Everywhere*) into a popular television series. Now one of China's most successful directors, Feng Xiaogang has adapted several of Liu Zhenyun's other novels into blockbuster movies—including *I Am Not Madame Bovary* (2016), about a woman who is falsely accused by her husband of having an affair; *Remembering 1942* (2012), about a famine in Liu's home province of Henan during the Sino-Japanese War; and *Cell Phone*, about a woman who discovers her husband's infidelity from text messages stored on his cell phone. In an interesting marketing maneuver, Feng Xiaogang's cinematic adaptation of the latter work, which was sponsored by the cell phone company Motorola, was released simultaneously with the original novel itself. *Someone to Talk To*, meanwhile, is also being adapted for the screen. The director is Liu Zhenyun's daughter, Liu Yulin, and the adaptation, which focuses on the second half of the novel, is scheduled to be released on November 11, 2017, which is "singles day" in China—fitting for a work that revolves around themes of loneliness and a continuous search for "someone to talk to."

Note

1 The original Chinese title, *Yi ju ding yi wan ju*, literally means "a [single] sentence is worth ten thousand sentences."

PART I
_____

LEAVING YANJIN

1

Yang Baishun's father was a tofu peddler. Everyone called him Old Yang the Tofu Peddler, though in the summertime he also peddled those bean-starch noodles called *liangfen*. Old Yang and Old Ma, a carter from Ma Village, were friends, though their friendship did not make a whole lot of sense, since Ma was often unkind to Yang. He did not curse or hit him, nor did he cheat him out of any money. No, he just held him in low regard, something that normally would stand in the way of a friendship. But Ma found it necessary to be around Yang when he told a joke. For Yang, when the topic of friends came up, Ma was at the top of the list, while Ma never once claimed the tofu and liangfen peddler from Yang Village to be his friend. No one knew why this was, and people simply assumed that they were friends.

When Yang Baishun was eleven, Blacksmith Li held a birthday celebration for his mother. Li made ladles, cleavers, axes, hoes, scythes, rakes, shovels, door hinges, and other metal implements in his Prosperity Blacksmith Shop. Most blacksmiths tend to be impatient men, but not Li. It took him up to four hours to hammer out a rake tine, but his slow, methodical work produced wares that were second to none. Before quenching, he stamped the word *Prosperity* on all his ladles, cleavers, axes, hoes, scythes, rakes, shovels, and door hinges. He was the only blacksmith for miles around, not because others could not match his skill, but because they were unwilling to put in the effort. People with placid dispositions tend to brood a lot, and brooders never forget a slight. Customers were always coming and going at Li's shop, and there was the danger that a careless comment would offend him. But the only person who could get under his skin was his mother, whose high-strung nature may have been the reason he was so unflappable. At the age of eight, he once took a slice of date cake without asking, for which she hit him on the head with a metal spoon, causing a wound that bled profusely. Most people forget the pain of an injury once it's healed, but he held a grudge against his mother from that day on. Unrelated to the wound itself, the grudge resulted from what she did after she hit him: she talked and laughed as if nothing had happened and went into town with friends to watch an opera. In reality, the grudge was not actually related to trip to the opera. But once he reached adulthood, they never again saw eye to eye on anything. Li was forty when his father died; five years later, his mother went blind. After taking over Prosperity Blacksmith Shop, he continued to tend to her daily needs, but he ignored all her requests. Most blacksmiths prefer a bland, coarse diet. So his blind mother would say things like "This food is tasteless. I want some beef."

"You'll have to wait."

Nothing would happen.

Or, "I'm bored. Yoke the donkey and take me into town, where there's something to do."

"You'll have to wait."

Again nothing would happen. He was not trying to provoke his mother; he just wanted to cure her of her impatience. It was time for her to slow down. He was also afraid that if he gave in to her demands, he would never hear the end of it. But the year his mother turned seventy, Old Li decided to hold a celebration.

"Don't waste your time celebrating the birthday of someone who won't live much longer," she said. "I'll be happy if you'll just treat me a little better." She poked him with her cane. "I wonder what you're up to with this so-called celebration."

"Don't think so much, Mother."

In fact, he was not planning the celebration for her sake. A month earlier, a fat blacksmith from Anhui named Duan had set up shop in town. He called his business Fatso Duan's Blacksmith Shop. Li would not have worried if Duan had turned out to be an impatient man. But he wasn't; like Li himself, Duan was unflappable. He too would take up to four hours to hammer out a rake tine, and that concerned Li. So he decided to show Duan what he was up against by celebrating his mother's birthday. It would be one way to show the newcomer that an out-of-town dragon should never try to outdo a local snake. No one else knew what was behind the birthday celebration. All anyone knew was that Li

4

had not been a filial son, and they assumed he'd had a change of heart. So on the day of the party, they came bearing gifts. Yang and Ma, both friends of Li, were among them. Yang, who had been selling tofu away from the village, arrived late. Since Ma Village was close to town, Ma was on time. Believing that the tofu peddler and carter were friends, Li left the seat next to Ma empty for the tardy Yang. Pleased with his attention to detail, he was surprised by Ma's objection.

"No, you have to seat him somewhere else."

"You two always talk up a storm, so that will liven things up," Li said.

"Will there be liquor?" Ma asked.

"Three bottles at each table, and no cheap stuff," Li replied.

"It's like this—joking with him when he's sober is fine. But as soon as he has a few drinks under his belt, he pours his heart out. It makes him feel good, and I wind up depressed." Ma added, "That has happened way too often."

Li realized that they were not best friends after all. For Ma, at least, if not for Yang. So his seat was moved to another table, next to a livestock broker, Old Du. Yang Baishun, who had been sent by his father to fetch water during the party, overheard the remark by Ma. The next day, Yang complained that he hadn't enjoyed himself at the banquet and carped that he'd wasted a good gift. His quibble had nothing to do with the food; he complained that he'd had nothing to say to Du, whose head smelled bad and whose shoulders were covered with dandruff. Yang assumed that he had been seated next to Du because he had arrived late. When his son told him what he'd heard, he slapped the boy.

"That's not what Old Ma meant. You've made whatever he said sound bad."

With his head in his hands, Yang crouched down in front of the tofu room while his son cried and said nothing for the longest time. Over the next two weeks he ignored Ma and refused to utter the man's name. But a couple of weeks later he was talking and joking with Ma again and went to see him whenever he needed advice.

Peddlers ply their trade by shouting, but not Yang. There are common shouts and there are refined ones. If you're selling tofu, then "Tofu for sale" or "Get your Yang Village tofu" are common shouts. For the refined variety, you need to make music and exaggerate your wares, like this: "This tofu, I ask you, is it tofu or isn't it? It is, but you can't treat it as mere tofu . . ." So what was it, this special tofu? It was touted as white jade, or pure agate. Not born with a silver tongue, Yang could not make up something like that; yet, though he hated common shouts, he tried out a couple—"Tofu fresh as can be, with none of this or that." But that just made him sound angry, so he chose a drum instead. By alternating between beating the skin and banging his stick against the sides, he was able to produce a bit of variety. He was blazing new trails, substituting a drumbeat for a shout as he peddled his tofu. Something brand new. When the villagers heard the beat of a drum, they knew that Old Yang the Tofu Peddler was on his way. In addition to selling tofu in the village, on market days he set up a stall in town, where he sold tofu and liangfen, which he combed into thin strips with a bamboo grater, dumped into a bowl, and added scallions, some herbs, and sesame paste. He made a fresh bowl for each customer. Old Kong of Kong Village sold flat-breads filled with donkey meat in the stall to his left. And to his right was Old Dou of Dou Village, who sold spicy soup and cut tobacco. Yang beat the drum in the village and in town, a steady tattoo from morning to night. At first it was new; but after a month of that, both Kong and Dou had had enough.

" 'Thud, thud, thud' one minute and 'crack, crack, crack' the next. Old Yang, you're turning my head into liangfen," Kong complained. "Peddling a little food isn't leading troops into battle, so is all that noise really necessary?"

Dou, who was more excitable than Kong and less given to speech, simply walked up with a scowl and put his foot through the drumhead.

Forty years later, when Old Yang was bedridden from a stroke, his eldest son, Yang Baiye, took over as head of the family. Most strokes affect the suf-ferer's brain and the ability to speak anything but gibberish. But Old Yang, whose mind was clear as ever, despite the paralysis of his body, had no trouble speaking. Prior to the stroke, he had been inarticulate and often got things all jumbled up; now his mind was clear as a bell, his tongue glib, his ability to keep things straight extraordinary. Spending all day in bed, he needed help for even the simplest activity, and this was where the stroke took its toll. His eyes and his mouth got the worst of it. He welcomed anyone who came into his room with a fawning gaze and answered every question he was asked deferentially. Before the stroke, he had lied as often as he'd told the truth; after the stroke, every word he uttered came straight from the bottom of his heart. If he drank too much water, he had to get up at night, so he drank nothing from afternoon on. Forty years had passed, and his old friends were either dead or busy with one thing or another, so no one came to see him. But then, on the fifteenth day of the eighth lunar month, Old Duan, who had sold scallions in the marketplace, came to see him, with two boxes of pastries. Yang reacted to seeing an old friend after all those years by clutching his hand and weeping. He quickly dried his eyes with his sleeve when a family member walked in.

"Can you recall the names of peddlers in the market, from east to west?" Duan asked.

Yang's brain was working fine, but after forty years, he had forgotten most of the friends he'd worked near. Starting from the east, he was able to count up to the owner of the fifth stall on his fingers, but no further. He recalled Old Kong, who sold flatbreads filled with donkey meat, and Old Dou, who sold spicy soup and cut tobacco, so he focused on those two, passing over the others.

"Old Kong had a thin voice; Old Dou was excitable. He destroyed my drum. But I got even by kicking over his cauldron and spilling his soup all over the ground."

"Old Dong, the castrator from Dong Village, remember him?" Duan asked. "Besides castrating animals, he also repaired cook pots."

Yang knitted his brow as he tried to recall, but he had no memory of the man who castrated animals and repaired cook pots.

"How about Old Wei from Wei Village? The west end of the market, the one who sold raw ginger, always laughing, struck by one thing or another, but no one ever knew what."

Yang could not recall him either.

"How about Old Ma, the Ma Village carter; you must remember him."

"Of course I remember him. He died two years ago." Yang was relieved.

"Back then it was all about Old Ma with you. No one else mattered. Were you aware that while you called him your friend, he was always bad-mouthing you?"

Yang quickly changed the subject.

"How can you recall something from so long ago?"

"I'm talking about the overall situation, not an isolated incident. You spent your whole life trying to get on the good side of people who did not consider you a friend and had no use for people who did. Everyone hated the way you beat that drum, but I liked the sound. I bought your liangfen just to listen to you beat that drum. I'd have liked to talk to you, but you ignored me."

"Not true," Yang quickly replied.

"See what I mean?" Duan clapped his hands. "You still don't consider me a friend. I came today to ask you one question."

"What?"

"You've lived a long life. Have you made any real friends?" Duan added, "You never thought about that before, but how about now that you're laid up?"

Yes, Yang finally got it. After forty years, when Old Duan, who could still walk, knew he was paralyzed, he'd come for revenge. He spat an answer to Duan: "Old Duan, I was right about you all along. You're no damn good."

Duan walked off smiling. Yang was still cursing him after he was gone. Yang's eldest son, Baiye, walked into the room. He was in his fifties. As a youngster, he was always doing something stupid, for which he'd received many whippings from his father. Now, forty years later, his father was bedridden and he had taken over as head of the family. Anything Old Yang wanted had to meet with his son's approval. Baiye picked up where Duan had left off.

"Old Ma drove a cart, you sold tofu, so there was no need to have anything to do with one another. Why in the world did you do everything you could to make him like you when he refused to treat you as a friend?"

Old Yang had no trouble getting angry at Duan, but his son was a different matter. If Baiye asked him a question, he damned well better answer. He sighed.

"I had my reasons. I wouldn't have been afraid of him otherwise."

"Did you cheat him, or was there something he could use against you?"

"There was nothing he could use against me if I had cheated him, and no way he could blackmail me if he had something on me, because I could just ignore him afterward. He outsmarted me the first time we met."

"Over what?" Baiye asked.

"We met at the farm animal market. He was there to buy a horse, I went to sell a donkey, and we struck up a conversation. Whatever we talked about, if I could see a mile down the road, he could see ten miles. If I could look ahead one month, for him it was ten years. I did not sell the donkey, and from then on he had the advantage any time we talked." He shook his head and continued. "No matter what it was, he could always outtalk me, so I looked him up when I needed advice."

"I see. So you took advantage of him whenever you needed a fresh pair of eyes. But what I don't understand is, why did he have anything to do with someone he felt was beneath him?"

"Do you think there was anyone else who could see ten miles down the road and ten years into the future around here? Old Ma never had any friends either." He heaved an emotional sigh. "He shouldn't have had to drive a cart all his life."

"What should he have done?" Baiye asked.

"The blind fortuneteller, Old Jia, said he was slated to start a peasant uprising, like Chen Sheng and Wu Guang at the end of the Qin dynasty. But he didn't have the guts. He was afraid to go out after dark, which kept him from being much of a carter, if you want the truth. It cost him a lot of business." He was getting increasingly excited. "A gutless man like him thought he was better than me. Shit, I was better than him! He never treated me like a friend, but it should have been the other way around!"

Baiye nodded with the understanding that those two were fated to be friends. It was lunchtime by the time they finished talking about Old Ma. Since it was the fifteenth day of the eighth lunar month, they ate flatbreads called *laobing* and a meat-and-vegetable stew. Laobing had been one of Yang's favorites all his life, but by the time he was in his sixties, and had lost most of his teeth, they were off the menu. The stew simmered till the meat and vegetables were mushy; he softened the laobing by dunking them in the hot soup. As a young man, he'd always eaten laobing on holidays, but after his stroke, he was no longer the one who decided whether or not he could eat them. Baiye had already settled on laobing and stew for lunch before they started talking about Ma, but Yang assumed that the decision had come as a reward for his straight talk about the years he sold tofu and liangfen. He ate till his forehead was bathed with sweat. He looked up at his son and flashed him a fawning smile through the steam from the boiling pot. His meaning was clear.

"Anytime you ask me something, I'll still give you a straight answer."

2

Prior to his sixteenth birthday, Yang Baishun considered Old Pei, the barber, to be his best friend, though few words ever passed between them. When Baishun was sixteen, Pei was already in his thirties. Pei lived in Pei Village and Baishun lived in Yang Village, thirty *li* apart and separated by the Yellow River, which meant they saw each other only a few times a year. Baishun never set foot in Pei Village, but Pei came to Yang Village to shave heads. Baishun often thought of Pei, even into his seventies.

Pei had not inherited the profession of shaving heads. His grandfather had woven mats for a living and sold shoes as a sideline. His father was a donkey trader who went to Mongolia each season with a backpack and a whip to buy the animals. It took a month to make the trip from Yanjin to Inner Mongolia, and, fast or slow, a month and a half to drive the donkeys back to Yanjin. That meant only four or five round-trips a year. Once he reached adulthood, Pei followed in the footsteps of his father, who died of malaria two years later. Pei joined a group of traders, making the trip to Inner Mongolia and back with donkeys. Though he was still relatively young, he thought like a much older man and earned as much each year as his father had. Married at the age of eighteen, he started a family, as expected. Buying and selling donkeys kept traders away from home eight or nine months of the year, and that led to romantic dealings on the road. But they were all casual relationships, nothing that might threaten the family back home. The other men gave the women false names and did not tell them where they were from. But Pei, the youngest among them, lost his head over a Mongolian woman named Siqingele, revealing both his real name and where he was from. Siqingele's husband was away tending a herd, so she survived by taking lovers, both for the pleasure and for the trifling bits of silver they left her as pocket money. She had another lover, a man from Hebei, also a donkey trader who traveled to Inner Mongolia, but he had left a phony name and address. Siqingele's troubles started when she got together with this man one fall. Her husband, who had been away for three months, returned to find her pregnant. Mongols don't much care about their women taking lovers to get by; though they are hot-tempered, thanks to all the beef and mutton they eat, they don't let a little sex get in the way. But pregnancy changes everything, since they would then have to raise another man's child. So women who take lovers need to keep an eye on the calendar. When the time is not right, they must forbear; the last thing they want is a little fun that leads to pregnancy. Siqingele had been careless with her Hebei lover, choosing the wrong time for him to enjoy himself. He had his fun, but her husband was livid and took a whip to his wife to get the man's name; she tossed in Pei's name in the process. So the Mongol left his wife and set out with his butcher knife, first to Hebei, where he failed to find the man he was looking for. Next he turned to Henan, heading straight to Pei Village in Yanjin, where he threatened to kill Pei. A peacemaker interceded, and Pei settled for thirty silver dollars plus the Mongol's travel expenses. But that was not the end of it. Pei's wife, Old Cai, tried to hang herself three times in three days, and even though someone always reached her in time, she was a different person after the attempts. She had been afraid of Pei before; now Pei was afraid of her.

"What are we going to do about this?" his wife asked.

"Whatever you say."

"Have nothing more to do with your sister," she demanded.

From lover to sister. Pei's head was spinning. Since his mother had died when he was only six, he had grown up under the care of his sister. They were extremely close, but Old Cai and Pei's sister were always at loggerheads. He knew exactly what was going on.

"She's already married, after all," he said, his head bowed, "so I'll break it off with her, starting today."

Cai was not finished.

"Do you plan to go back to Inner Mongolia?"

"Whatever you say," he replied.

"I don't ever want to hear the words 'donkey trader' again."

Pei had no choice but to put away his saddlebags and whip and give up the donkey trade. He now realized that the Mongolian husband had not come looking for him to settle a score or to demand money; what he'd wanted was to make Pei's life miserable. He may have been rough-hewn, but he'd managed that quite well. Siqingele's pregnancy was not Pei's doing, and it was his back luck to suffer what was intended for the Hebei man. Now that he could no longer trade in donkeys, Pei studied the craft of shaving heads with Old Feng from Feng Village. There was little to learn, and it took a mere three years to master the tricks of the trade. After apprenticing to Feng for two and a half of those years, Pei set out on his own to shave heads in neighboring towns and villages. Seven or eight years later, he had turned into a silent barber. His teacher, Old Feng, kept up a running conversation while he was shaving heads and knew pretty much everything that was going on in neighboring towns and villages. Pei hardly spoke a word while he worked; everyone agreed that master and apprentice could not have been more different. Though Pei hardly spoke while working, he often sighed, as many as four or five times per customer.

One day he went to Meng Village, where he shaved the head of Old Meng, a landlord who owned more than three hundred acres of farmland, worked on by a couple of dozen hired hands. It was nearly nightfall when he finished with the heads of Meng and his hired hands. Meng had a friend, Old Chu, a salt merchant from Luoning County in western Henan. He was passing through Yanjin on his way home from selling salt in Shandong and decided to pay Meng a visit. Since Chu's hair had grown long, he asked Pei to shave him. After a few swipes with his razor, Pei heaved a sigh; a few more swipes, another sigh. Upset by all that sighing, Chu jumped to his feet with only half his head shaved.

"Damn you!" he cursed. "Do you think I'm trying to get you to shave my head for free? I can't stand all those bad-luck sighs."

Pei just stood there, razor in hand, his face red from embarrassment, not saying a word. Meng rushed up to smooth things over.

"Good brother," he said to Chu, "he's not sighing, he's venting. It has nothing to do with shaving heads; it's just a bad habit of his."

Chu sat back down to let Pei finish the job after one last glare at the barber.

Pei had nothing to say on the road or at home, where his wife took charge of all ten household chores. Pei did what she told him to do and suffered a tongue-lashing if he didn't do it the way she wanted. Each time he felt like talking back, she brought up Inner Mongolia and the bastard child. That always shut him up. While there was nothing cruel about a tongue-lashing, joking about it to neighbors was. Pei turned a deaf ear to such talk, and everyone in neighboring towns and villages knew he was henpecked.

One summer, Pei went to shave heads at a large village of four or five hundred households and worked on a hundred or so men from thirty or forty of those households. He did not finish until noon of the third day. On his way home with his barber kit, by the bank of the Yellow River, he ran into Old Zeng, a hog butcher from Zeng Village. Zeng was on his way to Zhou Village to slaughter pigs. Since the trades of both men kept them on the road, they met up often and always had a good talk. On this day, they sat beneath a riverside willow tree to smoke and talk about this and that. When Pei noticed that Zeng's hair had grown long, he said, "I still have some hot water, so why don't I shave your head while we're here?"

Zeng felt his scalp.

"I probably should, but Old Zhou is waiting for me to slaughter a hog." He thought for a moment, then said, "Go ahead, do it. This way the hog will live a little longer."

So Pei took out his kit, wrapped a smock around Zeng, and washed his hair with hot water. Then he took the measure of the man's head and started in with his razor.

"Old Pei, are we good friends or not?" Zeng asked.

That surprised Pei.

"That goes without saying."

"Since it's just the two of us, let me ask you something. You can answer or not; it's up to you."

"What is it?"

"Everybody in neighboring towns and villages knows you're afraid of your wife. That makes no sense to me."

Old Pei paled, then turned red.

"You know how women are. It's nothing. I just don't want to fight with her."

"I know she's held something over you over the past few years. I'll go ahead and say it. It's better to suffer a sudden blow than long-term pain. You'll never get out from under this way."

Pei heaved a long sigh.

"I understand what you're saying. I'd have taken that sudden blow long ago if I could have, but it didn't work."

"Why's that?" Zeng asked.

"Everything would have been fine if she'd had nothing to hold over my head. But now that she's had a taste of it, she'll never agree to a quick solution."

He heaved another sigh. "It's all right though, because I have to think of the children. The problem is, where long-term pain is concerned, she can be unreasonable."

"If it was me, I'd beat her if she wouldn't listen to reason. Sooner or later she'd come around."

"If it was only her, that would be easy. But there's someone else who *will* listen to reason."

"Who?" Zeng asked.

"Her brother."

Zeng knew who he was. Cai Baolin, who ran a medicinal herb shop and had a large mole on the left side of his face. A smooth talker, he could argue a point to death; he was a man who could get a dead toad to pee, as the locals said.

"Every time we have a fight at home, she runs to her brother, who comes to have words with me. He'll start with one little thing and end up with ten, each with its own logic. I've been married to his sister for more than a decade, and how many arguments do you think there have been? I'm no good at talking, so I lose every time."

He sighed again.

"Everyone says it's good to use logic, but it actually makes things harder. In fact, I'm not afraid of an argument. What scares me is that one day I might lose control, pick up a knife, and kill someone. Let me ask you, can you kill someone over a phrase?"

The butcher was so alarmed by the question, he broke out in a cold sweat.

"Just shave my head, Old Pei. I talk too much."

Yang Baishun was thirteen when he met Pei. Before that he'd had a friend named Li Zhanqi, who was a year older. They were both studying *The Confucian Analects* at Wang's private school. People become friends for different reasons—they might have similar personalities, or they might help each other out. But not Baishun and Zhanqi, whose friendship developed over their affection for the same person, Luo Changli, a vinegar maker in Luo Village. Luo was a stumpy, pockmarked man, the latest in a long line of vinegar makers. He owned a small brewery that produced two vats of vinegar a day, which his grandfather and father then hawked in nearby villages.

"Come buy your vinegar!"

"Here comes Luo Village vinegar."

It was a small-scale business, but they earned enough to feed a family. Luo Changli did not care for the business, however, not because he had anything against vinegar, but because he liked something else better—being a funeral crier. Both lines of work required calling out to people, but he preferred to do it at funerals. He would never let vinegar making come before presenting himself at a funeral. Since he was not interested in the family trade, he was terrible at it—his product was bitter, like dishwater, not sour, as it was supposed to be. Other makers' vinegar was good for at least a month, but his grew moldy fuzz after ten days. Strangely, it was bitter before the fuzz appeared but turned sour later. Ordering funeral attendants about, not hawking vinegar, was the kind of work he liked. A young man with a long neck like that of a chicken, he had a sonorous voice, not the thin shrill of most people with chicken necks. He never suffered stage fright; the larger the funeral, the more spirited he was. At a funeral, he would change out of his usual black clothes and don white garb as he stretched his long neck and shouted:

"Attendees, come forward. Filial sons, take your place."

The white-clad filial sons would prostrate themselves and begin their laments.

"Attendees from Houluqiu, please offer your respects."

Then, "Attendees from Zhangbanzao, please move up."

Attendees moved forward in an orderly manner under Luo Changli's direction. Blessed with an indelible memory, he could recall a person's name after a single meeting in a crowd of people and never get it wrong. Seven days would pass between the time of the death and the funeral procession, and his voice never faltered. People referred to him as Luo the Funeral Crier, not Luo the Vinegar Peddler. Every family for miles around sent for him whenever there was a funeral, and Baishun and Zhanqi tagged along to watch. People attend funerals to pay their respects, but Baishun and Zhanqi went for the sake of watching Luo Changli. Of course, deaths were not a daily occurrence, so Luo had to make vinegar between funerals, which in turn created gaps in the boys' lives. They talked about Luo with gusto.

"Such a loud voice. You can hear him a mile away."

"Remember that time attendees from Xu Village caused a problem by not knowing the rules? He was so flustered even his pockmarks turned red."

"He's short, but he seems to grow taller when he shouts at a funeral."

"I wanted to say something to him the last time he came to sell vinegar, but I didn't dare say a word."

"How come no one has died around here lately?"

As their conversation heated up, one of them said, "I have to pee."

The other one didn't have to pee, but to keep the talk about Luo Changli alive, he offered, "I'll go with you."

Baishun's family lost a sheep in the fall of his thirteenth year. They had lost a pig before that. Having gotten drenched in rain the day before, Baishun was running a fever and had the shakes. Everyone in the family but him had gone out looking for the pig; he stayed in bed, hot one moment, cold the next. While he was still in a feverish daze, Li Zhanqi rushed over.

"Hurry," he said breathlessly. "Somebody just died."

"What?" Baishun was muddled from the fever. "Who died?"

"Old Wang from Wang Village. Come on, let's go watch Luo Changli."

At the sound of the name, Baishun's head cleared, his shaking stopped, and his fever retreated. He climbed out of bed and ran with Zhanqi to Wang Village, some fifteen li away. When they got there, they discovered that someone had in fact died in the Wang family, but that the funeral crier was Niu Wenhai, a cripple from Niu Village. Back then, a Yellow River ferry landing divided the county into East and West Yanjin. Where funeral criers were concerned, there were Luo of the East and Niu of the West, meaning those from East Yanjin would have Luo Changli as their crier and Niu Wenhai was crier for West Yanjin. Wang Village straddled the ferry landing, so confusion inevitably arose whenever one of their residents died. Some would hire Luo, while others hired Niu, which was what had happened on this day with Old Wang. The boys did not know what was happening.

"Something's wrong with Old Wang's family," Zhanqi said. "Why didn't they hire Luo Changli? Why go to Niu Wenhai?"

"Niu has a lousy voice and doesn't know how to stand or to sit. He'll ruin the funeral," was how Baishun saw it.

With the excitement gone, Baishun began to shake again and his fever returned. Zhanqi wanted to stick around to compare Luo and Niu to see just how lousy Niu was. Unable to wait for Niu to perform, the feverish Baishun managed to drag his shaking body the fifteen li back home. Everyone was home when he got back, and so was the missing pig. But a sheep had gone missing during the time he went to Wang Village to watch, unsuccessfully, Luo Changli perform. The pig had gone missing on its own, but the sheep was lost on Baishun's watch, a realization that immediately stopped the shakes. Without a word, his father, the tofu peddler, took off his belt. Baishun's brothers, Baiye and Baili, giggled with their hands over their mouths.

"Didn't I tell you to stay home to keep watch? Where did you go?"

Baishun knew he could not tell his father he'd gone to watch Luo Changli at Wang Village, so he lied.

"I went looking for the pig."

16

His father hit him with the belt.

"Li Bojiang said you went with Zhanqi to Wang Village to watch Luo Changli at a funeral."

Li Bojiang was Zhanqi's father. Baishun had missed the chance to see Luo Changli perform and only got to see Niu Wenhai, though that was not something he could explain, so he said, "Pa, I was shaking and running a fever."

That earned him another lash from the belt.

"Running a fever? How did you manage to travel thirty li? Now let's see if you have a fever or not."

Another lash and Baishun now had seven or eight blood blisters on his head.

"My fever's gone, Pa. I'll go find the sheep."

Old Yang tossed a length of rope at Baishun's feet. "Rope it and bring it back. Don't come home if you can't find it." Then he looked over at Baiye and Baili. "This isn't about the sheep. He's lying."

He continued angrily, "You come up with all sorts of excuses when I tell you to do something, but you manage to run off at the mention of Luo Changli even when you're running a fever. Am I your Pa or aren't I?

"Who's in charge in this house?" He glared at everyone. Now that he was off on a tangent, Baishun snatched up the rope and went searching for the sheep. He looked and he looked, from the afternoon till evening, but still no sheep, just a few jackals along the way. Where had that one-eyed sheep gone, anyway? Like Ma the carter, Baishun was afraid of the dark, especially because there were still wolves around at the time, so he retraced his steps and headed back. From somewhere in the cropland along the road came the hoot of an owl, scaring him so much he broke out in a cold sweat. When he returned to the village and neared his house, he did not dare go inside, because, unless something even worse happened, it would be hard for his father to forget the missing sheep. If, for instance, Baiye or Baili lost a donkey, then their father would forget the sheep and focus on that. But how could he make his brothers lose a donkey? Baishun gazed at his house, where a lamp silhouetted figures through the window. In the tofu shed, their donkey was snorting as it turned the millstone to grind beans. Then the light went out in the house, and all was quiet, except for the donkey snorts and the turning millstone, but he still did not dare go inside. So he went to Zhanqi's house, where he might be able to spend the night and ask about the differences between Luo Changli and Niu Wenhai. Li's house was pitch black when he got there, so Zhanqi must have been asleep. His father was weaving baskets by the light of a sesame stalk torch, humming a little ditty as he worked. That was a clear sign that Zhanqi had also gotten a beating. So he left and went to the threshing ground at the village entrance, where he planned to spend the night in a haystack. A night wind sounded like howling wolves as it blew across the treetops. Luckily, the sky cleared and a half moon crept into the sky at midnight. He began to shake again as he was assailed by hunger. When he finally fell asleep, it was a deep slumber, a dazed state in which he thought he heard the stampede of cavalry horses. At some point he felt someone patting him, and he awoke to see a dark shadow standing in front of him. He broke out in another cold sweat.

"Who are you?"

"Don't be afraid." The dark shadow bent down. "I'm Old Pei, the barber from Pei Village. I was just passing by."

The moonlight helped Baishun see the man's face; it was indeed Old Pei, who had shaved his head when he came to Yang Village. But they had never spoken.

"What's your name? Why are you sleeping here?" Pei asked.

The question aroused all the boy's pent-up grievances. Though this was the first time he had spoken to Pei, under the circumstances he felt like family, so he told the man everything—his name, his shakes and the fever, his trip to Wang Village to watch Luo Changli, whom he had failed to see, the missing sheep, the whipping from his Pa, and the fruitless search for the sheep that led him to sleep away from home. He even bent over to show the man the blood blisters. Pei let out a long sigh when the boy was done.

"I see. It had nothing to do with the sheep, but something else, something much more complicated." Then he touched the boy's head. "Aren't you cold sleeping here?"

"The cold doesn't bother me, Uncle. But wolves do."

Pei sighed again.

"This is none of my business, but I guess I'm in the middle of it." He took Baishun's hand. "Come with me, I'll take you somewhere warm."

This was the first time in the boy's life he had felt the warmth of someone's hand. As a tall man and a short boy walked away from Yang Village, Baishun tried to find something to say.

"Aren't you afraid of wolves, traveling at night, Uncle?"

Pei took a machete off his belt, sending its cold glint flickering in the moonlight. "I'm ready for them."

The boy smiled. Hand-in-hand, they arrived at the eastern edge of town, where Pei knocked on the door of an eatery run by a man named Sun. No one stirred inside, but he kept at it until a light came on, followed by Sun's curses.

"Who the hell is it? It's past midnight already."

But he laughed when he saw it was Pei, who often came by to shave Sun's head. In addition to shaving, Sun liked to have the tiny openings below his eyelids cleared and Pei would use a strand of horsetail hair on him, to his great delight. So Sun let them into the eatery, where he started a fire in the cold stove before washing his hands and making two bowls of mutton noodles.

"The mutton was enough for three bowls, but I used it all for you two," he said as he handed them the steaming bowls.

"Dig in." Pei knocked the ashes out of his pipe.

Baishun's face was bathed in sweat by the time he had polished off the noodles. He was crying when a rooster crowed, his tears dripping into the empty bowl.

"Uncle."

Pei waved him off wordlessly. Decades later that bowl of noodles would still be fresh in Baishun's memory, but he later learned that Pei had taken him to the eatery not because he pitied the boy but because of something else entirely.

It was a very long story: The day before the night encounter, Pei had gone to shave heads at Gong Village, a good-sized village with over two hundred families. But he had only a small clientele there, three families altogether, because Old Zang from Zang Village had a monopoly in the barber business there. Three families was still business, and besides, it wasn't far, only five li, so he came once a month, never letting the small amount of work stop him. It had been a nice day when he went to the village, but it started to rain after he finished around noon. It was a light rain, but it did not show any sign of letting up.

"Why not stay for lunch?" Old Gong said. "I don't want you getting sick from the rain."

"It's only five li. I can get home in no time."

So he borrowed a coir cloak and hurried back to his village. When he got to the entrance, marked by a cowshed, he saw a young man standing under the eaves to stay dry. He ignored the youngster and hurried on, but then the young man called out to him, "Uncle."

He stopped. It was his nephew, his older sister's son, Chunsheng. Sixteen years earlier, Pei's sister had married someone in Ruan Village, which was twenty-two li away. Her son, Chunsheng, now fifteen, had gotten up early that day to sell fabric in the county town and was caught in the rain on his way home, which was how Pei came to see him under the eaves. After the incident in Inner Mongolia ten years before, Pei's wife had forbidden him from having any contact with his sister, so the two families had no more interactions. Yet sometimes, when

19

Pei went out on barber business, he secretly made a detour to Ruan Village to see his sister. Running into his nephew just outside his own village put him in a bind. Normally, he would have a few words with the young man before sending him on his way, but it was raining and he could not possibly walk off and leave his own nephew under the eaves. So he braced himself and took the boy home with him. When they got there, his wife was making dinner, flatbreads to go with fried eggs, a rare treat. Pei and his wife had three children, two girls and a boy. That day happened to be the birthday of their second girl, Meiduo, and Pei had insisted on coming home in the rain mainly because of her. When Pei's wife saw Chunsheng, she made the dough thinner. Not a particularly perceptive boy, Chunsheng treated his uncle's home like his own. And since he seldom got to eat flatbreads, he gobbled up a grand total of eleven of them, rolled with fried eggs. The rain had stopped by the time they had finished, so he wiped his mouth and left. Pei's wife flew into a rage, complaining about how he'd shown up for no reason and eaten more than a dozen of the flatbreads. Why had he only come when they were having flatbreads? How did his mouth know that's what she was making? Did he plan to eat them out of house and home? He'd eaten his fill, while her daughter, Meiduo, was still hungry and had begun to sob. Pei complained silently about his nephew, not because the boy had eaten the flatbreads but because he was so clueless. If he had stopped at nine, then he would have eaten just a few of them; if he had stopped at ten, then it would be ten, no more no less. But, he had to have eleven, which was now turned into more than a dozen by his wife's count. He was upset with the boy, who cared only about his belly and had given no thought to his uncle's situation. How could he not understand the huge difference the last two flatbreads made? Pei would not have cared quite so much if his wife's complaints had ended with the boy; but no, she then moved on to the boy's mother, Pei's sister. Ever since open contact between the families had ceased ten years before, Pei and his wife had not mentioned the sister once, but now a few flatbreads had gotten his wife started again. If his wife had said some things that usually bother a sister-in-law, he could have let it pass. But no, she had to call Pei's sister a slut. Back when she was single, Pei's sister had been rumored to have engaged in a dalliance with a traveling salesman, but even if it had been true, it had happened seventeen years before. That, however, was not the point with Pei's wife, who started with the sister's rumored past, continued on with Pei's bastard child in Inner Mongolia, and ended with a comment that everyone in Pei's family was depraved.

"You're a depraved bunch, so why look elsewhere? Why not sleep with your sister and be depraved together?"

That did it for Old Pei. Enraged, he gave her a savage slap; things went downhill from there, and Meiduo's birthday was ruined. The situation got completely out of hand, not because his wife had started a fight but because she went back to her parents. Early the next morning, her brother showed up. He came in, sat down, and began reasoning with Pei, which was the last thing Pei wanted. This brother-in-law had a unique way of reasoning—he talked in circles. The fight between the couple had originated with some flatbreads, but the brother-in-law ignored that; instead, he went back several decades, starting with Pei's parents, who had fought as a young couple. His father had been a simple person, so his mother was "the reasonable one," though in fact she was not. If she hadn't died so early, the Cai family would never have agreed to marry their daughter to Pei. The brother-in-law talked on about the thousands of arguments Pei'd had with his wife since the day they were married. He himself had forgotten the reasons behind these quarrels, but his brother-in-law remembered every argument and every reason behind them; all the arguments and causes, like the endless thread on a magical needle, went on and on, longer and longer, until Pei felt that his head was about to explode. He had to credit the man for his fine memory. As he went on, the brother-in-law somehow turned Pei into Pei's mother, the unreasonable one, which caught Pei by surprise. From morning till noon, he rattled on before finally coming back to the issue of the flatbreads. But even then he could not stay on topic; instead, he brought up Pei's sister and the salesman along with Pei's Mongolian transgression. No one knew the truth about Pei's sister, but his own escapade was irrefutable. If it had been false, then his wife would have been wrong to make a far-fetched connection with the flatbread; but it was true and Pei was upset, not with anyone else but with himself. It would have been perfectly acceptable for him to hit someone who spouted a falsity, but it was wrong to slap his wife when he was upset with himself. By the time the brother-in-law had laid out all his ironclad logic, it was dark and they had to light a lamp. Pei, on his part, was becoming worried that he might go crazy from the brother-in-law's twisted talk. His only option was to pretend that he was persuaded he'd been wrong and to apologize to his wife and his brother-in-law. But his wife refused to let it go at that; she wanted to slap him back. So he turned his cheek to receive a slap from her, finally bringing everything to a conclusion.

Satisfied, the brother-in-law took his leave. Everything seemed back to normal, but that night Pei felt particularly unhappy as he lay in bed. How did all these unrelated matters—the flatbreads, the sister being a "slut," Inner Mongolia, and his parents—get all tangled up? No one could say for sure that his sister had been involved with the salesman, so how could he have let the brother-in-law twist the facts until they were somehow connected to his transgression in Inner Mongolia? How could one incident carry the consequences of two? Then it occurred to him that he had slapped his wife not because she had called his sister a slut but because she had insinuated that Pei ought to sleep with his sister. How in the world could his brother-in-law avoid that crucial comment and twist it into something else? He had slapped his wife and she had slapped him back; two slaps, but they were not the same. At the moment, his wife was out chatting with her friends, very likely joking about what had happened. With rage building inside, he climbed out of bed, picked up his machete to kill someone, not his wife, but his brother-in-law, and not just him, but his logic; not his logic either, but the twisted reasoning that had turned Pei into a different person. If he were to stay with this woman, they would surely have more arguments. It was clear that his nephew should not have eaten the eleventh flatbread, as it was clear that he would die from the twisted logic of his brother-in-law if it were to happen even a few more times. He could not complain if someone were to kill him, but it would be a great injustice if he were to die from twisted logic. With that incident in Inner Mongolia, he had been a scapegoat for the man from Hebei. That was bad, though not a great injustice to be blamed for someone else's fault, but it would be terrible if he were blamed for what he'd done. He set off in a murderous rage, which was how he ran into Yang Baishun. The boy's story about Luo Changli and the search for the missing sheep temporarily halted his desire for murder. A thirteen-year-old boy suffering the shakes had been forced to sleep away from home simply because he had wanted to see someone and had lost a sheep in the process. Was that twisted or what? How could he, a man in his thirties, go out and kill someone over a few flatbreads? If he carried out his plan, what about the three children back home? Everything in the world, it seemed, was caught up in twisted logic. So he heaved a sigh and took the boy by the hand to go knock at a door in town, the door to Old Sun's eatery, not his brother-in-law's house. Without knowing it, Baishun had saved the life of someone he had never met, the man who ran an herbal shop in town. His name was Cai Baolin; he had a mole on his left cheek and never passed up an opportunity to talk reason.

3

From the age of ten, Yang Baishun spent five years studying *The Confucian Analects* at Wang's private school in town. Wang's given name was Mengxi, also known as Zimei, in accordance with a practice common among scholars. His father, Wang Senior, a cooper in the county town, had a sideline of making tinplate kettles. Next to his shop was a pawnshop called Heavenly Peace, run by a man surnamed Xiong, whose grandfather had begged his way to Yanjin from Shanxi fifty years before. Upon his arrival, he had sold vegetables in the county town, before taking up shoe repair on the street. After the family settled down, he still could not rid himself of the habit of begging for food; over New Year's, he sent his children out to beg, even though they could afford to make dumplings by then. Practicing frugality had had its advantages. Old Xiong's father opened a pawnshop, which made it possible for the children to stop begging. In the beginning, they took in clothes and hats, candlesticks and clay pots, but people from Shanxi tend to have good business sense, so by the time Xiong's son took over, their customers mostly came to pawn houses or land, bringing in several dozen taels of silver every day. Xiong wanted to expand his business. Wang's cooper shop, located in the northeastern corner of Xiong's backyard, lent the yard a knife shape, with a narrow front and broad back. Xiong went to talk to Wang Mengxi's father about selling the shop, offering to buy a spot for the Wangs to build a new store. The cooper shop had three front rooms and Xiong would have been happy to build a five-room house and shop for them. With an expanded storefront, the Wangs could continue the cooper business and start new enterprises if they felt like it. It was a good deal, but Wang Mengxi's father steadfastly refused the offer; he would rather be a cooper in a three-room shop than do something else in a new shop with five rooms. His objection had nothing to do with the Xiong family; it was just that he had a different way of looking at the world. He did not much care if something was good for him; but if it was good for someone else, he would feel that it must be bad for him. Given the inflexible rejection, Xiong knew he could not possibly talk him around and had to give up his plan.

To the east of the cooper shop was a grain supply shop called Prosperity, owned by a man called Old Lian. When the Wangs repaired their roof one autumn, they made the eaves too long, sending water down on Old Lian's western wall whenever it rained. The Lian house also had long eaves, which had sent rainwater down on the Wangs' eastern wall for over a decade. But the wind blew from the northwest more often than from the southeast, so the Lians felt disadvantaged, and elongated eaves led to a dispute. Unlike Old Xiong of Heavenly Peace, who was mild and reasonable, Old Lian of Prosperity was a hothead who hated to lose. On the night the dispute broke out, he sent a clerk from his shop to climb onto the Wangs' roof, where he took down the eaves, relieving the roof of half its tiles in the process. A lawsuit ensued. Ignorant of the ins and outs of lawsuits, Wang Senior wanted to show the Lians who they were up against. The suit dragged on for two years, making it impossible for Wang Senior to continue his business. When Old Lian resorted to bribery, Wang Senior followed suit, but the Wangs were no match for the Lians where money was involved, for Prosperity handled tons of grain each day. Old Hu, the county magistrate at Yanjin, was so ineffectual that nothing was resolved after the two-year period. When Wang Senior sold the three-room shop, Xiong of Heavenly Peace bought it from the new buyer, and Wang Senior had no choice but to rent a small place in Dongguan to start over with his cooper business. Instead of being angry with Lian of Prosperity, who had filed the suit, he was upset with Xiong of Prosperity, who bought his space. As he saw it, Lian was just the front man for the suit, while the Xiongs were the real instigators. But there was no way he could get back at Xiong now, so he made new plans.

When young Wang turned twelve, his father sent him to study in Kaifeng, hoping that after ten years of hard work, his son would become an official and be sent to Yanjin. When that happened, Wang Senior would continue his dispute with the Xiong and Lian families—a gentleman does not mind waiting ten years for his revenge. But even planting wheat takes four seasons from sprout to harvest, and it would take tremendous patience waiting for Mengxi to grow up, make a name for himself, and become an official. Luckily, Wang Senior was a patient man. But a cooper who made a few basins and buckets a day could hardly afford his son's tuition and expenses. After holding out for seven years, he ruined his health and began to cough up blood; naturally, he could make no more barrels. After spending three months in bed, he knew his days were numbered, and he was about to send someone to bring his son back when Mengxi showed up on his own, his bedroll slung over his back. He came back not because he had learned of his father's illness; in fact, he had been beaten up in Kaifeng so badly that he came home with a swollen, bruised face and an injured leg. When asked about the culprit and the reason behind the beating, he would not say a word, except that he would rather stay home to be a cooper than go back to school in Kaifeng. The outrage over his son's failure and his own illness were too much for Wang Senior, who died three days later. But before he expired, he said with a sigh, "The whole thing was doomed from the beginning."

Wang Mengxi knew that his father was referring to the Lians and Xiongs, not the beating he'd suffered.

"Should we not have been involved in the suit?"

"I shouldn't have sent you to school." Wang Senior looked at his son's swollen face. "I should have let you become a murderous outlaw. That way, you would have been spared a beating and would have exacted revenge long ago."

For all intents and purposes, the episode was over. But after seven years of school in Kaifeng, Wang Mengxi was considered a learned person in Yanjin, for even Old Cao, who wrote petitions for lodgers of complaints, had only six years of education. After the death of his father, Mengxi became an itinerant tutor instead of taking up his father's trade, and stayed at it for over a decade. A slender man who sported a long robe and wore his hair parted down the middle, he looked well educated. And yet he was not only inarticulate but was a stutterer, a terrible trait for a teacher. Despite his accumulated knowledge, it did not come out easily, like dumplings in a teapot. During his first few years, he was usually fired within three months.

"Are you learned, Old Wang?" someone once asked him.

"Bring me pen and paper and I'll write you an essay," he said, red-faced.

"So, you are? Then why can't you explain things to us?"

"I just can't," he said with a sigh. "An impatient man talks too much, while a smart one treasures his words."

It mattered little how much he talked; he could not explain even the following phrase in *The Confucian Analects*: "The four seas may be impoverished, but heavenly fortune is inexhaustible." He kept trying to explain the meaning to the students, but after ten days, he still could not manage it, and vented his frustration on them.

"Do you know what Confucius meant by an inability to carve rotten wood? The sage was talking about pupils like you."

After seven or eight years, he finally managed to settle down with the Fan family in town. By then he was married with children and had put on weight. Everyone considered his hire to be a mistake, for there were other traveling tutors, like Yue from Yue Village and Chen from Chen Village, both more articulate than Wang. So why, instead of hiring either one, had Fan chosen Wang, who might have been muddle-headed but who knew what he was doing? Well, Fan's youngest son, Qinchen, was a bit on the slow side—not stupid, just not very bright. When someone told a joke during a meal, everyone else would laugh immediately, but he would not laugh until after they finished eating. So, Wang was slow with his tongue and Qinchen was slow with his thoughts; a slow brain was a perfect match for a slow tongue. That was why he was hired.

Wang gave lessons in Fan's cowshed, transformed into a private classroom after adding a few desks. He made a plaque with the words *Peach Planting Studio* out of wood from a horse trough and hung it over the door. Fan Qinchen might have been slow-witted, but he preferred a crowd and refused to go to school with only him and the tutor. So his father turned it into a private school that admitted children from other families. All these students had to do was bring their own lunches. They came from all around. Old Yang, the tofu peddler, had no plans for his sons to be educated, but he sent two of them, Baishun and Baili, along when he realized what a good deal it was to have to pay only for food. He had wanted to send his eldest, Baiye, but the boy was fifteen, too old for school. Besides, he needed him to help grind the soybeans, so he gave up on the idea.

With Old Wang's difficulty in explaining lessons, few of the students showed him any respect. Most were not interested in studying and simply sought an easy life by using the lessons as an excuse to shirk chores at home. Yang Baishun and Li Zhanqi, for example, wanted only to know who had died recently so they could watch Luo Changli perform. But as a conscientious teacher, Old Wang was often upset over the striking disparity between his understanding of *The Confucian Analects* and his students' abysmal lack of comprehension. So he often stopped in mid-lesson.

"You won't understand no matter what I say."

Take, for instance, the famous phrase by Confucius: "How delightful it is when friends visit from afar." The students all thought the sage was happy to have friends come great distances to see him. But Wang insisted that the sage was not happy; he was, in fact, sad. If he had said all he had to say to nearby friends, wouldn't it be a problem if a friend came a long way to visit? But because he had no nearby friends, he treated the ones from far away as friends. These distant visitors may or may not have been true friends, and in that phrase the sage was simply venting his displeasure. As a result, the students called Confucius a bad sage, which made Wang shed tears of sadness. The impossibility of communication between pupils and teacher led to a high student turnover and attrition rate. Those who left did so because they could not understand their teacher, and new ones came because they weren't aware of the situation. With pupils arriving and leaving, Wang ended up with students from every town and village; some were related and attended together, an uncle and a nephew, say, or two brothers.

Wang had a habit of taking solitary strolls on the fifteenth and the thirtieth days of each lunar month. He would set out at noon, roaming the neighborhood with long strides and not greeting anyone along the way. Sometimes he followed the main road; at other times he strayed into wilderness and made a path of his own. He worked up a sweat, whether in the summertime or in the depths of winter. At first people thought he was aimlessly roaming, but he kept at it month after month, year after year, until it became a pattern. On rainy days, he remained cooped up inside till veins bulged on his forehead. His employer, Old Fan, did not pay much attention to his roaming at first, but began to notice Wang's outings after a few years. One day, when Fan returned from collecting rents in the villages, he ran into Wang at the gate as he was putting on a jacket to go for his stroll. Jumping off his horse, Fan realized that it must be the fifteenth day of the month.

"I see you out walking year after year, Old Wang. What's it all about?"

"I can't tell you, Master Fan. It's too hard to explain."

So Fan did not pursue the subject.

Later that year, on the day of the Dragon Boat Festival, he invited Wang to dinner. As they ate, Fan again brought up Wang's strolls. By then, fairly drunk, Wang sprawled over the table and sobbed.

"Someone is always on my mind, and I get so pent up after fifteen days I have to go out for a walk. I always feel better afterward."

Finally Fan understood what was going on.

"Is this person still alive? Could it be your father? It must have been hard on him sending you to school back then."

"No, not him." Wang shook his head and kept sobbing. "I wouldn't go strolling for his sake."

"If the person is still alive, why don't you go look him up?"

"No, I can't do that, I can't." Wang shook his head. "I nearly died from looking for him years ago."

After pausing from the shocking revelation, Fan continued. "It's just that I'm worried you could run into an evil spirit out in the wild."

"Following along the stream, one forgets how far one has traveled," Wang intoned as he shook his head. "I'm not afraid of evil spirits. I'd go with one if it asked me to."

Seeing that Wang must be drunk, Fan shook his head and said no more.

Wang did not wander aimlessly; he remembered all the routes he traveled, even counted his steps. If you asked him how far a little shop was from town, he would say 1,852 steps, 16,036 steps from town to Hu Village, 124,022 steps from town to Fengbanzao, and so on.

Yinping, Wang's wife, was illiterate, but she worked alongside him at the school, where she checked the number of students and handed out brushes, ink, paper, and ink stones. Unlike Wang, she was a good talker, but she only gossiped about the neighbors, never about anything to do with the school. Once Wang started the lessons she went out to chat with the neighbors. She could talk up a storm, saying whatever came into her mind. Two months after they arrived, she had gossiped about every resident in town and, a month after that, had antagonized half the town's population

"Old Wang, you're an educated man, but your wife needs to watch her mouth," someone would say. "Why don't you talk to her about it?"

"You can reason with someone who is serious," he would say with a sigh, "but how do you talk sense into someone who's spouting nonsense?"

So he let her be, never bringing up people's objections. At home he ignored her, neither listening to her nor responding to her when she said something, so they led a peaceful coexistence as they went about their separate lives. Yinping had another flaw: she liked to take advantage of others, feeling good when she managed to do so, and bad when she couldn't. If she went to buy leeks at the open market, she would demand some free garlic; if she bought two yards of fabric, she would ask for two spools of thread. In the summer and autumn, she went gleaning in the field, and not just the harvested fields but those with untouched crops as well, plucking handfuls of grain to stuff into her pants. The closest field south of the school belonged to her husband's employer, which made it possible for her to take more from Fan than from anyone else. Once, when he went out back to check on the livestock in a newly completed pen, his steward, Old Ji, walked up in the space between the horses and the donkeys.

"Master, why don't you fire Old Wang?" he said.

"Why?" Fan asked.

"The kids can't understand a thing he says in class."

"That's why they need to learn. What's the point of having a teacher if they understand everything?"

"It's not because of that."

"Then what is it?"

"It's his wife. She's a thief, steals our crops."

"She's just a woman. What harm can she do?" With a wave, he continued. "And so what if she is? With fifty acres of land, why should I worry about a thief like her?"

Old Song, who was feeding the animals, overheard the exchange. He had a son studying with Wang, so he repeated the conversation to the teacher.

"What does it mean to have a friend visiting from afar? This is what it means," Wang lamented.

But Wang left the Fan family when Baishun turned fifteen, and shut down the private school. He left not because Fan fired him, or because he grew tired of the children who could not learn anything, or even because he was ashamed to stay after his thieving wife ruined his reputation. No, it was because something happened to one of his children. Wang and his wife had four of them, three boys and a girl. He was not inspired by his learning when it came to naming the children. The oldest son was Dahuo (Big Goods), the second son Erhuo (Second Goods), the third son Sanhuo (Third Goods), and the girl Dengzhan (Oil Lamp). The three sons were all well behaved, but the girl was a handful. When most children act up, they climb rooftops or treetops; but not Oil Lamp, who preferred to play with animals, not kittens or puppies but livestock. Barely six years old, she loved to spend time with the horses and mules, which presented a problem. One night when Old Song was feeding the animals, he spotted Dengzhan sitting on the back of a horse and whipping the animal.

"Giddy-up. I'll take you to see your mom at your grannie's house."

The horse neighed and kicked but failed to frighten the little girl. The three boys had never cost Wang any sleep; the worse they had done was, like other children, not to understand their father's lessons on *The Confucian Analects*. But Song complained to him frequently about his daughter's abuse of the animals.

29

"Say no more, Old Song. Just pretend she's one of them."

On the eighth month of that year, Song broke a hole in the soaking vat, which had been in use for fifteen years and was ready to break. He told Fan, who, without a word of reproof, told him to buy a new one. A bigger vat than the broken one was required, since they had bought more animals. When Dengzhan saw the new vat, with water flowing over the sides, she climbed up and began dancing on the rim. Used to her antics, Song sighed and shook his head but decided to let her be. He yoked the animals and took them out to the field. When he returned in the evening, he found the girl floating in the vat. He fished her out, but her belly was bloated and she was clearly dead. Picking up his pitchfork, he smashed the new vat and then sat down on a salt block to weep. Wang and his wife rushed over; Yinping took one look at the girl on the floor and, without a word, picked up the pitchfork to attack Song. Wang stopped her. Looking at the dead child, he said evenhandedly, "It's not his fault. It's hers." He added, "She was a troublesome child who brought us a great deal of trouble. Now she's dead and everything will be fine."

Back then, all families had broods of children; losing one was no big deal. For two days, Yinping had it out with Song, who gave her two bushels of rice as compensation, and that was the end of it. One day a month later, only five of the two dozen students showed up for class during a downpour. Instead of starting a new lesson, Wang told them to write an essay. After assigning the topic "One's biggest problem is not about others knowing you, but about you not knowing others," he sat staring blankly at the rain outside. Realizing that he could not possibly make the students write another essay for the afternoon session, he decided not to begin a new lesson and had them trace characters. He got up to find Yinping for some paper, but she was nowhere in sight, probably out gossiping. So he went home to find the paper with red grids at the bottom of Yinping's sewing basket, after which he went over to the windowsill to get his ink stone, with the intention of copying from memory a section of Sima Changqing's "Ode on the Mansion Gate," while the students traced characters. Two of his favorite lines in the Ode were "The sun is about to set, bringing despair / In the empty room, I sit forlornly." As he reached for the ink stone, he spotted a half-eaten moon cake, from a month earlier. Dengzhan had not finished the cake, which he had bought in the county town when he was buying textbooks for the children. He could see the marks left by her tiny teeth. The price for the Moon Festival treat was the same, but those in town had more of the filling called red and green silk. He had no sooner laid them down than Dengzhan had sneaked in to eat one; he caught her and gave her a good whipping. On the day the girl died, Wang had felt little pain, but now the cake with teeth marks brought him so much pain he felt as if a knife were piercing his heart. Putting down the ink stone, he walked to the animal shed, where Song, wearing a bamboo hat, was cutting hay. A month had passed, and Song had forgotten about the girl, so he thought Wang had come to tell him about his son misbehaving in class. Gousheng was a true piece of rotten wood that could not be carved. So he was shocked when, instead of complaining about his son, Wang walked up to the second new vat and began to wail. Once he started, he could not stop; he howled for three long hours, drawing the attention of all the employees and Master Fan.

After the good cry, Wang was once again his normal self, teaching *The Confucian Analects* when it was time to do so, going home to eat when mealtime arrived, and copying from memory "Ode on the Mansion Gate" when he felt like it. But he had become visibly more reticent. When the children were reading, he stared blankly out the window. Three months later it snowed. On the night the snow stopped, he went to see his employer, who was washing his feet. He saw the look on Wang's face.

"What's wrong, Old Wang?"

"I'm leaving, Master."

Surprised, Fan removed his half-washed feet from the water.

"You're leaving? Something's wrong?"

"Nothing is wrong; it's me who's not right. I miss my little girl."

Fan tried to talk him around.

"Let it go. It's been almost six months."

"I want to, Master, but my heart won't listen to me. When she was alive, I was annoyed with her time and again, and I even beat her sometimes, but now that she's gone, I think about her every day. I just want to see her again. I can't in the daytime, but she shows up in my dreams every night. There she's a good girl, standing by my bed and saying, 'It's getting cold, Pa. I'll tuck your blanket in for you.'"

Fan knew how the man felt, but continued to comfort him.

"It'll pass, Old Wang. Just give it time."

"I want to, but I can't, Master. I feel my heart is on fire and I'll go crazy if I don't do something."

"Would it help to go wail in the animal pen?"

"I tried that, in secret, but it didn't work. I couldn't shed a tear."

An idea hit Fan. "Go walk in the wild then. Take a stroll and you'll feel better."

"I did. I used to go out once every two weeks; now I go every day. It's no use."

Fan nodded to show his understanding.

"But where will you go? When your Pa was involved in that lawsuit, he lost the house and you had to come here. This is your home. In all these years I've never treated you like an outsider."

"I consider this my home, too, Master Fan, but I haven't been able to stop thinking about death these past three months."

Stunned by the revelation, Fan knew he had to let Wang go.

"Well, then you must leave. But I worry about you. Where will you take your family?"

"The girl told me in a dream to go west."

"You won't find her there."

"I'm not looking for her. I just want to find a place where I can stop missing her."

Early the next morning, Wang left Fan's house, wife and sons in tow. He had not been able to shed a tear for three months, but he began to cry at the sight of two yew trees that had grown as thick as a bowl from saplings when he'd arrived six years earlier.

Yang Baishun heard that Wang went west after leaving the Fan house with his family. They stopped every once in a while, but sadness would come upon him and they would set out again. They went from Yanjin to Xinxiang, from Xinxiang to Jiaozuo, from Jiaozuo to Luoyang, from Luoyang to Sanmenxia, and none of these places brought him peace. Three months later, after leaving Henan Province, they followed the Longhai rail line to reach Baoji, Shaanxi, where the sadness lifted from his heart. That was where they settled down. But he did not resume teaching, and no one asked him to teach. Nor did he pick up his father's old trade of cooper; instead, he made figurines out of blown sugar. His mouth was not adept at talking but was good at blowing figurines. In fact, he was so good they were lifelike, be they roosters or rats. On clear, windless days, he would put on a terrific show with figurines depicting Fruit Mountain scenes from *Journey to the West*, with monkeys spreading their arms to reach for fruit, fighting, picking lice from other monkeys' heads, and reaching out to beg for food. He could even make a human figurine when he was drunk; he would take a deep breath and produce a beautiful girl in her teens, slender with full breasts. But she would never smile; her head was lowered, as if she were crying.

"Is this your mistress?" people would tease him.

"No, it's a young wife."

"From where?"

"Kaifeng."

"Why doesn't she smile? It looks like she's crying. That's no good."

"She has to cry, or she'll die."

He was clearly drunk. By then he had put on weight and begun to go bald. But he seldom drank, and so produced few human figurines, though people all over Baoji knew about Old Wang from Henan, who lived by Zhuquemen in Luomashi and was good at blowing the "young wife of Kaifeng."

After Wang's departure, the students at Peach Planting Studio scattered. Baishun and Baili returned to Yang Village. Baishun, after studying with Wang for five years, was now fifteen; he had wanted to stay longer, since he had yet much to learn about *The Confucian Analects.* The teacher's departure came as a surprise. Back when Wang was around, Baishun had frequently played tricks on him. One winter day when he was twelve, Baishun and Zhanqi sneaked over to Wang's outhouse, where they drilled a hole in the bottom of his chamber pot, causing Wang to wet his bed when he used it that night. Now that Wang was gone, Baishun could not stop thinking about how good he'd been. Deprived of the excuse Wang had provided for him to stay at school, Baishun had to go home and make tofu at his father's side. He had no love for the work, not because of the tofu but because of his father. Not because his father had whipped him on account of a missing sheep, for which he'd ended up sleeping in a haystack and now bore a grudge. No, it wasn't that either. It was because, like Old Ma the carter, he did not regard his father highly. Luo Changli, the funeral crier, was the one who commanded Baishun's respect, and Baishun wanted to leave home to work with Luo. But it wasn't that simple: Baishun only liked Luo the funeral crier, not Luo the vinegar maker, recalling how Luo's vinegar grew moldy fuzz in ten days. But making vinegar was how Luo earned a living, while performing funeral rites was a hobby. In other words, he had to make vinegar in order to keep his hobby going. Every family used vinegar three meals a day, but who could produce a death in the family at every meal? Baishun was caught in a bind.

Baili, his younger brother, did not like their father either; he preferred Blind Jia, who played a three-string lute. Blind in one eye only, he used the good one to read fortunes. During his decades of fortune-telling, he had met countless people and had come up with his own philosophy of life. Everyone has his predestined lot in life, Old Jia would say, but people paid little attention to him. After reading other's fortunes, he felt terrible about his own, because, in his view, all the people had been born at the wrong time. No one was doing what he was destined to do, so all that running around was in vain, and everyone else was born to be an obstacle in his life.

The difference between Baishun and Baili was that Baili liked both of Jia's activities—playing the lute and telling fortunes, while Baishun only liked to watch Luo Changli perform at funerals. Baili went to Jia Village behind his father's back and asked to study with Jia, who then shut his eyes and touched the boy's hands.

"Your fingers are too thick to play the lute."

"I'll learn to tell fortunes with you," Baili said.

Jia opened his good eye and cast him a glance.

"You don't even know your own fortune, so how are you going to tell others?"

"Then what is my fortune like?"

"Long term you will have a life of toil, and will have to travel hundreds of li daily, because of your mouth," Jia said with his eyes shut. "Short term, you will see people's faces flash by, and nine out of ten of them will curse you under their breath."

Not only did Baili fail to study under Jia, but he was even given a lousy prediction about his life. He cursed Jia under his breath: Wouldn't I die from exhaustion if I had to travel hundreds of li every day? He decided that Jia was a terrible fortune-teller as he took himself back to Yang Village.

4

In the year Baishun turned sixteen, Yanjin got a new county magistrate called Old Han, who succeeded Old Hu, who was from Mayang in Henan Province. A man with a ruddy face, Hu had received the official title of Provincial Scholar during the Qing dynasty. His father was an herbal doctor who had cured some and killed others during his career. When other doctors finished their diagnosis, they dashed off a prescription, but not Hu's father, who hesitated on every single item on his list.

"You took a long time to write up the prescription, Old Hu," someone once said after the patient had left. "It seems harder than childbirth. Are you sure you got the illness right?"

"I did, of course. What I'm not sure of is the human heart."

"You're a doctor. Why do you have to worry about the heart?"

"Why not?" He sighed. "Even with the same illness, people are different. The same cure may not work for everyone."

"Quack. That is what makes a doctor a quack, and it's how he kills people."

After Hu had passed the exam and was assigned to Yanjin, all his Mayang relatives and neighbors came to see him off. With drums beating and gongs banging, he rode out on a horse, dressed in red and draped in green, to which everyone applauded. His father halted his horse.

"Son, everyone near and far congratulates you. I alone cry for your sake."

"I am not going to the execution ground, so what are you crying for?"

"You are good by nature, and can get along with your head buried in a book. But being an official is like traveling among jackals, and I am afraid you will suffer. You should return after a year but no more than three years if you haven't ended up in prison by then."

"When people take up a new post they get good wishes, but not me. You are spouting unlucky things."

"That was not what I really wanted to say to you," his father replied.

"What did you really want to say?"

"Don't lose hope if you lose the post. Come back to Mayang and I'll teach you herbal medicine. If you can't be a good official, then why not become a great doctor?"

But Hu stayed in the same position in Yanjin for thirty-five years. The longevity was not because he knew the ins and outs of officialdom or that his father was wrong in his prediction; it was not knowing anything and not knowing he did not know anything that led to his unlikely success. One prerequisite of being an official is receiving and sending off guests, as well as delivering gifts to superiors on holidays. After taking up his post, Hu did not receive or see off any guests, let alone present holiday gifts to his superiors. Yanjin was under the jurisdiction of Xinxiang Prefecture, whose magistrate was a covetous man named Zhu. During the holidays, every county magistrate delivered presents, all but Hu. Zhu was given to claiming to be an upright official, so the one out of ten county magistrates who did not give him gifts became his front. At banquets, Zhu was often heard to say to his superiors and colleagues: "People have accused me of corruption, but go ask Old Hu in Yanjin if he has ever given me anything."

More important than giving gifts to one's superior was flattery, specifically praising the accomplishments and virtues of a superior in public. It was, however, something unknown to Hu. He not only never flattered, but chose to say whatever came to his mind. Other officials adjusted to local customs; Hu, in contrast, continued to talk in his Mayang accent, which was all but unintelligible. Magistrate Zhu could not understand him, nor could his colleagues, let alone the people of Yanjin. When presiding over a court case, Hu gave his heavily accented judgment after the plaintiff and defendant had their say, but neither party had the foggiest idea what he had just said. Mutual unintelligibility meant that court cases were settled haphazardly, which, unexpectedly, led to peace for the people of Yanjin, who would only go to court when they had no choice, or when it was a life and death matter. They would suffer a minor loss if they did not go to court but might lose everything if they did. As a result, they tried to settle disputes among themselves, and their county appeared well governed. Now, with so few cases, Hu had nothing to do and developed an interest in carpentry. He looked listless at court, but when night came and the yamen was all lit up, he would shed his official's garb and change into a short jacket and pants to hammer out tables, chairs, stools, and cupboards. While other yamens were bathed in official, stuffy airs, those in Yanjin were shrouded in the smells of wood shavings and lacquer paint. His runners and constables, after changing out of their official garb, became his woodworking apprentices, which was why Yanjin produced so many fine carpenters. One would expect that the yamen runners would not want to be carpenters, but they were willing to do so because of the leeway Hu gave them, owing to his ignorance of yamen culture regarding court judgments and the intricacy of complaints. When Magistrate Zhu came for an inspection of Yanjin, he could only shake his head with a smile when he sniffed out the differences in Hu's yamen. With the reign of peace, Hu remained the county magistrate until he turned sixty, the stipulated age for officials to retire and return to their hometowns. Among all the colleagues who had come to Henan at the same time as he, either as county or prefecture magistrates, more than half had gone to prison, some had been executed, and others had lost their positions, just as Hu's father had predicted. Even Magistrate Zhu was sent to prison the year Hu turned fifty, which prompted Hu's colleagues to criticize him.

"Everyone says that Old Hu is a simple and honest man, but in fact that bastard is the worst schemer of all."

Hu did not go home after retirement; he stayed not because he had no home to go back to, but because after thirty-five years he had gotten used to everything in Yanjin, including its natural environment and climate. Yanjin had alkaline soil, with lots of niter, making the water salty and acrid; the locals and their livestock shook their heads after drinking the water, which lay behind Yanjin people's habit of head shaking. But it did not mean that they were unhappy about someone or something; it was merely a habit. When Hu first arrived, he suffered a great deal, with diarrhea every day, and he too got into the habit of shaking his head. After a few years, he no longer had diarrhea but suffered constipation when he went back to see his family in Mayang, where the water, devoid of alkali and niter, was bland. One can survive for seven days without food, but not seven days without relieving oneself; and of course, that too made Hu shake his head. So he stayed after retirement, turning Yanjin into his hometown. Using what he'd saved during his tenure as magistrate, he bought a house under a bridge over the Jin River, which ran through town, and became a full-time carpenter. At first, he was happy with the change of pace, but within a month, he began to worry about his choice. As magistrate, he had managed to snatch a few free moments to make tables, chairs, stools, and cupboards. But in fact there are many branches of carpentry—carpentry for houses, for carts, and for furniture, with the last the easiest to master. Carts were hard because of the wheels, shafts, axles, and spokes, but they were easier than house carpentry, which involved arched rafters, eaves, carved beams, and painted rafters. He had not wanted to be a mere furniture maker, but since he was in his sixties, he had a hard time learning the other two types of carpentry and contented himself with making common household items. In the past, he had copied the styles of others, but now, as a full-time carpenter, he wanted to make something new, different from anyone else's. That proved to be a challenge. Actually, it was fairly easy to be different from others but hard to make something different from his earlier work. He racked his brains in the day and studied piles of wood under lamplight until a rooster crowed in the morning, but still he did not know where to start. At times like this, he would shake his head and sigh.

"Everyone says it's hard being an official, but no one knows that it is even harder to be a carpenter."

When locals crossed the bridge late at night and saw the lights on in Hu's house, they too would sigh.

"Old Hu is still up."

Or, "Old Hu is racking his brains over carpentry."

In any case, Old Han took over as county magistrate after Hu retired to become a carpenter. In his early thirties, Han, a graduate of Yanjing University, had a mouth small enough only for a peanut to make it through, and he wore his hair combed back. Women with small mouths were a common sight, but not men. Han was from Tangshan, Hebei, with an accent that, to the locals, was almost as hard to understand as Old Hu's Mayang dialect. But that minor difference brought big trouble to Yanjin. Han was unhappy with the town the moment he arrived, not because the people weren't simple and honest. In fact, after thirty-five years with Hu as their magistrate, Yanjin was now enjoying a peaceful existence that included not picking up someone's lost item on the streets and never having to lock doors at night. Nor was it because Han did not like the pervasive smells of wood shavings and lacquer paint at the yamen after being used as a carpentry shop by Hu for years. No. It was because Han liked to talk; that little mouth of his was always in motion. For him, he was fine going without food for a day, but going without talking for a day would nearly kill him. In addition to hearing cases, he loved to talk to locals who could manage his Tangshan accent, and that in turn encouraged him to talk more. Being the county magistrate meant he could say whatever he wanted, whenever he liked, but after a few speeches, he despaired about the people of Yanjin; they heard what he said but understood nothing. So he decided to set up a school for the locals where they could learn to understand what he meant; he would begin with the students at the school before reaching out to the populace. Back then, Yanjin had only a few private schools here and there. In his thirty-five-year tenure, Hu had concentrated on making furniture, ignoring the need for a school. Building a school in those days was expensive, and where would a poor county like Yanjin find the money? Even if it was found, construction would take at least six months to a year, and Han could not wait that long. So he made do with a Catholic church, one that was big enough for three hundred people at Mass, presided over by an Italian priest whose Chinese name was Zhan Shanpu, or Old Zhan to the locals. Han had an announcement pasted on the church door, effectively turning it into a school.

"County Magistrate, I am not against your setting up a school," Zhan the priest said when he went to see Han. "But God will not allow you to confiscate his church."

Han smacked his lips.

"I talked to him yesterday and got his permission."

"Please don't joke about it like that, Magistrate. I'll file a complaint against you at the Kaifeng Church."

The Catholic Church was quite powerful in China back then; even the government had to concede to their demands every once in a while. So Zhan thought the threat would scare Han, but, to his surprise, Han slapped his thigh.

"Mr. Zhan, I'm afraid of many things, but if there's one thing that does not scare me, it is lawsuits. So hurry on over and come back quick. I'll be waiting for you here."

The ploy hit Zhan where he was weakest. The Yanjin church was part of the Kaifeng Diocese, but Zhan had issues with the bishop, a Swede named Regge Gustafsson, Old Lei to the locals. They had problems not because they could not get along; their issues rested on the phrase "and from the Son." It would not have been so bad if they had disagreed on something other than an interpretation of the Bible. With differing readings of the Bible, Zhan began to deviate more and more from Lei, who had long wanted to eliminate the church in Yanjin and merge it with another. Saying he would go to Kaifeng was an empty threat that failed to scare Han off. And by the following morning, the plaque above the church door had changed from "God Bless the East" to "Yanjin New

School." Now Zhan realized that Han was a worthy rival who had not seized the church on impulse. He had obviously been aware of Zhan's issues with the diocese.

After having found a building for the school, Han began the search for teachers in the county town, with an emphasis on knowledgeable people who were articulate. He wanted them not for their eloquence but for the ability to know what to say and what not to say. In the end he chose more than a dozen teachers who were all the quiet type. It was not that he liked them dumb; it was just that he did not want talkative people like himself. He knew he would always get to the point when he talked, but he wasn't so sure that talkative teachers know how to stay on topic, and it would be terrible if they did not. The selection of teachers was followed by recruiting students from the county, and naturally Han had his standards. He did not want youngsters who had never been to school before; they had to have attended at least five years of private school. Lest anyone forget, Han was setting up a school so he could talk to the people, and it would simply take too long to start out with uneducated children, like planting new saplings that required many seasons to grow. Only those with five years of schooling would understand what he had to say, so he accepted both boys and girls. His plan was part of his thoughts on changes in government structure; the future clerks in the government office would be selected from graduates of the Yanjin New School.

As we have seen, Yanjin was an impoverished county that, at the moment, could not support the students' education, so the parents had to pay tuition and fees. Han may have set up the school for his own purposes, since the students would end up working at the county office as clerks, an incentive that prompted many wealthy landlords to remove their children from private schools and send them to Yanjin New School. This development did not affect Old Yang, the tofu peddler, who had sent Baishun and Baili to study *The Confucian Analects* with Old Wang because it was free; they had failed to learn a thing. He would rather die than pay to send his sons to Han's school in town, in part because he had no intention of letting them work as government clerks; they would be his apprentices if they stayed home to make tofu, but if they became clerks, they would definitely show him no respect. Yet five days after the school opened, he changed his mind, not on his own account, but because of Old Ma, the carter, who was renovating his house and had asked Yang to go over to make some tofu. By the time Yang was done with that, it was nighttime. Ma assumed that Yang would go home straightaway after a day of hard work, because he lived fifteen li away. But after coming out of the kitchen, Yang stayed to chat, which displeased Ma, since they had no shared topics for conversation, and Yang always gained the most from their chats. As long as he'd known Yang, Ma had given him at least a hundred suggestions but got nothing but nonsense in return. To him, sharing a few coarse jokes was fine, but a heart-to-heart talk was out of the question. Worse yet, Yang was forever telling people that Ma was his best friend, and they appeared to be on equal footing, as if neither got the better end of any bargain. And there was more. Ma was tired from driving a cart all day and wanted to go to bed, which must be preceded by playing the panpipe for a while. That habit had started with his profession, a job he hadn't chosen at the beginning. But nothing else worked to his liking, after switching jobs, from bricklayer, to tile mason, to blacksmith, and to stonemason. Once he was back driving a cart, he kept at it for decades, getting into the habit of playing his panpipe on the road. Other drivers liked to shoot the breeze on the job, while he played the panpipe, so they thought it made him happy, while in fact he needed the music to forget what he was doing. As a result, horses on other carts would start moving when they heard the whip, while Ma's team would stir at the sound of the pipe, making it impossible for other carters to take over his horses. After a long time had passed, Ma developed the habit of playing the pipe before bedtime, like other people who like a nightcap before turning in. He played to keep the horses alert and to make himself sleepy, the same music for different purposes. He seldom went to bed early, but he'd had a busy, tiring day and wanted Yang to go home as soon as possible so he could play his pipe and fall asleep. At any other time, Ma would have said, "No chatting tonight. I'm too tired."

But he was compelled to sit beneath the locust tree to hear Yang's nonsense after seeing the sweat stain on the man's forehead following a hard day's work. Yang brought up this and that, and there was no end in sight, though Ma was not really listening. Then he brought up the topic of Han's new school in town, talking himself into indignation.

"Study? Why does it cost money to go to school? I have no money. All I have is this life of mine."

He spoke as if Old Han were sitting beside him, forcing him to send his sons to school. Ma was not interested in that topic either, but he knew he had to stop Yang at some point or the man would keep talking. The most effective way to stop Yang was to stump him with something he couldn't figure out right away and would go home to think about it, freeing Ma in the process. So he interrupted Yang.

"You're wrong on that one."

"What do you mean?" Yang was stunned.

41

"My son is too old now, but if he were younger, I'd send him to the new school. Attending the new school is about the same as working at the county government office, isn't it?"

"But that's exactly what I meant. I don't want them to work at the county office. I want them to stay home to make tofu with me."

"I don't mean to sound critical," Ma said, "but you really do have rat's eyes—tunnel vision. You never see beyond the tip of your nose. Let me ask you, do you know all about the previous county magistrate, Old Hu?"

"That carpenter? He did a terrible job with court cases."

"I'm talking about carpentry, not the court cases. Now that he's retired from his post, he makes furniture and sells it. He charges seventy yuan for a bench that costs fifty by other carpenters. A while ago he made an eight sages table, for which Old Li, who owns Source of Abundance, paid one hundred and twenty. Do you know why?"

Old Yang drew a blank, before venturing, "Because he's an excellent carpenter?"

"How could an amateur be a good carpenter at his age? It was simply because he was the county magistrate." He continued, "There are thousands of carpenters in the world, but Old Hu is the only one who has been a county magistrate. An eight sages table is nothing special, but when you add that it was made by a county magistrate, it becomes special. What Old Li has in his house now is no longer a table but a county magistrate. Your tofu business would not suffer if someone from your family worked at the county office. Then when that someone left and returned to make tofu, wouldn't Old Yang's tofu be just like Old Hu's table?"

The chat was a revelation to Yang. Ma the carter certainly could see farther than he could. Ma had gone on so long in order to keep Yang from chatting more, but Yang took it seriously, since he was used to getting Ma's advice. So he decided to send his sons to Han's Yanjin New School, not because of the school itself or the position of a clerk, but for tofu. The requirement of tuition forced him to pick one of his two sons. After that son spent some time in the county office, his tofu would be more than just tofu. As for the sons, if not for the sake of the county office, neither Baishun nor Baili would be interested in going, for it would be like being back at Old Wang's private school to suffer one more time. But the prospect of being a county clerk was enticing, even though no one knew whom Old Han would pick. The lucky son would be part of the county office and rise above everyone but Han himself. More importantly, he would be away from home, away from tofu, and away from his father. As mentioned earlier,

42

Baishun had wanted to work for Luo Changli and Baili for Blind Jia, just so they could be away; now that neither solution had panned out, the next best route was to go to the county office. Once there, they would cut ties with Old Yang and his tofu. So Yang decided to send a son to the new school on account of tofu, and both boys would be happy to go, also because of tofu. Back at Wang's private school, the two boys had vied to be the worst troublemaker, but now they fought over the chance to go, though, of course, Old Yang had the final say. For the first time in their lives, the boys fought to please their father, a tofu maker who did not care for tofu. He preferred crow's eggs, which were free. So Baishun got up early and went to the river behind the village, where he climbed seven elm trees to find crow's eggs. Baili, on other hand, brought his father a basin of steaming hot water around dusk.

"Pa, you must be tired from selling tofu all day. Here, take off your shoes and give your feet a good soak."

Yang had thought that Ma's idea was clever, but now he believed he had an even better idea: choosing to send only one son to school. They would believe they deserved it if he sent both of them, but now that only one could go, they listened to him. But soon he began fretting over which one to send, and the indecision had him running over to Ma's house again. Ma had made the comment to shut him up, and who would have thought that Yang had taken his words so seriously that it brought him back for more chatter? Now Ma rued his miscalculation, yet things being the way they were, he had to keep going down the allegorical path to the end; as a carter, he knew how hard it was to turn a cart around, let alone a person like Yang.

"Which one's smart and which one's stupid?"

Yang rubbed his beard and pondered.

"Well, Number Two's brain works better. Number Three's seems frozen."

Two was Baishun; Three was Baili. Suddenly seeing what Ma was getting at, he slapped his thigh and said, "Number Two has a better brain, so I'll send him."

But Ma shook his head. "No. Better to send the stupid one."

"Why? Isn't a good brain better for learning?"

"Of course, a good brain is better for learning. But if you want to get your money's worth, then the stupid one is a better choice. Look at it this way: people are like birds; with good brains, they flee the coop once their wings are strong. Only the stupid ones can be held back before they fly off." He continued, "Besides, what's the purpose of sending him to school to become an official? It's to come home and make tofu later. Tofu won't have a hold on the smart one; only the stupid one would come back to work."

Another revelation for Yang, who had to admire Ma's insight; but then he was fretting again.

"What if Number Two is unhappy with my choice?"

"Have them draw lots."

"What if it's Number Two who draws the right one?"

Ma harrumphed.

"I think it's you, not your third son, who's stupid."

Another revelation. Yang went home and began planning the lot-drawing event, which took place that night. Yang gave a rice bowl containing two slips of paper a good shake before placing it on the table.

"Take one. Whichever you get is your lot in life. And don't blame me if you don't get what you want."

Feeling apprehensive, neither boy wanted to be the first to pick. They even tried being nice to each other.

"Baili, you're the younger one, so you go first," Baishun said.

"You're older, so you should draw before me. I'd rather chop off my hand than draw before you," Baili said, keeping his hands in his sleeves.

So Baishun went ahead and the one he picked said, "No School." The other one would be "Yes School." Baili bowed to his brother and said, "Older Brother is kind enough to let me go."

So Baishun stayed home to make tofu with his father while Baili left to attend the Yanjin New School in town.

5

In February of that year, Yang Baishun began learning how to make tofu from his father, but that lasted only a month before they had a row. It started with the discovery of how his younger brother had been chosen for school, tacked on to his dislike of tofu and his father. One morning he left with his older brother, Baiye, who also stayed home to make tofu, to sell their wares in neighboring villages. Baiye normally took the eastern route while Baishun followed the western route. Old Yang had wanted to go with Baishun, with the idea to teach him some tricks of the trade and how to beat the drum. Old Yang had a special system of drumming—not just knocking out a chaotic tattoo of "dong-dong-dong" or "ka-ka-ka." He made different varieties of tofu, which required varying drumbeats. They had aged tofu, tender tofu, tofu skin, shredded tofu, and sometimes even tofu dregs, each type deserving its own drumbeat, which would tell the customers what he was selling that day. The skill took a month or more to master. Baishun would have preferred to shout like Luo Changli at funerals, but that was precisely what his father disliked and why he had opted for drum beating in the first place. They fought over that every day for two weeks.

"You want to change the rules after selling tofu for a couple of weeks, is that it? That's how renegades behave!" He laid down his drum. "It's not that I don't want you to shout. It's just not as easy as you think. All right, try shouting something."

Now that he'd been given permission to shout, Baishun did not know what to do. So he left the village, went off into a field, stuck out his chin, and tried yelling like his friend, Luo Changli.

"Come get your tofu!"

"Here comes Yang Village tofu!"

"Aged tofu, tender tofu, tofu skin, shredded tofu, even tofu dregs."

He sounded like a chicken with a knife at its neck, drawing laughter from his father. Even to himself, it sounded nothing like Luo, who shouted like a tiger in the forest, authoritative and powerful, imposing and orderly. Baishun sounded more like a sneak thief. At first, he thought it was a lack of experience, but a few days later, he saw that the difference lay elsewhere. He was selling a few blocks of tofu, while Luo's shouts announced the death of a real person. Using the funeral crier style to peddle tofu changed everything. But Baishun was not interested in shouting like a tofu peddler, so in the end he reverted back to drum beating, which saved his voice.

On this day, Old Yang had wanted to go out with Baishun. The day before, when he had driven his donkey to Qiu Village to buy soybeans, he'd encountered rain on the way home. Yang was unaffected, but his donkey suffered from a runny nose and the shakes the next morning; he cursed the animal before taking it to see Cai, the town veterinarian. Cai, as it turned out, was Cai Baolin, brother-in-law of the barber, Old Pei. He ran an herbal shop, with a veterinarian sideline. So Baishun went out on his own, taking a western route to a few villages, beating his drum along the way. Being new at the drum and not particularly interested in selling tofu, he did a terrible job. Everyone in the villages knew that Yang the tofu peddler was coming, but they had no idea what he was selling that day. By noon, after passing through seven or eight villages, he had sold only a few blocks of aged tofu and some tofu skin and none of the tender tofu, shredded tofu, or tofu dregs. He ate his lunch at the entrance to Xie Village, and then continued on to Ma Village, where his business suffered the same result. He kept at the drum— thud-thud-thud—but had only managed to sell three blocks of tofu dregs when Old Lü, the village cobbler, walked up with a pot of glue. He stopped at the sight of Baishun.

"So, now you're out on your own, I see."

Baishun told him the truth. "Not quite, but my Pa had to take our donkey to the vet." He pointed to his tofu cart. "Would you like some, Uncle?"

Lü ignored the tofu. "Don't you have another brother? You used to go to school together. What's he doing now?"

"He's attending school in town," Baishun said.

"Why does your brother get to go and you don't? Why should you be selling tofu?"

Too young to know better, Baishun told Lü about the drawing. The man burst out laughing when he heard the details.

"No wonder you're selling tofu," he said as he put down his glue pot. "Your brain doesn't work so well."

Sensing something in the man's comment, Baishun asked, "What do you know, Uncle?"

Lü looked around to make sure no one was around before telling the boy about the discussion Yang had had with the carter. Baishun had always thought his lousy luck had doomed him to a life of making tofu. It turned out that his father, Old Ma, and his younger brother had conspired to trick him; both slips had "No School" written on them. Baili had asked him to draw first, so he would get "No School" no matter which lot he drew. Baili did not even have to open the remaining slip for the chance to go to school.

The cobbler divulged the secret not because he had anything against Old Yang; his target was the carter. In addition to selling tanned hides, Lü also made leather jackets and pants, lambskin boots, whips, saddles, and harnesses; he even dealt in donkey and horsehides. He and Ma had never openly clashed. Their problem was simply the fact that they were the most calculating individuals in a village of more than two thousand. One was a carter, the other was a cobbler, and neither would capitulate to the other, which planted the seeds of discord. In public, they called each other brother this and brother that. Ma bought whips and harnesses from Lü, even a lambskin jacket two years earlier, which Lü had sold to him at a discount. But they sniped about each other in private, which was why Lü had taken this opportunity to undercut Ma.

To be fair, it was not Ma who had spread the story about the drawing to decide which son went to school. In fact, Old Yang himself had let the news slip when he was selling tofu in Ma Village to display his friendship with Old Ma. When Lü repeated the story for Baishun's benefit, he was actually targeting Ma, not Yang, but it hit the boy like a thunderclap. He was angry with his father, not the carter; he had never thought much of Old Yang, but he was shocked that he could sink so low. He overturned the tofu cart, sending its contents into the dirt and turning everything into tofu muck. Old Lü slunk away in fright. Baishun's fury then shifted from his father to his younger brother. Two summers before, when he and Baili were still at the private school studying *The Confucian Analects*, the tutor had asked his wife, Yinping, to watch them trace characters while he went to the market in town. No sooner had Wang left than Yinping

47

walked off to gossip with neighbors, locking the classroom behind her. That did not present a problem for the students. The room was a former cowshed, which meant that the back wall still had openings that had been used to clear the cow shit. The pupils crawled out through the openings and ran to the river to play in the water. While everyone stayed close to the bank, Baili showed off by wading out to the middle of the river with his hands up. He promptly fell into a hole and was swallowed up by the water. The other students got out of the water and ran off, except for Baishun, who was not a good swimmer, but had to risk his life to save his brother. He nearly drowned in the attempt. And this was how Baili repaid him, by hatching an evil scheme against him. Finally, Baishun's rage turned to the carter. He had never had problems with Old Ma, so why would the man conspire with his family against him? What upset him most was that it was a done deal, the rice was cooked, and there was no way he could turn things around. He stewed in anger until it was dark before pushing the empty cart back home. When he walked in, Old Yang, who had just returned with the donkey from the vet, was beating the dust off himself. Seeing the empty cart, he said happily, "So you know how to beat the drum, after all. You sold all the tofu."

Yang himself had never managed a sellout. Sometimes he sold half a load, sometimes less than half, but he always had some left. Since it all depended on the customers, it was impossible to say how much he could sell each day. At that moment, his oldest son, Baiye, came in with his cart. After heading east the whole day, he still had unsold tofu.

Ignoring his father, Baishun rammed his empty cart against the wall, sending dust flying in the yard, before blasting into his own room and slamming the door behind him. He did not respond when called to dinner that evening and refused to get up early the next morning, when his father told him to run the mill. Old Yang knew that something was up. So after breakfast, he took the cart out himself, heading west, selling tofu while gathering information along the way about Baishun's trip the day before. It was not until he reached Ma Village that he learned about the exposure of his lot-drawing scheme. As he was the one who had told others, he could not be angry at Ma, so the culprit had to be the cobbler, who had betrayed him to get back at Ma. After a day's work, he returned home, put down the cart, and went into Baishun's room. The boy was still in bed. When he saw his father, he grabbed a rolling pin and sat up, a fierce light glinting in his eyes. Yang knew this was serious. In the past, whenever father and son argued, it always ended up with Yang tying Baishun to a tree and whipping him, no matter who was in the wrong. After that, the matter would blow over. On this day, Yang had planned to do the same and whip the boy to solve the problem. But by the way Baishun was acting, Yang knew he would not mind having a real fight if his father started it; Yang Senior was intimidated, but not because he thought he would lose the fight. He was simply afraid that his family would be a laughingstock if people learned about the fight. He cursed himself for being so talkative and revealing the scheme, while holding off the thought of beating the boy. He put on a smile and began talking about Baili.

"So what if he gets to spend two years at the new school? He still has to come home to make tofu."

He continued, "Don't worry. Without going to school, you have a two-year advantage in tofu making. I promise you'll do just fine. Starting tomorrow, you'll get 10 percent of the profits and can save up enough to get married in a few years."

Then he whispered, "I won't tell Number Three about this."

He continued, still whispering, "I won't tell Number One either. He won't get a thing from selling tofu."

Yang thought he had succeeded with his clever talk, but Baishun ignored him, turned his back, and pulled the blanket over his head. He ended up sleeping the whole day and only got up for dinner, before going back to bed. He was supposed to work the mill at daybreak, but using a toilet visit as an excuse, he climbed over the back wall and left the house. He had finally managed to leave home. Or, put differently, he had finally found another reason to cut ties with his father and with tofu. He would feel no regret no matter where he went, so long as he could be away from Old Yang and tofu. But he began to fret as soon as he was out of the village. He had spent the past day and two nights fuming, without giving any thought to where to go. Now that he had left on a whim, he could not think of a single place to go. He had once considered working with Luo Changli at funerals, but he could not earn enough to support himself that way. Old Master Fan in town came to mind; he could work in his field. After studying at Fan's private school, he had observed Fan often enough to know that he treated his employees well. But harvesting wheat under a sweltering sun was not his ideal means of making a living. He must learn a skill, one with which he would be sheltered from the wind and the rain. Making and selling tofu was his only skill, and he knew no one from whom he could learn another. He was still clueless about which direction to take after walking five li when he suddenly recalled his third maternal uncle, Old Yin, who owned a salt field and, with a few workers, harvested salt by boiling the alkali soil. He pushed a salt cart through neighboring villages and, unlike Baishun's father, preferred to shout his wares.

"Good salt and fine soda powder!" he would shout. "Old Yin from Yin Village is here."

Salt and soda powder were also gathered under a hot sun, but, unlike harvesting wheat, it was a skill. Besides, he could shout when selling salt and soda powder, even though it was more akin to selling tofu than to performing funeral rites. Old Yang had pounded his drum for more than two decades, so naturally, it would have been awkward to switch to shouting. But Old Yin had been shouting since his first day, also for more than twenty years. Baishun thought it would sound natural to follow his uncle's example; though it could not compare with crying at funerals, he would at least feel pretty good doing it. He'd met this uncle during a visit at his grandma's, and would now approach him for a job. There was just one problem: Yin had gone bald, and, as a result, had turned ill tempered. On one occasion, Baishun had seen a worker carelessly let the water run from the salt pit into the soda pit. Yin had picked up a shovel and hit the man so hard he'd bled, though the man had stopped the water without even stopping to wipe off the blood. Baishun was apprehensive, but he had no other choice, so he decided to go see his uncle. Taking big strides, he headed for Yin Village, some seventy li distant, passing through Li Village that afternoon. Exhausted and hungry, he decided to stop for a rest at Zhangbanzao, where he would beg for something to eat. After entering the village, he spotted a group of villagers having their heads shaved under a locust tree by a large pond. The barber's stand was steaming; Baishun's eyes lit up when he recognized Old Pei. How could he have missed Pei when planning his future? He had not been sold on the choices that had come to mind, while the one he missed was right in front of him. What a happy coincidence. He felt like rushing up to tell Pei that he would learn to shave heads from him. It wasn't much, as skills go, but people's hair grew daily, so there would always be work. Compared with gathering salt and soda under a blistering sun, head shaving would allow him to work under a cool shade tree. Besides, he and Old Pei had met before, traveling from the threshing ground in Yang Village to Old Sun's eatery in town. They could be said to be companions in adversity. Now that he saw a bit of light, he felt much better about his future, and his hunger was gone. Pei was busy, surrounded by many people; obviously this was not the time to speak to him, so Baishun took off his shoes and waited outside the circle of customers. The crowd thinned as, one by one, the Zhangbanzao villagers left with newly shaved heads, until the last one was a man with a scabby head. Once that head was also shaved, Pei began packing up, wrapping the razor, scissors, clippers, comb, hair brush, and knife sharpener in a cloth. Baishun walked up.

"Uncle."

Exhausted from the day's work, Pei kept his eyes shut as he packed. Now they snapped open.

"You haven't had your head shaved yet?"

"Don't you remember me, Uncle?"

Pei took a close look but did not recognize the boy.

"You saved my life once."

He went on to tell Pei about the night two years earlier, the threshing ground, Old Sun's eatery in town, and in particular, the two big bowls of mutton noodles. Finally it all came back to Pei. Baishun had said Pei saved his life, but Pei knew deep down that Baishun was the one who had saved him by preventing him from killing someone that night. If he had, he would not be shaving heads today. So Pei warmed up to the boy.

"What are you doing here? Do you have relatives in this village?"

Baishun shook his head and then told Pei what had happened since they'd parted ways at Old Sun's eatery—the dissolution of Wang's school, the new school in town, the secret plot hatched by his father, his brother, and Old Ma against him, his discovery, and the decision to leave home. It was a different kind of twist, but a twist nonetheless. He sighed.

"Uncle, I have no place to go." Baishun began to choke up. "Please take me in. I'll be your apprentice."

Pei froze. "This is happening too fast." Puffing on his pipe, he began to think, and it was a while before he finally said, "I can't help you this time."

Baishun was disappointed.

"It's not that I don't want to. In fact, it's time that I find myself an apprentice, but it's not up to me."

Baishun knew that Pei was henpecked and, with such an important matter, what he said did not count. Baishun still wanted to plead his case, but Pei, knowing what the boy was about to say, stopped him.

"My wife told me to find an apprentice, and I did, six months ago. But he ran away last month."

"I won't run away once I start with you, Uncle."

Pei took a look around before saying to the boy, "He wasn't just any apprentice. He was my wife's nephew."

Now Baishun knew what was wrong.

"He ran away because he was no good. It had nothing to do with you."

Pei flashed an enigmatic smile.

"No, it had everything to do with me. I knew what was on her mind. She did not want me to visit my sister when I was on the road. She was also afraid I'd

51

keep some of the money for myself. I was already under her thumb at home, so why would I want someone to keep an eye on me outside? She wanted to play dirty, so that's what I did. I never beat her nephew, nor did I curse him; I just never passed on my skill. He nicked people whenever he shaved a head, so of course the customers were unhappy with him. Once in Ge Village, he cut the head of Old Ge the fence maker so badly that blood ran down the man's face. Ge jumped up and slapped him. It went on like that day after day, so what could he do but run way?"

Baishun got the picture.

"If I found another apprentice so soon after her nephew ran away, I might give myself away."

Now that Pei had told him the truth, Baishun knew he could not keep pestering the man.

"Since that's how things are, I'll go stay with my uncle at Yin Village for now. He's a salt maker with a bad temper. He beats his workers without provocation, and I'm sort of afraid of him."

"Why don't you stick it out with him for a while. We'll talk again when I can work things out on my end."

The sun had set while they talked, and Pei had to go home. It was time for Baishun to get on the road for Yin Village, and so, picking up the barber stand for Pei, Baishun left Zhangbanzao with him, chatting along the way until they reached a fork in the road, where they would go their separate ways. Baishun moved the carrying pole over to Pei's shoulder, and Pei walked off. But he turned back after a few steps.

"Let me ask you something. Are you any good with a knife?"

Startled, Baishun stopped in his tracks.

"What? You want me to kill someone?"

Pei laughed. "Not people, pigs."

The boy was confused. "I've never killed a pig."

Pei came back and set down his stand. "This will be good for you as long as you don't mind killing animals."

"How's that?"

"Old Zeng, the butcher in Zeng Village, is a good friend of mine. He told me once that he was getting old and wanted to find an apprentice, but had yet to find someone who worked out. His wife is dead, so he makes all the decisions at home. He may work with knives and cleavers, but he has a pretty good temper."

Baishun had run out of options, and this meant he would not have to work for his ill-tempered uncle.

"I'm not picky, Uncle," he said happily.

"Good. Let's go to Zeng Village." Pei was pleased.

Baishun shouldered the stand again as they headed to Zeng Village.

The next day, Baishun began his apprenticeship to pig butcher Zeng, while wondering when he would be able to apprentice himself with Pei. Zeng was a total stranger, while Baishun and Pei had a history. He saw Pei a few times after that, but the older man never again mentioned the apprenticeship. Over the next six months, Baishun grew increasingly familiar with Zeng, and so one day, while they were having a heart-to-heart talk, he mentioned Pei's old promise. He thought Zeng would be upset, but the man just laughed.

"You're too young to understand. He won't take you on precisely because you suffered hardships together."

"How's that?"

"Once people suffer hardships together, they can only be friends, not master and apprentice."

Baishun suspected that Pei had made up the story about his wife's nephew, which changed his opinion of the man.

6

Yang Baili, Baishun's younger brother, was expelled from Yanjin New School after only six months, though not because of anything he did. Back at Wang's private school, he had never paid attention in class when discussing *The Confucian Analects* and was always up to no good. But that was not the cause of his expulsion from Old Han's school, where a lack of diligence was not a problem so long as the student listened carefully when Han came to give a speech. What caused Baili's expulsion was that Han had gotten into trouble, though that had nothing to do with the New School. That fall, when Governor Fei of Henan came to inspect the regions north of the Yellow River, he made a stop at Yanjin, where Han spent a day showing him around. Being a chatterbox, Han rambled to the point that he got on Fei's nerves. Originally from Fujian, Fei's father had been a mute, which meant that Fei had grown up in a generally silent household and had himself become a man of few words. In his view, no more than ten useful phrases were uttered any day throughout the world. During his day in Yanjin, Han probably uttered more than three thousand sentences. From Han's chatter, Fei learned that Han had set up a school soon after assuming his post, and that in the six months since it opened he had given sixty-two speeches, amounting to one every three days. Han smugly told this to the governor as a means of demonstrating his "performance." Yanjin was under the jurisdiction of Xinxiang, whose commissioner, Geng, accompanied Fei that day. When they returned to Xinxiang the next day, Geng had lunch with Fei, who reported on his inspection trip that had taken him to five of the eight counties. He had little to say about the first four, but when he came to Yanjin he frowned.

"Who appointed Han as county chief?"

As it turned out, it was Geng himself. Han's father and he had been classmates at the Nagoya College of Business and Politics in Japan. Seeing that Fei did not like Young Han, he said, "He rose through the usual selection channels."

"I don't get it. That tiny mouth of his never stops yakking. Is he really magistrate material? Governing a large country is like making fine food. A single phrase ought to be enough for fifty years, but he gave sixty-two speeches in six months. About what?"

"Nothing much, really." Geng was sweating nervously.

"I can't imagine him saying anything important. He's barely out of school, so what does he know? All that talk, and he says nothing. That bothers me." Fei went on, "It's all right to talk, but he's setting a bad example for the students. What if they went around shooting off their mouths like him? Does he plan to turn everyone in the county into a chatterbox? If everyone were like him, all talk and no action, chaos would reign in the world."

"I'll talk to him about it," Geng said.

"As the saying goes, it's easier to alter the course of a river or move a mountain than to change someone's nature," Fei said with a somber look. "He's nearly thirty, not a child any longer. Can you really talk to him and get him to change? I doubt it, but maybe you're more skillful than I, and you could do it."

"I'm afraid not," Geng replied as he wiped the sweat off his forehead. "I'm not sure I can."

The day after Fei returned to Zhengzhou, Geng removed Han from his post, even though he did not agree with the governor's views on talking. What did being talkative have to do with the qualifications for a county magistrate? Besides, didn't Confucius say that one should never tire of teaching and should teach whoever wants to learn? Han did like to talk, but he hadn't done anything wrong; he just had this personal failing, not unlike his predecessor's carpentry hobby. It was precisely his talking without action that was a guarantee against stirring up trouble. But the governor meant business, so Geng decided Han had to go. He did not want to jeopardize his own situation over the young man. Han had come to Yanjin with great ambition and grand designs, but he ran into trouble with his habit of talking, like the proverbial crooked-mouthed mule that has to be sold for the price of a donkey. After only six months he would have to pack up and leave. When the news reached him, he ran to Xinxiang, where he tried to reason with Geng.

"Why did you remove me, Uncle? What did I do wrong?"

He began arguing his case with the actions of the European powers, and then the United States, before bringing up Japan's Meiji Restoration, which led to the advantage of opening new schools. Geng had felt sorry for him before he began, but Han's argument convinced him that he had made the right decision to remove him.

"My dear nephew, you are right and your arguments are sound. Your problem is that you were born in the wrong place at the wrong time."

Han looked at him blankly. "Where should I have been born—Europe, America, Japan?"

"Not necessarily. Your talents would not have gone to waste if you had been born in China at around the time of Confucius."

"I went to speak at the school not to teach but to save the country and our people." He was about to continue his reasoning when Geng stopped him with a frown.

"I did not assign you so you could return to the Warring States Period as a teacher, but for you to help the country and our people. How? You'd have been in your element in the time of the Warring States, for you would have been a fine negotiator who made a living with the mouth. But the mediator of those days talked to kings, not children. What good does it do to talk to children? You must talk to those in charge if you want to make a difference. If you were good at it back then, you got to wear the official seals of six states, bringing some of your good fortune to me. If you were no good, then, 'ka-cha,' off with your head. What I want to know, dear nephew, is how would you have managed by talking on and on to a head of state?"

Given the circumstances, Han sat woodenly, having been out-reasoned for the first time in his life.

When he returned to Tangshan, Yanjin New School closed up shop. As in Wang's last days, the students went their separate ways, their dreams of moving into the county office shattered, along with Old Yang's hopes for "county magistrate tofu." Baili should have returned home to work alongside his father, but he chose not to, not solely because he hated tofu and his father, like his brother, but more importantly because he had made a friend at the school, Niu Guoxing, a bigheaded fellow whose father was on the board of the Yanjin Fabricating Plant. The boys, who were in the same class but had no interest in school, often sneaked out of the classroom to catch cicadas with sticky bamboo poles and shoot birds with slingshots. In addition to these common interests, they became friends because they were good partners at "shooting the breeze," a Yanjin pastime with one person casually bringing up a topic, upon which another person builds, back and forth, continuing with it to create a story out of whole cloth. When done well, the story can go in a myriad of directions. It was altogether different from Han's speeches, which were grandiose but impractical, empty talk and nonsense. They had no idea what it meant to save the country and the people. Shooting the breeze, on the other hand, was based on concrete objects and people, leading to a lively story. Except for those days when Han came to give a speech, Baili and Guoxing never sat through a whole period in the class; they usually sneaked out when the teacher was writing on the blackboard. The teachers Han hired were all the quiet type, incapable of keeping the students in check. At first, Baili only knew how to catch cicadas and shoot birds; he was no good at shooting the breeze, and it took him three months of instruction from Guoxing to get the hang of it.

An example: Guoxing said, "The cook, Wei, at Grand Feast Diner in town used to smile at work, but he's been holding his arm and sighing over the past month. Why?" Baili gave some plausible answers, such as the man owed someone money, or had had a fight with his old lady. That upset Guoxing, for they were common reasons anyone could come up with, not shooting the breeze. After recovering his composure, Guoxing gave Baili a demonstration by answering his own question. "Remember that drama troupe that came to town from Hebei a month ago? Wei was infatuated with one of the main female roles and went to every performance over the two weeks they were here. It was as if he had lost his soul. When the troupe left for Fenqiu, Wei followed them there. Why? Because he wanted to have a little something going with her. And so one day late at night, he climbed over the theater wall and was backstage, where he saw the female lead's costume hanging by a bed. He assumed that the woman was in that bed, so he sneaked up, took off his pants, and whipped out his tool to carry out his plan. To his chagrin, it was not the female lead, but was a watchman who was guarding the costumes. Having once played martial roles on stage, the man beat up Wei badly, breaking his arm. Hiding his arm in his sleeve, Wei could not tell anyone about what happened. So lately he has been holding his arm and sighing." If this had occurred during the first three months of their friendship, Baili would have merely considered his new friend to be a superb bullshitter; but after three months, he had learned a thing or two about shooting the breeze, so he tried out his new skill, tentatively. "You say he nearly lost his soul? That's not what I heard. I heard he has been a sleepwalker since childhood, and nothing bad has come of it for more than thirty years. But last month he was walking in his sleep in a graveyard, where he ran into an old man with a white beard. This was not Wei's first time in the graveyard, but nothing had happened in the past. That night the old man whispered something to him. Wei nodded, and began sighing the next day. When stir-frying vegetables, he was so downhearted that his tears fell into the wok. When asked, he refused to say what the old man had said to him." When Baishun was done, Guoxing slapped him on the shoulder happily and said, "Well done." Then he followed up, "I know what the old man said. Wu, the owner of Grand Feast Diner, is a good friend of my father's. Wu told my father that it was bad luck to have a cook crying in the diner. He had wanted to fire the cook, but, to his surprise, business was better than ever. Many people came not for the food but to watch Wei shed tears. Obviously, they were so enchanted by the weeping Wei that they lost their souls." And so on. What they said could have been true or it could have been imagined, but it was certainly interesting. When they reached the climax, Guoxing said, "I have to pee."

Baili had no need to go, but he said, "I'll go with you."

After the school shut down, Baili refused to go home to make tofu at his father's side, and Guoxing did not want to part with Baili, since finding a good partner for shooting the breeze was hard. Nothing is better than having a bosom pal. So Guoxing pestered his father until he agreed to take Baili on as an apprentice at the fabricating plant. It was not a real factory, just a place where a dozen blacksmiths made wood choppers, kitchen knives, spades, scythes, hoes, plows, rakes, angle irons for wagons, stoves for diners, steel doors for shops, blunderbusses for shooting rabbits, and so on. They made pretty much the same things as Li's blacksmith shop in town, but their shop was larger, with more workers, almost a factory. After six months, Baili had yet to learn how to make even a spatula, because, as in school, he did not pay attention to what he was doing. He thought about catching cicadas and birds, and shooting the breeze all day long, and soon he focused exclusively on that, which pleased Guoxing no end. Baili's master could see that he was not cut out for smithing, so he told him to work the furnace, and he did such a terrible job with that simple task that he ruined a chopper the master was making.

"You know what people mean by undercooked?" he said with a sigh. "This is undercooked."

After six months, Baili had managed to annoy everyone in the shop. Old Niu could tell that the boy was no good for serious work, and wanted to send him home, but Guoxing did not want his friend to leave. He smashed a clock in protest.

"The problem isn't his lack of progress. I'm just afraid that he'll have a bad influence on you if he sticks around too long."

"Don't forget," Guoxing said, "I turned bad before he did. Let him go if you want, but I'll go with him, wherever he goes."

Old Niu sighed helplessly; he had no choice but to remove Baili from the plant and put him in charge of guarding the entrance, which made Baili very happy, as it gave him more time to shoot the breeze with Guoxing. On days when his friend did not come, he did it alone, in his head. Ideas soared in his head as he stood guard. Each person who came in interrupted his train of thought, and he would rudely interrogate whoever it was—it didn't matter who—for a long time before letting the person in. They cursed him silently, which in a way showed that the blind fortune-teller's prediction had been accurate.

He and Guoxing had a falling out a month after he started in his new job; it was related to, but not caused directly by, shooting the breeze. As we have seen, Baili had learned the pastime from Guoxing and got very good at it in six months. So good that he stopped using his brain for anything else. In the past, Guoxing had played the leading role, with Baili continuing the narrative; Guoxing could take the topic in any direction he wanted, like guiding the flow of water in a river. But that gradually changed. Baili had built his own ditch and could decide on the direction of the water flow, not necessarily following Guoxing's lead. They also had problems with topics, which Guoxing had monopolized in the past. He could say anything he wanted, but now Baili offered his own topics. By spending his days guarding the gate, his imagination had time to run wild, so he was well prepared when they got together at night. Guoxing, however, had to rush to catch up, and after a while, Baili had the upper hand in both topics and the order of their narratives, with the frequent result that Guoxing would be stuck in Baili's train of thought.

Now that Baili was taking the lead, consciously or not, he began to behave as if he were Guoxing's equal. Guoxing, on his part, did not mind losing at the pastime, but it did not please him when Baili sought equal footing in their daily life. He slowly lost interest in shooting the breeze with Baili. But the direct cause of their fallout was a girl from their former school, Deng Xiuzhi, nicknamed Erniu, whose father was the owner of Big Shot on East Street in the county town. Big Shot was just a general store that sold rice, flour, soy sauce, cooking oil, vinegar, matches, lamp shades, hemp cords, woven baskets, and the like. A stumpy girl, she wore her hair in two thick braids, but she had a pleasant face with thick brows and large eyes, as well as dimples when she smiled. Back at New School, Baili and Guoxing had been too busy catching cicadas and birds and shooting the breeze to pay her any attention, so neither boy had ever spoken to her. When Guoxing ran into her one day after the school was shut down, she cast a casual glance in his direction, which he took as a sign of her feelings toward him. Upon his return, he used that as the opening of their breeze shooting one day, beginning with that glance, then back to their school days; a relationship that began in shyness advanced into intimacy that included kissing and going to bed. Guoxing even added some romantic clichés, such as a morning breeze and a waning moon, and waking up from a drunken stupor. Knowing it was part of the routine, Baili paid his words little attention, but Guoxing turned serious. Not brave enough to see her himself, he wrote a letter that began with "Dear Sister Xiuzhi, when you read this letter it will be like talking to me in person . . ." He then gave the letter to Baili to deliver to Erniu. Baili would have carried out his mission without a word if this had happened six months earlier, but now he was reluctant because he felt that he was Guoxing's equal.

"What's the point in writing her a letter if you've done you-know-what already? You get to have a good time with her, but what's in it for me?"

Guoxing viewed Baili as heartless and ungrateful, a "white-eyed wolf." But he wanted to see the girl so much that he handed five yuan to Baili, who agreed to deliver the letter. Three days went by, and Baili thought his friend had tricked him. The letter could only be delivered at night, because he had to guard the plant entrance during the day, and yet he went round and round on East Street three nights in a row and failed to run into the girl. Guoxing was unhappy; in his view, walking around town was useless. Baili ought to climb over their wall. Since he did not want to part with the money Guoxing had given him, Baili had no choice but to go back to the Deng house. Instead of climbing over the wall, he went up onto the roof to check things out. He had to discover where her room was before he could find her. The Deng house was shaped like a box, with a courtyard, unlit at the moment, in the middle. He couldn't see a thing. People were going in and out of various rooms, but it was impossible to tell who those shadowy figures were. It was easier when they stayed in a room, casting a shadow on the window to show Baili where each of them lived. In the main room were an old man in a skullcap and an old woman who was threading a bobbin winder, likely Erniu's parents. In a room in the eastern wing a man and woman were arguing, with a baby crying nearby, possibly her brother and sister-in-law. That left a window on the western wing, where the shadow of a woman moved about, probably the girl. Baili was getting numb after three hours sprawled on the roof, when the lights went off in the rooms one by one. He climbed off the roof, tiptoed over to the western wing, where he planned to push the letter under the door. That would have been a resounding success had she been in the room. But she had gone to Kaifeng to see her aunt three days earlier, which was why Baili had not been able to spot her on the street. In her room that night, instead, was the younger sister of Erniu's mother, who had come to visit. Having suffered from diarrhea for two days, she had just lain down when she felt another attack coming on, so she got up to use the outhouse. She pulled open the door and was face-to-face with a dark figure, frightening them both. This maternal aunt of Erniu's was a spinster, still unmarried in her late thirties. Seeing the shadow, she thought it was Erniu's father coming to take advantage of her, for he was in the habit of making suggestive comments. In a hurry to use the toilet, she had no time for any shenanigans, so she raised her hand and slapped Baili. With a yelp, he fell to the ground, rousing everyone in the house, who relit the lamps. Erniu's brother thought that Baili was a thief come to steal goods from the general store and, still fuming from a fight with his wife, hung Baili up on a date tree in the yard to whip him. It took only two lashes for Baili to reveal the truth, showing them the love note from Guoxing as proof of his innocence. Deng untied him after reading the letter, for he knew Old Niu at the plant, and he decided not to make a big deal of children's capers. Besides, his daughter's reputation might suffer if anyone heard about it. Guoxing was greatly displeased with Baili the next day, but not because Baili's failure might affect his prospect with Erniu. He was upset because Baili had betrayed him after taking his money. How could he be friends with someone like that? They continued talking to each other, but a wall had risen up between them and they stopped shooting the breeze altogether.

In the eighth month of the same year, Old Wan, a purchaser for Xinxiang's locomotive depot, came to town and stayed at the plant. The Xinxiang depot was in charge of maintenance on the section of railway between Beijing and Hankou, which meant they required a large quantity of railway spikes. The depot chief was a relative of Old Niu, who naturally got all his business, and Wan came once every season to buy railway spikes. Originally from Shandong, Wan was in his forties with white brows and a habit of constantly opening and closing his mouth. He wasn't yawning; he was exercising his jaw, making a "ka-beng" click. Niu had yet to make all the ten thousand spikes Wan needed by the time the man arrived; he was about three thousand short, which was why Wan stayed at the plant. With nothing better to do, he went out for a stroll in town. The rules at the plant required an exchange with the guard when entering but not when leaving, unless a load of product was involved. Out of politeness, Wan greeted Baili when he saw the young man sitting at the entrance. The greeting set Baili off, because he was once again making up stories in his head and Wan had interrupted him. He decided to get back at the man by stopping him with questions. Others would have cursed him silently when Baili stopped them, but Wan loved to talk. He knew no one else in Yanjin, where he had nothing to do but wait for the spikes; instead of being upset over Baili's questioning, he enjoyed the chance to talk with the young man. Clicking his jaw, he told Baili everything: his name, where he was from, where he worked, why he was in Yanjin, following up with spikes, leading to the rail tracks, the trains, the locomotive depot, the number of people working at the depot, and his purchasing job. Wan got Baili so interested in railroads and trains that the young man forgot about his own mental activity. At first he just listened, but then he began asking questions, and that turned into an animated conversation. Wan asked him about Yanjin, to which Baili responded by telling him about all the interesting places. He continued with amusing stories about the town, beginning with Old Wei from Grand Feast Diner running into the graybeard in the graveyard and ending with his own misadventure the previous month, when he was tied to a tree and whipped after climbing onto the roof of Big Shot. Wan roared with laughter. After losing Guoxing as a breeze-shooting partner, Baili could only conduct a solo act, with no chance for a real back-and-forth now that he had finally mastered the skill, after six months' practice. It was like thunder with no rain. Lucky for him Wan showed up, and though it wasn't true breeze shooting, it was better than nothing. They went back and forth, whiling away a whole morning. As if a burden had been lifted from his shoulders, Baili felt light and happy, while Wan was intrigued by a guard who looked like a boy but who had a surprising ability for conversation. Over the past four decades, Wan, a chatterbox himself, had yet to meet his match, and was shocked to find a kindred spirit at the Yanjin Fabricating Plant. Over the next three days, instead of visiting any of the pleasure sites in town, he came to the entrance to shoot the breeze with Baili, after which they became friends who could talk about anything. When the rail spikes were ready and Wan was about to cart them away in a hired wagon, they saw each other again at the entrance. Both felt sad about having to say good-bye.

"Whenever you come to Xinxiang," Wan said as he jumped down off the wagon, "you must come see me at the locomotive depot. Just ask for Big Mouth Wan. Everyone knows who I am."

"Anytime you come to Yanjin, you must stop by the plant. Go to Yang Village if you can't find me here."

Wan got back on the wagon after they waved good-bye. The wagon had traveled for only about one li when he jumped off and ran back.

"I forgot to tell you something."

"What is it?"

"Two of the firemen at the depot just left, and we're hiring. Interested?"

"What does a fireman do?"

"Shovels coal into a locomotive boiler. It's hard work. Firemen work in three shifts, so you'd have time off. I'm a good friend of the guy in charge of hiring, Old Dong, and all it would take is a word from me if you feel like coming. But maybe you don't want to leave the plant."

Baili would have not wanted to go if this had been two months earlier. He had come not to guard the entrance but to shoot the breeze with Niu Guoxing. Now that they'd had a falling out and no longer kept up their pastime, there was no point in sticking around. Maybe he would find a new place to shoot the breeze if he left for the Xinxiang Locomotive Depot with Wan.

"Only an ass would want to stay here. I'll go with you. But I'm going so we can see each other more often, not to be the stoker."

"That's what I had in mind, too." Wan clapped. "Go get your stuff and come see me in Xinxiang three days from now."

"No need to wait three days. If you wait, I'll go get my stuff now."

Wang laughed. "You're certainly eager to go."

That morning, Yang Baili slung his bedroll over his shoulder and left the plant on Wan's wagon. Everyone was glad to see him go, and Old Niu even chanted a few lines of a sutra: "Amita Buddha. Old Wan is a good man. He helped rid me of a terrible worker."

Guoxing was the only one who felt a bit lost when he heard that Baili was leaving. He had expected his friend to stay a long time and was surprised that he would up and leave. When Baili was around, they had fought often, but now that Baili was leaving, Guoxing was reminded of all the things they'd done together. He ran to the entrance, hoping to talk his friend into staying, but Baili was sitting in Wan's wagon and was on his way. Guoxing saw that he was having such a good time talking with Wan that he didn't even turn back to look. A rage rose up inside. How had he managed to get away from here? Wasn't it all because he could shoot the breeze? And where had he learned to do that? Hadn't he, Guoxing, taught him little by little? Now he up and left, without even saying good-bye. Guoxing had tried to help Baili, but ended up helping an enemy. Gnashing his teeth, he cursed, not at Baili but at himself:

"I'll be a son of a bitch if I ever help anyone again."

7

Baishun had been learning how to slaughter pigs with Old Zeng for more than six months. Zeng was in his early fifties, with a fair complexion, medium build, and small hands and feet. From a distance, he looked more like a scholar than a butcher. Yet when he was working, it was as if he had suddenly grown large hands and big feet and was several inches taller. A three-hundred-pound pig was turned into a cat-sized pet in his hands. Other butchers needed three hours to butcher a pig, while he would finish the job an hour into the process and, after placing meat, bones, and guts in neat rows, he would sit on his haunches smoking and chatting without a drop of blood on him. Old Pei, the barber, had told Baishun that Zeng had been an ill-tempered youth, flying into a rage at the slightest provocation; but after butchering pigs for three decades, wielding a butcher's knife and cleaver all day long, he had become mild mannered. Zeng also killed chickens and dogs for customers, a sort of sideline job. When Baishun first came, Zeng let him practice on chickens and dogs before moving on to pigs, not just to practice his skill but also to work on his nerves. Baishun had not flinched at killing a chicken or a dog but recoiled when he was asked to kill an animal standing right in front of him. They were hogtied, but they clacked and they howled, and once they cried themselves out, they just looked at him with tears in their eyes. He shut his eyes the first time and, naturally, his knife missed the critical point, making the animal suffer twice. But just about anything can be mastered with the passage of time, and once he got into the rhythm, his heart grew hard and cold. All it took was a single thrust of the knife to stop the crying animal from making any more noise, and the job was quickly done. That got him thinking. For all creatures that roamed the world, this sort of ending was faster and neater. No other end was that easy. He felt a sense of pleasure when it was done. So in three months' time, he began to get fidgety if there wasn't enough work for several days in a row.

"It's time for you to learn to slaughter a pig," Zeng had said.

Zeng's wife had been dead for three years. Baishun was given board but not room with Zeng, but not because there wasn't space for him in the five-room house. Though not in the best shape, two of the rooms had brick walls and a tiled roof, and the other three were made of rammed earth; they all leaked when it rained. One of the rammed-earth rooms was used to store firewood. Zeng's sons, who did not get along with their father, did not want a stranger living in their house. As with Yang and his sons, Baishun and Baili, who did not want to be tofu makers with their father, Zeng's sons did not want to be pig butchers like him; they didn't oppose his taking on an apprentice, but they refused to let the apprentice move in with them. They said that the rooms were empty for now but would be theirs when they married in the near future, and it would be awkward to kick him out soon after he'd moved in.

Baishun had landed a job but had no place to sleep. Since jobs were harder to come by than lodging, he was not about to quit. He would have moved in with relatives or friends if he'd had any in neighboring villages, but the closest village was, in fact, Yang Village, fifteen li away, and he had no plans to go back there now that he had left home. He knew he could make do with other aspects of his life, for a while at least, but he had to sleep every night, and a haystack was out of the question. In the end, he was forced to knuckle under and return to Yang Village; cutting ties with his father and tofu had not been as simple as slitting the throat of a chicken or a dog. The two villages were separated by the Jin River, which Baishun crossed twice each day. In the early morning, he showed up at Master Zeng's house to go to work; at the end of the day, he saw the master home before returning to Yang Village. Luckily, the ferryman, Old Pan, was a friend of Zeng's, who slaughtered pigs for him twice a year, so Baishun did not have to pay the ferry fare.

Old Yang had been stunned when Baishun left, and he thought the boy would never be back. He was gratified that Baishun had not gone far; the boy had only managed to travel fifteen li to work for a butcher who didn't even offer him a place to sleep, forcing him to commute. He had been wrong to trick Baishun with the lot-drawing plot, but now he felt that Baishun was wrong in choosing butchering over tofu making. So father and son were even. Sometimes, when Baishun rushed home bathed in sweat, Old Yang mocked him.

"What's your rush? Who says you have to hurry like this just to learn a skill? That's too much trouble."

Or, "My tofu mill didn't shut down because you didn't want to learn the trade. I can make it without you."

Or, "One of these days, I'll go visit Old Zeng. I'd like to know how a virtual stranger could make my son travel thirty li a day, while *I* can't make him do anything."

Zeng was actually the one who felt sorry over Baishun's commute.

"I could have let you move in, but I didn't want you to suffer their cold shoulder on a daily basis," he said, knocking his pipe against a table leg. "The one goal in life is not to suffer unnecessary gloom."

"Master, I don't mind running over early every morning, but I'm frightened at night. I don't want to run into a wolf."

"Then we'll finish early from now on. If it gets too late, instead of coming back, we'll spend the night with the customer. I don't believe any of them would say no."

The master and apprentice enjoyed lively conversations. At first, Baishun was reserved around Zeng, but once they knew each other better, they talked freely, back and forth, on the way out for work and back to the village, making the trips seem shorter. They shared information about their families and the people they both knew before moving on to what was on their minds, like confidants. Baishun had treated Zeng's place as a stopgap measure before going to study head shaving with Pei; that moment did not come, and Zeng did not mind. He taught the young man the ropes in affairs between master and apprentice, and Baishun decided to stay put. Butchering pigs was not his ideal job, for what he wanted most was still to be a funeral crier, like Luo Changli. But that was not a viable trade, and he didn't know what to do. Zeng laughed when he heard Baishun's story.

"You like to shout, don't you? Well, there are shouts in our line of work, too."

"Really? Who does the shouting?"

"What, not who. It's the pigs. And it's squealing. A funeral crier shouts for the dead; the pigs squeal before they face the knife." He continued, "We see people eating pigs, never pigs eating people. So funeral shouting isn't a money-making proposition, but making pigs squeal is."

That sounded reasonable to Baishun, easing his mind enough to stay on. But with no place to live and the discomfort of seeing his father's mocking face every day, he was unsettled. As for the widowed Zeng, his biggest concern was finding another wife. But it was also time for his sons to be married, and they had different views as to who should get married first, father or sons. The family was not well off enough for all three to get married at about the same time. Who would go first was one of the causes behind the problems between father and sons, as well as the reason they would not let Baishun move in; their father was their real target, not Baishun. Zeng had secretly sought the help of a matchmaker several times, but none of the prospective matches had worked out; either he did not like something about the woman or the woman found something lacking in him. So he had to put the matter aside. Baishun did not want to harp on his lodging problem, for every mention was like picking at the master's scab; Zeng, on other hand, talked on and on about whether he ought to remarry. Any fresh subject can grow stale after time; Zeng never tired of talking about his marital problems, but Baishun grew tired of listening to him. Once, as they were returning from slaughtering pigs in Cui Village, fatigued from foot travel, they sat beneath a willow tree by the Jin River to rest, seeing that it was still early and they did not have to rush back. Zeng smoked and complained about stingy Old Cui; they had finished butchering pigs for the man by lunchtime, but not a shred of pork had shown up in their food. Had he known that Cui was such a miser, he would not have worked for him. Before long, he was talking about remarriage again, but this time Baishun cut in before he got started.

"If you want to remarry, Master, why not just go ahead and do it? You keep talking about it, but what good does that do? You're just talking to make yourself feel good, is that it?"

"Who wants to remarry?" Zeng rapped his pipe against the tree trunk. "Wouldn't I have already done that if I wanted to? I'm just talking."

"But you talk about it every day, and that can only mean one thing. You really want to."

"There's no suitable match, even if I did want to."

"That's because you're so picky. You want a good match, but have you thought about how good a match you are? If you weren't so choosy, you'd have been married long ago," Baishun said with a slightly censorious look. "But it's really not because you're choosy, is it? I know you're afraid of those two brothers."

Those two brothers were Zeng's sons, the old man's sore spot. Stiffening his neck, Zeng replied, "Who's afraid of them? I'm still the head of the household."

An awkward silence between them lasted awhile before Zeng sighed, knocking his pipe against the willow tree.

"I'm not afraid of them. I just don't want any gossip. They're in their late teens and I'm in my early fifties. How would it look if I fought with my sons over who got married first? Actually, I don't care what people say that much. Just think about the problems we have already. Life would be even harder if I went ahead and got married."

"That's because your sons are not being sensible. They can wait because they're only in their late teens. But not you. You're in your fifties, and it will be too late if you wait till you're in your sixties. What would be the point in getting married then?"

That got Zeng thinking.

"What you say makes sense," he said after a moment.

In the spring of that year, Zeng made up his mind to get married before his sons did. No longer choosy, he told the matchmaker not to worry about him as long as the woman found him to be a suitable match. With his requirements removed, everything was easier this time; a prospect was quickly located, the younger sister of the man who sold flatbreads with donkey meat in Kong Village. On market days, Kong set up his stall with Old Yang to his left and, to his right, a spicy soup and tobacco stand by Old Dou from Dou Village. We have already seen how Zeng and Kong argued with Yang over the way he liked to beat his drum. Kong's sister had lost her husband just before New Year's, an ideal opportunity. It was Pei the barber, not the matchmaker, who brought the two together. Pei befriended Kong when he came to shave heads in Kong Village, and Kong trusted him enough to marry his widowed sister to Zeng, a friend of Pei. The betrothal gifts were sent over on the second day of the third lunar month, with an agreement that the wedding would be held on the sixteenth of that month. Baishun was happy for his master, not because he had finally taken action and would stop talking about it, or because he could vent his unhappiness with the two sons. Baishun secretly hoped that the new mistress would take charge. When the sons were in charge, they would not let him move in, and things might be different if the new mistress took over from them. Since they were both family outsiders, she might be willing to let him stay in the house. So he looked forward to her arrival, hoping she would be tough enough to intimidate Zeng's sons. He was, in fact, more eager than Zeng for the day to arrive.

He was keenly disappointed when the new mistress moved in. First, her looks. Baishun had met Kong before; the seller of donkey meat cakes was a stumpy man with small eyes, but he was clean and neat from head to toe, and had a pleasant look and a soft feminine voice. Baishun expected his sister to be a woman with slender limbs. Imagine his surprise when, on the night of the sixteenth, the new mistress climbed out of the sedan chair. In the light of lanterns, he saw she was tall and had a long, narrow face with high cheekbones, thin lips, and dark, dry skin. There were even freckles in the hollows beside her nose. He got another surprise when she spoke in a loud, hoarse voice that sounded like a man's, if you could not see her. How could brother and sister by the same mother be so different? The brother looked like a woman and the sister a man. Baishun had advised his master not to be too choosy with his remarriage prospects, but he hadn't expected the master to overcorrect himself so much as to give up all criteria. To be sure, her looks did not affect Baishun. After she arrived, he realized that she might look like a man, but she talked and acted like a woman. She combed her hair into a bun early in the morning and put on a bit of rouge; she could cook and do needlework. Over the past three years, the Zeng household, devoid of a woman, was a mess, with a moldy, gamy odor everywhere. In three days, she turned the place inside out, making it clean and tidy. What pleased Baishun was her mild temper, despite her appearance. She smiled before speaking to anyone and always said the right thing. If there were two ways of saying something, she could turn criticism into praise.

But it was precisely her good nature that dashed Baishun's hopes. He had expected that Zeng's sons would not get along with her, and he could benefit from the discord, like the fisherman in the folktale who gets both a clam and a sandpiper whose beak it has caught. He was disappointed that the first thing she did during the first days of her arrival was to make a new lined jacket for each son, that and new shoes. They were happy with their new outfits. Then she told them that their marriages would be taken care of once the wheat was harvested. These were not empty promises, because she already had two women in mind, nieces from different sides of her family. She told them she was busy with household affairs, but would personally see to the nuptials once she'd put things in order, and everything would work out fine. The sons, expecting to be hostile toward their stepmother, were just waiting for an opportunity for a good fight, but were pacified by the new jackets and the promised wives after the harvest. In fact, they were grateful to her. Their own father had fought with them over many things, while the stepmother was doing everything she could to make them happy. Now they began to vie to get on her good side.

And all Baishun could do was brood. He realized how clever the mistress was, disarming the two sons with lined jackets, new shoes, and a promise, truly like slaying your enemy without drawing blood. What disappointed him the most was her indifference to his exhausting daily commute, the same as Zeng's sons, although she treated him like everyone else, smiling before speaking to him. She echoed the two sons when it came to Baishun's housing situation. In other words, he might have been able to talk the sons around before her arrival, since they had been unhappy with their father. But it was so much harder now with her in the house, and, as the mistress, she thought everything over, making it nearly impossible for Baishun's situation to change.

Zeng's reaction was quite different. For three years he had gone back and forth over whether he ought to remarry. In addition to his concerns for his sons, he was also worried that he might marry someone like his late wife. Pei the barber had once told Baishun about the wife, calling her a shrew. In the first three months of her marriage to Zeng, she had argued with him and everyone in the neighborhood, always choosing the harshest expression when there were two ways of saying the same thing, so that in her mouth praise turned into criticism. After an argument at home, most people remain upset for a while, but not her; she ate, drank, and fell asleep as usual, leaving Zeng to fume alone. His youthful ill temper changed because of his occupation, but also because of her—she had worn him down. Kong's sister never argued with him; she always wore a smile and never uttered a harsh word. At mealtimes, she offered him the first bowl of rice and refilled it when he finished. Before bed each night, she brought him hot water for his feet. Zeng could not have imagined anything better. Within a month, his gaunt face filled out and he no longer spoke in a low voice; his spirits raised, he forgot all about Baishun's housing problem. He had brought it up from time to time in the past, but no longer. He might even have shared his wife's view that this was the way it should be. In the past, he did not care how far they had to go to butcher pigs, but now he would say, "No more than fifty li."

"Why?" Baishun would ask.

"So we can come back the same day."

Baishun could only stew. In the past, he had always hoped to travel long distances, since they could spend their nights at customers' houses, and Baishun would not have to make the nighttime journey back to Yang Village. Now, the master wanted to return every night, so they never traveled any farther than fifty li, which meant that Baishun had to rush home each night. That did not upset him as much as the fact that the master no longer talked like his usual self. They had been open and direct with each other in the past, but now Zeng gave up on straight talk. He did not want to travel far for his own sake, but he said, "You won't have to go home in the dark if we leave early and come back early."

Baishun said nothing, not because he had nothing to say, but because he didn't know how to start. With a third person between them, everything had changed. He sighed over the fact that the master became a different person the day the mistress arrived.

On the day before the Dragon Boat Festival, they went to work in Ge Village, which was within the fifty li limit. But they were working for the head of the village, Old Ge, a minor landlord who owned a bit more than four acres of land. He was the take-charge type, someone who had to decide everything—important matters such as buying or selling land and insignificant details like adding another lamp to the house. He was off at the market when Baishun arrived with Zeng. The Ge family had three pigs: one black, one white, and one spotted. They were all grown animals but, without Ge's instruction, they did not dare choose which one to slaughter. So Baishun and Zeng waited for Ge, who returned in the afternoon. He pointed at the spotted one for the master and apprentice to get to work. It was dark when they were finished and had packed up to leave. It began to rain, a drizzle quickly turning into a downpour. Zeng watched the rain splash into puddles.

"Looks like we can't make it back today."

"We could if we want to," Baishun said sulkily.

Zeng reached out to catch some rain in his hands. "We'll get sick going home in this rain." He turned to Baishun. "What do you think?"

"You're the master, so I'll do whatever you say."

Old Ge came over. "Don't go. Stay the night. It's my fault, so I'll feed you dinner."

So they stayed. After dinner they were put up in Ge's cow pen. At midnight Baishun heard Zeng sigh.

"What's wrong?"

"Turns out I'm an ingrate."

"Why's that?"

"It's all your fault," Zeng said.

"How so?"

"You were the one who urged me to remarry. I just dreamt about my late wife. She was wiping tears with her sleeve, saying I'd forgotten her. Come to think of it, I haven't given her a thought since I remarried. Not once in the last month." He continued, muttering to himself, "She's dead, so what's the point of talking about it? She fought with me all the time when she was alive, didn't she?"

He got up to smoke. "What's the point?"

Listening to the rain on the roof, Baishun felt terrible. On the surface, the master was saying he missed his deceased wife, but in fact he was commenting on how wonderful it was to remarry. If that was how the master felt, then why did he have to say it that way? The more positive the master felt about his second marriage, the worse Baishun felt about the woman, not because he was still hung up on his housing problem but because, after changing everything in the household, she began to tighten her grip, leaving him no breathing room. For instance, based on master and apprentice conventions, the master got to keep everything they earned from their business; the apprentice was not paid. But while the pork belonged to the customer, the intestines—heart, liver, lungs, and stomach—were given to the butcher, who then shared some with the apprentice. In the past, the master pocketed the money and Baishun carried the innards in a wooden bucket to the master's house, where Zeng would then say, "Take whatever you like, Baishun."

If there were ten pieces, Baishun would usually take three and leave seven for the master. On his way home, he would take the innards to Old Sun's eatery in town, where he'd enjoyed a bowl of noodles with Pei the head shaver late one night years before. At the end of the month, Sun would tally up the total and Baishun earned a bit of money. Now, with the new mistress, it was different. When he carried the innards back, the master would smoke his pipe and Baishun would brush the dirt off himself while the mistress divided up the innards. She would say with a broad smile, "Here's your share, Baishun."

He still got three pieces, but in the past he'd chosen them himself. Now he was given the items, the same result, but it felt different. He cared less about the innards than about the difference between taking and giving. With this new mistress in his life, the whole damned world had changed, not just his master. He felt as if weeds had sprouted in his heart.

As the lunar year came to an end, the master's legs began acting up. It was an old affliction from his younger days, when he stripped to the waist while spiritedly butchering pigs, even in the coldest months. He would bare his arms and chest, wearing only unpadded pants, as he wielded a knife to turn a fat pig swiftly into slabs of meat, dazzling the eyes of onlookers, who erupted into loud cheers. He never expected his theatrical act to become a health concern; his arms were fine but not his legs. After he turned forty, he stopping baring his arms, but his legs often ached so much he could barely walk. It had been five or six years since he last experienced those pains, and he hadn't expected them to surface again this year. Now he could not walk, let alone go out to butcher pigs. But New Year's, the busiest time for a butcher, was just around the corner. He lay in bed and fretted.

"It's all right, master," Baishun said. "We'll just miss it this year. Your legs will be better in the spring."

"It's not just about the earnings. I don't want to lose customers to other butchers."

Two butchers in the immediate area, named Chen and Deng, were Zeng's rivals.

"Then what do we do? No one will deliver their live pigs to us."

"These legs are no good." Zeng slapped his legs before banging the bowl of his pipe on them. "Why don't you go alone, Baishun?"

Baishun was startled. "All in all, Master, I've killed only about a dozen pigs, plus a bunch of chickens and dogs, and you were watching me each time. Do you think I could just go out like this? Could it work?"

"Normally, I'd say no. It takes three years to be a good butcher, and you haven't been at it for even a year. But things are what they are, and it's not only about slaughtering pigs. Losing a bit of money is not that important. Chen and Deng would be thrilled to know I can't do my job any longer, and when I think about their reaction, my heart aches as if sliced by a knife." He paused and thumped the edge of the bed.

"It's settled, then. I'll take the order, as usual, but you're to go by yourself."

"What if the customer refuses?" Baishun said, clearly worried.

"There's only one way out. We mustn't tell anyone about my legs." He added, "We'd have to close up shop if people knew I could no longer slaughter pigs. But the customer won't know if you carry my flag into battle, as they say. They'll think that any apprentice of Old Zeng's can't be too bad. I'm sure about that at least. If anyone asks why you're by yourself, just tell them I got a cold the night before, so I'm staying home to get better."

Starting on the sixth day of the last lunar month, Baishun was rushed into solo work. He was anxious without his master around. After the master's re-marriage, Baishun had been annoyed by Zeng's double-talk when they went out together. But now, traveling all alone, he was unnerved, bereft of peace and quiet.

Baishun's first solo pig belonged to a man named Zhu who lived at Zhu Stockade and was one of Zeng's oldest customers. He was startled to see Baishun show up alone.

"Where's your master?"

Baishun followed Zeng's instructions. "He was fine yesterday but woke up with a cold this morning."

"Are you sure you can manage, young man?" Zhu eyed him dubiously.

"It depends. Not compared to my master, but compared to last year I'm much better now. I didn't know how to kill a pig back then."

Amused by his response, Zhu laughed but, with no real objection, took the pig from the pen. Baishun did a decent job tying up the pig, turning it over, and hoisting it onto the board, but he lost his nerve when he picked up the knife. He managed to kill it with a single thrust but used too much force when opening it up and punctured the intestines, sending colorful contents all over the board and turning it into a sauce shop. He missed the major veins when letting the blood, and the chest cavity filled with blood. When cutting off the head, he cracked the snout; now the head could no longer be considered whole. He failed to do a clean deboning job, littering the board with pieces of meat. Old Zhu was so upset he stomped his feet angrily, but instead of screaming at Baishun, he cursed Zeng.

"Damn you, Zeng. What did I do to deserve this?"

It took Baishun five hours to finish work on the pig. With his padded jacket soaked in sweat, he hurriedly packed up. It was evening by then, but he didn't dare stay for dinner, nor did he take the innards with him. He rushed back to Zeng Village and forgot about wolves along the way.

After dispatching ten pigs, however, Baishun improved, though speed remained a problem. Zeng could kill a pig in an hour, while Baishun needed four. But he no longer punctured the intestines; he did a clean job letting the blood, kept the head whole, and deboned nicely. If a customer complained about his slow pace, he just lowered his head and quietly cleaned the bones. The complaints stopped when he neatly laid out the meat, bones, and innards. That went on for twenty days, and he started to see the upside of working alone. Zeng had always decided where to go and how far they would travel. Now it was up to Baishun. Since remarrying, the master had wanted to go home every night, limiting their work to within fifty li. The limitation was now abolished. Baishun had never liked the fifty-li limit, since it meant he had to return to Yang Village each night. Without the limit, a customer could put him up. When he started out on his own, he obeyed the limit, but it took only ten days for him to break the rule. He managed to stay with a customer every three or four days. Once he could manage the business all by himself, he began to have ideas, and new complaints about the mistress cropped up. Back when the two of them went out, the master had taken the money and Baishun had received three of the ten pieces of innards. Now that the master could no longer work and Baishun took over, he still had to return to Zeng's house after work. The mistress took the money and

Baishun still got three pieces. In his view, the mistress was being unreasonable. He never expected to receive the pay, but at least something ought to change with the innards, since he was doing two men's work. Yet the mistress merely smiled when he walked in with a bucket over his back.

"See, your master was right, Baishun. You're cut out for major work."

Or, "What does being forced to use drastic measures mean? This is what it means."

But smile or no smile, all Baishun received was three pieces, upsetting him as he walked home with his share in hand. On the twenty-third day of the month, he went to He Village to slaughter a pig. Old He, a man with his hair parted down the middle, loved to talk. After the usual greetings, Baishun got to work, but Old He stuck around, squatting nearby to chat. After talking about this and that, Old He, who owned a small oil mill, began to complain about the price of sesame, which reduced his profit. Then he mentioned Baishun's master, Old Zeng, and was soon on to Zeng's new wife. Baishun was fine before that subject arose, but once Old He talked about Zeng's wife, Baishun's resentment flared up and, impulsively, he began to complain about her as he cleaned the bones. He talked about how she wore a smile on the outside but was vile inside, how she was miserly with the apprentice, and on and on, pouring it all out. Baishun complained only about her, nothing about the master, and felt so much better afterward. With a sigh, Old He said, "She looks so nice. Who'd have thought she could be so two-faced."

Baishun promptly forgot what he'd said. On the twenty-sixth day, Old He went to the market, where he had lunch at Kong's flatbread stand. They talked about the New Year's celebration and how difficult it was to get through it. Giving He's purchase at the market a glance, Kong asked if he'd had a pig slaughtered. The tofu stand run by Old Yang, Baishun's father, was next to Kong's stand. Years earlier, Yang had gone to He Village to sell tofu and gotten into an argument over the accuracy of Yang's steelyard. An enmity formed between the two men. When Old He was asked about the pig, he took Kong to a spot behind the wall and repeated to Kong everything Baishun had told him. When Baishun was at He's house, He knew only that the youngster was Zeng's new apprentice, and had no idea that Baishun was Yang's son. Later, when he learned of the relationship, he even regretted letting Baishun do the job. Now when he saw Old Yang at his tofu stand, he recalled Baishun, and a perfect opportunity for revenge presented itself. Baishun had said much on many subjects, but now Old He put all else aside and focused on the boy's complaints about the mistress, with ample additions and free embellishments. Baishun's mistress was the younger sister of Kong, who was upset by what he heard. When Old He left, Old Kong suppressed the urge to kick over Yang's tofu stand. But being a smallish man, he thought he might not win in a fight, so he changed his mind, quickly gathered his things, and left for Zeng's house. His sister was in the kitchen, where Kong told her everything he'd heard from Old He. As soon as her brother left, she put down the ladle, went to the main room, and repeated everything to Zeng. After several repetitions, the contents had changed. Baishun had complained only about the mistress, nothing about the master, but when it reached Zeng, it was all about him—he was mean and miserly; he had space but refused to let the apprentice move in; and sometimes he didn't even let the apprentice take home some of the innards. That night Baishun came home as usual, with the bucket of innards over his shoulder. Putting it down, he waited for the mistress to collect the fee and divide the innards, so he was surprised that instead of seeing her, he heard the master call him from inside.

"Come in here, Baishun."

He went in. The master was lying on his bed, as usual, with the mistress standing nearby.

"Let me ask you, Baishun. You've been with me for almost a year. How have I treated you?"

Sensing something in the question, Baishun said, "You've treated me well, Master."

Zeng rapped his pipe against the edge of the bed.

"What did you say to Old He then? You told him I was mean. I want you to explain to me how I've treated you meanly, so I could change."

That sent Baishun into a panic. He knew someone had squealed on him.

"I didn't say that, Master. Don't listen to that nonsense."

Zeng slapped his palm on the edge of the bed.

"Everyone knows it's true, but you deny it. You'll gain my respect if you stand by what you said. Now I'm upset because you deny your own words. Put your hand over your heart and think. How did you end up here? What were you like when you first got here, and see what you have now? I'll get Old Pei the barber over tomorrow, and we'll have a reckoning."

Baishun wanted to offer an explanation, but Zeng's face turned steely dark as he got angrier and angrier.

"You think you've learned everything, don't you? You think I'm lying in bed like I'm dead. No one has said anything bad about me in my thirty years of pig slaughtering. Now my own apprentice has stabbed me in the back, like taking down a bridge after crossing the river." He slapped himself twice. "I thought I could tell a person by looking in his face. I damned well deserve this."

The mistress went up to take his hand.

"Don't get so worked up. No matter what, he's your apprentice." She turned to Baishun. "You're the one to blame, Baishun. If you were unhappy, you should have told him in person, not criticized him behind his back."

"Let him criticize me." Zeng pointed at Baishun. "I deserve it. I was a dumb ass to take him on as an apprentice."

Knowing that the situation was grim, Baishun got down on his knees.

"I was wrong, Master. I did say those words, but that wasn't what I meant."

"What did you mean?"

Baishun had wanted to say that the target of his complaint was the mistress, not the master, but with her standing there, he could not utter a word. His hesitation only made Zeng angrier.

"No need to say any more. From tomorrow on, you go your way and I'll go mine. You're no longer my apprentice and I'm not your master. We'll have nothing to do with each other. From now on, I'll call you Master when I see you."

"With what you just said, Master, I'll lose my place in society."

"Did I do that? You have made *me* lose my place in society." He smashed a lamp shade. "Starting tomorrow, no more slaughtering those goddamned pigs!"

8

On the twenty-ninth day of that year, Baiye, Baishun's older brother, got married. He was nineteen. Back then, that was not too young for a man to marry, though Old Yang had not planned to have him marry that soon. It was a big deal for a tofu peddler to marry off a son, and it was very expensive. Even if they had the money, a family with a small business like theirs could not expect to find a suitable girl waiting on the doorstep to marry one of the sons. There was also the human factor. In people's eyes, the Yang family did not get along well with others, but Yang himself did not look at it that way; he believed he had many friends and that he was well liked. But when a son takes a wife, he starts having ideas, and Yang would have liked for his son to wait a couple of years and to help him make tofu. More important than tofu making was the fact that he had three sons, two of whom had issues with him, which in turn affected his views on sons in general. Baishun and Baili were now both gone, leaving Baiye home to work with him. Those who had left were far away, while the one beside him could not seem to do anything right. A single wrong phrase would make him bear a grudge for a week or more. But how can anyone not say the wrong thing every once in a while? As a result, Yang's unhappiness with his older son began to outstrip his dissatisfaction with the other two, though he never said so. Baiye, on his part, had looked forward to getting married since the age of seventeen, not so much because he wanted a wife but because marriage would let him establish a household of his own and live away from his father. When that happened, he would no longer have to mill soybeans for free, like a mule. Grinding the beans was not as important as getting away from his father and from the need to listen to him. Yang early on sensed Baiye's intention, which deeply upset him. So he kept putting off the marriage. Father and son ground the beans together, each harboring his own thoughts. With Yang making all the decisions, Baiye could *think* whatever he wanted but could not *get* what he wanted.

This year everything was different. The Yang family was not looking for a wedding, but a wedding found them. In Yanjin, weddings seldom took place before a year had passed after exchanging the betrothal gifts. The Yang family began talking about the marriage on the twenty-fifth of the month, and the wedding would be held on the twenty-ninth, a grand total of four days. Old Yang was just a tofu peddler, so only the daughter of a barber or a donkey trader would be considered a good match; and yet their new in-law was Old Qin, from Qin Village, some twenty li distant. The Qin family, with thirty acres of land and more than a dozen workers, socialized only with well-to-do families in the area. A big man, Qin had a round head and small eyes that never stopped blinking, some twenty thousand times a day, compared with two thousand by the average person. Contrary to common beliefs about people who blink too much, Qin was not keen on thinking too much. With a hoarse voice, he rarely spoke above a whisper, but he loved to reason, although his reasoning was different from that of Cai Baolin. The herbalist Cai would not let others talk as he tried to win them over with his reasoning. Rather than offer his own argument, Qin let others do the talking.

"No matter what I do, I can't figure this matter out. Would you mind explaining it to me?"

Then he listened while whoever it was talked, starting from the beginning, giving all the details and every twist and turn, leaving nothing out nor condoning any doubts. But perfection does not exist anywhere in this world, and every story has more than one side. So as the person talked on, holes began to open up in the reasoning, and Qin would quickly exploit the flaws.

"Wait, wait. I'm getting confused here. Explain it to me again."

When one hole in the argument was plugged, another would appear elsewhere, and another, until there were no more, and he would win the argument without having to say a word. He might stop pushing for even more explanations, but he would not let you off the hook now that he had won.

"It was you who said that," he would say, blinking rapidly.

And that was why he never had to use his head when dealing with others; they would eventually come around to his thinking on their own.

Qin, who was approaching sixty, had four boys and a girl. He liked the boys fine, but he cared most about the girl, who had been born when he was forty. Qin might reason with his sons, asking them to explain things to him, but he never did that with his daughter, Manqing. He had even sent her to a private school and later to Yanjin New School, where she'd learned to read. Under normal circumstances, Qin would rather die than marry his only daughter to a tofu maker's son, not to mention the fact that she had already been betrothed to the son of a granary owner on North Street in town. Old Li, the owner of Source of Abundance, also ran a Chinese medicine shop, Heal the World, next door to the granary; the two shops took up half the block. At mealtime, four tables were needed to serve the clerks and all the rest. A talkative man, Li liked to stand on tiptoes out on the street and declare, "If you're well, you eat my grain, and if you're ill, you take my medicine."

That sounded a bit arrogant to most people, but it was only in the way he talked. Deep down he was a decent, if not terribly thoughtful, man with few ideas. And yet he and Qin, a man with too many ideas, were friends. With the help of livestock trader and sometime matchmaker Cui, the two families had arranged a marriage between their children the year before. Li's son, Jinlong, had also attended Yanjin New School, so he and Manqing were classmates. After the betrothal gifts were exchanged, they'd settled on the twenty-ninth day of the last lunar month to hold the ceremony, aiming for double happiness, with a wedding and New Year's. The families had frequently exchanged visits. Over various holidays, Jinlong had come to pay his respects to his future father-in-law. Unlike his father, Jinlong was not the talkative type. When sitting with Old Qin, he quietly listened to the older man and was never bothered by the silence when Qin stopped talking. He nodded or shook his head to express his views on all matters. When Qin was with others, he listened; now Jinlong, his future son-in-law, assumed his role while he became the talker.

"Damned if he isn't better at keeping his composure than I am."

He had nothing against the young man. But less than a month before the wedding, Jinlong abruptly changed his mind, though not because he did not like the Qin family or Old Qin. Earlier that year, he had been drinking with some sleazy friends. When they were playing a drinking game, he had a row with a friend, Wei Junren, also from New School. Jinlong had called Junren a stupid dick, upsetting his schoolmate so much that he retorted, "Who's a stupid dick? You don't even know that your own fiancée is missing an ear. You have no right to call other people names."

Thinking that Junren was joking to hurt Jinlong's feelings, a friend reached out and slapped him. That really angered him. He swore he was telling the truth, saying he'd heard that from Deng Xiuzhi, another classmate. When she entered school, Manqing had first spent a few nights at Xiuzhi's house. According to the girl, Manqing had lost the ear at the age of two; it had been bitten off by a pig while she was napping in the cool of the yard. That was why she let her hair down—to cover the left side of her face. Xiuzhi was the love interest of Niu Guoxing, whose family owned the Yanjin Fabricating Plant, where Baili had once worked. He had been tied to a date tree and beaten by Deng Xiuzhi's father when he was delivering a love note to her on behalf of Guoxing, his best friend and partner in shooting the breeze. Junren had revealed the secret out of momentary anger and had no intention of ruining the marriage plans. But Jinlong's head nearly exploded at the revelation, which came as a great loss of face in front of everyone. Upturning the table still laden with food and drinks, he stormed out and went home to his father to break off the engagement. Old Li, the owner of Source of Abundance and Heal the World, was shocked when he heard about the missing ear.

"That's Old Qin's fault. You should not hide things, even if you're selling a pig, let alone marrying off a daughter. If it had only been a mole, there'd have been no need to say anything. But it's a missing ear. Why didn't he tell us?" Old Li complained.

"But we have been friends for years," he added unhappily. "How can I tell him we want to break off the engagement? He's wrong this time, but if there's an argument, I'm not sure I'd win."

So he tried to talk his son around.

"It's just an ear. She's not missing anything else. Besides, it's covered with hair."

"It's not just about the ear." Jinlong glared. "It's about telling the truth. We only know she's missing an ear, but do we know what else might be lacking? You may be afraid of him, but I'm not. I'll go see him. If you're afraid to break off the engagement, then you marry his daughter."

Li knew his son well; Jinlong was not talkative, but he was stubborn. Once he made up his mind, nothing, not a team of nine oxen, could turn him around. It did not please Li to have his son marry a girl with a missing ear either, so the engagement must be broken off. But he would never let his son go on his own to get it done. Since Jinlong did not care much for talking, a few words could easily start an argument, and then it was only a matter of time before a fight broke out. Li did not want his son to argue with Qin, or even worse, get into a fight. He held his son back by asking the matchmaker to explain things to Qin. So Cui went and told Qin, who angrily retorted that his daughter was not missing an ear, just an earlobe. And it hadn't been bitten off by a pig out in the yard when she was a little girl, but by a rat in her room. It was only an earlobe, after all, not an important organ and not worth mentioning. Then he dragged his daughter out of her room and pulled the hair back to show Cui. Indeed, both ears were there, minus one earlobe. Qin asked Cui to sit down.

"Old Cui," he said, "I don't understand this at all. I hate to get you involved, but I ask you, should we break off the engagement on account of an earlobe? Breaking it off by itself is not a big deal, but why must they exaggerate and turn an earlobe into an ear? Explain that to me or I won't let you go."

Cui was a livestock trader; matchmaking was only a side job. He started to panic when he realized that the matter had gotten complicated, one error turning into another. He did not like to reason with Qin, since he could easily lose an argument even if he was in the right. In the case of ear versus earlobe, Qin was not entirely in the wrong.

"This does not concern me," he said. "I'm not the one who wants to break off the engagement. It's all Old Li's fault. He shouldn't have listened to the gossip." He quickly got to his feet.

"I'm going back to tell him everything. I'll explain the situation and you'll still be in-laws, because you should be."

But it was too late. Not because a missing ear could not be downgraded to a missing earlobe or because the Li family would refuse even that. Li's son, Jinlong, had left home, not to run away but to go south with Niu Guoxing, the son of the fabricating plant owner, to buy medicinal herbs in Hangzhou. Obviously, the trip was just an excuse to get away, leaving a mess for his father to clean up. He did not even say he was leaving.

"It's that damned rumor." Li wrung his hands. "They turned an earlobe into an ear, and he left without a word. The twenty-ninth is around the corner. What am I going to do?"

Cui relayed the news to the Qin family. Qin realized that the little bastard Li Jinlong had pulled a fast one on him. For the first time, someone had gotten the better of him, and he was livid.

"Go tell Old Li that we could have worked things out, but not now, after the way they messed with me. If we break off the engagement over an earlobe, it will turn into an ear when people begin to gossip. His son ran away, and it's his job to get him back. If they don't come for the bride on the twenty-ninth, my daughter will not marry him. I will deliver myself to their house in her place. When that happens, it will no longer be about breaking off an engagement, but about something altogether different, and it won't end until we make some sense out of it."

That hit Li hard, especially since he was used to running to Qin for advice on important matters. Li had started out with only the granary, Source of Abundance; it was Qin who had suggested that he buy the herbal shop next door. Now it brought in more than the granary, which meant he was indebted to Qin. But his son was gone, and how was he supposed to get him back? Someone said they'd gone to Hangzhou, but who knew where they'd really gone? The two families were at loggerheads. It was already the twentieth, and there was no sight of Jinlong, who obviously did not plan to come home for the New Year's celebration. Li was a nervous wreck, like a man sitting on a carpet of thorns, so fearful that Qin would come reason with him that he himself felt the urge to flee. Qin, on the other hand, was talked around by his own daughter. He'd had a few drinks and was cursing the Li family when Manqing walked in.

"I know you're worried, Pa, but I want to ask you something."

"What?"

"Are you trying to prevail over them or are you marrying off a daughter?"

"What do you mean?"

"If you're trying to prevail over the Li family, then we'll continue the brawl. They'll lose out in six months or a year and, with the way you are, eventually you'll be able marry your daughter off to the Li family and be vindicated. But the enmity and bitterness will never go away, not even after I start living with them, which means I will suffer a life of misery over an earlobe. In that case, it will be about more than just an earlobe."

"I'm a reasonable man, so naturally I understand all that," Qin said with a sigh. "But how do we deal with the broken engagement? I can't let them cast you off like a broken tile. That would make your life miserable. I'm upset because I've backed you into a corner, not because they reneged on the arrangement."

Since dropping out of Yanjin New School, Manqing had had little to do but read vernacular fiction from the Ming and Qing dynasties. She read about women from wealthy families who suffered setbacks in their marriage prospects and decided to marry themselves off when they had no way out. They married oil peddlers, woodcutters, even beggars, and all of them ended up with happy lives.

"I used to focus only on people's appearance, but I've learned I must pay attention to what goes on inside. The human heart is the deadliest thing in the world. I don't mean that people are vicious, but when something happens we tend to assume the worst. From now on, I will appear defective in people's eyes, flawed over a missing earlobe. If you really love me, Father, let's not pin our hopes on one person. Starting today, we must take every prospect into consideration, rich or poor. I'll marry the one who truly wants to spend the rest of his life with me and does not let my earlobe bother him. We'll tell him about the earlobe, because that is the only flaw I can reveal. I will remain single if you disagree, even if the Li family has a change of heart." She was in tears when she finished, the sight of which caused her father to curse.

"Damn you, Li, you and your Li ancestors! You've made a mortal enemy out of me." He then turned to his daughter.

"I've used logic all my life; it's you who understands what is important. At the end of the day, we have to agree that wealth and poverty are as changeable as water. A rich man can harbor worries, while a poor couple might have a good life together. Coarse corn muffins can be tasty if you're happy. You'll be miserable all your life, no matter whom you marry, if you don't understand this logic. But if you do, there is little that can bother you. I'm in my sixties and can die free of worries now that I know you understand this important point."

Most people could not out-reason Qin, even if it took three days, but his daughter was able to talk sense into him. Early the next morning, he told one of his clerks to ask Old Fan, another wealthy merchant in town, to come by. He shared with Fan his new views on his daughter's marriage. Fan himself was an in-law of Old Li, who had married his second daughter to Fan's eldest son. Qin asked Fan to be his messenger, for an established merchant carried more weight than Cui the matchmaker. Qin spoke in measured tones. First, he was ending it with the Li family. No more talk about a marriage and no more communication between the two families. Second, the engagement gifts would not be returned, not even a needle or a spool of yarn; instead, they would be distributed among beggars. Third, he would be willing to discuss marriage prospects with anyone, wealthy or not, if his daughter's missing earlobe was not an issue. Fan was stunned into silence when Qin finished. The serious matter over with, they enjoyed a smoke together. Fan was most impressed by the third condition, since it had come from Manqing herself. When the message was relayed to Li, the owner of Source of Abundance and Heal the World was similarly impressed.

"This is a delicate matter, with layers of meaning. How could a mere girl see more clearly than I?" He shook his head. "It's my son's loss. He has eyes but was not lucky enough to see what's good for him, and we have missed an opportunity to have a terrific daughter-in-law," admitted Li. "So be it," he said with a clap of his hands. "I'll be a despicable person in Old Qin's mind until the day I die. It's my own fault for not coming up with a solution."

The incident had nothing to do with Old Yang, but he figured he might benefit by getting a daughter-in-law for practically nothing. The missing ear had been a sticking point for the Li family, though it had turned out to be just a missing earlobe. Yang would not have cared if the girl had only one ear. What mattered was the prospect that he would form a connection with a wealthy family. He would lose nothing if it didn't work out, but if it did, it would be like bringing down two birds with a single arrow. Like a stuffed bun dropping from heaven, it was his to catch. But, being the indecisive type, he hesitated for two days before going to see Old Ma, who had worked out the idea of sending Baili to Yanjin New School a while back. That had fallen apart in the end, but Yang, who focused on gains and ignored losses, could not pass up such a good deal. Ma had also heard of the incident, but he knew it was just a face-saving show by Qin to resolve a dispute between two established families, hoping to shake off the bad aura while proving that his daughter was missing only an earlobe; it would also show that the Qin family, and especially his daughter, had spunk. There was no need for a tofu peddler to get involved. In other words, it was a stage play not to be enacted in real life. Ma was amused by how seriously Yang had taken it and began to feel contempt for the tofu peddler. The contempt was compounded by his anger over the trouble caused by Yang's revelation of the lot drawing for the New School. In the end, Ma decided to play a trick on Yang, handing him a momentous defeat. Instead of stopping Yang, Ma showered him with earnest encouragement.

"That sounds like a wonderful deal. Getting a daughter-in-law for free is better than selling tofu for a whole winter. Actually, it's more than that. Once you're linked to the Qin family, the Yang name on tofu will carry more weight," Ma explained. "Your son's studies at New School did not pan out, but you can make up for the loss by associating with the Qin family."

Ma was not done.

"I don't mean to nag, but you had better get a move on, or someone may get the jump on you."

Yang went home happy. He got up early the next day, the twenty-fifth, changed into new clothes after washing up, and hurried over to Qin's house. After Old Qin had spread the word, everyone knew that it was all for show; no one took him seriously, and not a single family had come with a proposal. Within days Qin had put the idea behind him. So when a tofu peddler came to propose marriage, Qin felt like laughing but could not. Having made it public, he had to deal with Yang. Incredible though it might sound, the show was enacted in real life after the two men had a conversation and a marriage bond was formed. Yang, the tofu peddler, did end up with his food from heaven. He arrived at the Qin house in high spirits, but began to lose heart when he saw the grand mansion with its three outside courtyards and three inside, like a yamen, with a team of well-fed donkeys and horses in the stable and neatly dressed farmhands walking in and out. It was not his first visit, but he had come only to sell tofu in the past and had stayed at the gate to deal with the cook. He had never actually gone into the yard. Now he traveled through the courtyards and entered the main room, where Qin fixed his beady eyes on him from where he sat, in an imposing armchair. He silently waited for the trembling Yang to speak first. The silence persisted, with Qin refusing to speak and blinking leisurely at Yang. Finally Yang could stand it no longer and decided to back out.

"Let's forget it, sir." He turned to leave.

Qin would have let the matter drop there if Yang had not said that, but now that he had offered to leave, Qin decided to speak up.

"Hold on. Why did you come if now you want to forget it?"

"I was wrong, sir." Yang was downcast. "This is what they mean by a toad trying to eat swan meat."

"Tell me, why do you think your son is a toad?"

"He's not good at anything but making tofu."

"What's wrong with that? A thousand acres of fertile land cannot compare with a marketable skill."

"He's an unworldly boy and not a good talker."

"What's so good about being a talker? I use reason instead of words, and look where that's got me with my daughter's marriage."

"He can't read."

"That bastard in the Li family knows how to read. A bad seed who can read is worse than a decent boy who can't."

"Let's not take it any further, sir. My family is dirt poor."

As they talked, Yang sounded less like someone coming to propose a marriage than someone trying to wreck his own chances. Manqing was listening in. Qin's announcement to listen to any marriage proposal had been only a pose, and now he was having fun at the expense of the inept tofu peddler. Manqing, on the other hand, was serious. When no one showed up after the word was out, she assumed that either her missing earlobe was to blame or that no one wanted to get involved in a messy issue. In her view, no one understood what was on her mind. Then Yang had shown up. Unaware that he was scared stiff, she liked what she was hearing, so she parted the curtain and said, "Let's settle on the Yang family, Father."

The two men were stunned.

"Don't be in such a hurry," Qin said when he realized that his daughter was serious. "We've just started talking."

"No need for more talk," Manqing said. "Other families will say only good things about their sons, but Mr. Yang has done nothing of the sort. Where are we going to find a family like that? I have seen Mr. Yang's son, who has been here with him to sell tofu. He gave us a third more than we paid for. If this is how he is selling tofu, I'm sure he'll be the same with other matters. He does no one wrong, while others may take advantage of him."

Manqing did not have all the facts. Yang Baiye had given them tofu not because he was a shrewd businessman but because he was venting his anger at his father. Yet in her eyes, it was a positive character trait. Qin was flustered when he realized that his clever scheme had turned against him.

"This is only the first round. We mustn't jump into it. We need to give it more thought."

Like the ladies in distress in her novels, Manqing took out a pair of scissors and, with a snip, cut off a hank of hair.

"Stop toying with me, Father. I know you were not serious, but I am and I *will* marry him. If you have any more objections, I'll leave home tomorrow and become a nun on Mt. Yunmeng."

The determined look on his daughter's face told Qin that there was nothing he could do; something truly bad could happen if they continued to wrangle over this. He had been out of his mind to agree with her method of finding a husband, but now that he had taken the proverbial eight steps, he could not turn back. Qin had known Yang only through his profession before this night, but he sensed that the tofu peddler was an honest man. In fact, he didn't care even if Yang weren't. What kind of trouble can a tofu peddler cause anyway? But Qin had misread Yang, who could well cause mischief and did not play by the rules when he set his mind on something. He would not have come with a marriage proposal if he'd played by the rules. Qin's misreading led him to believe that poverty was the only thing his daughter would have to endure in Yang's home, so he said to Manqing, "You lack my patience. I would never decide such an important matter after only a few exchanges. I don't want you to regret your decision today." Qin sighed and continued, "This is a first for me."

So the matter was settled, and Yang had no idea how it had come about. Coiling another lock of her hair, Manqing said to Yang, "You have to promise something if you want me to be your daughter-in-law."

"What is it?" Yang said as he wiped the sweat from his forehead.

"We'll consider this a form of engagement, and I want the wedding to take place four days from now. That's the twenty-ninth."

Qin knew what she was thinking; her original wedding with Li Jinlong had been scheduled for that day. Yang was hesitant.

"We won't have time to make the preparations on such short notice."

"What preparations do you need to make?" Qin rebuffed. "Your son is getting married, but I'm the one who will prepare everything for your family."

An overjoyed Yang left for home. Property and connections made it possible for other families to marry off their sons, but it had taken Yang only a few words to gain a daughter-in-law. Serendipity, not connections, was what mattered here. Neither Yang nor Ma had expected that. Yang was still grateful to Ma, though, since he had helped him this time, despite the wagon driver's failed attempt to help Baili get into school. When Yang told his wife about the marriage, she was equally thrilled, but not Baiye, who actually looked peeved. He had been grumbling about his father's inattention to his marriage prospects, but he had a different complaint now that Yang had found him a wife.

"I'm not missing any body parts, so why did you find me a wife without an earlobe?"

Yang kicked him in the shin.

"You're not missing an earlobe but you have a hole in your head."

Reprimand, not praise, made an impression on Baiye, a true good-for-nothing who would cause more complications if he were to have his way. He never raised a stink when he was scolded or punished. His lack of drive was the reason he had stuck with the tofu trade, while his brothers had both struck out on their own. On second thought, he realized that he would have to wait forever to get a wife without this opportunity. The girl did have only one earlobe, but she would soon be sharing his bed and, moreover, as a married man, he could demand a division of the family property. All things considered, it was a good deal, and he gave his consent.

A wedding ceremony was held in the Yang house on the twenty-ninth day of the last lunar month. It had been clear the day before, but tiny snowflakes began to fall in the night and continued on into the wedding day. It was such an unusual marriage that people came from all over to watch, though they seemed to be there not for the wedding itself but to see the missing earlobe, or maybe for the intriguing stories it spawned. The crowd surged forward with cries and shouts when the bride was about to step out of the sedan chair, toppling the earthen wall in the yard and littering the snowy ground. An old woman's leg was broken amid the chaos during which Manqing alit from the sedan chair. Yang Baiye and his father had been to her home to sell tofu, but she had never been to Yang Village. In the novels she devoured, a young woman from the wealthy family would marry into a poor but neat home, and the husband would be astute despite his impoverished state. He might be an oil peddler or a woodcutter, but he had once been a refined scholar who composed poetry and painted. She felt a chill rise up inside when she looked around. The Yang house was dilapidated, with leaning ramshackle rooms in danger of toppling surrounding a badly tended yard on which the snow had turned muddy from the trampling of the crowd. She had expected the run-down house but not the filth and the mess. Her disappointment mounted when she saw the way Baiye carried himself as he rushed up with a piece of red satin to form a tie with her. He had dressed in everyday clothes when he'd gone to sell tofu at her house, giving the impression of a simple, honest man. But now, wearing the borrowed, ill-fitting costume of a groom, consisting of a hat and a long robe adorned with a red satin knot on his chest, he ran over like a goofy monkey. At the sight of Manqing, he laughed foolishly. He did not know why he laughed or what he was laughing at. Baiye was not an idiot, but his face froze in shock when he was confronted with the sea of onlookers. His true colors were there for all to see. Manqing lost hope at the first thing he said, having misinterpreted her dark look as unhappiness over his impoverished state.

"Don't worry," he said. "I've saved up a bit from selling tofu behind my father's back."

She sighed, hit by the realization that real life was different from what was in novels. But she had come up with the idea and it was too late for regrets; she teared up amid the wedding music, not over her wrong choice of a husband, but over her avid reading.

After selling a donkey, Old Yang was able to put up a banquet of sixteen tables, though his house was not big enough for all the guests. He asked to use the two brick rooms in the house of his neighbor, Yang Yuanqing, who agreed only after Yang gave him two large squares of tofu. It was a festive wedding, all things considered. As his son was marrying the daughter from a wealthy family, Yang had been concerned that something might go wrong or not be done well, and would draw criticism from the Qin family. Everything went smoothly at the wedding, and he did not hear a peep from his in-laws. But something did go wrong after the ceremony, though it was caused by Baishun, not by the groom.

Baishun had no place to go after the fallout with Zeng, the pig butcher, so he returned home. Having already learned the butchering skill, he could have gone solo and started out on his own, but the convention of the trade made that impossible, for he was now known as an ungrateful apprentice. At first he had considered going to Pei Village to see if the barber would take him on. But it was Pei who had made the introduction for him to apprentice with Zeng, and Baishun would have trouble explaining the intricate reasons for the fallout, even though he had a different version than his mentor. He might even make things worse and be blamed for something that was not his fault. So Pei was out of question. Next he thought about going to work again with Yin, the salt maker, except that salt making was limited to spring, summer, and fall, since the alkaline soil froze in the winter. He had to wait until the following spring. Another option was doing farm work, but there would be no hiring till the spring. All doors were shut to him, and he was out of options. The person he liked least was his father, and the last job he wanted was to make tofu, and yet he had to return to his father's side like a defeated soldier, stripped of his armor and weapon. Yang was immensely pleased to see his son slink back like that, but he changed the way he expressed his pleasure this time. Instead of making a sarcastic remark with a gleeful look, Old Yang said seriously, "I don't need any help making tofu."

Baishun caused a scene at his brother's wedding not because he was upset with his father, nor because he wanted to vent his frustration over his defeat, and not even because he wanted to complicate matters out of unhappiness over his older brother's marriage. It was simply because his younger brother had come home, having seemingly changed into a different person after working as a fireman for the Xinxiang railway maintenance department. The first thing he noticed was how Baili dressed. As a country boy who worked as a fireman, he spent his days shoving coal into a boiler, and, covered with soot, was hardly recognizable. For his older brother's wedding, however, he took off his work clothes and put on a newly bought suit, complete with tie and a top hat, looking like a man who had returned home covered in glory. In fact, his job on the train had not been going well, though not because it was hard, dirty work. It was because he was the only fireman on a locomotive pulling more than a dozen cars. He enjoyed not a single moment of rest from the moment he got on board until the train reached its destination; his padded jacket and pants were drenched in sweat when he finished his shift. It was far worse than his old job, gate guard at the Yanjin Fabricating Plant, where he could sit under the sun gazing out all day long. Old Wan, it seemed, had tricked him. What bothered Baili more than the work itself was the fact that both Engineer Wu and his assistant, Su, were his bosses. He did not enjoy talking with either of them, though not because he liked to shoot the breeze and they were the quiet type. On the contrary, they were talkers, too; it was just that they talked about different things. They were gossip-lovers who talked about the Zhang family's brother-in-law, who'd had his leg broken after stealing from them; or about the head of the Li family, who'd been found in bed with his son's wife, not by his son but by his own wife; or about the fight between the Wang and Zhao families over a dog that had nearly killed someone. None of this appealed to Baili because it was too realistic for breeze shooting and required no imaginary transitions. In the story about someone out walking at night when a white-bearded old man comes on the scene, Wu and Su did not care for the fabricated appearance of the old man, which to them was nonsense; they preferred real stories about the people around them. But they were Baili's superiors, which made them the masters of the locomotive space. They did not mind Baili's joining in on their talk, but it upset them if their underling changed the topic or the direction of the conversation. They would talk the whole way, as the train traveled from Xinxiang to Beiping, or Xinxiang to Hankou, or on the return trips. All Baili could do was add coal to the boiler, his mouth idle. No one ever died of idle hands, but an idle mouth can be harmful. Whenever he had time off, he went back to see Old Wan and pour out all the words he had held back on the trip. As the purchaser, Wan was away eight out of ten days, and Baili seldom found him in his office. He had to leave with all the things he wanted to say unspoken, but it felt different holding them in on the way back, as his belly seemed on the point of bursting. That was when he was most keenly aware of his mistake of taking on the job as a fireman. He would recall the prediction made by Blind Jia, who played the three-string lute. Jia had said that Baili was destined to travel hundreds of miles each day because of his need to talk; he had known what he was talking about. Baili stayed on at the maintenance department, not because he loved his job, but because he dreamed of getting out of the locomotive and becoming an attendant in the passenger cars. As a waiter, he would walk down the aisles adding water to the passengers' cups and sweep the floors, nothing more. With more than a dozen cars transporting a thousand or more passengers, he would surely be able to find someone to shoot the breeze with on the twenty-four-hour journey to Beiping or to Hankou. But changing from fireman to attendant meant switching professions, since the maintenance department was in charge of the locomotives and tracks, while the service department dealt with the passenger cars. Wan could find him a job in a locomotive but not one in a passenger car, so Baili had to stay where he was while continuing to search for someone to talk to. He really believed that he deserved better, but his job turned out to be helpful at his brother's wedding. The guests would have been laborers like Old Ma the carter, Old Li the blacksmith, and Old Liu the donkey seller if Yang's son had married someone with a comparable family background. But with the Qin family as their in-laws, they had different types of guests, wealthy men like Old Fan from town, Old Feng from Fengbanzao, Old Guo from Guoliwa, and Old Jin, who managed Peace and Prosperity Silk Shop in the city. They did not have to come, of course, but, knowing that their friend Qin hoped to shake off the bad aura and make it a dignified wedding for his lobe-less daughter, they put aside whatever required their attention and showed up in their fancy donkey carts, which lined the snow-covered avenue. Neither the Yang family nor their friends had ever seen such a display. Ma and Liu, who were used to shouting, were too intimidated to entertain guests on the bride's side. When the banquet started, Li and Liu cowered in the kitchen, while Ma, a man who normally put on quite a show, was awestruck.

"I've got a sick foal at home," he muttered, "so I have to hurry home now that I've seen your boy's wedding."

He sneaked down the alley and out through the rear of the village. Suddenly, Baili's presence made a difference. A fireman did not amount to much in the world of trains, but in the Yang family, he was someone with a bit of status.

Eight of the sixteen tables, laden with delicacies, were occupied by guests from the bride's side; the other eight were taken by members of the groom's party, each given a bowl of mixed stew. Manqing's two older brothers, plus Fan, Feng, Guo, and Jin, sat at the main table, up front. Others in the bride's party were seated behind them, all but Yang Baili, who had been plucked out to sit next to the guests of honor. Being a fireman might not have been something to brag about, but Baili had spent six months away from home and had seen a bit of the world. Moreover, his talent in shooting the breeze put him at ease with the other guests; he began talking as soon as he was seated, possibly because he had been cooped up in a locomotive too long, and treated his brother's wedding as an arena to shoot the breeze. The guests ate and drank, as Baili talked to a captive audience. Doing so in a suit and top hat felt different from doing it outside a factory in work clothes. No longer focusing on what happened in Yanjin, he switched to interesting events that had taken place on his round trips. His life on the train was monotonous—shoveling coal all day long—but since he was shooting the breeze, the boring days became entertainment. For instance, one day the train ran over a young woman crossing the tracks. When it came to a screeching halt after the accident, he saw a red fox fly out of the woman's body and vanish without a trace. Who was that woman? None of the banquet guests ventured a guess. It was neither a woman nor a fox. It was a tree transformed into a ghost. Years earlier, when the railway was under construction, trees were cut in the northeast to serve as railroad ties, and this tree was among them. She made an annual presence to frighten people on the day the tree was cut down. At night the train's headlight shone more than five li in the distance. One night they saw a man riding on the column of the train light, yelling, "I could let go of my livers and lungs, but I want my heart back."

He was not an immortal but a real human, a pot mender from Handan who had died a wrongful death after a lawsuit, showing up on the light to cry foul when he failed to get justice in the human world.

The wealthy guests knew what a locomotive fireman did for a living and thought that Baili was comical, but his stories were more suitable for people like Niu Guoxing and Old Wan than for moneyed guests. Naturally, they felt that Baili had gone overboard with the pot mender's demand to reclaim his heart, that he was laying it on pretty thick. None of them laughed, but a five-year-old boy, Jin's grandson, was scared into crying. Baili had wanted to tell them the cause of the pot mender's wrongful death, with all its fascinating details, for it was no ordinary case. But he couldn't, not with the boy crying. In the end, he did not get his fill of shooting the breeze, although the guests thought he had gone far enough. At wedding banquets, guests needed to show respect to the host; as the saying goes, they should do it for the Buddha if not for the monks. So they listened and joined in with a titter now and then, and no one made a fuss over it. The banquet ended as they ate and Baili talked. The men were humoring him and Baili did not feel sated with talk; but he was a different person in the eyes of Baishun, who thought his younger brother had been elevated to equal status with the rich men. Unlike Baili, Baishun had spent the past year learning to be a butcher and had kept company with pig's giblets. Worst yet, he had offended his mentor to the point where he'd had to quit and come home to constant jabbing from his father. On the day their older brother got married, the two younger brothers received totally different treatment; Baili sat at the table for the guests of honor, while Baishun did not make it to any table, for his father had given him a task—shoveling dirt in Yang Yuanqing's outhouse. When a banquet guest tied his pants cord and walked out after finishing his business, Baishun was to quickly shovel dirt into the toilet to cover the filth. It had been Yuanqing's condition when Old Yang asked to use his rooms for the banquet; Yang had to promise to keep the kitchen and toilet clean. In Baishun's view, Baili and he had been equals two years earlier at Old Wang's private school, but now the difference between them was like night and day. How had that happened? Baishun traced the origin back to the time they were trying to enter Yanjin New School. Had he been the one who got in, he would be the one wearing a suit and a top hat. It was precisely because their father had tampered with the lot that Baili was able to walk out of Yang Village into Xinxiang, on to Beiping and Hankou, while he was reduced to the state of having no place to live. He was right about the phony drawing, but left out everything else; he thought only about how Baili got to attend Yanjin New School, while glossing over the fact that after the school was dissolved, Baili met Niu Guoxing and later hooked up with Old Wan. If Baishun had been the one who got to go, Baili might not have become good friends with Guoxing, since he did not know how to shoot the breeze; consequently, he might not have met Old Wan, and would have had to return to Yang Village in the end. Amid his angry indignation, Baishun naturally cared only about the outcome; besides, he was ignorant of what had happened in Baili's life.

It was late afternoon when the banquet ended and evening by the time all the guests had left. The more Baishun thought about it, the angrier he got, though now his ire was no longer directed at his father and younger brother, but at Old Ma, after further exploration of the cause. Ma would not have been his intended target if he hadn't used the outhouse shortly before slinking away. Ma had meant to relieve himself, but he was so awed by the Qin family that he forgot what he wanted to do once he was in the toilet. Since he was there, he thought he ought to do something, so he spat, but he missed and left a sticky gob on the side. He looked up when he was done and saw someone waiting to cover his filth. Ma was too preoccupied to see that it was Baishun, but to Baishun, Ma had done it on purpose. He had not come to use the toilet; all he'd planned to do was spit for Baishun to clean up. That, when compounded with the New School and lot-drawing incident, grew into something much bigger. Ma had been the one who'd given his father the idea to temper with the lot in order for Baili to attend New School. Baishun had never done anything to Ma, so why would the carter set him up and hurt him like that? You can say a thousand bad things about someone under normal circumstances and do no harm, but a phrase alone at a critical moment can transform a person. Ma had made it possible for Baili to become a fireman, and now he had helped Baiye get a wife, concentrating his vile intentions on him, Baishun, alone. They must have been karmic enemies in a previous life.

In fact, Baishun's anger toward Ma was misplaced. Ma had been Yang's accomplice owing to a strange combination of circumstances. Put differently, he had worked with Old Yang and Baili, making him one of the perpetrators of an offense against Baishun. It made no difference whether he was an accomplice or a perpetrator. What galled Baishun was how Ma ignored him after committing the offense and, worse yet, even spat in the toilet. That was more than he could take. He had worked from morning to dusk, covering filth left by a ceaseless string of guests coming to use the toilet, and did not get to eat until after dark. He left the toilet only once the guests had gone home, and found something in Yuanqing's kitchen to eat. Unhappy and irritated, he took a few sips of the liquor from the banquet, which helped drown his sorrows and led to more drinking. As dizziness took over, the flames of anger burned even brighter, turning the gob of spit into an eternal feud with Ma. Everything would have been fine without the liquor, but now the effects of alcohol brought out a desire for revenge. With anger emboldening his scheme, he left Yuanqing's kitchen and returned to his house, where he went straight to the cow pen and picked up a butcher's knife before heading over to Ma's house. With him around, who knew how much more he might suffer at the vile man's hands? Ma must pay for that gob of spit.

As dusk deepened, the snow fell more heavily, but undeterred, Baishun trudged one step after another toward Ma Village. Since beginning his apprenticeship with Zeng, he had slaughtered more than three hundred chickens, eighty dogs, and at least forty pigs. Killing the animals was a way to make a living, so he was nervous at first, since they were harmless. As time passed, however, he got used to it, and needed only the flick of his knife. Killing Ma this time was going to be different. He had never killed a man, but the fires of anger removed the fear. All the resentment and hatred would be erased once he plunged in the knife; just thinking about it brought a sense of gratification. A drunk normally stumbles as he moves forward, but not Baishun, who sped along on steady feet, as if buoyed by wind. At this moment, he said to himself, his older brother was having a good time with his new wife in the bridal chamber, while Baili, who would return to his job as a fireman in Xinxiang, was probably shooting the breeze with someone. His father could be plotting how to take advantage of his new status as the in-law of a wealthy family. No matter what they were doing, by the next morning they would know that Ma had left this world. Another wave of euphoria rose up as he imagined the shocked look on their faces. He was killing Ma to get rid of the man, but he was also doing it to show the others, with whom he had formed an enduring enmity. As he walked on, under the influence of alcohol and his wild imagination, he soon reached the entrance to Ma Village. A northern wind blew over and brought something up to his throat; he ran to the threshing ground near the entrance. His knees buckled; he fell onto the grain stalks and threw up. His stomach felt better and his mind cleared. He discovered, to his surprise, a boy next to him when he stood up to wipe his mouth. He had actually stepped on the boy, a scrawny little thing with big eyes. He looked to be twelve or thirteen and, dressed in thin clothes in the heart of winter, was shaking uncontrollably. Baishun thought he must be a homeless beggar who was making the haystack his home as the year neared its end.

"Who are you? You scared me," the boy said in a trembling voice before Baishun could say anything.

Baishun threw up again.

"Don't be scared. I'm a butcher from Yang Village. I'm just passing through. What's your name? Why are you sleeping here?"

The boy looked down wordlessly, so Baishun repeated his questions. The boy began to cry and told Baishun his name was Laixi, from Ma Village, and that he was not a beggar. His father was a donkey seller named Old Zhao. Laixi's mother had died the year before, and his father had remarried a woman with three kids of her own. He had been well treated by his stepmother, who did not beat or scold him, except that she never gave him enough to eat. Six months earlier, a momentary lack of judgment had led him to steal one of her bracelets and pawn it in the market to buy some flatbreads. When she found out about it, instead of telling his father, she waited until her husband left home to sell donkeys and jabbed the boy's navel with a large nail at night. The punishment was not solely for the stolen bracelet. When the theft was made public, rather than blame the boy, people blamed the stepmother for mistreating her stepson; if she had given him enough to eat he wouldn't have stolen her bracelet. Her reputation was ruined, all because of him, she thought. Laixi did not dare bring it up with his father after he returned, afraid that the punishment would lead to his discovery of the theft and who knew what else. Pricking his navel was only the beginning; it had not stopped there. From then on, she meted out the same punishment whenever he made a mistake, which was why he slept outside when Zhao went on his donkey-selling trip. He still had to be on guard, however, for sometimes she would come looking for him, and he got into the habit of sleeping in different spots. He was fast sleep when Baishun stepped on him, and he had thought she'd come to get him again. Laixi pulled up his thin jacket to show Baishun, who could see, under the reflecting light from the snow, more than a dozen nail holes around the boy's navel. Some were scabbed, while others still had pus. The deplorable sight made Baishun forget his own troubles.

"So many twists and turns to one story," he said with an emotional sigh. "Aren't you cold sleeping here?"

"The cold doesn't bother me, Uncle. Wolves do, though," Laixi said.

By now Baishun was sober. He recalled how years before he had slept on the threshing ground in his village, where he'd encountered Pei after losing a sheep. Now here was a boy who had lost his mother and got a stepmother, who had his navel pricked over a bracelet, and who had a home but couldn't go there. The boy's stepmother sounded worse than Zeng's new wife, a hypocrite with a phony smile. Baishun thought that he, an eighteen-year-old man, had actually fared better than the boy, even with the injustice he'd suffered thus far. It wouldn't be hard to kill Ma, but what would he do afterward? Everything in the world, it seemed to him, contained injustice. With another sigh, he said to the boy, "It's really none of my business, but I'm here, so what can I do? Come with me. I'll take you to a warm place."

He took the boy by the hand and they walked out of Ma Village together. The sky seemed to hang lower now; the snowfall got heavier, sending down flakes the size of goose feathers all around them. The young man and the boy braved the snowstorm as they headed toward the lights in town. Without knowing it, Laixi had just saved the life of a man, Ma the carter, who loved to play his pan-pipe on his cart before going to sleep.

9

One day, at the age of seventy, Yang Baishun recalled how he had met the Catholic priest Zhan in Yanjin at the age of nineteen. It was an important event in his life, for he would not have come to the county town otherwise and would not have gotten married if he hadn't come. Baishun had apprenticed with Jiang the dyer before meeting Father Zhan, whom he had met back when he was working for Zeng the butcher. Zhan was an Italian whose uncle, also a missionary in China, had been stationed in Beiping, Fujian, Yunnan, and Tibet. He returned from Tibet at the age of fifty-six and settled in Henan to head Kaifeng's Catholic church. At the time, the Kaifeng Church supervised branches in northern Henan's thirty-two counties. Zhan had followed in his uncle's footsteps, arriving in China at the age of twenty-six, and was sent to Yanjin, where there was not a single Catholic. Zhan, a man with a high nose and blue eyes, did not speak a word of Chinese. More than four decades later, now fluent in Chinese as well as the Yanjin dialect, his nose looked flatter and his eyes were a muddy yellow. As he walked down the street, hands clasped behind his back, from behind he looked like an old scallion peddler. At six feet two, he was taller than the average Yanjin resident. Given to snorting before opening his mouth to talk, he was not cut out to be a missionary. Most likely he knew all the sermons by heart, but he could not squeeze much out, like dumplings in a teapot. There was a difference between Zhan and Baishun's teacher, who'd criticized his students when he could not pour his knowledge of Confucius into them. Zhan was always calm as he tried to pass on God's word. When he jumbled his message or lost the thread of his sermon, he simply snorted and started over again. After several false starts, he would likely present a different God to his Chinese audience.

Zhan's uncle was still the head of the Kaifeng Church when he arrived in Yanjin. With its alkaline soil, Yanjin was susceptible to crop failures, caused by either drought or flood. Of its three hundred thousand residents, only some ten thousand managed to fill their stomachs daily, which was why people from Yanjin tended to be gaunt. God would take pity on them. With high hopes for his nephew, Zhan's uncle allocated enough church funds to build a church on North Street in the county town. He had originally planned for only a chapel, but the materials bought with the funds were sufficient to build a structure with sixteen windows on both sides, one that could accommodate a hundred or more people. Zhan was better suited to be a builder than a priest; one of his maternal uncles was a mason, and, having grown up with his maternal grandmother, he had learned quite a bit about construction from watching and listening to his uncle. He bought the common variety of bricks, tiles, and wood but altered the usual construction by using dark bricks on the western and northern walls and building mud walls on the east and south sides. Tiles covered the part of the roof with no direct sunlight, and straw mats and bamboo strips were used on the sunny side. When they ran out of wood, he bought thirty Yanjin elms. Hence, he built a church with thirty-two windows by using materials for one with sixteen, a building that could accommodate three hundred. Over the following four decades, the roof leaked only after ten days of rain; in other words, the church stayed dry for nine days during a rainy spell. But a church that could house three hundred people remained mostly empty; Zhan managed to convert only eight people in more than four decades.

Then Yanjin got a new magistrate, named Han, who set up Yanjin New School and drove Zhan out of his church to use the space for classes. The Catholic church was now Han's school, partly because Zhan had so few followers and partly as a result of his conflict with the current head of Kaifeng's Catholic church, who made it difficult for Zhan to file a complaint, since they disagreed on religious doctrine. Han would not have had the audacity to infringe on church territory if it had enjoyed a large following in Yanjin. And yet, having only eight believers never discouraged Father Zhan. Even in his seventies, he still ran around Yanjin all year long, rain or shine. Back when Baishun was apprenticed to the butcher, they sometimes ran into Zhan as he spread his message in the countryside. The butcher and the priest would sit beneath a willow tree at the village entrance and smoke pipes. Once, as they sat there, Zhan tried to get Zeng to follow the Lord.

"Why would I follow him, since he and I have never smoked together?" Zhan snorted.

"If you came to believe in him, he would know who you are, where you come from, and where you are going."

"I know all that already!" Zeng said. "I'm a butcher from Zeng Village who kills pigs in other villages."

Zhan's face turned red from the effort to be eloquent and he could only shake his head and sigh.

"You can't put it that way." Then he nodded after giving the butcher's words some thought. "But you're right, actually."

It would appear that instead of converting Zeng, the butcher turned the tables and won him over. So he fell into a prolonged silence and sat quietly for a moment before blurting out, "You can't say you have no worries, can you?"

Indeed, he could not. Zhan had struck a nerve, for the butcher had been fretting over whether he ought to remarry and which of his sons he should marry off first.

"You're right. All people have worries."

"Who would you go to if not the Lord when you have worries?" Zhan clapped his hands.

"What can the Lord do for me?"

"He would let you know right off that you're a sinner."

"What does that mean?" Zeng did not like the sound of that. "How can he know if I've done something wrong if we've never met?"

The conversation came to a premature halt, so they sat quietly for a while before Zhan spoke up again.

"Jesus's father was also a laborer, a carpenter."

"Different vocations, different worlds. I'm not going to listen to a carpenter," Zeng said dismissively.

Baishun paid little attention to Zhan while the two men were chatting, but he was envious of Zhan's acolyte, named Zhao, the son of a local scallion peddler. A young man in his twenties, Zhao made a career of riding Zhan on his bicycle to spread his message. Zhan had ridden his French Philippe bicycle as a young man, but decades later, as an old man with a bent back and bad eyes, he took on an apprentice and taught the young man how to ride. Now Zhao rode him around, ringing the bell as they went, informing everyone that Zhan had arrived. Zhao kept quiet when Zhan preached and dozed alongside the bicycle. Sometimes Zhao tied a rack to the bike to carry scallions to sell in the village while Zhan was on his mission. The priest did not mind. Baishun ignored Zhan and studied the way Zhao sold the scallions, examining the bicycle when the young apprentice dozed off. Once, he mustered the courage to walk up and touch the handlebars.

"This thing must be hard to handle," he said to Zhao. "It's faster than a horse, and you could fall on your face if you didn't know how to ride it."

The bike did not really interest Baishun, who was mostly curious about the flexible relationship between Zhan and his apprentice, who sold scallions instead of helping his mentor with his work. Baishun had a far more restrictive relationship with Zeng and his wife. Doing anything else was out of the question, of course, but Baishun's hands were tied even when he did exactly the same as his mentor. After they butchered a pig, he had to wait for Zeng's wife to distribute the giblets, and sometimes he did not even have a place to sleep after killing pigs from dawn to dusk. So, using the bicycle as an excuse to chat up Zhao, Baishun asked about the relationship between Zhao, the priest, and the Lord, and how Zhao had worked it all out. But Zhao was not interested in chitchat, focusing instead on the bicycle, taking Baishun's hands off of it.

"Your hands are sweaty," Zhao said dismissively. "Don't soil the chrome."

Zeng believed that a butcher was the equal of a priest, but the hierarchy between the apprentices could not be ignored. So Baishun made a point of ignoring Zhao the next time they met.

Baishun never returned to Yang Village after his aborted plan to kill Ma, a plan he actually felt he had carried out. And not just Ma—in his mind, his father and Baili had also died at his hand. He had wanted to kill Ma in real life, while his father was the first to fall in his imagination, since he was the one he saw every day when he ground soybeans. He had little to say to his father now, and even less before he "killed" him. When his father was pacing beneath their date tree, Baishun mentally sneaked up and clubbed him to death. His next target was Baili, the jabbering locomotive fireman. Baili was sleeping in the maintenance office when Baishun watched himself cut off his younger brother's head to keep him from ever shooting the breeze again. Ma the carter was the last to go, as Baishun saved his mortal enemy, the devious man with a bellyful of tricks, for last. He envisioned the carter walking toward him as he plunged a knife into the man's belly and sliced it open, spilling colorful intestines all over the ground. He could not return to the scene of the crime, so he stayed away, but this time it was different. The first time he left home, he did it out of spite, but this time he left feeling despondent. Leaving home was easy;

where to go was the question. After what had happened, he could not think of a single person in all of Yanjin with whom he could stay. He felt as if he had offended everyone, though that was an exaggeration; there were some he did not get along with, but now all of Yanjin disgusted him. He had to leave the place if he was to amount to anything. So he headed for the ferry landing amid swirling snow the day after he parted with Laixi; he would cross the Yellow River to find temporary work in the unfamiliar city of Kaifeng. All he knew was that it was a big place, with lots of people, which meant there were enough doors that could open to him, promising a better life than in the countryside.

The snow had forced Old Ye, the ferryman, to pole to the other bank when Baishun reached the landing. He turned to go home but was reminded that he had no home to go back to, so he went to Old Ruan's diner to spend the night. When he walked in, after pulling aside the door curtain made of half of a blanket, he saw three customers sitting on the floor by the fire. One was foreman Gu from a dye shop in Jiang Village; the other two were his apprentices. Baishun recognized one of them, named Song, whom he had befriended back in the private school. Old Gu, a man with a square head, was taking the apprentices to Ji County to buy merchandise before the end of the year. The so-called merchandise was fabric and yarn for the dye shop. They were snowed in after returning from Ji, unable to cross the river to the dye shop, so they came to Ruan's diner. Baishun sat down with them by the fire; Gu ignored him, and Baishun did not dare strike up a conversation, whereas the foreman's cold shoulder stopped Song from chatting with him. So he spent the morning listening to the three men go on about the dye shop. They had a shared wish for the snow to stop soon, but it got heavier as the day wore on, and by the afternoon, the sky had darkened. They had to bed down for the night at the diner. Baishun lay down next to Song, giving them an opportunity to whisper and catch up. Song had been with the dye shop ever since leaving school.

"I don't mind working at the dye shop. It's better to stay with what you know than try something unfamiliar," he said to defend his inability to make much of himself.

But Baishun envied Song, who did not have to leave home to find work. He sighed when Song asked how he was doing. He told his friend what had happened, starting with his failed attempt to enter Yanjin New School, his apprenticeship with the butcher, his older brother's wedding, his lack of options, and his plan to cross the Yellow River to find work in Kaifeng. He had moved several times over the past two years, never staying in one place for long, though not by choice. Things just kept going wrong for him. He was worried about traveling to Kaifeng, since he knew nothing about the place. The more he poured his heart out, sharing the complicated, twisting turns in his life, the more agitated he grew.

"Perfect," Song said with a clap of his hands. "The dye shop is looking for someone to tend fires. Would you be interested in the job?"

"I'm at the end of my rope, so it doesn't matter if I'm interested or not." Baishun's mood brightened. "It's better to tend fires for someone I know than try my luck in an unfamiliar place like Kaifeng."

"I couldn't agree with you more. You get picked on if you're new to a big city." Song added, "I'll speak with Old Gu tomorrow and see what he thinks."

"He didn't look too friendly to me," Baishun commented. "It might be a tough sale. But it would be great if he took me on. You'd have a friend nearby." That did not sound quite right, so he added, "I don't mean you need a friend nearby. It's me who needs someone. These past couple of years have taught me that I can't make it on my own."

"You have decades to go yet, so forget those thoughts," Song said to console him.

The snow had stopped and the sun was out when they awoke the next morning. Song told Gu what Baishun had been through over the past two years, with no place to go, and asked the foreman to take on his friend.

"He's moved around a lot over the past couple of years and seems not to get along with people wherever he is," Gu said. "He could be hard to deal with." He added, "I'd like to help a friend of yours, but you know what our boss is like. He doesn't mind a slow learner, but he won't tolerate a difficult worker. I don't want to be responsible if your friend causes trouble."

Gu walked outside to see that Baishun had carried several dozen bundles of fabric and yarn to the ferry landing. At dawn, while the dye shop employees were still asleep, Baishun had gotten up to move the bundles for them. When Old Ye poled his ferry up, Baishun carried them onto the boat, working up a sweat and looking like a steamer with heat rising out of his head.

"Look," Song said to Gu as he pointed to Baishun.

"What's there to see?" Gu spat on the ground. "I wouldn't have minded if he hadn't done that, but it just goes to show that I was right about him. The boy is crafty. I don't want someone like him."

Baishun had brought everything onto the ferry when Gu walked up and saw that the top half of the young man's padded jacket was soaked through in sweat. He and his apprentices stepped onto the boat. Baishun would have wasted his sweat if he had tried to talk to Gu, so he didn't. He did not try to take credit for his hard work, nor did he want to know if Gu would take him on. In fact, he didn't say anything. Instead of getting on the ferry and crossing the Yellow River with the three of them, Baishun changed his mind and jumped off to wave good-bye to Song. The gesture caused Gu's resolve to waver, as he thought that Baishun might be a simple, honest boy after all.

"Come on, young man. You can present yourself to the boss at the dye shop. It's your luck if he hires you, but don't blame me if he doesn't."

Baishun jumped on board, and the four of them crossed the river.

Jiang's dye shop, Grand Fount of Peace, had eight large cauldrons that were more than three meters in diameter. A fire burned day and night under cauldrons that contained one color each—red, orange, yellow, green, indigo, blue, purple, and black. After a piece of white fabric or spool of white yarn was placed for two hours in a boiling black cauldron, it came out as inky fabric or black yarn, or whatever color the cauldron held. Jiang's dye shop, one of two within miles, employed more than a dozen men. In his fifties now, as a young man Jiang had been a tea merchant who had generally plied his trade around Yanjin and other cities between Jiangsu and Zhejiang, but also other provinces when the opportunity arose. As he grew older, the travel got harder, so he opened a dye shop with the money he'd made from selling tea. A bony man with a hooked nose, he had been a good talker back when he sold tea, and every tea merchant traveling the same areas knew about Jiang the hook-nosed chatterbox. Strangely, however, he turned taciturn when he reached the age of fifty. Like quitting smoking, giving up the conversation habit is not easy, and most people fail at it. But not Jiang, who quit and never reverted back to his old talkative self. In fact, he sort of went overboard, for sometimes he rarely said a word all day. He was now given to brooding when something came up, a new style that confused others. For instance, he would think long and hard over something before producing a commonplace utterance. No matter how much time he took, nothing spectacular ever emerged from between his lips. Yet though it might be an ordinary phrase in others' ears, it was not ordinary to him, especially after he'd invested so much thought in it, and he would be upset if someone treated it as nothing special.

When Baishun showed up, Jiang glanced at him before casting his eyes downward, deep in thought. Song tried to help his friend. "Just to tend the fires, Boss. He's a good kid."

Jiang turned his gaze on Song and lowered his head again for more deep thought. A long time passed, but instead of saying anything, he merely waved his hand as a sign for Gu to hire Baishun.

Gu did not send Baishun to tend the fires, however; instead, he told Old Ai, who was in charge of the water supply, to do it and had Baishun take over Ai's job. So now Baishun was responsible for getting water, not much of a skill, but then neither was tending fires, he realized, after giving both positions some thought. As a newcomer, he had to consider himself lucky to have a job, but it only took him ten days to see how tough a job it was. The water was not for the kitchen; it was for the cauldrons, all eight of which required eight large, brick tanks to rinse the fabric and yarn before it could be hung on poles to dry. Each tank was more than six meters long, and the water had to be changed every third day, which meant more than six hundred trips to bring enough water each day to rinse out all the colors. The well was close by, under a locust tree in the yard, but it took time and strength to winch the buckets up from the deep well and carry them into the shop. Baishun had to get up at the rooster's crow and did not knock off until the stars were out in the sky. Still he failed to have the water changed two out of every three days. He began to feel that tending the fires was much better than carrying water, which also showed what a cunning man Gu was. The foreman had agreed to take him on, with the intention of showing him who's boss. The work at the dye shop would come to a stop if the water was not changed in time, and Jiang was upset before Gu had a chance to rein in Baishun, though the boss never cursed or hit anyone when he was unhappy. He simply stared at the tanks with their colors getting darker and called Baishun over to fix his eyes on the young man. Jiang had yet not said a word to him since his hire, for he was in the habit of staring at people when they did something wrong. After the stare came the contemplation with his head lowered. It was creepier to be standing in front of someone worrying you than being hit or cursed, in which case Baishun hurriedly picked up the buckets to draw more water from the well.

In retrospect, slaughtering pigs with Zeng was easier than carrying water, despite the abuse from Zeng's wife. Sometimes, when he'd gone out with Zeng, they would take a break to chat under a willow tree. One thing, though: Zeng provided meals but not a room, so he'd had to travel thirty li every day, while Baishun had a place to stay at the dye shop. A month went by, and he found a way to carry less water. Water in the three tanks with lighter colors—orange, yellow, and blue—needed to be changed every three days, and he was diligent about that, while the water for the five darker colors would not show any difference even if he were to replace it every five days. At first he'd tried replacing the water in all eight tanks, which was why he could not keep up with the lighter ones. Now he handled his job with ease, and without Jiang pondering the tanks, life was better.

By the time spring arrived, Baishun had gotten to know all the workers. It had been only a dye shop to him when he first arrived, but after a while, he learned that there was so much more to consider than dyeing fabrics. The thirteen workers came from five different places: five from Yanjin, three from Kaifeng, two from Shandong, one from Inner Mongolia, and the last two from down south in Zhejiang, men Jiang had met earlier while selling tea. With different backgrounds and personalities, understandably, not everyone got along; Baishun found he had more to say to some, and less to others. For him, his co-workers could be divided into six groups depending on the levels of conversation possibilities. He had first believed that those from the same area would be natural friends, but after a while he learned that there tended to be barriers among them, and it was easier to make friends with someone new. For example, his friend Song kept his distance from other Yanjin workers and was friendly with a beefy man from Inner Mongolia, called Talhis Khan, who had a tiny glazed lantern hanging from his right earlobe. Everyone called him Old Ta. A generally pleasant person, Ta enjoyed picking on newcomers. Back when Baishun first came and had trouble changing the water in time, Ta stared daggers at him and muttered things in Mongolian, while even the boss only brooded with a fixed stare. Baishun did not need to know Mongolian to sense that Ta was not complimenting him. Since he could not be one of Ta's friends, his relationship with Song faded over time. He also discovered that the foreman was not especially loyal to the boss. Gu and Jiang were related on their mothers' side. Though they were about the same age, generational seniority determined that Gu was Jiang's maternal uncle. Gu acted differently with Jiang around. When the boss was away, Gu did not care if the employees wasted dye or firewood, sneaked food, played tricks, or goofed off. He ignored his duties as foreman and focused on matters outside his range of responsibilities. He loved to gossip and larded his talk with embellishments, while everyone else simply talked among themselves. One simple thing could be turned into something twisted and complicated in his mouth. The employees paid lip service to his role as a foreman, but they all hated him. They worked and ate together at the dye shop, yet each had his own private thoughts.

And there was more. Jiang had two wives, the first in her fifties and the second in her twenties. Song once told Baishun that Shunli, a senior worker from Shandong who called himself Wu Dalang Junior, had something going with the second wife. Shunli was more a Ximen Qing than a Wu Erlang, two characters from classical fiction. Everyone at the shop but Jiang knew about the affair. Baishun was worried for Jiang's sake, but puzzled too. Jiang spent his days contemplating the world, so how could he fail to know this? When he heard that Jiang had been the talkative type before he turned fifty, Baishun knew there had to be a reason behind the boss's change. He could not have simply changed his personality. Having been through quite a lot over the past few years, Baishun was convinced that there was a reason behind everything and that every reason had twists and turns. Who knew which turns Jiang's change had come from? At the dye shop, with its host of problems, Baishun sometimes felt that his head would explode worrying about the Jiang family and Jiang the boss. As an apprentice to the butcher, he had found the relationship with Zeng and his wife too complicated to handle and had hoped to gain some peace by coming to the dye shop. It was worse, to his great disappointment. In fact, it was mostly because Baishun, after all he had been through, was more mature, which manifested itself mostly in his decision to stay out of trouble. At a place with so many workers and complications, Baishun kept one thing in mind—not to be too close to or too distant from anyone, including Song, who was no longer a close friend or the companion that Baishun had hoped him to be. Steadfast in remaining a faction of one, he hoped to hold on to the job of carrying water and, by taking it one day at a time, learn to be a dyer at some point.

But that did not happen. He'd lost the job by the fall, not because he'd gotten on Jiang's bad side or quarreled with anyone, but because of a monkey. Besides staring and brooding, Jiang preferred nights over days. He mainly slept during the day, when the dyeing was under way, and emerged from his bedroom at night, when the fabric and yarn were laid out to dry; that was never done during the day, for the sun would bleach them. At sunset, sixteen tallow lamps were lit around the eight tanks, sending ropelike black smoke crackling as it rose. The waterlogged fabric and yarn were heavy as lead, requiring the workers, all stripped to their waists, to drag them out of the tanks onto the drying poles. Every day they laid out several hundred bolts of fabric and hundreds of bundles of yarn, in all colors. Huffing and puffing, they were sweat-soaked an hour into the work. Engaged in the hard work, side by side, they forgot what they said about each other and the problems among them. Jiang would walk over to watch them, wordlessly, of course. At other times, he would focus on something concrete, a person or something that had happened. If someone did something wrong, he stared at the man. But at night, he was looking at a scene with all his workers engaged, so he did not focus on a single person. After fixing his eyes on the scene, the totality of the work, he would then lower his head and lose himself in thought. Or, if the workers were pulling fabric or yarn out of the tanks, he would pace the area, in contemplation, hands clasped behind his back. Oblivious to the rousing scene, he treated it as a backdrop as his mind moved on to something completely detached from what was going on in front of him. Day or night, he was always ruminating, but what was he thinking anyway? Baishun had no way of knowing.

Jiang also raised a monkey, as he shunned interactions with humans, something with which Baishun could identify, since he shared the same misanthropic attitude. Their reasons for this tendency, however, were different. Baishun had suffered at others' hands, so he was wary of people; but he could tell that Jiang was simply fed up with humans and transferred his feeling to a monkey. When Baishun was hired, Jiang had a monkey called Jinsuo, Golden Lock. Being a newcomer at the time, he devoted his attention to doing his job well and nothing else. When he finally got the hang of carrying water two weeks later, he began to notice a monkey crouching under a date tree in the yard. It was an old tree, with cracked roots, but the branches were weighed down by heavy fruit. Someone told Baishun that after eight months, the monkey had the same schedule as his owner, dozing under the tree during the day and waking up at night. Looking around with its shifty eyes, it might nimbly leap onto a wall and snatch someone's hat, put it on its own head, and chatter as it waved to them. Sometimes it hung upside down from a branch and swung back and forth, sending green dates to the ground. Had a person done that, Jiang would have angrily fixed his gaze on the person. But with the monkey, he just shook his head and laughed, sometimes even bending down to pick up a date and pop it into his mouth.

Yanjin saw lots of rain the year Baishun was hired. Rats, the dye shop's biggest pest, ran amok when autumn arrived. They chewed the yarn, the fabric, even the dyes. Gu went to the market and bought rat poison, which he spread out on the roofs and the ground under the eaves. More than five dozen rats died within days. Golden Lock, the monkey, got cheeky at noon one day, when no one was paying attention; thinking the poison was brown sugar, it finished off a whole pack and died that night. Gu knew that he was in big trouble. Jiang stared at the monkey before turning his gaze on Gu, and then lowered his head to think, making Gu shake fearfully in the process. They might have been related, but at this moment, Jiang was only his boss.

"I'll make it up to you, Boss."

Jiang looked up, gazed at Gu, then was once again lost in thought.

"It's dead," he said after a protracted silence, "so how could you make it up? It would be a different monkey."

Ignoring Gu, he went to the market to buy another monkey, and this one he called Yinsuo, Silver Lock. He had picked it from a litter of five baby monkeys, believing that the gentle-looking animal would not be as mischievous as Golden Lock, whose rascally nature had cost it its life. When he brought the monkey back, Jiang realized that Silver Lock might seem gentle, but it was unsettled, either because it was newly separated from its siblings or because it was in a new place. Day and night, it patted his head and chattered over and over. That would not have bothered Jiang if the monkey had done it only at night, but he could not sleep well with Silver Lock making a racket during the day. Convinced that it needed training, Jiang adopted the same method he'd used on his workers; he neither hit nor cursed the monkey. Instead, he got out of bed, sat across from it, and glared before lowering his head to think. As with the workers, Silver Lock did not know what Jiang was all about and was intimidated by his gaze and silent contemplation.

Baishun had to laugh when, on his many water-carrying trips, he saw Jiang staring at the monkey. Staring and ruminating actually worked on all creatures. It took Jiang ten days to make Silver Lock behave like his predecessor; the monkey began to doze off under the date tree during the day and turned active only after nightfall. But Jiang did not let his guard down, for he knew that it takes a year to train a monkey. To prevent Silver Lock from ingesting rat poison, Jiang chained it to the date tree all day long. Baishun had just arrived when Golden Lock was around, so he stayed away from the monkey. Now with Silver Lock, Baishun felt like an old-timer, while the monkey was the newcomer; Baishun could see his earlier self in the monkey and felt drawn to the creature. When he took a break under the tree after two hours of work, he developed the habit of rubbing the monkey's head. During the day, Silver Lock would open its eyes, glance up at Baishun, and then fall back asleep. At night, the lively monkey returned the favor. Man and monkey exchanged smiles, giving Baishun the illusion that Silver Lock was a real friend; no trouble could arise from this friendship. To be sure, Baishun dared touch the monkey only when the boss was away. If Jiang was around, he wouldn't even look at it when he walked by with his water buckets. When he was sure Jiang was somewhere else, Baishun would put down the buckets and walk up to greet the monkey, whose arrival improved Baishun's life. He invariably thought about Silver Lock when he carried the water.

Another rainstorm hit the area on the fifth day of the eighth lunar month. The rain stopped the following day, but the clear sky only brought stifling heat. Baishun was soaked through after a morning of hard work and was drenched again midway through the afternoon after breaking for lunch. He stopped and took a drink of water from one of the buckets. When he was done, he noticed that Jiang was still sleeping inside, so he tiptoed over to the tree. Silver Lock, chained as usual, was dozing off, bathed in sweat. Baishun patted its head gently and woke it up. In the past, Silver Lock would go back to sleep after giving Baishun a glance. But on this day, the monkey stayed awake with a dazed look. Silver Lock pointed at its mouth and then at the buckets off to the side. Knowing the monkey was thirsty, Baishun brought over one of the buckets, and Silver Lock leaned against the rim to take in big gulps of water. When it was done, the monkey wiped its lips before mopping Baishun's sweaty forehead with its paw.

"Hot enough for you?" Baishun asked.

Silver Lock stared; obviously it didn't understand. Baishun pointed at the dates. "Want some?"

The dates had turned red by then and looked lovely among the green leaves. This time Silver Lock understood what Baishun said and nodded. "Wait here. I'll get you some," Baishun said.

Silver Lock nodded but then it chattered and clutched Baishun's shoulder, pointing to itself and to the tree. Baishun knew the monkey wanted to climb up and get the dates. Ultimately, carelessness led Baishun to mistake Silver Lock as a true friend and forget that, unlike dogs, monkeys take a year to train and domesticate. Seeing that Jiang wasn't around, Baishun took it upon himself to unchain the monkey, utterly unaware that Silver Lock was not what he thought; it showed its true colors as soon as it was free. For days, it had been pretending to be as docile as Golden Lock. But instead of going up the tree for the dates, it reached over and scratched Baishun. Caught off guard, Baishun fell to the ground. He touched his face and found it was streaked with bloody claw marks. Silver Lock dragged the chain along as it leaped up into the tree and then to the roof. Baishun scrambled onto the roof, but by then it had reached the wall and from there bounded across yards and from rooftop to rooftop. Baishun chased it all the way to the entrance of the village, where sorghum grew vast and dense; Silver Lock was nowhere to be seen, having disappeared into the field.

Baishun did not have the courage to return to Jiang's shop without the monkey, but not because he was afraid the boss would ask for compensation. He suspected that Jiang would not do that; nor would he hit or curse him. Jiang would apply the usual method of gazing and ruminating with his head down, just as he had dealt with Baishun when he could not change the water in time or when Silver Lock first arrived. Baishun shuddered at the image of Jiang doing that to him again. Gu had been laid up for three days after Jiang had used the method on him when Golden Lock died of rat poison. Besides, it wouldn't be the same for Baishun this time, though not because Gu was the foreman and he was a new hire. The difference lay in the causes and outcomes; one monkey had died and the other had run away, with differing repercussions. Gu wasn't entirely responsible for Golden Lock ingesting rat poison, while Baishun was the sole culprit for setting Silver Lock free. He did not mind being hit or cursed or paying for the loss even; but just imagining Jiang looking at him, lost in thought, his head down, was enough to make Baishun tremble in fear. Who knew how long Jiang would brood after his trouble with both monkeys? Gu had fallen ill after the silent treatment from Jiang, when he wasn't completely responsible. Baishun thought he would die this time after setting the monkey free. In traditional plays, people are always dying from missing a paramour. In his case, Baishun could easily and actually die if Jiang stared at him like that. Once again, he found himself an outcast, all because he refused to be subjected to Jiang's method of punishment. He followed the main road and walked on aimlessly. After spending over six months at the dye shop, he had developed an attachment to the place and was sad to leave without saying good-bye. His schoolmate Song had been a great help in getting him the job and would surely suffer because of Baishun, even though their friendship had cooled. Song would get either a tongue-lashing from Gu or the silent stare from Jiang, the thought of which sent pangs of guilt through Baishun's heart. He had to kick himself for being fooled by a monkey; he would not be in such a sorry state if he hadn't treated it as a friend. Even an abyss has a bottom, but the heart of a monkey is unfathomable. These thoughts filled his head as he walked until the sun was about to set and he ran into the priest and his apprentice.

It was the fifth day of the eighth lunar month. Zhao had pedaled Zhan to Wei Village. It was a remote place located in the northernmost corner of Yanjin and eighty li from the county town, but Zhan was not prepared to give up on it. The trip went smoothly, as did the preaching, for Zhan was able to say what he'd come to say. He failed to convert anyone, but that did not upset him, for it was a common occurrence. Zhao, on the other hand, managed to sell five bunches of scallions. The return trip went well at first. They talked about the heavy rainfall that year and the possibility of another flood in the fall. Zhao said it was fine with him, that floods do not stunt the growth of scallions. In Zhan's view, the flood had been caused by the Lord's wrath over Yanjin residents' refusal to believe in God all these years. At some point they reached Wushilipu, where a steep hill required Zhao to pedal really hard. They heard a "ka-cha" as the front axle snapped, sending both riders to the ground. The bicycle was more than thirty years old, ripe for problems. They both knew how to fix a punctured tire and a broken chain; they carried inner tubes, metal wire, a hammer, and a pump with them wherever they went. But a broken axle could only be replaced in town. They could neither ride nor push the bike in such a state, so Zhao carried it over his shoulder and Zhan had to walk the fifty li back to town. On a stifling hot day, Zhao was tired and drenched in sweat after ten li but still fared better than Zhan, who was approaching seventy. Battered by fatigue and sleepiness, he held on to his apprentice's clothes, dozing off and stumbling along the way, which meant it would take longer than usual to get home. No longer in the mood to chat, they forged ahead for another ten li before Zhan plopped down on the roadside, too tired to go on, while the young man was still strong enough to keep at it, even with the heavy load of a bike. That was when Baishun rushed toward them, afraid that Jiang would send someone after him upon discovering the missing monkey and worker. He was also worried about wolves when night fell, which was why he traveled at such a frenzied pace, not caring where he was going. He knew the priest and his apprentice, and had even touched the bicycle once, but on this day he was too absorbed in his flight to see them. Zhao called out to him.

"Hey you, stop."

The shout sent a fright into Baishun, who thought that Jiang's people had caught up with him after all. He froze in the middle of the road and did not take a breath until he recognized Zhan and Zhao.

"What's gotten into you?" Zhao asked. "Why are you in such a hurry?"

"N—nothing," Baishun stammered, for he had yet to recover. Besides, he didn't know where he was going.

Zhao just looked at him.

"Nothing, you say? Well, how about I give you something to do?"

"What do you have in mind?" Baishun asked.

"I'll pay you fifty coppers to carry the old man into town," Zhao said as he pointed at the bike on the ground.

Baishun was put at ease when he realized it did not involve the dye shop and the monkey. He looked at the priest while carrying out a calculation in his head. He didn't know what to do or where to go next, and he could earn fifty coppers carrying the old man into the county town. A flatbread cost five, so fifty could buy ten. He had no money, since he'd left his personal belongings at the dye shop. Besides, he did not have to worry about wolves if he traveled with the two men. After giving the proposal some serious thought, he knew it was a good deal, so he nodded.

But he felt he had been duped the moment he picked up the priest. The old man might have been in his sixties, but at six feet two, he was heavy. And indeed it felt to Baishun that the priest weighed around two hundred pounds, and within one li he was bathed in sweat. The fifty coppers would not be easily earned. Lucky for him, he had gotten stronger after spending the past six months carrying water. They took a break every three li on their return journey. Now that he did not have to walk, Zhan regained his vitality on Baishun's back, which led him to think about his vocation and about the man carrying him.

"Say, you, what's your name?"

"Yang Baishun."

"Which village did you come from?"

"Yang Village."

"You look familiar."

"I was apprenticed to Zeng the butcher."

"I know him. I don't see him. Where is he?"

"I quit slaughtering pigs and went to work at a dye shop."

Uninterested in the reasons behind Baishun's change of profession, the priest went straight to the matter at hand. "Do you know me?"

"Everyone in the county knows you. You want people to believe in God."

The priest was pleased, satisfied that he hadn't wasted all these decades. He patted Baishun on the shoulder.

"Do you want to believe in God?"

Zhan had asked the same question thousands of times and received a "No" each time. After a while, it became a simple routine question and he never waited for an answer before offering his own.

"Do you want to believe in God? Probably not." Zhan was not prepared to hear Baishun blurt out, "Yes, I do."

That was all Baishun said, but it stunned the priest, as if Baishun had been the one posing the question.

"Why?" Zhan had to know.

"Back when I was with the butcher, I once heard you say that if I believed in God, I'd know who I was, where I came from, and where I was going. I'm clear on the first two, for I know who I am and where I came from. But I've been bothered by the third question for years. I simply don't know where I'm going."

Zhan slapped his leg and said, "That's mainly what God wants to show every-one. The first two are about the past, and they're secondary."

"Will you help me find a job if I believe in God?" Baishun asked.

It dawned on the priest that they were talking about the same thing but for different purposes. That stopped him, but only for a moment.

"But you say you're working at a dye shop. Why do you need another job?"

Ignoring the question, Baishun pointed to Zhao.

"I'd like to be like him, believing in God, riding a bicycle every day, and selling scallions."

Zhao was outraged before Zhan got the full implication of Baishun's answer, though not because Zhao was afraid of losing his job to Baishun. The apprentice was incensed that Baishun would convert in order to trick the priest to get a job. But instead of pointing out the flaw in Baishun's intention, he sneered.

"Don't listen to him. I knew right away, though I decided not to say anything. Look at the bloody scratches on his face. He must have had a fight or escaped from somewhere, maybe after killing someone."

"That's rubbish." Baishun defended himself. "I didn't have a fight and didn't kill anyone. I just didn't want to work at the dye shop any more. I saw a rabbit on my way, and it kicked me when I tried to catch it."

Zhan snorted while studying the young man's profile. He didn't look like a murderer. After spending four decades in Yanjin, the priest had managed to convert only eight people and hadn't found even one in recent years, until now, on a chance encounter. To be sure, believing in God meant different things to them, but Baishun had sounded straightforward with his answer, which was unusual in his experience. That alone meant the young man might be a good candidate; besides, it was precisely because he had a different objective in mind that he needed God to show him the way. Baishun could be his ninth Yanjin convert, the priest decided.

"Let's talk about the job later. You want to believe in God, so would you let me give you a Christian name?"

"What do you have in mind?" Baishun hadn't expected that.

"Your family name is Yang." Zhan considered the fact for a while. "You'll be Moses Yang then. It's a wonderful name."

Hoping for an auspicious portent, Zhan had chosen Moses for Baishun, who, like the real Moses leading the Israelites out of Egypt, would save the Yanjin residents from their suffering, as the priest hoped to make Catholicism the religion of Yanjin before he died. Baishun, on his part, did not think much of the name; he accepted it purely on account of a job prospect. He decided he would be Moses Yang if he got a job, and if not, he would change back to be Yang Baishun. It was a just a name for others to call him; he would never use it. Besides, nothing had gone well for him as Baishun, so he didn't hesitate.

"I don't mind changing my name. I've had enough of Yang Baishun anyway."

Despite their different intents, what Baishun said fit the priest's plan quite well. Greatly pleased, he snorted noisily and said, "Amen. What you just said means cutting yourself free, and bringing you closer to the Lord. You'll be Moses Yang from now on."

The three of them continued on to the county town, with Zhao pursing his lips to show his discontent while Zhan and Moses Yang chatted away.

10

Moses Yang did not get to pedal the bicycle or sell scallions like Little Zhao after becoming a follower of the Lord; he was sent to split bamboo at Old Lu's bamboo workshop on North Street in Yanjin's county town. The priest had found him a job, but it wasn't what Moses had wanted, though not because he hated bamboo or because he preferred Zhao's job. He realized that, after his conversion, the priest seemed to be a different person from the one Baishun had run into as a butcher's apprentice. Moses had been envious of Zhao, who, as the priest's apprentice, could pedal a bicycle all day long and sell scallions while Zhan spread his gospel. Baishun had also been attracted to the unrestrained relationship between the priest and his apprentice, which was not just unrestrained but actually too free, as he discovered after spending time with the two men. Or, put differently, Zhao was not really Zhan's apprentice; he was hired help. Not a believer himself, Zhao usually sold scallions with his father and spent little time with Zhan when they weren't out on the road. The priest got Zhao to take him to the countryside on his bicycle because he couldn't ride the vehicle himself. At two hundred yuan a day, Zhao made pretty much the same as he did selling scallions, which was why he had agreed to the task. He could also sell scallions in the villages while the priest preached. It had nothing to do with being a believer or not. In all likelihood, the loose relationship would have made it possible for Baishun to take over Zhao's job once he became Moses Yang. But Moses was new and had yet to learn to ride the bicycle, so he couldn't take over without the skill. To be sure, he could learn; Zhao had had to learn to ride from Zhan. The problem was, Zhan was in his early sixties back then, not too old or too busy to spend a whole month teaching Zhao how to ride a bicycle. He had even damaged the vehicle a few times. Now that the priest was nearly seventy, he wanted to devote every one of his dwindling days to spreading the gospel. Besides, he had only one bicycle and could not set it aside for Moses to learn; Zhao was the one he could rely on for his preaching trips. Moses Yang could learn at night when the bicycle was idle, but the old Philippe bicycle kept breaking down, even with the utmost care, and would likely turn into a heap before Moses mastered the skill, which was why Zhan was opposed to the idea in the first place. Moses didn't care if he got to ride the bike; it just didn't feel right for an outsider to be on it, while he, a true follower, had to split bamboo elsewhere. What kind of apprentice was that?

Wary of Moses's design on his job, Zhao pulled a long face when the priest asked him for a ride.

"Not today. My legs hurt. Go get someone else."

The priest did his best to mollify the perturbed young man.

"Do it for the Lord. Didn't you see we had another natural disaster this past fall?"

Yang Baishun had converted and changed his name because of a job, but now everything had turned out differently than expected. Granted, he could simply turn his back, quit the job, and take back his old name. But it wasn't that easy to leave Zhan and find another job, even though this one hadn't gone as he'd wished. Zhan had used connections and had gone through considerable trouble to find him the job at the bamboo workshop. With no one to turn to in the county town and no immediate job prospects, Moses Yang had to settle for what was available, following the Lord and splitting bamboo. In the beginning, he had thought he would be a true believer, a follower of Zhan, like a monk or a nun reciting sutras in a temple. Life would have been easy that way. So he was surprised to see that Zhan, like Luo Changli the funeral crier, could not afford to support an apprentice through his trade alone.

Zhan never did get his church back after the county magistrate had seized the building to use as a school. It should have been returned to the church after the school was dissolved and Han had returned to Tangshan when Governor Fei fired him because he was a blabbermouth. But a new magistrate, a man named Shi from Fujian, had replaced Han. After the dismissal of Han, Commissioner Geng of Xinxiang should have been the one to pick a new magistrate, but he did not want to make the choice, since the governor had fired Han. Geng decided to ask for a recommendation from the governor, who suggested Shi, a section chief under Fei. The governor had been judicious both when firing Han and recommending Shi, which convinced Geng that Fei was definitely governor material.

A man of few words, Shi was a completely different magistrate, and he had no desire to set up a school. He was very much like his old boss in that neither talked much, the difference being that Shi enjoyed listening to others. However, the kind of talk he liked was not everyday conversation, but that spoken in dramatic plays. A play usually lasted two to three hours, during which the actors chattered away and sang arias on stage. So the first thing he did after becoming magistrate was to form a drama troupe. In the past, the residents of Yanjin had been too poor to even fill their stomachs, so all they could afford were a few plays by wandering troupes. They could not support a permanent troupe, and itinerant actors would starve to death if they decided to stay. The county was on the brink of financial collapse. With the arrival of Shi, the county would have to put up the money to install a troupe. So shortly after he assumed his post, he quietly checked out the merchants to see what could be done for the county's finances. Finding nothing via an open investigation, he switched to secret inquiry. Two weeks later, he found three possible sources: Jiao the salt merchant, Shen the timber man, and Kuang the opium den owner, all of whom were running illegal businesses, conducting fictitious transactions, or evading taxes. Without a hint of reluctance, Shi arrested them, tossed them in jail, and confiscated their properties, thereby enriching the county coffers overnight. The county residents clapped in appreciation when they saw the new magistrate punish the lawless merchants and improve county business practices. Shi's next move was to put on plays for the residents. Yanjin's residents preferred Henan clapper plays, but not Shi, who was originally from Fujian, though he didn't like Fujian opera either. As a young man, he had attended school in Suzhou, where he had happened to watch a local Xi opera and fell in love with it. So he brought a Xi opera troupe all the way from Suzhou. Since they had no venue to put on plays, he remodeled the church-turned-school and turned it into a theater. When the troupe put on its first opera, Shi and people from his office were the only audience, for the actors sounded more like screeching cats to the locals. Echoes were heard in a space that could accommodate three hundred people, but unfazed, Shi attended performances every day. After a while, the residents began hearing something new in the screeches, finding them more polished than their own clapper plays, which explained why a form of opera from a distant province enjoyed popularity in Yanjin, a Henan inland city.

Shi's love for the opera differed from Han's penchant for conversation and education, which were tied up with national salvation and the survival of the Chinese people. For Shi it was just a hobby, similar to the carpentry of another magistrate, Old Hu, and ensured peaceful coexistence with others, from the governor to Commissioner Geng.

When he was first driven out of his church, Zhan found a temporary replacement in a temple abandoned by a monk years before, in a place called Xiguan. With his knowledge of construction and a diligent approach to the work, he was able to fix it up to the point that it no longer leaked when it rained. Convinced that he would get his church back, he was elated for a while after Han was fired, only to be disappointed by the arrival of Shi, with his plan for opera performances. Rather than lose faith, Zhan went to see Shi and told him the background of the site, with a request to have the church back. Shi was congenial as he said with a smile, "It's an unalterable principle that an object should be returned to its rightful owner, but I took over the spot from Han. You have the right to ask for it back, but I'm not the person to talk to. You need to go see him."

Han was no longer the magistrate, however, and had left for Tangshan. What was the use of seeing him? Zhan complained that the government should not seize church property time and again. Still smiling, Shi cut the priest off. "Based on what you say, Mr. Zhan, I have to admit that Han did the right thing. What do you mean by seize property? This land belongs to China. There was no church before you came, so it was you, Mr. Zhan, who seized our property, and, moreover, you have been trying to confuse and poison the people's minds. Let me be perfectly frank. I don't mind if you want to preach, but you cannot turn things around, and, most importantly, do not try to blackmail the government. We can coexist peacefully if we stay clear of each other, but if you try to blackmail the government through your church, I will tell you that I don't believe in anything but a phrase from our sage Confucius. That is, I do not bother myself with the bizarre or the supernatural. I don't care how powerful any religion is; I will ban it if it breaks the law. It's nothing personal, just a way to ensure peace in our corner of the world."

He continued, still wearing a broad smile. "You're not stupid, Mr. Zhan, so go on with your mission and stop interfering with government."

Zhan did not know how to react. How was he interfering with government by wanting his building back? Besides, Shi was using the site for opera performances, which had nothing to do with government work. But now Zhan knew that the new magistrate was even tougher to deal with than his predecessor. He realized that he could continue with his church work if he let go of the building, but might have to leave if he insisted on getting the site back. After witnessing how Shi had punished the illegal merchants, Zhan knew he had to be contented with the temple. He could not help sighing over the fact that he was a Catholic priest living and working in a dilapidated Buddhist temple. What upset him most was the Kaifeng Church, which never made things easy for him. When Zhan's uncle died, his successor did not share Zhan's interpretation of doctrine. Bishop Lei had long wanted to eliminate the church in Yanjin, which had managed to convert only eight people, and merge it with others. He could not bring himself to do that to a man in his seventies, so he kept the old priest around out of compassion, but gave him less money each year, intending for the Yanjin church to die out on its own. The funds were barely enough to support Zhan alone, which was why he could only offer his new convert, Moses Yang, a place to live. Yang had to find a way to provide for himself. Back when Baishun was with the butcher, it was board without room, and now, as Moses Yang it was room but no board. He hadn't paid much attention to the old priest when he was traveling with the butcher, and had never imagined that he would be Zhan's apprentice a year later. A year can go by in a blink of an eye, but to Moses Yang it was more like a lifetime ago. He sighed and went to the bamboo workshop.

Old Lu, the owner of the workshop, had a hoarse voice, which was why he spoke so loudly. He preferred to shout, even with something quite trivial, not to emphasize its importance but to stress the fact that it was he who said it. No one could tell what was critical and what was not, since everything he said was at the same volume level. He was reluctant to take Moses Yang on when the priest broached the subject, not because he did not like the young man but because Moses gave a wrong answer to one of his questions. Zhan had gone to see Lu one night and got him to agree to hire Moses. Zhan told Moses to go to the workshop on his own when he went out to preach the following morning. Old Lu did not feel that taking on another apprentice was a big deal, but he felt obligated to ask the young man some questions, since he was new. So he smoked his pipe and asked Moses where he was from, what he had done before, and where. It was a simple routine to Lu, but not to Moses, who decided to be careful with what he said. Recalling his experience at the dye shop, he thought it might arouse suspicion if he were to say he had had several jobs. With that in mind, he hid his previous work at home selling tofu and later slaughtering pigs with Zeng, and told only about his employment at Jiang's dye shop, where the dye had caused a rash on his hands and feet, forcing him to quit. Everything would have been fine if he had mentioned the other jobs, and it did not matter how many jobs he'd had, because Old Lu was not Old Gu. As luck would have it, Old

Lu was annoyed that Moses had worked for Old Jiang, a former tea merchant, for Lu himself had sold tea until he was too old to travel and opened a bamboo workshop with money earned from the tea trade. He had met Jiang, the man with a hooked nose, while selling tea and did not get along with him at a time when he had not yet quit talking. They were both from Yanjin so, in theory, they should have helped one another when they were buying tea in the Jiangsu and Zhejiang area or selling tea in Inner Mongolia or Shangxi. But they were never close, their conversation was often strained, and they were competitors. When they both quit, one opened a dye shop and the other a bamboo workshop, further proof that they had little in common. Old Lu immediately sent Moses away, saying he did not need more workers when he heard about the young man's former employer. Naturally he had no idea that Moses had fled Jiang's place on account of a monkey. Moses returned to the temple to spend the rest of the day wondering why he'd been sent away. On his return that evening Zhan went to the workshop on North Avenue to see Lu, and learned of the man's change of heart. After persistent questioning, he realized that Old Lu had vented his ire at Old Jiang on Moses.

"You shouldn't be doing that, Old Lu." The priest took a puff on his cigarette. "The Lord says to forgive your enemy. Jesus was crucified because one of his disciples betrayed him. He knew that beforehand, but did not run away."

Not being the Lord, Lu refused to forgive Jiang or Moses Yang, but he didn't say so. Instead, he focused on Zhan's Lord.

"Why didn't he run when he was about to die? Something wrong with his head?"

That brought on a lengthy explanation from Zhan about why the Lord did not flee. He kept at it, but not because he was dead set on a job for Moses at the bamboo. With so few converts in Yanjin, he was always trying to get people to believe in God, and no one ever came to him for any favors. He might know a lot of people in Yanjin, but they were his friends only insofar as he did not ask favors. Once he did, a crack appeared in the friendship. Lu was one of his closest friends, without whom he would have had trouble finding Moses a job on the spur of the moment. The job was not critical, but it would mean losing his ninth convert, and that was a big deal. He brought up the blind man Old Jia, when Lu was still unmoved after he brought up the Lord. Jia was Lu's cousin, a fortune-teller who played a three-string lute. Back when Old Wang's private school shut down, Baili, Moses Yang's younger brother, had gone to Jia, but the blind man had told him to leave. Old Lu had never liked that cousin; nor did he care for the blind man's fortune-telling or his lute.

"What does a blind man know about fortune-telling?" Lu was once heard to say. "If he's so good, why couldn't he have foreseen his own fortune?"

The priest had met Jia on one of his preaching trips, and they'd gotten along nicely, though Zhan was against fortune-telling. In his view, everyone's fortune was in the hands of God, and there was nothing to tell. When he first arrived in China, he could not speak Chinese and could not appreciate Chinese opera or musical instruments. Now, more than forty years later, he was fluent in the Yanjin dialect but still could not bring himself to enjoy Chinese opera or music, except for Blind Jia's three-string lute. The priest usually left a village after he finished his sermon, but he always made a point of going to hear Jia play when he did God's work in the blind man's village. Given his sense of pride, Jia did not play for just anyone who showed up, but he usually did for the priest, because he liked the fact that a foreigner appreciated his music. Jia could play happy melodies such as "Shooting the Geese," "Counting the Grain," "Zhang Lian Sells Fabric," or "Liu the Big Mouth Gets Married," as well as sad tunes like "Second Sister Li Visits the Grave," "Snow in June," "The Woman from the Mengjiang Family," and "Wailing at the Fort." The former did not move the priest, who shook his head and smiled when Jia finished a happy melody. Not so with the sad ones about Second Sister Li, Dou E, Mengjiang, or Wang Zhaojun, women suffering injustice, which made him lower his head and sigh.

"The suffering in the songs is precisely what the Lord wants to alleviate." Zhan would bang the table and say emotionally, "That's why God is here."

That outburst was sometimes followed by a heartfelt reaction to how Jia managed to show what was on the Lord's mind, which led him to shake his head and sigh. Why would someone who could understand God's mind refuse to follow him? He would try to convert Jia, who once gave him a surprising response.

"Why do I need to follow him if I understand what he's thinking?"

There was nothing Zhan could say to that, so he gave up.

Zhan and Lu had met thirty years earlier, and the priest had tried to convert him when he was still a tea merchant.

"I'm too busy. I'll follow him if you can get the Lord to help me sell tea."

Zhan tried again when Lu changed professions and was greeted with a similar reply.

"I'll follow him if you can get the Lord to help me split bamboo."

Over the decades, Lu traveled on a parallel course with the Lord. Despite his nonbelief, Lu liked the simple, straightforward priest, who never slacked at his job even though he'd converted only eight people. He was also impressed by his persistent preaching trips, for he knew there was not another man like the priest in Yanjin. Just about everyone else would have given up when there was no result in sight. They became friends, and when he was drinking with other friends he often said about the priest, "The Lord has not treated Zhan fairly. If he weren't a priest, he could have made a bundle selling tea by now, and he wouldn't have to live in a dilapidated temple."

When Zhan realized that Lu would not relent, he knew that he and the Lord were not important enough to Lu, and not merely because of his disagreement with Jiang. The priest was reminded of Lu's cousin, the lute player Blind Jia. Maybe Lu would listen to his cousin, if not to him and the Lord, he reasoned.

"If I can't convince you, I'll go get Jia to talk to you."

Unaware that Lu did not like his cousin, Zhan thought that family connections would carry more weight than he and the Lord combined. In fact, the priest meant more to the blind man, but Zhan said, "When I tried to get you to believe in God, you said you would if the Lord would help you split bamboo. Now the Lord sends one of his followers to help you, so why don't you take him on?"

Having no use for his blind cousin, Lu did not want the priest to bring him over to pester him. Moreover, he was amused and exasperated by Zhan's illogical reference to the Lord and splitting bamboo. He smiled unhappily and agreed to take on Moses Yang, simply to avoid further conversation with the priest and the need to deal with his cousin. Hence, the blind man who was not even there managed to accomplish what the priest and the Lord failed to do, and Moses Yang became the fortune-teller's unintended beneficiary.

From that day on, Moses went to split bamboo at Lu's shop in the day and returned to sleep at the temple at night. Splitting bamboo wasn't difficult, especially for Moses, the one-time apprentice of a pig butcher. He knew how to use a knife. Even though it worked differently at Lu's place, a knife was still just a knife, and he quickly mastered the skill. His problem arose at night, though not because he had trouble falling asleep. The temple was too run-down to stop the wind from blowing through, which was perfect for a good night's sleep in the summer. His trouble came from the priest, who returned from his mission work at about the same time as Moses and wanted to sermonize to him. Other apprentices served a single mentor, while Moses Yang was split in half, serving one master in the day and another at night. He was exhausted after working all day splitting bamboo, so naturally he dozed off while listening to the priest. He went to work each day tired, and it dawned on him that following the Lord was no easy task. He kept at it for a month before concluding that he could not keep burning the candle at both ends; he had never felt such a need for sleep in his life. If he dozed off, Zhan was patient enough to wait till he woke up to continue, but not Lu, when Moses fell asleep at work. Dozing off led to bamboo split the wrong way. To his credit, Lu could take the loss of some bamboo, but the mistakes got in the way of the one thing Lu enjoyed: listening to loud, noisy Shanxi opera. Like the new magistrate, he did not appreciate Henan clapper opera, even though it was local. He had often passed through Shanxi on his way to Inner Mongolia to sell tea bricks and heard his share of opera. He was not a born opera lover, however. He became one owing to the characteristics of Shanxi opera, which required the performers to yell until they were hoarse as the opera reached its climax; the voices turned steely hard and rose up after a brief pause. He liked it not because of his own hoarseness but because of the pause after the high point and the following rise in the singing. It touched a place deep down in his heart, a spot unknown to him before; now that he had found it, he was hooked—unlike Shi, who preferred operas from the south and could afford to support an opera troupe. As the owner of a bamboo workshop, Lu was not rich enough to do the same with his favorite Shanxi operas, whose performers never came to Yanjin; besides, he would likely have been an audience of one if they had shown up. The possibility of watching an opera every day put the new magistrate in a good mood; a longing for a chance to enjoy his favorite opera continued to build until Lu began to go over in his head the plays he had seen over the years, such as *The Story of Su San*, *Huang Guiying's Undying Love*, *Capturing the Traitor*, *The Tryst of Dian Can and Lü Bu*, *The Treasonous Royal In-Law*, and so on.

Lu did not set aside a time to review these operas in his head; he could start anytime the mood struck him, including when he was watching the apprentices split bamboo. He never sang along; he just mentally called up the lines, going through an entire performance with gestures and a range of facial expressions. People who knew what was going on could tell when gongs and drums were banging and clanging in his head; people who were in the dark mistook these as signs of mental instability. It was, in a way, similar to Yang Baili's shooting the breeze in his head when guarding the gate at the plant, but different in that the former focused on exaggerating real and invented events, and fabrication was allowed, which Lu could not do, for he had to memorize the sung lines, which were paramount in an opera. Though creating fantastic stories out of nothing was difficult, remembering lines was equally challenging, maybe even harder. A man in his late fifties, Lu did not have the power of memory he had once enjoyed. Sometimes he rocked his head and sighed because he had become one with the dramatic episode in his head, but at other times he could be sighing over his failure to remember certain lines and was forced to pause, stewing in anger at himself.

Moses Yang was terrified, convinced that his boss was having an epileptic fit the first time he saw Old Lu reviewing an opera in his head. He laughed when he found out what was going on. He did not know that there were many different sighs, only that Lu sighed when he was reviewing an opera. Moses might puncture a bamboo pole when he dozed off while watching and laughing at Lu. The pole would make a strange noise, interrupting the performance in Lu's head or erasing lines he had just recalled. Either way, he was roused out of his mental opera house, for which he whacked Moses in the head with the ruined pole. He did not complain about the disruption of his mental performance or for ruining the bamboo pole; instead, he yelled at the top of his hoarse voice, "Damn it! You're going to ruin me, just like Old Jiang."

Without knowing it, Jiang had been implicated in Moses's mistake, and he looked around, momentarily unsure of just where he was.

Zhan received a letter from Italy one afternoon. His maternal grandmother and his parents had died over his four decades in China, and his younger sister was the only one who wrote to him from home and, of all the people he knew, the only one who idolized him. He had no one in Yanjin, and his uncle, the one in Kaifeng, had been dead for fifteen years. Before the old man died, Zhan had received instructions from his uncle; they had talked about nothing else. So his sister was the only person he could open his heart to; but with her being so far away, letter writing was their sole means of communication. It was hard to recall what he'd written to her during the four decades of correspondence, but it was likely all about his mission work in Yanjin, its magnificent church, and the spread of Catholicism manifested in many thousands of believers. In her view, Zhan had to be the all-time best Italian missionary in China, someone their family and all of Italy could be proud of. One wondered what she would have thought if she'd known the truth.

In one particular letter, she told him that one of her grandchildren, an eight-year-old boy, had just been baptized. The boy was full of admiration for a maternal uncle who was doing such a splendid job spreading the gospel in the distant land of China. Zhan had no idea what she'd said to the boy, who added a few lines in his childish handwriting to the sister's letter: *Dear Uncle, We have never met but you remind me of Moses when I think of you.* The boy must be saying that, like Moses leading the Israelites out of Egypt, Zhan was rescuing the Chinese from suffering. No one else had given him such high praise, not since Zhan started mission work, so his mind was in turmoil long after he finished reading the letter. He spoke in a loud and sonorous voice that evening when he conducted Bible study with Moses Yang.

For his part, Moses was feeling low after being hit over the head that day at the workshop, so he dozed off shortly after Zhan started. Too keyed up to notice his drowsy convert, Zhan went on and on, beginning with the Lord, the belief, and baptism, and following up with the need to change from the old and adopt the new, emphasizing the importance of a transforming mind. This was by no means a new sermon for Zhan, but he had always brought up the topics one at a time, and that night marked the first time he had brought everything together. When he lost the thread of his sermon or got the order wrong, he simply snorted and started over. It was barely dark outside when he began, and he was still at it at daybreak. It was by far his best sermon ever, in his estimation. Over the past forty-odd years, he had conducted maybe four or five such thorough, satisfying sermons. Moses Yang failed to catch pretty much all of it, and, in his view, Zhan had never been as long-winded as this night. There was a glow on Zhan's face when he finished, but for Moses it was daybreak, his head had barely touched his pillow, and he had to get up for another day at the bamboo workshop. His head felt as heavy as a millstone as he sat on the stool; he might as well have been splitting bamboo in his dreams, for he ruined just about every pole. Another opera was put on Lu's mental stage, a major one called *Wu Zixu*, about a man from the Chu kingdom who engaged in fights all his life to avenge his father's death, which eventually forced him to flee his hometown. Years later, he led the army of another kingdom to vanquish his own homeland, unaware that soon he would be framed by an evil minister and killed by his new king. Before he died, Wu gouged out his eyes and placed them on the tower over the city gate so he could see the destruction of his second homeland. The opera was unwieldy, but Lu did not stumble in his re-creation, unlike previous times, when he encountered many bumps. After a few drinks, he had slept well the night before and woke up refreshed. He decided to give *Wu Zixu* a try, and would move on to something else if it didn't work out. To his surprise, there were no glitches from the moment he started, and he was able to recall the lines in spots that had always given him trouble in the past, imbuing him with a new sense of vitality.

Unfortunately, Moses broke a pole shortly after Lu was really getting into it, interrupting the mental performance with its jarring noise. With everything going so smoothly for him that day, a rare occurrence, by all accounts, Lu had no time to stop and berate Moses; ignoring the noise, he continued on with his play. But he was just getting the opera going again when another sound of breaking bamboo came up. Wu Zixu was fleeing from home, like an abandoned dog, and even before he reached Shaoguan, Moses had ruined eleven poles. Lu's eyes snapped open and, leaving Wu Zixu hanging, he headed to the backyard, returning shortly with a bundle under his arm, Moses's bundle, to be precise, with his clothes and a few valuable items. As Zhan was in the countryside preaching during the day, the temple was unguarded, so Moses had left everything at the workshop to ensure that no one stole from him. With his eyes on neither the broken pole nor Moses, Lu threw the bundle out onto the street and shut his eyes as he shouted hoarsely, "Hey, you. Fuck eight generations of your ancestors. Get out of here."

Fired while he was still dreaming, a jobless Moses Yang had to pick up his bundle and return to the temple. He did not think he was to blame this time; it was Zhan's fault for preaching all night along. Zhan was responsible, so Moses went to him for another job. Besides, he was getting fed up with working at Lu's shop. Zhan was limited in his ability to find another job for Moses, who had walked in with his bundle; he had nearly exhausted his persuasive power to get Lu to accept Moses, and on such short notice, he could not find anything else so quickly. Moreover, he had a different view of Moses now that they had been together for two months. The young man dozed off whenever the priest started Bible study. Zhan could forgive him if it had happened once or twice, but something was seriously wrong with Moses if he was tired every day. Maybe Moses Yang wasn't one of God's people after all. Even the priest's eight-year-old grandnephew in Italy was aware of how important the Lord and Zhan were, saying that Zhan was like the real Moses. In contrast, the Moses before him, who was nearly twenty years old, could be blind to his impassioned sermon the night before. Someone like that was unsalvageable. To his credit, the priest was not unsympathetic to Moses's tiring work at Lu's shop, but no matter how tough, could it be worse than what the Lord had gone through, being crucified so he could awaken mankind with his blood? Zhan thought of himself, a man in his seventies, as someone who spent his day preaching, with not a moment of rest, and devoted his nights to teaching Moses the meaning of Christianity. All Moses had to do was sit down and listen, which was less demanding than preaching.

Zhan began to regret his earlier decision. Perhaps he had been wrong trying to make Moses Yang his ninth convert. He could forget a person's motive for conversion, which in Moses's case was a job. But Zhan felt deceived when

Moses failed to take him and the Lord to heart after he got the job. He didn't mind the deception, for that had happened to him before, but he was too old for that now. If he were young, Zhan could always make up for what he had lost to the deceptive person, but now the trickery would affect not only him but also the time he had to spend to do God's work. After devoting nearly every night to the young man over the past couple of months, Zhan began to lose interest in Moses's situation, since nothing seemed to get through. The priest did not feel like doing anything more for Moses; meanwhile, he thought that Moses ought to strike out on his own and temper his will through setbacks. He might learn a valuable lesson and return to the fold one day. The Lord was interested in tempering and testing, wasn't he? But alas, Moses Yang was not cut out for those kinds of trials and tribulations, although not because his heart wasn't in it. He simply hadn't had the time, like Zhan. Without a job, he wouldn't be able to eat, and how was he to follow the Lord on an empty stomach? Zhan could not help him out, so he left.

Moses Yang roamed the area around Yanjin, taking any temporary job that came up. He thought about his earlier plan of going to Kaifeng, but things had changed so much that heading to Kaifeng now felt different. The place had not seemed intimidating before his experience at Jiang's dye shop and Lu's bamboo shop; after the setbacks, he wasn't sure if he could do well so far away from home. So he stuck around the county town, waiting to see if anything better would turn up. He started out as a porter at a Yanjin warehouse and made good money, but he had to leave when the warehouse didn't have enough work to keep him. Taking up his old profession at the dye shop, he carried water for the shops along the street, filling his stomach when someone needed water and going hungry when no one required his services. At night, he returned to the warehouse to sleep in the shed. Compared with his earlier days, he felt unfettered, and didn't always get to eat. With no more sermons at night, he could sleep well, yet he began to suffer from insomnia now that he could sleep all he wanted. A sauce shop owned by a Duan family was directly across from the warehouse. When he woke up at night, he looked over at the lanterns by the shop door, one showing the name of the owner and the other the goods it sold. Duan and Sauce swayed when a breeze blew over.

Now that he had left Zhan and his Lord, he could change his name back to Yang Baishun, but why bother, since no one cared what the water carrier was called? Besides, Zhan had given it serious thought before coming up with the new name for him, and it would seem fickle to change it. People around town knew his name was Moses Yang and called out to him, "Moses, fill our vat, would you?" He couldn't go to them one by one and explain why he wasn't Moses Yang, but Yang Baishun. One day he recalled the story of Moses in the Bible and had to burst out laughing when he thought about himself, the Chinese Moses, carrying water in Yanjin. Time went by, whether he was able to fill his stomach or not, and soon it was the end of the lunar year.

Before the year was over, Yanjin had its annual community festival. It usually took place around the fifteenth day of the new lunar year, though the residents continued to refer to it as the end of the year. A man named Feng, who lived on East Street, was a good rabbit hunter. He went into the mountains to shoot rabbits and smoke the meat to sell on a street corner. Born with a harelip, Old Feng loved festivities more than anything, so as a natural organizer, he served as head of the festival committee. He would get a hundred people together before the year was out, dress them in colorful clothes and paint their faces to walk on stilts and beat gongs and drums in a parade through the town. The performers were from all walks of life, but on this day everyone got to play someone else, either a mythical or historical figure like Gong Gong, Gou Long, Chiyou, Zhu Rong, King Wen of Zhou, King Zou, or Da Ji; or fictional characters such as the Monkey King, Pigsy, Monk Sha, Chang E the moon lady, the King of Hell, and demons; or stock characters in popular opera, such as Sheng the leading man, Jing the painted face, Dan the leading lady, Mo the old man, and Chou the clown. They did not need a serious replication, just a general resemblance. The festivity usually lasted seven days, from the thirteenth to the twentieth of the first lunar month. On the fifteenth day of the year, Old Feng got the people together again to put on a show for the residents, but something was different. In years past, when Old Hu was the magistrate, he had paid no heed to what was going on outside his window, including the annual festival, as he engrossed himself in woodwork. Later, when Little Han took over, his short tenure covered the New Year period and the festival. Han preferred orderly talk, with him giving speeches to the people, so naturally the festival, with its demonic figures jumping around, felt chaotic to him. He didn't appreciate the dust that performers kicked up either. So he went out, took a look, and said with a handkerchief over his nose, "You want to know what a mob is? This is it." And that was why a school was important.

Old Shi, the latest magistrate, held different views from his predecessors, not because he didn't like disorder but because it meant different things to him. He was against disorder in daily life, but a man dressing up as another person to parade the street was actually peaceful; he was, after all, an opera lover who enjoyed watching actors talk and sing on the stage. To be sure, a community festival was different from an opera, which had only a few actors. The former, consisting of a hundred people playing someone else, meant more than peace to him; the county would be well governed if all the residents wanted to be someone else. Starting on the thirteenth day of the first lunar month, Shi had his stately armchair moved to the Jin River bridge, where, with a fur coat draped over his shoulders, he sat high up to look down on his subjects putting on the festival show, ignoring the opera in the church-turned-theater.

When the performers spotted him on the bridge, they doubled their efforts to put on a more splendid show than previous years. Shortly after daybreak each morning, gongs and drums were heard banging loudly as the performers danced along the Jin River, enjoyed by thousands of onlookers. By nightfall, you could easily fill large baskets with shoes that had fallen off the feet of people in the crowd. It was still the heart of winter but was turned into spring by Old Feng's festival troupe, as even the spectators were bathed in sweat from running after the performers. Shi remained in his chair up on the bridge throughout the day, not bothered by the cold or hunger; he did not return to his office for a noon nap after eating a few steamy hot buns brought over by his attendants.

But something went wrong on the third day. It was nothing major; Old Deng, an important actor who played the King of Hell, fell ill. Owner of a sundry store called Chief's Shop, Deng had a daughter named Xiuzhi, who was called Second Sister at home. It was she who had misspoken, turning Qin Manqing's missing earlobe into an ear and ruining the marriage prospect between Li Jinlong and Manqing, who later married Moses Yang's older brother. Deng had felt fine the night before, but woke up with a stomachache on the third morning; it hurt so much he rolled around on the bed. Thinking that tapeworms were the cause, the family sent for Old Chu, the town's herbal doctor, who, after pressing Deng's abdomen, said the pain was caused not by tapeworms but by entangled intestines. It was likely one of the worst problems in the world, when things inside get all tangled up. What did people mean by a mess? This was it. He would write out a prescription, and either it would help smooth out the intestines and cure the disease or it would kill the patient. Deng passed out from the excruciating pain, as his family members wailed.

Feng was worried sick when he heard about Deng's illness once the troupe was out on the street, but not because he cared whether Deng lived or died. The festival simply could not do without the King of Hell. It shouldn't be a big deal to miss one role in a troupe of a hundred, but Feng did not think about it that way. For him, every role in the troupe was irreplaceable and indispensible, because, with one role suddenly missing, the chain of festivity would be broken. Without the King of Hell, there would be no reason for the demons, since the king would put the demons on trial later in the celebration. By extension, the people in the human realm would have a shaky existence without those in the underworld, and with no one on either side, legends and operas alone would not be able to hold up the world.

Feng told the gongs and drums to stop before embarking on an urgent search for another King of Hell. But where would he find one on such short notice? He went to see Old Wang the basket weaver, Old Zhao the cobbler, Old Li the vinegar maker, and Old Ma the pear peddler. They either were not nimble enough to be on stage or abhorred the disorderly scene, like their previous county magistrate, or did not want the role to get in the way of their business. After spending the morning on a futile search for a new King of Hell, Feng had the troupe remain idle. His forehead was beaded with sweat, but that was nothing compared with what Old Shi was going through on the bridge. He sent someone down to find out what the problem was and then to tell Feng, "Just start your performance, and forget the King of Hell for now. Don't make all these people wait."

He added another instruction: "You can keep looking while the show is going on."

The magistrate's instruction notwithstanding, Feng felt he would not be able to face himself or others if he started without a King of Hell. Halting his search, he went to the bridge to give Shi a personal explanation of the significance and consequence of the role.

"I've always been a patient man," Shi replied with a smile. "This should not be the only time I'm too eager."

He continued, "We'll do it your way. Things never work out if we try to wing it. So go on with your search and we'll wait."

Feng hurried off the bridge and went to see Old Li the blacksmith and Old Wei the cook, but neither was a good candidate; they enjoyed the performance but ran off when Feng broached the subject. The more Feng hurried to find someone, the more evasive the substitute seemed. As he looked into the multitude of spectators, Feng spotted Moses Yang, who was turning his head this way and that way to see what was preventing the performance from taking place. With his face, his build, and his height, Moses was not a bad fit, and besides, it was nearly noon, so Feng decided to settle for what was available and plucked Moses out of the crowd to ask if he would be willing to play the King of Hell. Moses had always enjoyed a festivity like this and had once been an admirer of Luo Changli, the funeral crier who could always have a scene under his control.

Luo was as good as Feng in his ability to make things happen his way. Moses had once played a part in his village festival, but had gradually lost his interest in festivities after taking several wrong turns in his career path. So far he'd been with his own father, making tofu, a pig butcher, a dye shop owner, a priest, and the owner of a bamboo workshop, and each change had taken an edge off his personality, removing the possibility of merrymaking from his life. Or, put differently, he forgot there was merrymaking in the world. Now that he was away from all those people and had regained his freedom, he watched the performance every day at the expense of earning money from carrying water. With no money, he had to go hungry. He was excited at the offer to join the troupe, but felt intimidated after seeing what the others had been doing over the past few days.

"You, what's-your-name. Do you really think I can do it?"

"Have you done anything like it before?" Feng was impatient.

"I have, but it was back in my village. This is my first time at something this big."

"You don't have to dazzle the crowd," Feng tsked. "You'll just be there to make up the total."

He took Moses Yang to Old Yu's coffin shop and painted the young man's face before giving him the costume. Yang was so nervous he was sweating when Feng applied the paint.

"I'm not trying to kill you, so why are you shaking like that?" Feng was losing his patience. "See, the paint has smudged."

"I'm not afraid, Uncle. This is abnormal sweat from hunger. I've missed several meals already."

Feng gave Moses a few flatcakes from Yu's kitchen. After washing them down with a bowl of water, Moses tied stilts to his legs and joined the festival troupe. A bit tense at first, he trembled, but no longer from hunger. He missed cues from the drums and gongs and fell a few times, making the onlookers laugh. Soon, however, he was able to get into the role. With newfound energy from the flatcakes, he danced to the beat of the drums and gongs, even with a bit of flair. Moses Yang, Yang Baishun, was the good-looking one among the three boys in his family. He was tall and blessed with large eyes, a handsome young man whose looks went unnoticed until his face was painted and he was dressed in colorful costumes. Deng, the sundry store owner, looked uglier each day he played the King of Hell, eventually turning the fear-inspiring figure into a shriveled old man. Now with Moses Yang, the King of Hell was a striking young man who looked trustworthy but roguish, shy yet outgoing. Every body movement, every smile, and every frown made him look more like Pan An, the handsome scholar of old, than the King of Hell. Moses Yang was Yang Baishun again, especially when he added a move from his village, "face-dragging," to his current performance. "Face-dragging" was unique to Yang Village, something unknown to the county town residents. It required the performer to cover his face with both hands while lifting his shoulders and spreading his legs, and then slowly dragging his hands away before his face is completely visible to the spectators. Moses danced and revealed his face little by little, as if in a trance, causing such a stir among the onlookers that they shouted their approval. Feng, who hadn't held out much hope for a stopgap replacement, had been worried that Yang would do a terrible job. It was no big deal for one man to fail at his role, but it could ruin the whole performance with considerable consequences. Imagine his surprise when he was treated to a fantastic dance that changed people's view of the King of Hell.

Feng was all smiles when that day's performance ended; he took the young man aside and asked him all kinds of questions. Feng had planned to use Moses for that day only, while he continued to search for a suitable King of Hell. He didn't have to; the original king had recovered from his illness. Old Chu was wrong; the pain was caused not by tangled intestines but a tapeworm. The herbal concoction did not smooth out the purported mess inside; it expelled the worm. He was cured, even with the wrong diagnosis. But Feng did not ask Deng again; he chose to let Moses play the King of Hell for the remaining four days of the festivity. Moses got to eat flatcakes every day, plus a bowl of spicy soup for lunch and dinner. Feng decided that Moses would be his choice again the next year.

No party lasts forever. The New Year's celebration was over after the twenty-first of the month, and the rousing communal celebration came to an end. Gongs and drums had been beating to the high heavens the day before, but only abandoned shoes were left by the river on the twenty-second. Gone were the troupe members, as they all returned to their old lives to resume their jobs: Feng, the head of the troupe, back to sell smoked rabbits; Du, the God of Fire Zhu Rong, to be a tailor; Old Yu, the seductress Da Ji, to make coffins; Old Gao, Pigsy, to make millstones; and Moses Yang, the King of Hell, to deliver water. What people heard by the Jin River early in the morning were now the intermittent shouts by Old Nie, peddling soy milk from his shop.

On the twenty-second, Moses Yang happened to be delivering water to Old Lian, who ran Prosperity on East Street, which was the grain supplier involved in a lawsuit with Old Wang, the teacher at the private school. Wang survived Lian's tactics but not the lawsuit. By this time, over a decade later, Old Lian had died, and his son, Lian Junior, had taken over. In addition to a large water vat in the kitchen, the Lian family had four large vats in the granary, in case of a fire, and three more in the backyard stable to store water for the half-dozen animals transporting grain. Each vat required seven trips, making a total of fifty-six trips to fill eight vats. It was a major client for anyone delivering water. But there was more than just delivering water. First, the remaining water must be scooped out before new water could be poured in, and the vats had to be swept clean with a brush. After cleaning the vats, Moses went to the well to bring water in. The well was two li away, quite a distance, so he managed to fill only four vats after a morning of hard work that had him bathed in sweat. But it was a job, and he couldn't complain; it would be much harder if he didn't have one. After taking a break by the well, he stood up and resumed working, forgoing lunch altogether. Someone called out to him just as he was walking onto the street with his full buckets.

"Hey, you there, stop."

Moses turned his head to see Old Chao, a clerk at the county government office, in charge of processing paperwork. Chao also lived in town, on North Street, which was why Yang thought Chao needed him to deliver water to his house.

"You'll have to wait till this afternoon. I'll bring you water after I finish with the Lian family and get a bite to eat."

"It's about a government matter, not water."

During the lantern festival, while everyone had been out watching the festival troupe by the river, a group of thieves had taken advantage of the occasion by stealing thirty silver dollars and a parcel of women's hair ornaments from Old Jin's Peace and Prosperity Shop on South Street in broad daylight. Shi started an investigation, after the Jin family reported the theft. Moses thought he was under suspicion for the theft when Chao mentioned a government matter, so he quickly replied, "I had nothing to do with what happened on South Street, Uncle. I deliver water. I'm not brave enough to pull something like that." As if that weren't enough, he added, "Besides, I was performing at the festival. You saw me."

"I want to see you precisely because of the festival." Chao flicked the chain in his hand.

Convinced that Chao was going to use the chain on him, Yang was so frightened he dropped his buckets and spilled the contents all over the ground. Chao laughed before telling Yang why he needed to see the young man; his visit was on behalf of the county magistrate, not because of the theft. Besides opera, Shi had a hobby of growing vegetables, not for consumption but as a way to keep a low profile, like Liu Bei of the Three Kingdom Period. It was a bit over the top for a mere county magistrate to want to keep a low profile, but he was serious, and no one could say anything about it. There was a small plot of land behind the county government building; Old Hu had used it to store his woodworking materials, while Old Han had let it stay fallow. Upon his arrival, Shi had his underlings clear the area and turn it into a site for personal cultivation, which explained why Shi walked around a vegetable garden with his hands clasped behind his back. He actually needed someone to work the garden, and he'd had someone, a distant uncle of his from Fujian. Shi's father had died when he was little, so he had grown up poor, and the uncle had frequently helped his family out. He hired the uncle to tend the garden after assuming the position but had not expected the uncle to be more interested in government affairs than in growing vegetables. The uncle held the erroneous view that Shi should follow his advice, as he had done during his younger days. When he saw that Shi paid no heed to his job and spent his time and energy on operas, he called him a terrible official; moreover, he went out to take on lawsuits and helped the plaintiffs, as if he were the magistrate. Shi had chastised Zhan for interfering in government affairs and frightened the priest off when he had come to get his church back. Now his uncle interfered with his work while neglecting the vegetable plot, making it impossible for Shi to carry out his self-cultivation. Shi did not know what to do with this benefactor of his youth. As if that weren't enough, shortly before the end of the year, the uncle tried out another antic; taking a page from popular opera, he put before the county building a large drum that was more than three meters in diameter for the residents to beat when they had a complaint. Shi had put up with his uncle's escapades to that point, but this time the old man had gone too far. Shi told him what he thought, unaware that his uncle was also petty, in addition to his penchant for meddling in government business. Peeved, he quit and went back to Fujian with his final declaration: "I'm not upset that the county magistrate is a terrible official; I just feel sorry for the suffering residents of Yanjin."

Shi simply smiled and let him go, for he had grown weary of this uncle of his. Later, when he went to watch the festival, he spotted Moses Yang among the performers and was impressed with the splendid job Moses had done in the role. Shi asked around and learned that Yang delivered water to shops along the streets, with no place to call his own, which gave him the idea of hiring the King of Hell to tend his vegetable garden. To be sure, he wouldn't have trouble finding a replacement for his uncle, but he thought it would be interesting to have a King of Hell in the garden as he conducted self-cultivation, since growing vegetables was not his true focus.

Moses Yang was confused when he learned of the job offer from the magistrate. Chao did not find Moses's reaction unusual and went up to pinch his ear.

"Damn! It makes me angry just looking at that stupid face of yours. How does a water carrier deserve such a cushy job? One moment you're more or less a beggar and the next you're going to work at the county office."

Years before, Yang Baili, Moses Yang's younger brother, had attended Yanjin New School, with his eye on a job at the county office, but had never made it. Who would have thought that, without even going to school, Moses Yang could accidently fulfill a dream of his brother's by simply performing at a New Year's celebration? It was normal employment, even if he would be growing vegetables, and he would no longer have to deliver water and go hungry when no one needed his services. Besides, tending a vegetable garden at the county office was different from doing it in his village. Back when he was studying the classics with Wang, he had read the sage's comment that one's study improves through diligence and deteriorates from too much merrymaking. No one could predict that Moses would find employment not through diligence but through merrymaking at the Lantern Festival. He had to shake his head and sigh over the strange turn of events.

"I've always thought my benefactor would be a person or the Lord, but it turns out to be a New Year's festival."

11

As the saying goes, when good luck comes calling, no door can keep it from entering. Moses Yang was married three months after starting his new job at the county office.

South Street in the county town was the site of Jiang's cotton shop, where family members fluffed and ginned cotton, while others pressed the seeds to make oil to bottle and sell. They also replaced the worn cotton in blankets with new material. Jiang's cotton shop naturally was owned by a man surnamed Jiang, who had three sons, Jiang Long, Jiang Hu, and Jiang Gou. Everyone in the family, men and women, young and old, worked at the shop year-round and walked around with cotton fluff in their hair. Whenever someone walked down the street with a head of white, the residents knew the person belonged to the Jiang family. Before the sons were married, Jiang Long and Jiang Gou could talk about anything, while Jiang Hu, the taciturn son and a loner, kept everything to himself. Since they had married one at a time, five years before, they no longer spoke to one another, owing to problems not between the wives but between the brothers. As the father and three sons ran a business together, the daughters-in-law were always gossiping about who worked harder and who didn't, who earned more and who earned less, who got the heavy work and who didn't. As time went by, the discord among the women spread to the brothers. When there was a rift, no one could do anything right, and good intentions were misconstrued as scheming. The rift did not affect business at the shop, but turned the life of a family of a dozen people upside down.

On the sixth day of the fifth lunar month, the family dog killed one of their chickens. After kicking the dog, Old Jiang took the dead chicken into the kitchen for his wife to stew in a clear broth. The Jiang family had a simple diet and rarely saw meat or chicken on their dining table. After the father took the chicken head, Jiang Long's and Jiang Gou's sons were drooling over the rest of the chicken. Old Jiang tore off the drumsticks and gave one to each of the boys. Jiang Hu had a daughter named Qiaoling, who had been out playing that day. When she returned, there were no more chicken legs on the platter; they were in the hands of her cousins. She walked up with the intention of snatching one for herself. Jiang Long's son was five years old, and Jiang Gou's was two, so naturally she picked on the younger one. The boy held onto it with all his might. Hu's wife, Wu Xiangxiang, slapped her daughter.

"You eat whatever is your share. You don't have a share today, so forget it."

She was obviously talking about something other than the leg. Qiaoling opened her mouth wide and began to cry. Jiang Gou's wife was unhappy when she saw the little girl try to take the leg from her son, but she said nothing. She did, however, have to speak up after Xiangxiang used the drumstick as a pretext for something else and slapped her daughter all for show.

"It's just a chicken leg. What's the big deal?"

"The children are too young to know what's right, but what about the grown-ups?"

A quarrel ensued, and one dispute brought out eight more, one of which involved Jiang Long's wife, so she joined in. Soon all hell broke loose. Old Jiang quickly went out to buy a rabbit leg from Old Feng for the little girl, but her mother snatched it away and flung it out the door. The dog ran off with it. The melee lasted into late afternoon, so no one got to work on time and none of them cared to eat when dinner was ready. That night, Old Jiang called his second son into the main room.

"It's my fault; I forgot that a chicken has only two legs." The old man banged the bowl of his pipe on the table. "Go talk to your wife. No need to quarrel like that."

Hu had been quiet throughout the women's bickering, but now he spoke his mind.

"The rest of you can quarrel all you want, but not me. I want some peace and quiet."

Old Jiang was shocked when he got a drift of what his son was hinting at. "What do you mean?"

"All parties must come to an end one day. I want to strike out on my own."

Old Jiang knew his second son well; the young man never said much but always knew what he wanted. There was nothing extraordinary about wanting to strike out on his own, but now he was using a drumstick as an excuse to split up the family, which could only mean that he had not been taking his father seriously for some time. This went beyond a mere drumstick. Not wanting to be shown up by his son, Old Jiang asked his wife's brother over early the next morning to split up the family property. In addition to the cotton shop on South Street, the Jiang family also owned a three-room house with a storefront on West Street, which Jiang had inherited from his father. The place was currently rented out to a tofu maker. With the property he received from the family, Hu set up his own household and abandoned the cotton trade; instead, he moved to West Street, got the tofu maker to leave, and, with the stove and pots ready, began selling steamed buns. He gave up on the cotton business not because it led to a family split, but because he did not want to live the rest of his life with a head of white fluff. He called his shop Jiang's Steamed Buns.

Separated from his family in housing arrangements as well as in trade, he more or less cut off ties with his parents and his brothers. Their life was more peaceful than before, as husband and wife steamed and sold buns, even though they had done better financially working in the family cotton shop. Hu was born frail, not as robust as his brothers, who often said he was sneaky. After two months of kneading dough for the buns, he found his arms getting thicker and his hands stronger, with well-defined muscle tone. Sometimes his wife muttered as she worked the dough, "They can go their way and we'll go ours. We won't go hungry by leaving that cotton shop."

"No more of that nonsense," Hu stopped her. "Can't you say something useful?"

Not given to speech, he hated the talkative type. To him, nonsense meant talking about what has already happened, while saying something useful takes care of what's coming up ahead. When he wasn't tending the business, he also joined up with his friends, Old Bu and Old Lai, to buy scallions in Shanxi and sell them locally as a way to make enough to remodel the storefront house. The tofu-maker had not taken care of the place. The walls were blackened from stove smoke, which would not have mattered much if the walls themselves hadn't turned hollow. Even the bases were spongy from standing water. A stomp of the foot sent mud flying off the wall. The roof also needed repairs. It leaked when it rained and water continued to drip for hours after the rain had stopped. In addition to fixing up the old rooms, he wanted to add a side room, plans for which consumed much of his time and energy. Leaving town to buy scallions exposed him to the elements, and was much harder than staying home to work the dough. But it was a profitable business that made money faster than selling buns. In the space of a year, he managed to remodel the three rooms and build a new one. He was mildly addicted to the scallion trade, and traveled to Shanxi with his friends whenever he had time, even after he stopped going year-round. He had much more to talk about with the two men than with his own brothers; buying scallions to him was as much for the opportunity to talk to someone as for resale.

Just before year's end, two years earlier, he had gone to Taiyuan with his friends. They all rode on donkey carts and chatted along the way, arriving in the city seven days later. Taiyuan "chicken-thigh" scallions were the size of pig knuckles, with a pungency that went straight to your nose; they were spicy but not bitter, making them a hot commodity back home. After loading their carts, they headed back without stopping for the night, hoping to make market day in Yanjin on the twenty-third. They reached Qinyuan, on the border between Shanxi and Henan, three days later, but the weather changed, with a gusty northern wind that brought snowflakes. The snow-laced Shanxi wind was cold and strong. The men were cold but not in as bad shape as their donkeys, which were sweating and shaking from the chill. Afraid that the animals would fall ill, they went into town, deciding to stop for the night, even though the sky told them they had two more hours before dark. They found an inn that also took donkey carts and horse wagons, tethered their donkeys in a shed, and fed them. They added a fire to warm the animals before walking out to find a diner for a hot meal to warm themselves. They checked out several places, but didn't like any of them; either they were too cold or too expensive. Finally, they found a small diner in Xiguan that sold giblets soup. The place looked clean, the prices were reasonable, and it was warmed by giblets bubbling in a large wok. Since it was getting dark, they decided to go in. It was mealtime, and people traveling for business were forced by the cold to stop at Qinyuan, so the diner was full. They were lucky to find a group of diners finishing up and vacating a table for them, so they sat down and ordered three bowls of giblets soup, plus thirty fried cakes. The cakes had already been made, so they could start with them while the soup, which had to be prepared for each customer, required a wait—for them and the other diners. Customers loved the soup, partly because they got free refills, so no one ate the cakes first, wanting to eat it all at the same time. The three friends waited for the better part of an hour before the soup was brought out. They buried their heads in the bowls and were slurping away when the door curtain parted and in walked three travelers, two men and a woman. With no other vacant spot, they sat across from Jiang Hu and ordered three bowls of soup and thirty fried cakes. The men had a Shandong accent, while the woman was obviously from Shanxi, and from their conversation it seemed that they were mule sellers. As they waited for their soup, the two men flirted with the woman, who did not appear to be either man's wife, judging by the way they talked. She seemed to be a temporary companion they had hooked up with on the road, for she joked around with both men. Hu and his friends had seen enough loose women like that on their trips, so they paid them no heed as they continued to eat. Old Bu, who by nature could keep nothing to himself, eyed the woman and, as if that weren't enough, whispered something to Old Lai. They sniggered, which, combined with their whispering, irked the two Shandong men, who took the behavior as maliciously motivated. One was tall, the other short, but they were both beefy. The short one spat in Lai's direction and cursed: "What are you whispering about, motherfucker? Tell your granddad here where it itches and I'll scratch it for you."

Old Bu lowered his head to stay out of trouble, but not Old Lai, a tough guy back in Yanjin, who feared no one. He snapped back, and an argument started. A waiter brought the soup out and tried to mediate, but the Shandong man took a step back, picked up the bowl of soup, and aimed it at Lai. Lai also took a step back to prepare for the imminent fight. Seeing the two in that pose, Hu put down his flatcake and got up to stop them. Normally, he would have called the man Dage, older brother, as a form of respect, but their accent made him switch to Er-ge, second older brother, because the most famous Er-ge in Shandong was Wu Song, the tiger slayer, while Dage was a cuckold and murder victim.

"Er-ge, my brothers here did not know any better. We're all travelers far from home, so please accept my apology on my friend's behalf?"

But the Shandong man would have none of it, partly because Jiang Hu looked frail, and his soft voice made him an easy mark.

"An apology isn't enough for me. They have to call her Mother." He pointed to the woman. But he was wrong about Hu. He could have either left Hu out and continued to argue or got on with his business, but he should not have asked Hu to apologize to a woman like that. He had no idea he should not have angered Hu. Without another word, Hu kicked the bowl of hot soup out of the man's hands, grabbed him by the hair, and pounded his head on the table over and over, not stopping even when the man began to bleed. Everyone in the diner, including the other man, the woman, Bu and Lai, and all the diners, was stunned, never expecting frail-looking Hu to have that kind of temperament and strength. What happened next was even more shocking. The tall man had been caught off guard when Hu grabbed his head, and he was too dazed to respond; when he finally recovered, he took out a knife and buried it in Hu's chest. Blood spurted and sprayed the wall when he pulled the knife out. Hu slumped to the floor, and his friends rushed to help him, while the two men and the woman ran out and disappeared without a trace. Bu and Lai gave chase, but it was pitch black under a sky blanketed by snow. Hu gasped for air on the floor before he took his last breath, while blood continued to seep for a moment. Bu and Lai took the diner owner to the county government office to file a report, but they did not know the names of the perpetrators or where they lived. The accent alone was no help. The woman was from Shanxi, but obviously had no fixed residence. They could be anywhere, and there was no way to find them. With no alternative, Bu and Lai took Hu's body back to Yanjin three days later. Bu talked to Lai about the cause of Hu's death. They would not say they had been the cause of the trouble that had led to Hu's murder; instead, they would tell his wife that Hu had been killed in a fight with someone in Qinyuan. He had been well and alive when he left for Shanxi, but returned as a corpse. Cradling their child, his wife wailed and passed out from grief several times. The bright red New Year's couplets were replaced by white ones for a funeral.

Wu Xiangxiang, now a widow, kept the bun shop going by herself. When Hu had been around, the shop seemed lively, even though he never said much. Now the place was desolate without him. She had become an outsider to her in-laws, who, from Hu's father down to his brothers, all expected her to remarry soon. To them, it was a great loss that their son and brother was dead, but her remarriage would mean nothing to them; besides, they would get the newly repaired bun shop back. Xiangxiang had thought of remarrying, since she was still young, but it was not easy for a widow with a child to find a suitable match. Moreover, she realized that her in-laws wanted her to remarry so they could claim the shop, which made her hold onto it, out of spite. When people do such things, they tend to forget the reason behind them, as they focus solely on irritating others, which in turn ruins their own prospects. A year went by and nothing changed. Old Jiang was not concerned, since Xiangxiang's daughter was, after all, his granddaughter, even if the woman herself was now an outsider. Hu's brothers, on the other hand, were anxious to see her go, so they formed an alliance against her despite their prior issues with each other. Of course, they would not do anything openly. Instead, after midnight each day during the second half of the month, when there was no moon in the sky, they sneaked from South Street to West Street while the town slept, climbed onto the roof of the bun shop, and stomped their feet to frighten her. They started out together but then began taking turns; one could sleep while the other bedeviled her.

But they had misjudged her. If they had not tried to intimidate her, she might have considered remarriage, but she steeled her heart and put the matter out of her mind after their antics. Moreover, she changed the shop's name to Wu's Steamed Buns. But being alone and constantly harassed was no way to live, so she decided to find a man to come liven up the place. No suitable one showed up among those she checked. She wanted someone with passably good looks and a good temper, and he had to be able to talk. There were plenty of eligible men for each criterion, but none who would meet all three. One might have a good temper but was too timid to keep a robust appearance. Another would be bold, but so bold she feared he would overpower her and take the bun shop away. Once she found a man from Ju Village whose wife had just died. He had a loud voice and sounded fearless, but knew to defer to her. The downside was his three children, whom she would have to support the moment they were married. She sighed over the difficulty of finding the right person. The matter remained unresolved for more than a year, a difficult time. But one day she chanced upon Moses Yang.

By then Moses had tended the magistrate's vegetable garden for four months. He had never grown vegetables before, but as a country boy, he had seen enough to know the basics. As the saying goes, a country boy would have seen a pig run even if he'd never eaten pork. He fertilized the plot behind the county office as soon as the soil thawed in early spring and then turned it. The county office kept no farm animals, so he had to do it by hand, one shovelful at a time, until the plot was furrowed. Then he crushed the clumps of clay with a rake to smooth the surface before planting eggplants, beans, radishes, spinach, hot peppers, scallions, garlic, and medicinal herbs, all personally specified by the county magistrate. Moses added trellises for sponge gourds and bottle gourds at the corners. With the planting done, his job switched to watering the sprouts; along with them came weeds, so he weeded before loosening the soil to retain the moisture level. After three months he found that tending a vegetable plot was more exhausting than delivering water, which had fatigued him only when there was work, and he could take a break if no one needed his service. But now he never enjoyed a moment's rest; there was always something that required his attention, from dawn to dusk. The work was hard, and yet he was happy. In the past, he'd had to wait to work; now the work waited for him. Nothing was more onerous than having no work to do. Besides, he had sole authority to decide how he wanted to manage his time, unlike the old days, when storeowners would tell him how much water they wanted and when. Granted, he was kept busy all day long, but he could choose what to do first, as long he made sure the plot was well maintained. He was much happier when he had autonomy. And there was more—he ate better. Delivering water to stores had not been steady work, which meant he hadn't always earned enough to eat. As lowly as he was now as a gardener, he was at least a government employee and entitled to eat three meals a day. He was reassured that he no longer had to worry about where the next meal would come from.

The forty or more clerks at the county office complained about the cook, Old Ai, calling him a lousy provider after being served the same dish—stewed pork slices with vegetables—for too long. To Moses Yang, the stew was delicious, at least at first, for it had plenty of grease and a good texture. After three months, people were talking about how the vegetable garden tender had put on weight. Yang's only complaint about life at the office was the clerks; it was so much easier delivering water alone than trying to get along with all those people. It had been taxing back at the dye shop, where he'd had to deal with a dozen workers; now there were several dozen of them, each slicker than the next one. The clerks, like Old Ta the Mongolian at the dye shop, picked on Yang because he was new, giving him errands like delivering a letter, buying cigarettes and liquor, or moving desks or chairs, despite the fact that he was occupied with the garden. Even the cook had him buy oil and soy sauce at the market or bring back a basket of steamed buns two out of every three days. So Moses was also their errand boy. He could curse them all he wanted silently, but he knew that a job like this was hard to come by. Moreover, in dealing with people over the years, he had gotten used to being taken advantage of, in addition to his disinclination to join a clique, which always led to trouble. Whenever he was called, he put aside his garden work to do what was asked of him; he would curse them silently, but wear a smile.

The magistrate had hired Yang to tend the vegetable garden so he himself could lie low, and he had not anticipated the additional duties piled onto Moses. He shook his head and smiled when he saw the clerks order Moses around and make him run like a spinning top, showing no sign of displeasure toward either them or Moses. Since his smile was directed at the clerks, they felt justified in picking on Moses, while in fact it was all to his advantage, though he acted like a loser. They were not deep thinkers. Everyone in the office shared a view that "Moses" was not much of a talker, but was one hell of a worker. He was able to survive and get a solid footing because he was quick to carry out their requests.

In Old Shi's view, Moses's relationship with the clerks was a perfect example of keeping a low profile.

Shi would stroll around the vegetable garden with his hands clasped behind his back whenever he had a free moment. Moses had taken the liberty to plant two rows of Indian asters and canna lilies in an open spot in the front yard. He watered them daily. Shi had hired Moses mainly because he had done such a fine job as the King of Hell, who was in charge of life and death; his life-snuffing demons unhesitatingly took people away if the king set a time for the death. But now Shi's King of Hell was bending over, occupied by hard work and devoid of the awe-inspiring airs at the festival; he gave a direct, succinct answer when Shi asked him a question. Just looking at his King of Hell made Shi laugh. Moses never said anything more than required to Shi, not because he was cautious, like the clerks, but because the somber, reserved magistrate intimidated him. In fact, Moses often trembled when speaking with Shi, which had escaped the man's attention.

One day Shi made his way into the garden and stood by the canna lilies to watch Moses hoe the plot.

"What's on your mind when you work, Moses?" he asked after watching awhile.

This was precisely why Moses was afraid of Shi, who was always tossing off questions like that, all about things that he had never thought of before. Moses stood up and thought about the question for a moment.

"Nothing."

"That can't be true," Shi said. "Everyone thinks about something when they work."

"Sometimes I think of Luo Changli," he said after a pause.

Then he proceeded to tell Shi about Luo, a vinegar peddler with a loud voice who was unmatched at funerals and good at directing mourners. Moses said he loved hearing Luo shout more than anything else in the world. The revelation caught Shi by surprise, not because of Luo, but because of Moses, a manual laborer who knew to appreciate a funeral crier. He could not help but think of Moses's role at the festival; a performer who played the King of Hell loved to hear Luo shout at funerals. The two were connected with death, and it seemed natural for Moses to move from funeral crier to the King of Hell. Shi shook his head and smiled again.

Something happened on the sixteenth day of the fourth lunar month that changed Shi's view of Moses. There was no indoor plumbing back in Shi's day, so he had to use a chamber pot, like everyone else. As a reserved man, Shi had the same tendency as other reserved individuals in their secret fondness for eroticism. There was nothing unusual about that, but Shi's predilection was a bit different, in that he preferred male over female sex objects. That was no big deal either, except that he liked them only on the stage, which was why he enjoyed opera so much. He was mainly looking at the male actors when he went to the theater. Back then it was mostly handsome young men in female roles. As someone who had grown up in the south, Shi did not appreciate tall, strapping northern men. They gave their gender away in how they carried themselves and in their movements when they played female roles. That was why he could not bring himself to enjoy the Henan clapper dramas. He'd gone to school in Suzhou as a young man and fallen for the effete male actors there, which was why he'd brought a Wuxi opera troupe all the way to Yanjin. To be sure, there were other types of southern operas, but to him, the male actors in Wuxi opera looked more like women than those in the Min or Yue operas. Not women but better than women, mind you. Su Xiaobao, a seventeen-year-old male actor with a lovely face, was a member of the troupe he had brought out. Fetching on stage, he was taciturn and reserved once he shed his costumes, a perfect fit for Shi's preferences. Shi had hired this particular troupe precisely because of the young actor, and he went to the theater every day to watch him perform. Shi had gone to watch the New Year's celebration not because he was tired of the Wuxi opera; Xiaobao had had to return to Suzhou during the period for an uncle's funeral. The stage looked suddenly empty, so the magistrate left to enjoy the town's festival performance. If he hadn't, he would not have found Moses Yang, who thought the festival had helped him find a new job. In fact, he should have been grateful to Xiaobao, or maybe to Xiaobao's uncle, who had died at just the right time. Shi went back to the theater when Xiaobao returned.

After a performance, the magistrate would summon the actor to his residence, where they would spend the night together. It may have been a bit unseemly for the head of a county to consort with a male actor, but, unlike Old Hu's woodworking hobby, it was a personal preference with no national salvation implications. Old Xu, the governor, and Old Geng, the commissioner, just smiled when they learned of it. Some might suspect that the two men were engaged in something untoward, but in fact they spent the night in bed talking, nothing else. To be more precise, they did not talk with their mouths, but with their hands. They played Chinese chess while talking with their hands; yes, talking, a sort of "mental masturbation," which was where Shi differed from other men. All he asked of Xiaobao was for him to keep his costume and face paint on as they talked with their hands. They did not do that every night, for that would have been exhausting. Just once every ten days, on the fifth, the fifteenth, and the twenty-fifth of each month, taking it slow and easy, to enjoy the moment. Since no one actually knew what was going on, people thought they must be doing whatever two men normally did in bed. It would be hard to convince them, especially those at the county office, that a man and a "woman" did nothing physical when they spent the night together. Shi did not care what others thought, and he maintained his usual somber demeanor, which made his subordinates fear him even more, though not because he was their boss. They were fearful because they could not determine what went on in his head.

Shi went to an opera performance on the fifteenth day of the fourth lunar month and spent the night at his residence with the actor in full stage regalia. The moon was big and bright, but they ignored it as they carried on a game of chess. They played all night, concluding at daybreak with a most unusual game, which they called "Wind and Snow Paired." It always ended in a stalemate, but the overall arrangement was unorthodox and the moves ingenious. They had not started out with a plan for every move to turn out that way; they simply changed their tactics according to circumstances, until they saw the grand play they had constructed. The game was filled with intrigue and strategy, but the black-and-white chess pieces moved in a seemingly amorphous and chaotic fashion, a union made in heaven. It was a state of ultimate gratification many people tried but few obtained. Victory was not the goal of hand talking; anyone with that in mind was vulgar and uncouth. The players aimed at going hand in hand to a place they'd never been before; they played not just to play, not even for the game, but for that union made in heaven. They wrapped their arms around each other and wept sorrowfully. Both men were the quiet type, but now they were weeping over a game of chess, sobbing to the depths of their souls.

The county employed a man called Gan, who had a big head and a booming voice that sounded like a gong, to sweep the floor. Moses Yang was closer to Gan than to any of the clerks, but they became friends not because their jobs put them on the same status level, nor because Gan wasn't as crafty as others. Gan loved to pontificate even though he swept the floor for a living. The desk clerks worked with pens and had nothing to say to Gan. Moses was the vegetable gardener and a newcomer, a ready-made pupil for Gan. For his part, Moses needed someone to teach him the ins and outs of the office. So they became friends.

On the thirteenth day of the fourth lunar month, Gan's wife gave birth to a baby boy in the countryside. He asked for a week's leave of absence to go home for a celebratory banquet. He came to the vegetable plot before he left, sighing over and over, which puzzled Moses.

"Why do you look so unhappy? You have a son."

"It's not about the baby. I'm worried about what will happen here while I'm away."

"It's just the floor. I'll sweep it for you."

"Sweeping the floor is nothing. The key is the chamber pot in the magistrate's quarters."

Old Gan emptied the magistrate's chamber pot every morning, sometimes bringing it out to the garden to fertilize the vegetables.

"I've gone through everyone at the office, but can't find anyone I can confidently turn the job over to."

"A chamber pot? That's no big deal. I'll do it for you. I'll empty and clean it before putting it back."

"I feel I can trust you, but how is your hearing?"

"What do you mean?"

Gan sat Moses down and explained to him what was involved. It was not just emptying the contents; timing was crucial, though not because it must be emptied at an auspicious hour. It just had to be done at the right moment, immediately after the magistrate got out of bed. He would disturb the man's sleep if he went in too early, but it would look terrible to have a chamber pot still in the room if he went in after the man was up and about. So he must wait and listen outside the window, and then enter when he heard stirring inside and empty it right away. Not too early, not too late, perfect timing for a job well done. It became clear to Moses once Gan was done explaining.

"I'll get up early every morning and listen outside his window for stirrings. I'll go in as soon as I hear him getting out of bed."

"Well, that's the best I can do." Gan sighed. "Make sure you do it right."

Moses now had an additional task besides tending the garden. He got up just before daybreak on the first morning to wait outside Shi's window. An hour later, when he heard the magistrate cough, he sprang into action. Shi was surprised to see him.

"What are you doing here?"

"Emptying the chamber pot; Old Gan's wife had a baby and he went home."

Shi said nothing more, and Moses walked out with the chamber pot. Everything went smoothly the following morning as well. But Gan forgot one thing before he left for home. During his seven-day absence, there would be a fifteenth day of the lunar month, the night Shi and Xiaobao would have their "hand-to-hand," and Moses must wait until Xiaobao left the bedroom. Gan had not mentioned that. On the morning of the sixteenth, Moses got up to wait outside Shi's window. Shi and Xiaobao were sobbing in each other's arms when Moses reached the window; mistaking the noise as a sign of the magistrate moving about, he opened the door and walked in without thinking. What he saw— Magistrate Shi sobbing in the arms of a fully costumed actor with a painted face—so stunned him that he let out an involuntary cry. His cry tore the two men out of their deliriously happy state, which was not so bad, since they were sobbing over the game of chess; but it looked extraordinary in the eyes of an outsider. Xiaobao recovered first and returned to reality from a state he'd never reached before; he pushed Old Shi away and turned to face the wall. Shi was still dazed as he tilted his head and saw Moses standing there. He flew into a rage when he too recovered, though not because he didn't want Moses to see them together. He was incensed that he and Xiaobao had not cried all they wanted yet, and might never be able to do it again. They could have gone to a place they had never been before if not for Moses Yang stumbling in on them. Everything was ruined now. Overcome with exasperation, Shi was incoherent and turned to Xiaobao, instead of Moses.

"What's going on?"

Still facing the wall, Xiaobao did not answer. Moses, who was shaking from fear, mustered enough courage to say, "I'm here to empty the chamber pot."

A chamber pot had ruined a perfect union. Shi was furious. No longer his reticent self, he looked up and shouted, "Get out of here!"

Moses ran awkwardly back to the vegetable garden as fast as his legs would carry him, leaving the chamber pot behind. Knowing he had made a huge mistake, he thought he would be fired soon, but Shi did not tell him to leave; he just stopped talking to him. Moses mistook that as a sign of the man's leniency, but in fact Shi was never lenient. He was simply too infuriated to do anything at the moment, that was all. He was angry not only at Moses, though the gardener was the culprit; starting with Moses, everything in the world disappointed him. A King of Hell stood out at the festival, but once he had been brought down to tend a vegetable garden, he was as muddle-headed as everyone else. Everyone made Shi unhappy. He could fire Moses, but most likely his replacement would not be any better than Moses or his interfering uncle. He was too discouraged to even fire Moses.

For his part, Moses could not fathom what went on in Shi's mind, and he began to live in fear, though he managed to keep his job. He worked the garden, feeling that a sword hung over his head; he had not felt such trepidation before, not even when he first started working at the county office. He worked harder than before, as a way to make up for his error, and acted unhesitatingly when one of the clerks sent him on an errand, unaware that disaster can turn into good fortune for some people. Moses got to know Wu Xiangxiang from his frequent bun-buying trips for Old Ai the cook. In fact, Moses and Xiangxiang had known each other back when he delivered water to the shops. In addition to selling buns at her store, she had also set up a stall at the intersection, where a flag inscribed with "Wu's Steamed Buns" stuck out of a misty steamer.

Whenever Moses did not make enough money delivering water, he went for a bowl of soupy rice at Old Zhan's Congee Shop in Beiguan. But he bought buns from Xiangxiang when he had extra cash. Something was different when he bought from her now, but not because he was buying a basketful to feed dozens at the county office. It was his status that had changed. Xiangxiang had not paid Moses any attention until he came as an employee of the county office. Truth be told, he had caught her attention even before that. Like everyone else at the festival four months earlier, she had noticed the King of Hell, who was unlike any King of Hell she had seen before. But in her mind, she never linked herself with the man who performed at the celebration. She realized that he could do more than perform only after he started working at the county office.

None of the people engaged in the various trades on the streets had taken Moses seriously when he delivered water to them. Now that he was a county employee, they saw how the magistrate favored him, but were unaware that he had recently fallen out of favor. He was simply different in their eyes. Next to Xiangxiang's stand at the intersection was a shoe repair stall run by Old Zhao the cobbler. Moses wore down his shoes easily when delivering water and had to have them repaired often. Zhao was peeved after Moses had asked him to put the charge on credit twice and pulled a long face when he showed up after that.

"I'm running a business here. You have to pay first."

No money, no shoe repair. With his new job in the vegetable garden, he wore out his shoes just as easily, so he asked Zhao to work on them when he went to buy buns for the cook. Zhao put other shoes aside to work on Moses's first and never asked to be paid. He was unhappy if Moses insisted on paying.

"Are you shaming me, Brother? It's something I do, no big deal."

Or, "Are you afraid I might ask you to return the favor?"

As time went by, Xiangxiang began to look at Moses differently and asked around about his background. She was disappointed to learn that, besides delivering water, he had worked at a bamboo shop, a dye shop, and a pig butcher's, all manual labor. Her heart sank when she heard that his family was in the tofu-making business, but the Yang family status went up a notch in her mind when she was told about the Yangs' in-laws, the wealthy Qin family. She dug deeper and lost hope; Moses had left home after a row with his family, so he was alone with nothing to call his own, neither house nor land. And yet he was an attractive candidate precisely because he was alone, that and the fact that he worked at the county office. She would be marrying a water deliveryman if he had continued his old trade, but now with him working at the county office, she would get more than a husband; a backer was the support she badly needed. Wu's Steamed Buns would then carry the prestige of the county government, which was exactly the plan that Moses's father and Ma the carter had had in mind when they plotted to send Baili to school. Moses, being alone, would normally be a terrible catch with no property; but that suited her need to have a man marry into the family. He would not bring with him any necessary complications, and, more importantly, having nothing to his name meant he would defer to her.

One afternoon Moses was in the garden picking insects off the plants. Still a novice at the line of work, he knew only to work hard and had no idea how best to go about it. All the vegetables—eggplants, beans, spinach, and gourds—grew nice and tall, but insects showed up when the leaves were about the size of a human palm, and left holes on the leaves. The magistrate frowned and shook his head when he noticed the holes. Vegetables tend to attract insects, which would not have been an issue, but to Moses, who had felt guilty since walking in on the weeping Shi and Xiaobao, it felt like a major offense. He was afraid that Magistrate Shi would do more than just frown at the holed leaves. Being new to the vegetable-growing business, he ran to Old Gong, who had his own vegetable plot, to determine the cause. Gong ignored him the first time he went. Moses was smart enough to take a bag of tobacco along on his second visit, and Gong told him the insects came from the fertilizers he had applied earlier. Moses had thought that the more fertilizer the better, unaware that too much chicken droppings would breed insects. The best remedy to root out the problem was to bury tobacco in the ground, where it would ferment and kill the eggs. So Moses put aside other work in the garden and bought enough tobacco to get rid of the eggs, while catching the live insects one at a time. He lit a lantern at night to continue the work left over from the day. Come mealtime, he brought food back from the kitchen and ate as he worked, not leaving the plot for five days. On this day, he had just finished lunch and was catching insects by flipping over the eggplant leaves, which attracted more pests than the other plants. He had also seeded more eggplants, and they took up more than 40 percent of the plot, while everything else occupied from 20 to 30 percent. He worked until sunset, when he heard someone call out from behind.

"I need to talk to you, Moses."

He turned around and saw a head sticking above the wall. A closer look told him it was Old Cui, the animal broker. Moses went back to catching insects.

"I'm busy."

"You'll regret it if you don't stop to hear me out."

"I'm already full of regret. I shouldn't have put down so much chicken droppings. And I shouldn't have planted so many eggplants."

"This is more important than chicken droppings and eggplants combined. I found you a wife."

Moses recalled that Cui had a side job as a matchmaker. Finding a wife was good news. But he had never had dealings with the broker; worse yet, Cui had often taunted him when he was delivering water. Moses thought Cui must be toying with him as he passed by. There could have been a gang of idlers on the other side of the wall waiting to have a good laugh at Moses's expense.

"I hear your mother has died," Moses replied. "So save the wife for your father."

Moses bent down for more insects and refused to look up, no matter how much Cui tried to get his attention. Finally, Cui lost his temper.

"Fuck you. I find you a wife, but you act like you're something special. When I find matches for the rich, I at least get a banquet, even if it doesn't work out in the end. Now see what I get instead? A cold ass for my warm face." He was getting carried away. "You want to be snooty? Fine, I'll go tell her it's off. I won't die without this match, but you'll be a bachelor forever."

Cui went on and on until his voice grew faint. Moses turned back again, but Cui was nowhere in sight. He ran over to the wall. Still cursing, Cui was walking by the Jin River, quite a distance away. If he hadn't cursed Moses or walked off, Moses would have thought that Cui was having fun at his expense. But now, with Cui storming off like that, Moses realized that the man could have been serious, so he climbed over the wall and stopped the broker when he caught up with him.

"Tell me what's on your mind, Uncle." He grabbed him.

"Let go. I'm busy."

Moses was further convinced by Cui's attitude that it was not a joke.

"You and I have to get a drink today, Uncle, no matter what."

"Let go. I really am busy." Cui tried to shrug out of Moses's grip, but only half-heartedly. They walked along, one shoving, the other tugging, until they reached the Jin River bridge, where there was a place called Grand Feast Diner, with a cook named Old Wei. Years before, Yang Baili and Niu Guoxing had used the cook as the subject of their breeze shooting, making up a story about

Old Wei, who loved a stroll at night. One evening, Wei ran into an old man with a white beard who whispered something to him that made him cry while cooking in the diner. He might have sobbed back then, but not anymore; now he served liquor and no longer worked in the kitchen. Wei knew both Cui and Moses and thought that the two, a donkey broker and a vegetable gardener, would just order a bowl of braised noodles. He was in for a surprise, however; Moses ordered a platter of chunky beef, a plate of goat intestine stewed in soy sauce, a rabbit head slow-cooked in sauce for each, plus two liang of hard liquor. Wei knew the two men had something serious to discuss. Cui and Yang tucked in when their food arrived. Moses, who was dining with Cui for the first time, realized that Cui was a true donkey broker, someone with an incredible appetite, likely developed during his extensive travels. The meat was gone in no time and the liquor bottle quickly went dry. Moses ordered two bowls of vegetable and pork stew, as well as three more liang of liquor. The stew came, steamy hot with cabbage, tofu, seaweed, and pork slices. Cui devoured his stew and downed some liquor before finally putting down his chopsticks to smoke.

"Who is she, Uncle?" Moses asked.

Cui told him it was Wu Xiangxiang, who had first talked to Old Sun, a professional matchmaker on East Street. She had taken a mutton leg to see Sun, who had agreed, but then changed his mind when he learned the background story and the reason behind her remarriage. Her long-standing enmity with the Jiang family, the house for the bun shop, and the two feisty Jiang brothers were all signs that this was more a powder keg than a marriage proposal. Sun knew that he would be helping her if he succeeded, but if not, it could turn explosive, hurting everyone involved, including himself. But he would offend her if he turned down the job and told her why, so he feigned a stomachache that prevented him from leaving the house. He then turned the matchmaking job and the mutton leg over to Cui, who brokered marriage proposals only when he wasn't buying and selling donkeys. He was good at the regular job but lousy with his side job, probably because he didn't do it often enough to hone his skill of persuasion to turn two out of ten matches into marriages. Rarely succeeding wasn't a problem; the problem with him was the tendency to create more complications. The match between Lin Jinlong and Qin Manqing the year before had been broached by none other than Old Cui; as we know, that ended with Manqing marrying Moses Yang's brother on account of a missing earlobe. Cui, with his substandard matchmaking talent, liked to think of himself as Sun's equal. Considering Cui someone with no sense of propriety, Sun gave Cui the difficult job so he would finally realize how hard it was to be a matchmaker.

Indeed, Cui was not experienced enough to see the danger lurking behind the match; he did a quick check on the couple and accepted the mutton leg before going to see Moses for what ought to be a simple job.

Moses knew Wu Xiangxiang, at least by sight. She was short, with small eyes and mouth, a button nose, and a red mole between her brows. Not a beauty, she had fair skin, white like newly steamed buns, which overshadowed the flaws and gave her a unique look. On a dark face a red mole looks like a mouse dropping, but against a fair complexion it is a small cherry. Moses knew she was a widow with a child and had seen her plenty of times when he bought steamed buns, but the idea of the two of them becoming a couple took him by surprise.

"That thought never occurred to me." He added, "What are my chances, Uncle?"

Cui's big appetite was for food only, not for liquor. When the effects of seven liang of alcohol overtook him, he tended to pour his heart out, which was a bit like Moses's own father, Old Yang the Tofu Peddler. Cui sprawled over the table and grabbed Yang's hands.

"I'll do it for you only, not for anyone else."

Those were clearly the words of a drunk. The two men had had little to do with each other, so no such friendship bound them, not to mention the fact that he had cursed Moses earlier. But Moses didn't care; he said, with his hands still in Cui's, "I'll come to your door to show you my gratitude if it works out, Uncle."

"What nonsense is that?" Cui banged the table, upset by Moses's reply. "Are you trying to make me look like I'm doing this just to get something from you?"

"That's not what I meant, Uncle. I tend the county vegetable garden, so what do I have to show my gratitude? I just meant I'd be eternally grateful, that's all."

Cui leaned back and waved his hands dismissively.

"I'm afraid the conditions might make this marriage hard to manage. There's a whole range of them. I was able to take care of most of them, all but one. It's something only you can decide."

"What is it?"

"There's nothing to talk about if it doesn't work out, of course, but if it does, you'll be marrying *into* her family."

Moses was speechless. A woman marries into most marriages, but not his. He opened his mouth to say something, but Cui gave him a searing look.

"And that's not it. There's something else if you want to be married to her."

"What is it?"

"You have to change your surname, since you're marrying into her family. You'd be a Wu, not a Yang anymore."

Another shock for Moses. Every man gets to keep his own name when he marries, but not him; he would have to take hers. Dumbfounded by the two conditions, he hesitated, unable to come up with an answer, which angered Cui. As a matchmaker, Cui wanted more than just something to eat and drink or a present or two, which set him apart from Sun, the professional matchmaker. Besides the material reward, what he wanted most was the chance to make a match; for him it was fun, something new. He matched buyer with seller as a donkey broker, and was always on the lookout for an opportunity to match a man with a woman. Naturally, sometimes he didn't get to have his fun, like the matchmaking deal with the Li and Qin families. He'd been caught in the middle and had taken lots of hostility, without much of a say. But with Moses Yang, Cui thought he could talk sense to the man, patronize him, even make up for the unpleasant experience elsewhere. On the other hand, he would have been disappointed if Moses had agreed right away; the hesitation gave him an excuse to patronize him some more.

"I thought you were someone who knew what was good for him, which was why I decided to help you out." Cui spat on the floor. "I didn't expect you to hem and haw before I even finished. Go take a piss and look at yourself in it. Do you think you're good enough to hem and haw? Your father makes and sells tofu for a living and you tend a vegetable garden. You have nothing to your name, no house, no land. Wu Xiangxiang can always find someone else if she doesn't marry you, but you'll probably die a bachelor if you pass up this opportunity. You may work at the county office, but you're not the magistrate. You grow vegetables! I'm angry not because you're hemming and hawing. I'm angry because you have no sense of who you are. Don't force yourself if you just want to find a wife but not marry into her family; you can keep your family name if you think it's worth so much. It's clear to me now. You're right to hesitate; it's my fault. I was blind to who you really are. I do this out of the goodness of my heart, and you make it look like I'm setting you up. What I don't understand is, what do I get by setting you up? And just what do you have that's worth setting you up for? We'll wait and see, if you don't believe me."

Cui had twisted the whole thing into something else, and, as he went on, he began to lose his temper for real. Irritated, he stood up, forcing Moses to put his hesitation aside and grab hold of Cui, who struggled out of Moses's grip while shouting at Old Wei behind the counter.

"Tell us if this makes sense to you, Old Wei."

Wei was a busybody. He kept working, but his ears were pricked the whole time. Cui's shout was all he needed to share his ideas.

"I heard it all. Cui is doing the right thing."

They all started talking at once, with Moses trying to pacify Cui before turning to Wei when he saw that Cui was white with anger.

"This has happened too fast," he said to Wei. "I need time to think."

Moses returned to the vegetable plot after leaving the diner and sat on the ground to consider the proposal. It wasn't just sudden; it was unusual. Take the idea of marrying into her family, for instance. It was the opposite of what other people did, and it didn't feel right having everything turned upside down. That was one thing. It would be a big deal for anyone, whichever way it was done, naturally, but in his case, there was more to it than that, as explained by Cui. He wouldn't have been lucky enough for this to happen to him if she weren't thinking about marrying a man into her family. If it were done the normal way, with a man bringing a woman into his family, Wu Xiangxiang would not have chosen him. But even if she had been willing to marry into his family, how would he accomplish that without a house or some land? He would have to take her back to Yang Village, and who could say if she would be willing to leave the city? And besides, he would object, since he did not want to see his father again; but even if he didn't mind seeing his father, the old man would not have a room for him to live in with his new wife. On the other hand, he could save himself a lot of trouble if he were to marry into her family.

Then he thought about the name change. Other men got to keep their names when they got married, but not him. He would have to change his name. But wait, hadn't his name been changed once already? He had changed it to Moses Yang and followed the Lord in order to get a job. He'd stopped being Yang Baishun with the name change, but he had since found a job and a new self over the years since the change. By now he was no longer the old Yang Baishun, and there was no need to get hung up on appearances. Being called Moses instead of Baishun was certainly different from actually giving up the family name, since that amounted to abandoning ancestors. But he had never felt that his ancestors had done him a lick of good since the day he was born; in fact, they had given him more trouble than he could handle, the worst of which was becoming a laughingstock over changing that trouble-causing family name. Besides, Wu Xiangxiang was a widow, like a used chamber pot, and he could not afford to buy a new one. She was a widow with a child, so he would have to raise someone else's offspring after the wedding. He wasn't sure he could do that.

Most importantly, he would have jumped at the offer if this had happened four months earlier, when he was delivering water; he wouldn't have minded being married into her family, changing his family name, or marrying a widow with a child back then. He'd had no other option at the time, so the proposal would have looked like a gift from heaven, and he wouldn't have given it a second thought. But now he was working at the county office, a steady job, even though he only tended a vegetable garden. He believed that he would regret changing his name to marry a widow if the job were to be permanent, giving him the chance to make a name for himself. On the other hand, having offended the magistrate the month before, he felt a sword hanging over his head, though he still had a job. He would continue to work the plot if Old Shi's mood did not change, but he would be penniless, back on the street delivering water, if the magistrate was unhappy and fired him. However, there was a steamed bun shop waiting for him if he married Xiangxiang. In brief, it was fundamentally up to the magistrate, not Moses, if he were to accept the marriage proposal; but Moses had no idea what was on Shi's mind. He thought he'd been doing just fine, but now, with a marriage prospect, he had a lot to think about. Worst of all, there was no one he could talk to about his situation. Suddenly, he thought of Zhan, one of the few trustworthy people he knew. The priest was not good at his job, but he never harbored ill will toward anyone. So Moses left the vegetable garden and headed to the temple in Xiguan. Zhan, who had just returned from the countryside when Moses got there, was sitting on his bed smoking, looking much older than only a few months before. The priest did not seem surprised to see him.

"Amen. I knew you'd be back sooner or later."

"I'm back, but I'm not back like that, sir." Moses assumed that Zhan had misread the reason for his visit.

"I don't mean you're back to be with me again." Zhan knew why he'd come back. "I just knew you'd have something on your mind."

"Right." Yang nodded. "I'm back to ask your view on something. Let's forget about who I am and where I came from. I'm just not sure where I'm going this time."

Moses told the priest about the marriage proposal, about Wu Xiangxiang, and about her conditions, giving all the details and the twists and turns, including the magistrate. As mentioned earlier, Zhan had had an argument with Old Shi over the church property, so he reacted immediately.

"That Old Shi is not one of the Lord's flock." He then glanced at Moses. "Son, this will mark the first time I talk to you not in the name of God but as your elder. You can pin your hopes on others for minor matters, but with something this important, you should never, ever depend on others to determine your future," Zhan advised. "What do we have that we can depend on?" The priest was referring to the county magistrate, before making clear his concern over Moses' predicament. "We cannot complain about others' harsh demands if we cannot depend on ourselves. We have so little to offer, so we cannot say they did not warn us beforehand." The last phrase was obviously about the marriage and the name change. Zhan banged the bowl of his pipe on the side of the bed and sighed. "What is sorrow? It is that which goes against our wishes."

"So you don't want to give me any advice then, sir?"

"It's so complicated that I ought to stay out. As an elder, I would find it hard to advise other people, but with you, I'd suggest that you marry into her family."

"Why?"

"Because deep down you are willing."

"I wouldn't be here if I was."

"To the contrary. You wouldn't still be talking about it if you were not willing. Coming to me for advice is proof that you are."

Moses was about to say something when the priest raised a hand to stop him.

"You're right to want it, Moses. You are doing so much better now than when you left. You know who you are, and when you do this you'll know where you're going."

Moses Yang had barely heard a word the priest said in the past when he talked about the Lord, but on this day he understood everything, now that the subject was Moses Yang. Every word hit the mark, making Moses's eyes moist.

On the thirteenth day of the fifth lunar month, Moses Yang married into Wu Xiangxiang's family on West Street and changed his name to Moses Wu. The process, from proposing the marriage to the wedding, took three days, one less than it took his brother, Yang Baiye, to marry Qin Manqing. It was a major event in Moses Wu's life, but he did not ask his father's opinion, though not because the tofu peddler would object to him marrying into his wife's family. He didn't think his father would care; in fact, Old Yang might react just as he had with Baiye's marriage, a gift from heaven. Moses did not want to see Old Yang again because he had mentally slain his father before leaving home the second time. He did not say anything to his brothers either. Cui the donkey broker was impressed when he saw that Moses had not notified anyone in his family.

"I underestimated you. You may be young, but you've already renounced your family."

The wedding wasn't bad. As a diligent worker ready to help anyone in the county office, Moses Wu had established himself there. Many employees at the office would have attended the banquet if not for Moses's status as a vegetable gardener. Only two people from the office planned to show up, Old Gan the ground sweeper and Old Ai the cook. The magistrate was astounded that his gardener, the King of Hell, was marrying into a woman's family with a name change. Moses Wu had been irresolute about the marriage, but in the end he impressed Magistrate Shi as someone who was capable of bold, decisive actions, someone who marched to his own drummer.

Magistrate Shi had his personally calligraphed inscription delivered to the wedding: "Bold and Decisive." Moses Wu did not know what to say. The other employees, who had not planned to attend, changed their minds after learning of the calligraphy from the magistrate himself. Among the guests were Old Zhan the priest and Old Lu the bamboo workshop owner. Zhan's gift was a silver cross for best wishes, though probably it was meant for Moses to never forget the Lord, while Lu gave Moses several bamboo chairs. Moses was not surprised to see the priest, but was moved to see Lu, for whom he had worked for a while, though the relationship had not ended well. After the wedding, Wu Xiangxiang had the county chief's calligraphy framed and hung over the entrance to Wu's Steamed Buns; she kept the bamboo chairs for customers waiting for their buns. The silver cross, however, was sent to the silversmith, Old Gao, next door, to be melted down to make herself a pair of teardrop earrings.

12

Moses Wu got beaten up one day, six months after the wedding. Yanjin had a night watchman named Ni San, or Ni the Third, a swarthy, heavyset man whose head reached the top of a door, with lots of skin tags on a face framed by reddish hair. He never buttoned his shirt no matter the season, showing off a chiseled chest that had turned burnt red after decades, a different color from the rest of his body. Ni's grandfather had been the first in Yanjin to pass the imperial examination at the provincial level, had become a *juren*, and had served as magistrate in Luzhou, Shanxi. Ni's father had not taken after his own father, for he did not like to study and had no interest in an official position; rather, he enjoyed feasting, drinking, whoring, and gambling. By the time he died at the age of forty, he'd squandered everything his father had saved as a magistrate. People thought he should have lived longer, but he said, "One day in my life is ten years for other people. I've enjoyed every minute of it."

Ni San grew up in extreme poverty and worked as a night watchman. Starting at seven in the evening, he struck his clapper every two hours until the fifth watch, shortly after daybreak: one strike for the first watch, two for the second, and so on. Still under the influence of his family's former background, Ni had a couple of afflictions. First, he sought an easy life, and, though he was an impoverished watchman, he did not take a day job. Second, he never let his poverty get in the way of his love for the bottle, which meant he was usually drunk by nightfall. He stumbled around town sounding his clapper, passing street corners with his eyes shut; no wonder he often announced the wrong watch. Which is why, to this day, the people of Yanjin ignore the watchman's clapper. The watchman was also required to shout things like "It's fire season, so be careful with lamps and candles." But Ni skipped that entirely. Such an irresponsible watchman should have been replaced, especially since more than five decades had passed since Ni's grandfather was the prefectural magistrate. But none of the county magistrates could spare even a moment's attention for the night watchman's clapper; they were too busy with their personal hobbies—woodworking, talking, or watching opera. Ni got married when he was twenty-five, to a cross-eyed woman who gave him a baby a year, with no gaps between them. Ni frequently beat his wife when he was drunk, for no other reason than her productive belly.

"Damn. Are you a woman or a pig? I can't touch you without you having another baby."

She spent much of her time at her parents' house to avoid his fists and hands. Even with that tactic, she still gave him seven boys and two girls in ten years. Luckily, none of the children were cross-eyed. Seven boys and two girls sounded auspicious, but it was hard for a night watchman to support such a big family. He had always been law abiding, though quite lazy. As a young man, he'd never broken the law, despite the family destitution. Later, after the children arrived, each year was harder than the one before, and he began to care less and less about dignity. He still did not break any laws; he would just grab things from the market stalls when they didn't have anything to eat at home.

"Put it on my bill. I'll pay you later," he would say.

No one knew when that "later" would be. The food vendors knew Ni well enough to avoid trying to stop him, since all he took was a handful of scallions, a bit of rice, or a strip of pork. That emboldened him, though he never took more than he needed. All he wanted was to have enough to eat and drink that day; he would return the next day if he needed more. But he could be verbally abusive when drunk.

"Don't tell me an entire town can't afford to feed Ni San," he would complain as he snatched something off a stall.

The vendors did not mind the petty thefts, but they could have done without the verbal abuse. Yet no one said anything, not after he walked off with the "loot," avoiding trouble over a few outbursts. Moses Wu had gotten to know Ni San and had even delivered water to his house. Naturally, he did it for free, in a way, because Ni never paid him. Knowing that everyone was afraid of Ni, Moses left after filling Ni's water vat without a word. He steered clear of the man when he saw him on the street, which made Ni unhappy.

"Why are you avoiding me? Do you owe me rent or something?"

But Ni was an impartial arbiter whom people sought out when a dispute between families erupted, and the county magistrate either did not care enough to deal with it or was too incompetent to make sense of the suit. There was only one caveat: whoever talked to Ni first won the case. Ni would go immediately to the house of the accused after hearing the complaint. If he was drunk, he would start smashing things as soon as he walked in the door. If he was sober or if there were too many in the house for him to win a fight, he would produce a length of rope and put on a show of hanging himself at the person's door. A fight was easier to deal with than a man planning to kill himself. Though angry, they laughed at Ni San, who boasted a grandfather who had been a juren, but had sunk so low as to threaten suicide in order to resolve a dispute. Eventually, the accuser would drop the suit out of frustration and then talk with Ni, smoothing things over until everything was fine. After a while, when Ni showed up at someone's door, he would be greeted by a conciliatory face.

"We know, Old Ni. We'll talk it out as long as it's nothing serious."

Which was why the vendors allowed him to take what he wanted. Moses had minimal dealings with Ni, and yet one day Ni beat him up. Moses had done nothing to incur the man's wrath or require his arbitration; he simply had not invited Ni to his wedding banquet. Why had Ni waited six months? Moses left the county office six months after the wedding—that was why. Moses had asked Xiangxiang if she wanted him to leave his job and work at the bun shop with her, like a monk who recites sutras daily, and nothing else. But she'd had her eyes on Moses purely for the county office connection, which she hoped would bolster the shop's appeal. So she told him to keep tending vegetables for the same reason that she had hung Shi's calligraphy over the entrance. Moses was happy with her decision, but not because he preferred working the land to kneading dough; staying at the county office was his only chance to improve his role in life. Backed by the bun shop, he was able to take bolder steps in the garden. Moses helped Xiangxiang by getting up at the crack of dawn to prepare the dough and steam the buns. He headed to the vegetable plot after daybreak, while she took her load of buns to sell on a street corner. In a word, they had a good life together. He left the county office six months later, not because he had suddenly grown tired of the work, or because Xiangxiang had changed her mind, or even because he'd offended Shi again and was fired. Shi was the one to leave, after disaster struck, though not because he had failed as a magistrate, like his verbose predecessor, who had been removed by his superior on account of mistakes. Shi's problem was his superior and patron, Old Fei, who was fired and cost Shi his job in the

162

process. Fei lost his position as governor not because he did a bad job; in fact, it was trying too hard to be a good governor that got him fired.

By then, Governor Fei had been in office for ten years. Several changes had taken place within the Nationalist government over that decade, but Fei remained solidly installed in Henan, which earned him seniority. Unfortunately, he got careless owing to his seniority and offended the new prime minister, a man by the name of Huyan. Minister Huyan was nearly fifty, no longer a young man, but young for a PM. Fei, like Shi, was reserved and taciturn, the exact opposite of the new minister, who was more like Little Han, the chatterbox. Huyan was an animated talker, who gestured like brandishing a manure fork and peppered his speech with points one, two, and three, not stopping even after he had reached point ten. Hours would pass like that. He believed in laying everything out plainly, like poking at a wick to turn up a lamp; when people had clear guidance, they would know what to do and nothing would be amiss. He called that the correlation between knowing and doing.

Fei found it hard to get along with the new PM. One day there was a meeting at the PM's office, attended by three dozen governors from all over the country. Border affairs were the focus of that day's meeting, a topic that had little to do with Henan, an inland province situated in the Central Plain. Huyan started out with the border regions, but moved on to the inland areas, leaping from Heilongjiang to Hebei, from Hebei to Shanxi, from Shanxi to Henan, where he paused. He said a few good things about Henan before adding his criticism and then paused. That went on for two hours. As he was from the central government, he had never worked at the local level and, unfamiliar with regional affairs, got his facts wrong in every one of the eight points he brought up. His comments either were too vague to make any difference or were turned around due to a lack of intimate knowledge about the situation. He followed up on the eight points with his recommendations for improvements, all of which were incongruous with the issues. Old Fei nodded with his mouth shut, though he was unhappy with the eight points of criticism raised by the minister. Huyan walked from table to table to toast his governors during the post-meeting meal and resumed talk on the topic when he reached Fei's table, adding point nine to his criticism. He even patted Fei on the shoulder when he was done.

"Am I or aren't I right, Old Fei?"

Fei would have simply nodded and let it pass if they'd been at a meeting, but he felt he had been put on the spot when Huyan refused to drop the subject while they were eating and drinking. Having downed a couple of drinks, he could control himself no longer. A quiet man with a stubborn streak, he did not think much of the new PM, who was not his equal in seniority. He pushed the man's hand away and said, "Sure, you're right. But your solution would bring the people of Henan to the brink of starvation within three years." And he wasn't done. "A worse problem than that are the connections officials rely on for their positions and promotions, not their performance."

He was obviously referring to Huyan, who had managed to become PM with no experience as a provincial governor purely because he knew how to build connections. His face darkened as he pointed at Fei.

"So you mean I should hand my position to you then?"

"Why should it be me?" Fei shot back. "My last name isn't Huyan, and I don't shout 'hoo-yah'!"

With no prior enmity between them, it would have blown over easily if they had been arguing in private. But in front of all the other governors, Fei's words were too strong, ensuring the animosity of the PM, who, three days after the meeting, sent someone to Henan to look around. Nothing turned up from the open investigation, but secret inquiry showed that Fei had been involved in corruption that amounted to a million yuan. Once the damning report was published in the paper, Fei was arrested and thrown in jail; the downfall of a corrupt official earned applause from people all over the country. Huyan's motivation was not purely personal; as a new PM, he knew from Fei's retort that his own position was shaky, and he brought Fei down to show the other governors what he was capable of, should they dare to have any wrong ideas. It was a case of killing a chicken to warn the monkeys. Everyone knew, however, that Fei had been one of the more upright governors, since he had only amassed around a million yuan in ten years. His colleagues sighed over his fate; he was, after all, an old rooster, so how had he committed the mistake of a young chick? Since Fei had been the one who recommended Shi, Old Geng fired Shi the day after Fei was arrested. Shi had started a vegetable garden for self-cultivation to keep a low profile, but that turned out to be in vain. The actor Su Xiaobao came to see him off the day Shi packed up to go back to Fujian. Xiaobao took him by the hand and sobbed. Shi did not shed a tear.

"Everyone laughed at me for self-cultivation and keeping a low profile, but in fact I have gotten a lot out of it."

"I can't believe you're still making quips at a time like this."

"But what I'm saying is true," Shi said seriously. "Several thousand years have gone by, and these chicken-shit people are still playing tricks. We're doomed." He continued emotionally, "Too bad we have to stop hand talking."

"I'll go with you," Xiaobao said, still holding Shi's hand.

"We could talk with our hands because I was the magistrate. Now that I'm no longer in that position, it would be pointless for you to come with me." He added, "Hand talking involves more than just the hands."

Shortly after Shi's departure, Geng appointed Old Dou, a distant cousin on his grandmother's side of the family. Fei had picked someone he knew to replace Little Han, so Geng felt justified in selecting one of his own. A former army man, Dou had once been a deputy regiment commander and had retired after a battlefield bullet ruined one of his legs. He had a bad temper and a foul mouth, with a signature phrase, "Don't fuck with me, I'm a goddamn soldier."

The soldier naturally was not interested in self-cultivation or a vegetable garden, since his natural inclination was military activity—target shooting. The first thing he did after taking office was to raze the garden and turn it into a shooting range, filling Yanjin with gunfire from dawn to dusk and giving newcomers the impression that war had broken out. Public safety in Yanjin actually improved thanks to the magistrate's hobby, as criminals from out of town no longer dared set foot in their town. The newly safer Yanjin, however, meant nothing to Moses Wu, except for the loss of his job once the garden was turned into a shooting range. Dou walked all over the plot in his boots, turning the vegetables Moses had planted in the spring into mush. Moses had not lost his job after offending the former magistrate, Old Shi, but he was fired the first time he met the new one.

"Growing fucking vegetables? Get out of here."

So Moses Wu did, returning to Wu's Steamed Buns to prepare dough. He was sad over the loss of the job, but he congratulated himself for marrying into the bun shop, which meant he did not have to return to the streets to carry water. Indecisive about the marriage proposal, he had sought advice from the priest, who was able to see through his situation and encouraged him to accept it. Zhan had been a failure at mission work, but had given Moses good advice at a critical moment, for which the young man was grateful. What Zhan did not get right was his advice for Moses to not pin his hopes on Shi, who was unreliable; it turned out that Shi's replacement was the unreliable one.

Moses was not disturbed about going home to work the dough, but his wife, Wu Xiangxiang, felt she had been duped. Her plan was not just to find a man, but also to find a backer. Now the backer strategy had failed, and Moses Wu was just Moses Wu, a man with no house or land, no money, no one to turn to. She regretted her calculation, oblivious that she was not duped by Moses, by Old Shi, or by Old Fei. She was, in the end, a victim of the prime minister. But it really did not matter who had tricked her. With Moses Wu being plain old

Moses Wu, the buns sold at Wu's Steamed Buns were just that: buns. Xiang-xiang was so outraged by the turn of events that she snatched Shi's calligraphy off the entrance and whacked it to pieces; keeping it there would have made her a laughingstock, now that the calligrapher had fallen. She had thought that losing the backer meant a loss in the sale of buns, never anticipating that Ni San would come to beat up Moses Wu the day after he left the county office and returned to prepare bun dough. It was a humiliation to be fired from the county office, so he wanted to lie low at home for a few days before showing his face in public. But that was not how his wife looked at it. In her view, he needed to make up for the loss of his job by taking her place at the market, in addition to preparing the dough and steaming the buns, so she could take care of other matters at home. Moses did not want to run into people he had known, such as Old Zhao the cobbler, Old Feng the smoked rabbit peddler, or Old Yu the coffin shop owner. Convinced that they would want to know all the details about his loss of employment, he could not offer a decent explanation. But he couldn't tell his wife that he was too embarrassed to go out, so he said he'd never sold buns before and that his experience in selling tofu could not be of any help. Different trades were like different worlds, so he would like to wait a couple of days.

"I don't know how to cry out for customers." He scratched his head.

Wu Xiangxiang blew her top. "You had little to do when you were working at the county office. Now you have no job and you mean for *me*, a woman, to be out there so *you*, could sit around as the master of the house, is that what you're saying?"

She was not being completely unreasonable. So he got up before dawn the next morning to prepare the dough and put the buns in the steamers. He then loaded the cart and left as soon as it was light out. Only days before, he would have been on his way to the county office at that time, the thought of which made him nostalgic for Old Shi and the vegetable garden. As he was walking along, pushing the cart, Ni San bounded out of a side street and yelled to him.

"Hey you, stop right there."

Moses stopped. Ni came up and looked at him out of the corner of his eye.

"Why didn't you invite me to your wedding banquet? Wasn't I good enough to be your guest?"

Moses felt like laughing but didn't dare. The wedding had been six months before. Why was the watchman complaining about it now? Besides, even if the wedding had been held just the day before, they were neither friends nor family, so why must Moses invite him? He hadn't even told his own family, so why should a watchman, an outsider, learn about it? It had nothing to do with whether he thought the man was good enough or not. Moses thought that Ni was drunk, so he decided to ignore the watchman and turned to walk off. To his astonishment, Ni ran up, kicked over the cart, and sent the buns rolling across the ground. He followed that up with a kick at Moses before pummeling him in the face with fists the size of vinegar jars.

"Who's your backer? How dare you look down upon Master Ni? I've been stewing in anger for half a year. Today I'm going to show you that Master Ma the deity has three eyes, and is no one to mess with."

In an instant, Moses was a mass of contusions and welts, bleeding from his nose and his mouth, like a sauce shop. They quickly attracted a crowd of market-going gawkers, none of whom dared intervene when they saw Ni San, who straightened up once he was exhausted from punching; he pointed a finger at Moses.

"Get your ass back to your Yang Village. You don't belong here. If you don't leave, I'll beat you every time I see you."

With that threat, he stumbled off. Moses got the sense that Ni beat him up not because of the wedding banquet but because of something else. On that same afternoon, Ni San also went to beat up Old Cui the donkey broker, who had done the matchmaking, so viciously he even broke one of Cui's arms. The beatings taught both men something they had not known before—this was a marriage that should not have taken place. It was more complicated than just the union of two people. When they gave the matter serious thought, they suspected that the Jiang family must have put Ni up to it. Jiang Long and Jiang Gou had obviously given Ni enough money for the man to avenge them. No one had dared touch Moses when he was a county employee, so they'd waited until this day, after Moses was fired. Cui, who had suffered by association, directed his anger not at Ni but at Old Sun the professional matchmaker. Sun had known the deal was detrimental to his health, so he'd gotten someone else to take over; Cui did not think that the beating was uncalled for, but he felt abused by Sun's deception. So Cui let Ni off the hook and, instead, with his injured arm in a sling, went to East Street to see Old Sun that night. The news traveled fast, and Sun had heard about the beatings. He feigned sickness when he saw Cui through the door curtain. He moaned and kept his eyes shut when Cui walked up to his bed.

"I'm getting old. I get sick all the time," Sun said weakly. "This time it's much worse than before. I haven't been able to eat or drink a thing for five days."

Cui flipped the blanket off. "You damned liar. You think I'm going to let you off the hook, don't you? You old fool."

Seeing that the man meant business, Sun sat up and, giving up the pretense, apologized repeatedly.

"It's my fault, I know, Old Brother." He paused. "It's been six months, and I thought it was over and done with. I didn't expect them to rake up the past. It was meant to be a prank, and I'm sorry you suffered because of it." He added, "Let's take care of that arm of yours first. Whatever it costs, I'll pay."

He saw no change in Cui's angry face. "You can hit me if you're still upset."

Cui almost laughed, despite his anger. He vowed to never again deal with human matters, only donkeys for him from then on, which was exactly what Sun expected.

Moses Wu was dazed; Ni's powerful punches had caught him by surprise, each one of them in the face. He sat up, wiped his face, and saw his hand covered in blood. When he picked up the dirt-covered buns to put them back into the basket, they turned red; even the basket was stained. Being beaten up in public was more humiliating than being driven from the county office. He could not bring himself to sell the buns, even if they weren't smeared with blood and covered in dirt. He could not go home with that blood-streaked face either, so he pushed the cart over to the former warehouse to get some water to clean the buns. After wiping down the basket, he pushed the cart back to the shop. It was so humiliating to be beaten up on the street that he planned to hide the incident from his wife until he had recovered enough to deal with the matter. He just needed an excuse to explain to Xiangxiang why he had turned around and come back so quickly. He decided on a stomachache. He walked in the door, hand on his belly, only to discover, to his surprise, that she knew all about it. She was sitting, awash in tears, in one of Lu's bamboo chairs. Knowing he could not hide it from her, he took his hand off his belly and adopted a light-hearted tone:

"It's nothing. I said the wrong thing and we got into a fight."

"Don't pretend you hit back."

"I'm fine. No serious injury." Moses knew he had to own up.

"I married you not only because you worked at the county office," she said, ignoring his reference to injury.

"What else then?"

"I heard you were a pig butcher and thought you might be sort of rugged. I didn't expect you to be beaten up on the first day you went out to sell buns."

He had forgotten about his former profession, but now he felt the blood rushing to his head with that reminder.

"I was never this humiliated when I was alone. We might as well close the shop if you're going to get beaten every day," said Xiangxiang.

"You probably think they're targeting you alone, don't you?" She went on, "Actually, what they have in mind is to chase us out of town. I'll go pack up if you have a place for me and my kid, but if you don't, and you plan to stay with us, they won't let that happen."

She wasn't finished yet. "When the kid's father was alive, not even a fly, let alone a man, dared touch me. We're helpless now that he's dead.

"My poor man." She banged her hands on the floor and wailed. "Why did you have to die so young?"

She seemed to be crying over her dead husband, but Moses was the target; her complaints about him sounded like a taunt. Either way, he had to agree with her. He could let it go if Ni San had beaten him up just because he felt like it, but he had no place to go if they meant to run the family out of town. Alone, he could go anywhere and fill his stomach with whatever job he could find. Now, with a wife and a child, he could only return to Yang Village, and he wasn't sure she would want to go. If she didn't mind going, he would. He had effectively cut all ties with his father when he decided not to tell him about his marriage six months earlier. He'd had a tough life over the years, stumbling from job to job, from butchering pigs to carrying water at the dye shop to being Zhan's apprentice to splitting bamboo to delivering water on the streets to tending vegetables at the county office to being married into Wu's Steamed Buns. A long, treacherous road had finally led to a quiet, peaceful life, and now people wanted to get rid of him. He felt cornered by a lifetime of setbacks and by Ni San, an unrelated third party.

Xiangxiang was crying louder now, and the louder her wail, the higher the flames of anger in his heart, until he spun around and stormed into the kitchen. He came out with a knife left behind by Jiang Hu.

"What are you going to do with that?" Xiangxiang stopped crying at the sight of the weapon.

"I'm going to kill Ni San."

She spat on the floor and said, "I knew that's what you'd come up with. Ni San beat you up, but do you know who was behind it?"

It all became clear to Moses now. He walked out with the knife, and, like Old Cui, chose not to go see Ni San. Instead, he raced toward Jiang's Cotton Shop on South Street to see Jiang Long and Jiang Gou. By the time he reached the intersection, the fires of anger had died down, replaced by a sense of trepidation. The brothers were both bigger than he was, though not as beefy as Ni San. Moses thought he might be able to handle Ni, but not the two brothers together. Besides, he had once been a pig butcher, but had never killed a person. Several years before, he had thought of killing Old Ma the carter, a plan he'd abandoned upon reaching Ma Village. All he'd done was mentally murder all those who deserved to die; he doubted he would have the guts to really kill someone. So why did he take a knife if he lacked the nerve for murder? It occurred to him that his wife was no ordinary woman. If something similar happened in another family, he was sure the wife would try to hold the husband back to prevent further complications, while his wife had talked him into murder right after he had been beaten up. But he couldn't possibly turn around and go home after he'd walked out the door with a knife. If he did, he would not be able to face anyone, even if he didn't mind her laughing at him. It was nearly noon, and the market was packed with shoppers. The knife in Moses's hand told anyone who knew about his marriage that the powder keg was about to blow. They put aside what they were doing and followed him for some entertainment. Those who hadn't known needed only to ask around to get the full story, and they too fell in behind the gawkers. Moses could have turned back if no one had known, but he had no way out now, trailed by a contingent of onlookers. Forcing himself to keep going, he finally reached the Jiangs' shop, where a stoneroller was half-buried in the ground ten or fifteen feet outside the door. Moses took a step back and placed his foot on the stone as he mustered the courage to shout, "Come out here, you inside the house."

The two Jiang brothers had indeed been the ones who had gotten Ni San to beat up Moses and Cui. Not only were they incensed that Wu Xiangxiang had married a man into her family and taken the bun shop from them, but they were also outraged that from start to finish it had taken her only three days, which had left the Jiang family with no chance to react. The rice was cooked. They could not do anything at the time, because the county magistrate had handpicked Moses to work his vegetable garden. After Shi was removed and Moses fired, they gave Ni five yuan to beat up Moses and Cui, who had been the matchmaker but had nothing to do with the shop. Beating up Moses was not just to vent their anger; it was in fact an overture to an opera, to be followed by the main acts. They were going to follow it up with more beatings until they drove Moses out of town, which would also drive out Xiangxiang and her daughter. Before her remarriage, they'd had no excuse to get rid of her; Moses's appearance gave them the perfect one. They could get the shop back while venting anger that had been stewing inside for six months. The brothers had seen Moses deliver water, doing whatever he was asked to do, the perfect example of a coward. Later, when he tended vegetables at the county office, he had also been sent on errands, running around all day like a spinning top. They surmised that he was clearly a man with no backbone who would flee after the beating; if he didn't run at first, they would continue until he skipped town. It surprised them that Moses had actually decided to do something about the first beating and had come looking for them with a knife.

The Jiang brothers would have gone to fight it out with Moses had their father not stopped them in time. When he saw the knife in Moses's hand, the old man knew from experience that someone could die, and the problem would go beyond the bun shop if that happened, no matter who was killed. No one came out after Moses shouted. But a wolfhound as big as a calf roared out the door and came at Moses. It was Old Jiang's idea to send a dog to scare him off and bring an end to that day's encounter, so they could figure out what to do next. No one could have anticipated the opposite result. Moses would not have known what to do if the two Jiang brothers had shown up, but he perked up when the dog stormed out. Back when he had apprenticed with Zeng the butcher, Moses had practiced on dogs before trying his hand on pigs. Murdering someone frightened him, but killing a dog was taking up his old trade. So he waited for the dog to get near before turning sideways to avoid the charge and grabbed one of its hind legs as it turned. The dog slumped to the ground the moment he raised the knife and brought it down, opening a gash from its neck down. Blood splashed all over him, while the multicolored guts spilled out onto the ground. The swift action earned a loud "Ah" from onlookers. Moses, blood splattered now, was so impressed by his own heroic action that he yelled out even louder, "The dog is dead; it's your turn now."

Moses would likely have lost if the brothers had come out to fight two to one. They would have shown their faces before the dog was killed, but not now; they were cowed after seeing that Moses meant business. He had killed a wolfhound with one sweep of his knife. Or more aptly, it was precisely because there were two of them that neither came out. Seeing the knife, their wives stopped their husbands from going, waiting for the other to move first; the blood-splattered man out there was clearly ready to risk his life, so why would they let their husbands go meet their deaths? In the end, Old Jiang, not the brothers, came out, dressed in a long robe and a skullcap, and stood by his door.

"Young nephew." He looked at Moses Wu. "You're mistaken. The one who beat you wasn't from the Jiang family."

Moses knew the Jiang family was frightened when he saw an old man come out and shift the blame.

"Old Uncle, we're both grown-ups," Moses said. "So let's drop the act and be honest with each other."

"Don't listen to gossip from vicious people. Let's not become enemies."

Moses was even more certain of the Jiang family's fear as the old man insisted on that line of talk. He wasn't going to die today, he knew, but he mustn't push them too far either.

"I'm being nice because of you, Old Uncle. My usual way would be to storm in with my knife; I wouldn't have waited for someone to come out. I might not be able to take your whole family down, but I'd kill as many as I ran into, like the dog over there. I didn't plan to go home alive when I came this morning. I'd even the score by killing one, and any more would be a bonus."

"We can't let it come to that, Young Nephew, no matter what has caused this." The old man was shaking from fear as he went on. "I know there's been a misunderstanding, but you're a sort of stepson to me now that you're married to my former daughter-in-law. So would you listen to an old man? Let's not let this go any further. You've shown me what you're made of, so go home, please."

Moses took a menacing step forward and raised his knife to smear the blood on his face.

"I need a promise from you before I'll go home."

"Of course. I won't let you go home empty-handed." Jiang fell into Moses's trap.

"So what do you say?"

"We'll forget everything in the past and the two families will have a friendly relationship from now on."

Moses spat on the ground to show his rejection, to which the old man reacted by slapping his thigh and saying, "And two gourds of cottonseed oil for you to fry some buns."

The cotton shop had an endless supply of the oil expelled from cottonseeds after the cotton was picked. Moses knew it was time to back down before more complications arose.

"I don't want the two families to have a friendly relationship, Old Uncle."

"Then what do you want?"

"The two families will never have anything more to do with each other."

"You're right." The old man slapped his thigh again after thinking over Moses's suggestion. "It's come to this. Having a peaceful relationship means no relationship at all."

Carrying the two gourds of oil, Moses walked back to West Street, covered in blood from head to toe. By then there was a huge crowd of gawkers, many more than during the New Year's festival. "Moses Wu Wreaks Havoc in Yanjin" became a popular story, and people were talking about it decades later. In fact, fear caught up with him as he was on his way home—cold sweat dotted his back and his legs nearly buckled. He considered himself lucky to have gotten away with his life. Wu Xiangxiang threw her arms around him and gave him a big kiss when she saw him return home in victory.

"My dear!"

Moses stood still, still covered in dog's blood. Feeling as if he would fall apart any moment, he was also hit by the sudden realization that the woman kissing and calling him "Dear" was anything but dear to him.

The bun shop had made seven pots of buns every day when Jiang Hu was alive. They would let three large basins of dough rise the night before and get up at cockcrow to knead the dough to form enough buns to fill three steamers, each of which would have seven layers of steamers containing eighteen buns. When they were ready, they loaded the 378 buns into two large baskets. It would barely be light out when the baskets were put into the handcart to take to sell. If all the buns were sold in the morning, they would steam another four steamers of buns to have 504 more that would last into the night. When it turned dark, a castor oil lamp was lit and the sales continued until Ni San came out to strike the first watch. It would be time to start mixing the dough to let the flour rise again. After Jiang Hu's death, Wu Xiangxiang steamed only four steamers of buns, two in the morning and two in the afternoon, with no night sales. Once she'd married Moses into her family, she changed back to seven steamers, with exactly the same practice and the same numbers of buns to be sold in the morning and into the night. Ni San was stunned to learn of the "havoc" wrought by Moses, someone who hadn't said much and avoided Ni every time they ran into each other. Ni had not expected him to have the balls to kill someone. Unsure of what Moses was all about, Ni softened his attitude toward him, not in word but in deed. He still cast sideway glances at Moses and sometimes even spat on the ground to mean "I know you're a killer, but do you dare kill me?"

As we have seen, Ni grabbed whatever his family needed to make a meal from the vendors in the market: scallions, rice, or pork. He had also taken buns from Jiang Hu in the past. But once Moses took over, Ni never took another one, a show of grudging respect. On his part, Moses had simply made an empty show of strength and killed a dog under unusual circumstances, so he did not use the incident as a pretext to pick a fight with Ni. They maintained a safe distance.

Time flew, and after six months Moses realized he did not like the steamed bun trade. He didn't mind the hard work of mixing the dough to let it rise, kneading it, and steaming the buns; on the contrary, he didn't like the easy work of selling buns, not because he didn't like buns or didn't like selling them, but because he hated having to talk to people all the time. A couple of years earlier, when he was working with the butcher and was still called Yang Baishun, he'd had to go solo on trips before New Year's when his mentor was sidelined by rheumatism in his legs. Moses had dreaded the prospect of having to deal with people. The fear was different his time, though. With butchering, he usually had only one customer, which meant he would visit at most one family or two each day, so it hadn't been too hard to bear. Besides, the focus was killing a pig, and talking to people was secondary. He had prepared enough set phrases to use with the owners, since it didn't matter whose pig he was slaughtering.

But there were too many buyers with too much to say when he sold buns, each with a unique look, temperament, and way of talking. As a vendor, he could not be his usual self when he talked to customers; he could say what was on his mind elsewhere, but at the market he must keep up with the customers and change his tune with each one. When the day was over, he was exhausted, but from talking, not from selling buns. By the time Ni San came out with his clappers, Moses usually felt he was on the verge of collapse. He realized he would rather be delivering water, when he thought about it, because all he needed was physical strength, not words. In fact, customers usually didn't care for a talkative water delivery-man. Sometimes acquaintances, such as Zhan the priest, Lu the bamboo shop owner, and Little Zhao, the priest's scallion-peddling assistant, would walk by his stand; Moses enjoyed chatting with them and felt good about it.

After giving his situation more thought, he sensed that life was exhausting not simply because of the work; what was more tiring than selling buns was the fact that he and Wu Xiangxiang did not get along, though not because she had instigated him into attempted murder. It was worse than having to kill someone when he had little to say to her in daily life. Killing someone takes only a moment, while life with her would go on for a long time. Moses had difficulty handling small talk with customers, but she didn't. They were worlds apart in how they handled things.

Wu Xiangxiang did not treat Moses gently when she saw how tired he was from talking to customers. He had been terrific at turning the King of Hell into a handsome scholar, but with her he became a mute. She didn't mind it much when he was quiet with others, but he had nothing to say to her at home when they worked together, whether mixing and kneading the dough or steaming the buns. He could not bring himself to say anything, even when they were in bed doing what husband and wife did at night. She was upset, but could not do or say anything when he climbed on top of her wordlessly and got to work; to her it was worse than not doing it at all.

Wu Xiangxiang's father, a tanner, was also a quiet man, while her mother was quick-tongued; he barely uttered ten words a day, and she had to say a thousand. Verbosity did not always mean she had the upper hand, because reason and logic were what won an argument. With Xiangxiang's father, however, he had little to say and even less persuasive power to make up for it. Her mother, on the other hand, could say enough to drown out whatever he managed to say, whether she was making sense or not. Everyone in Wu Village knew that Xiangxiang's mother wore the pants in their family and treated her father as if he wasn't there. In this regard, she took after her mother, but with differences. Xiangxiang's mother was illiterate, so she could talk forever, but she was mainly a quarreling nag. Xiangxiang had had three years of schooling, where she had learned the skill of persuasion that enabled her to zero in on a core issue and shoot holes in people's arguments. Her first husband, Jiang Hu, had also been a man of few words, but she was not able to gain mastery over him, for he'd had a hot temper and would beat her at the slightest provocation. Moses, who had subdued the Jiang brothers, was actually a cowardly man in every respect, and she realized that the incident had been his one and only display of manliness. Emboldened by her new realization, she found no need to fear him, and subdued him whenever she could. Gradually she became the head of the household, taking charge of nearly everything, like her mother before her. She acted like the man of the house, while Moses was the wife, which was actually an apt illustration of their marriage, as Moses had married into her family.

Sometimes Moses went out to sell buns alone, but at other times Xiangxiang went with him, depending on what needed to be done at home. The customers would only talk to her if they were both present; they would ignore him as if he wasn't there. Some of the loafers would flirt and verbally take advantage of her, but she dealt with them handily. Once, one of the loafers picked up a bun and hefted it in his hand.

"This one isn't big enough."

She knew what he was insinuating, so she retorted, "I could steam one as big as a mountain, but could you handle it?"

"It's not fair enough, not as white as that one," he said with his eyes on her breasts.

Xiangxiang was famed for her fair, white skin.

"That bun is fair and white. You'll have to call me Mother if you eat it."

Xiangxiang and Moses also sold New Year's stuffed buns. With that in mind, a loafer once said, "Ai-ya! This one isn't stuffed."

Or, "There's no meat in the stuffing."

She was not deaf to his innuendo, so she spat on the ground and said, "I could put a whole cow in there and it would ram the life out of you."

The loafers tried but never got the upper hand with her, to everyone else's great delight. This was mere banter, not something to be serious about, so Moses laughed along with them. Knowing he could not have thought of the retorts, he was impressed by how fast Xiangxiang's mind worked. Or maybe her glibness had been suppressed when she was married to Jiang Hu and only now got a chance for full play, to be herself again, with Moses. The buns went quickly with her around, as if the customers came not for the buns but to hear her abuse people verbally. Without her around, Moses had trouble selling the buns, and sometimes there were still some left by the time Ni San came out. She chastised him when she saw him come home with buns remaining in the basket, a minor scold when she was in good mood and a major reproach if she wasn't. She could go on and on until he felt his head was about to explode. Did he have to relearn how to talk and get things done after twenty years? How would he do that? Moses evaluated his situation. He was always being chided by someone, always being put down by people; there was probably no end to that. Then he had a second thought. After Old Shi left and the new magistrate fired him, he was doing better than the old days, when he had been delivering water; he had a home, he had enough to eat, and he dressed better. What else could he do and where could he go, if he didn't want to be under Xiangxiang's thumb? He had to rely on her for his livelihood, so he took it silently when she berated him; it wasn't just because he wasn't eloquent. Once he figured that out, he put it out of his mind. He would fight back if he had a response to Xiangxiang's complaints; if not, he would keep quiet. Most of the time, of course, he couldn't think of a good rejoinder.

Wu Xiangxiang's daughter, Qiaoling, was five. She had been a handful all her life. Someone had had to watch her at play even before she was two. If not kept under close supervision, she would either break a lamp shade or set fire to the kindling in the stove and nearly burn the house down. She came down with a major illness when she was three. It started out as a minor ailment, diarrhea, after eating moon cakes during the Mid-Autumn Festival. Neither Wu Xiangxiang nor Jiang Hu thought much about it and simply gave her some pills from a traveling medicine man. The diarrhea stopped, but she ran a fever. Her father had to look for a legitimate pharmacy. Hu took his daughter to see Old

Miu, who owned an herbal clinic on North Street called World-Saving Hall; he prescribed some herbal medicine, but the fever continued and her neck stiffened. Hu then took her by wagon to Three-Ingredient Hall in Xinxiang. Some medicine from the doctor there managed to bring her temperature down and returned her head to the right place, but the diarrhea made a comeback. Fortunately, it was worms; small worms the size of sesame seeds, a dozen or so in each batch of feces. The worms, though small, wrought havoc in the stomach. Qiaoling constantly cried out with her hands on her belly; in a month, she was reduced to skin and bones. So this time her father hired another wagon to take her to Gourd-Hanging Hall in Kaifeng, where he got some medicine from a doctor there. Finally, the worms were gone, only to be replaced by a facial rash. That required another wagon ride, this time to Restoring-Health Hall in Ji County. Three visits and over twenty doses later, the rash began to fade and she regained her weight, slowly looking more like a human girl. In six months, father and daughter had traveled to just about every herbal clinic in the neighboring area of a hundred li. The diarrhea was a minor illness, an ant, but it had gone around and around until it had grown bigger and more serious, now an elephant. Her father had wanted to save trouble and had ended up spending ten times as much time and money.

What upset her parents was the fact that Qiaoling recovered from her illness but lost her pluck. She had been a terror of a girl, and now she was timorous, though not in the normal sense. A timid child was usually afraid of everything, but not Qiaoling, who was only afraid of the outside world. She was scared when it got dark outside; she ran home when a commotion broke out on the street and other children ran out to see; she cried when a kid had hit her after a quarrel. Yet she was a totally different girl at home, continuing with her antics of playing with a lamp shade or fire in the kitchen and talking back to her mother. She defied her mother, going after a chicken when Xiangxiang told her to chase away a dog. Qiaoling was still afraid of the dark at home though and slept with her mother before Moses came. After the remarriage, she had to sleep alone, with every light in her room lit.

Xiangxiang could not bring herself to love the girl wholeheartedly, for Qiaoling was like a dog that only barks at home, its tail between its legs. Moses had little to do with the girl at first, but later, once they knew each other better, they realized they had one thing in common—neither liked the outside world. He had little to say to his wife but not to his stepdaughter; on her part, Qiaoling talked back to her mother but not to Moses. They had a lot to talk about, and there was no room for backtalk.

Every ten days, Moses traveled forty li to Bai Village to buy bleached flour from Old Bai's mill. He could have bought it from the mill in the county town, but it would have cost a little more, amounting to four extra yuan for two thousand *jin*. Four yuan was one day's profit from the buns. So he went there every ten days, a round-trip of eighty li, which took a whole day. Moses did not have to sell buns on that day, and Qiaoling usually asked to go along. Moses was a virtual mute with others but quite a talker with the girl.

"Did you have a dream last night, Qiaoling?" Moses might ask.

"I did."

"What did you dream about?"

"My bed was flooded."

"What did you do?"

"I rode on the back of a cow."

She called him Uncle, not Daddy, which had been Wu Xiangxiang's idea; it wasn't changed, because the girl had gotten used to it. It didn't matter to Moses what he was called; starting with Yang Baishun, he'd become Moses Yang and ended up as Moses Wu, so he didn't mind whether he was called Uncle or Daddy.

"We have to come back early today, Uncle," the girl would say the moment the donkey cart left town.

Moses knew that Qiaoling was afraid of the dark, and they would have to travel at night if they didn't get on the road early enough. He looked up at the sky before teasing her.

"The sun was way up there when we left. I'll have to load the flour at the Bai Village, and we need to stop on the way for something to eat. It'll be dark before we get home."

"You'll have to let me get under the blanket and close the opening if it gets dark."

Moses always made sure to take a blanket along. The girl would crawl under it when it was dark, and Moses would secure the opening with a hempen cord so she could then feel that the dark night was being kept away from her.

"I'll do that, but you have to stay awake to talk to me."

"I won't fall asleep. I'll talk to you."

In fact, she fell asleep under the blanket most of the time. She would stay awake for a while, but be asleep before she'd uttered ten sentences. He hadn't liked the fact that Xiangxiang had a child when they were first married, but now he was glad to have the girl around. The family of three went through thick and thin together, and life went on. What was unusual was that Xiangxiang had yet to get pregnant after they had been married for some time. She didn't care either way; she might give birth to a tiny Moses Wu, which was not a particularly exciting prospect. He didn't dare say anything, since she seemed unconcerned. Besides, it wasn't something he could have just because he wanted it.

Winter came on the heels of fall, and soon it was the end of the year again, time for everyone to get ready for New Year's, the busiest time for the steamed bun business. Xiangxiang and Moses added three more steamers, but they still ran out. On the twenty-seventh day of the last lunar month, Xiangxiang stayed home to check the accounts while Moses tended the cart. Customers swarmed around Moses, keeping him busy with his hands and his mouth until his forehead was bathed in sweat. Old Feng, who sold smoked rabbits on East Street, came up to him.

"The buns aren't white enough," Feng said.

Moses looked up to see Feng and smiled, knowing the harelip man was joking.

"Feeling the itch for it again?" Feng said.

Moses stared, not knowing what Feng was referring to.

"It's the end of the year, time for the New Year's Festival. You have to join us."

Moses laughed when he realized what Feng wanted, reminded that Feng was the head of the festival organization. Since the last festival, Moses had tended the vegetable garden at the county office before moving on to steam and sell buns, so he had put the festival out of his mind. If he hadn't played a role the year before, he wouldn't have been hired at the county office, nor would he have gotten married. Everything was different this year, precisely because he was married. He would agree to participate again without hesitation if he were still delivering water. The Lantern Festival would last seven days, and taking part in it meant putting the business aside; he knew he couldn't make the decision without checking with Xiangxiang first. They wouldn't be as busy then as they would be at the end of the lunar year, but still lots of people would come to visit relatives and watch temple celebrations, and they would all want to buy buns. When he got no answer from Moses, Feng knew the man had to check with his wife first.

"Let me know before the year is over. The King of Hell will still be yours if you want it. I'll get Old Deng to play the matchmaker." He added, before walking off, "Remember how the festival last year brought you such good luck. You may get even luckier this year."

Moses shook his head and smiled. There was no way the festival would bring him good luck every year. He'd had his share, and it wouldn't be easy to get more. On the other hand, Feng's invitation had awakened a dormant desire to join the festival, despite the fact that he had just about forgotten all about it. He wanted to take part, not just for the fun; the festival had something "unreal" about it, compared with his daily routine. "Unreal" was a local Yanjin expression, like "shooting the breeze." Moses would leave his daily life behind by taking part in the festival to play someone else. He had enjoyed watching Luo Changli at funerals years before, particularly because Luo's shouts invoked something unreal. Life felt too settled when he did nothing but knead dough and steam buns to sell, which was why he needed something unreal for a while.

He didn't finish until Ni San came out that night, though he did manage to sell every bun from ten steamers, because it was near the end of the year. Xiangxiang was happy to see him come home with an empty cart. After washing up, Moses seized the moment and brought up Feng's invitation when they were in bed. They did not always get along, but they had been working together since they were married, and he deserved a break after working so hard for more than six months. He was surprised to hear her say no without a moment's hesitation. She refused, but not because she didn't like the festival. In her mind, Moses hadn't been doing well selling buns and, instead of working doubly hard to make it up over New Year's, he was actually thinking about having some fun. Their business would be badly affected if he were absent for seven days, but that wasn't what bothered her most. He just seemed inattentive; she had wasted her breath over the months trying to teach him things. She was displeased not because of the business, but because of the wasted energy on her part. But she focused on the business when she said to him, "Who's going to take care of the business if you go have fun?"

"I've thought it through. We normally get up before dawn to knead the dough from the night before. I'll get up shortly after midnight to get everything done, and you'll have buns to sell later."

"So I'll be selling the buns while you're having fun. In that case, you don't have to steam the buns at night, and I won't have to sell them in the day. We can both take a break."

Knowing she wasn't serious, Moses tried a conciliatory measure.

"Okay, we can take turns. I'll sell buns every other day."

She hadn't been too upset at first, but she blew her top when he tried to bargain with her. She was angry not because he was bargaining to have fun, but because she had misread him; she hadn't expected him to come up with the idea of taking turns. He never took what she said to heart, so she had thought he must be the simple-minded type, and now, because of his plan for the festival, she realized that far from being simple-minded, he actually knew how to make plans. He just never said what he was thinking. If he had been making plans, it could only mean they didn't see eye to eye, and he had been intentionally ignoring her ideas. So she hadn't merely been wasting her breath; she had, in fact, been deceived. Her brows raised, she let loose her anger.

"You say you want to attend the festival, but what exactly do you have in mind? You haven't said much since we got married, and you loaf. What have you been thinking, anyway? You've never treated this place as your home, I suppose. You're simply living off the two of us, aren't you? Now that you've filled your stomach with food and drink, you want to have fun. I might have let you if you hadn't pestered me like that, but now that you have, I won't let you, no matter what. Don't think about going anywhere this year, and you're going to do my share of the work too. You get up at night to prepare the dough and steam the buns, and go out to sell them later in the day. I'm going to stay home and rest. You have so much energy you ought it use it working instead of playing."

As she went on, Moses saw she was getting further and further off topic; she was not talking about the festival anymore. He hadn't wanted to fight back, but he was reminded of a phrase, an effective phrase that did not come easily to him, and he had to say it.

"I'm your husband, not your worker. Even a worker gets a few days off around New Year's. I'm going to go, and I don't care what you say."

She was speechless; he had never been so adamant before. It didn't bother her, though, since she could find ten more comebacks for a single demanding outburst of his. But she didn't say anything; she took a blanket and went to sleep with her daughter. He was left to sleep alone for three days in a row. With her in the room, Qiaoling did not need to have lights on anymore, though. The quarrel meant a terrible New Year's for the couple, and Moses did not join Old Feng in the performance when the Lantern Festival came around. He went out every day to sell buns. Xiangxiang would have come along if he hadn't brought up the festival, but now, true to her word, she stayed home and Moses had to go out alone.

"It serves you right. You shouldn't have had different plans."

He sighed every time he went out. The celebration did not stop just because he couldn't make it; it went on for seven days, from the thirteenth to the twentieth, just as the year before. Little Du, the house painter, was the King of Hell this year, while Old Deng was assigned to play a matchmaker because of his poor performance as the King of Hell in previous years. Every day, they banged gongs and drums as they danced and paraded down the street. Through the sea of spectators, Moses stole a glance or two while dealing with customers; sometimes he ignored the show, keeping his head down as if the festival weren't happening. But the more he tried to ignore it, the more he thought about it. At night, Moses would, like Old Lu mentally going through an opera, run the whole performance over in his head. He was lying beside Xiangxiang, but in his head gongs and drums were banging away, as the performers, including Gonggong, Chiyou, Daji, Zhurong, Pigsy, Monkey King, King of Hell, and the Moon Lady, were raising their shoulders and picking up their legs, tilting their faces up and stomping their feet, frowning or smiling, even "pulling the face." He didn't miss a step as he mentally followed the troupe from East Street to West Street, from South Street to North Street. He eventually fell asleep during the performance and continued the parade in his dream. Once, he dreamed that the troupe was missing a performer and Feng was anxiously looking for Moses to save the day. In another dream, he was sitting in front of a mirror to paint his face, but he was doing a terrible job no matter how hard he tried, for he was painting the face of the Moon Lady, not the King of Hell. Dressed as the Moon Lady, he danced away from the troupe and eventually flew toward the moon as a woman, his long skirt fluttering in the wind. That scared him awake. A rooster was crowing outside the window, and he felt as if he'd just returned from another world. The rooster crowed before dawn, time to get up and steam the buns. When that was done, he loaded the cart and went out to hawk his wares. With his mind busy for three days like that, he was exhausted, even though he'd stayed away from the festival. On the morning of the seventeenth, he was tending the cart as usual when he dozed off. Some of the boys lighting firecrackers came up to take the buns from his baskets when they saw him fall asleep. Fortunately, he had sold more than half of the buns in each basket. He snapped out of his sleep and chased after the children. He grabbed one, and another ran off. Some boys spat on the buns when he caught them, and those buns were worthless even if he had them back. By the time he went home with an empty cart, Xiangxiang had already got wind of the children's prank. In the past, she'd seldom lost her temper when Moses was bullied, but now she was infuriated that even children dared take advantage of him. Besides, how could such a worthless man even dare think about performing in the festival? Her anger this time was different, though. In the past she was angry because she could complain or berate him and yet fail to make any difference in how he behaved. She wouldn't have minded so much if he simply remained that way, but no, he had to scheme against her. So he knew how to scheme against his wife, but was tormented by even a group of children. She slapped him without saying a word when he walked in the door.

"You lose face, but not just for yourself, you know," she added after the slap. "You've also lost face for my ancestors, all three generations of them."

She had never hit him before. He wanted to fight back, but he didn't, even though she was no match for him. All he did was curse: "Fuck you!" Then he turned and walked away, a gesture that meant he was cutting ties with her.

He left the bun shop and went straight to the warehouse. It had been more than a year since he'd been there, but it seemed like only the day before when he left. The months he'd spent with Wu Xiangxiang felt like a dream. The porters for the warehouse had all gone home for the New Year's celebration, for there was nothing to carry during this time of year. There was no one around, and Moses liked the quiet. The gongs and drums started up again out on the street, obviously getting near the warehouse. He was alone and unfettered, free to watch the performance, but he wasn't in the mood; he was ashamed to show his face. As thoughts went through his head, evening came, and it was time to sleep. He had been so eager to leave the shop to spite Xiangxiang that he had forgotten to take his bedding along, so he had to make a bed in a pile of straw. In the corner were several large, discarded hemp sacks, too tattered to use for the goods, but good enough for him to spread out and cover himself. He spent the next day at the warehouse before hunger got the better of him and he quietly went across the street to buy a few flatcakes on credit. A day and a night had passed. He figured Xiangxiang might regret her action after thinking about the incident; her anger might have subsided and she would come looking for him, or she might want to pick another fight. But to his chagrin, she did not apppear. She might be so angry that she wanted to sever ties with him, and his life at the bun shop would come to an end. He might have to resume his old profession, delivering water again, going hungry at times. Now he regretted leaving the shop out of momentary anger when she slapped him. The relationship would not have broken irrevocably, even if they'd fought, but after cutting ties with her, how was he going to reconnect? It was nighttime again, and still there was no sign of her. He sighed as he spread the sacks out to make a bed. He sat up when he heard a noise just as he was about to fall sleep; it was Qiaoling, still breathing hard while standing there. He thought she had come with her mother, who would be waiting outside after sending Qiaoling in to get him. He had been fearful when Xiangxiang hadn't come for him, but now he felt like sulking again.

"Tell your mother to come in. I want to talk to her."

"She didn't come with me."

"Who did you come with then?"

"No one."

"Did your mother send you?" He was apprehensive again.

"She told me to never talk to you again. I came on my own."

"Aren't you afraid of the dark? How did you come all the way out here to see me?"

"I miss you." The girl began to cry. "It's time to buy flour tomorrow."

Moses cried too. He got up, took the girl by the hand, and returned to the shop.

13

A jewelry shop called Qiwen Hall, run by a man named Gao, occupied the spot next to Wu's Steamed Buns. It was a called a "hall," but Gao was both owner and clerk. His grandfather had fled a famine in Shandong to Yanjin, where he gathered cow dung for a living; his father was a traveling peddler who pushed a wheelbarrow from village to village selling needles and thread. Gao apprenticed with a silversmith and rented the storefront after his mentor died. Now in his thirties, he forged silver bracelets, rings, earrings, hairpins, and tiny bells for children's winter caps or pendants for their tiger-head slippers. There was another silver shop in Yanjin, run by Old Cao, on South Street. Gao worked more slowly than Cao but produced finer jewelry, which was why his silver ornaments showed up on most Yanjin residents. Customers could buy new silver jewelry or trade in old jewelry at Gao's shop; they could also bring in silver ornaments for him to polish until dull, dark surfaces regained their shiny luster. For a more thorough cleaning, the pieces were soaked in a solution to make them look brand new. Gao could also melt a piece and remake it in a style that pleased a customer better, such as the Italian silver cross given by the priest to Moses and Xiangxiang as a wedding present. As we recall, she had it turned into a pair of teardrop earrings.

Gao was of average height, with a fair complexion and nice features, which, at first glance, made him look more like someone from south of the Yangtze River, not from up north in Shandong. He enjoyed talking to his customers as he worked, but he was quiet at other times. The topics were never silver jewelry, but gossip of what went on out in the streets, for the conversation lessened the tedium of his work. He talked slowly in a soft voice, pausing frequently, but was logical and articulate. No matter how twisted the events on the streets, he could recount them in detail, keeping everything neat and coherent. Each time he gave an elaborate narration of an event, he picked up his small sandalwood hammer and banged it on the silver piece he was working on as a way to conclude his story. He had three favorite phrases that he inserted at critical junctures of his narrative as a transition to pass on his judgment or to offer his own solution after rejecting others.

The first one was: "You can say that, but you can't do it that way."

The second: "You can do that, but you can't say it that way."

The last: "If you ask me, I'd say it was wrong from the start."

Ninety-five percent of the incidents were wrong from the start, after he verbally combed through them. What was the point of talking about them if they were wrong from the start? Nothing. He just needed to talk.

Every once in a while Moses Wu took a break from the busy work of kneading dough and steaming buns. He could sell buns on the street only on clement days, for no one came out to buy buns when it was raining, which gave him a day off. The rain was never a problem for Gao, the silversmith, who worked indoors. Moses did not feel like staying home when it rained, so he often went to Gao's shop for the simple pleasure of hearing the man talk. Not an articulate man himself, Moses abhorred people who were talkative or gossipy, all but Gao, whom everyone but Moses considered to be a chatterbox. Throughout his twenty-one years, Moses had considered most matters in the world too messy or complicated to explain clearly. To Gao, however, everything had its cause, and anything could be explained.

Timid Qiaoling stayed home most of the time. But she and Moses had another thing in common—delight in Gao, although for different reasons. Moses liked to hear Gao talk, whereas Qiaoling enjoyed watching him hammer away to produce all sorts of lovely things. So she often followed Moses to Gao's place, like his tail, and Gao frequently shared an oil fritter with the girl.

As time went by, Moses and Gao became friends, starting with talking about what took place on the street. Moses spent most days on the street selling buns, which gave him the opportunity to learn what had happened to this or that person. He would commit to memory anything he could not understand and wait for a rainy day to get Gao to offer his analysis. Later, once they knew each other better, Moses began opening his heart to the silversmith, who would listen attentively before resolving issues for him. But Gao would only pass judgment on what happened on the street; for instance, he would examine Moses Wu's spat with a customer and determine who was in the wrong, but he clammed up when it involved private matters in the Wu family. Moses's biggest problem was not out on the street, but at home, as he and Xiangxiang simply did not get along. She had goaded him into attempted murder after he was fired and beaten by Ni San. She had not let him take part in the festival, which had led to two months of awkward interactions, and she had slapped him when children had stolen buns from his basket and had not gone looking for him when he'd spent a night at the warehouse. Gao would listen to his tale of domestic strife but merely sigh along with Moses, who thought the silversmith was trying to stay clear of trouble. But no, Gao provided a convincing reason why he did not want to get involved, verbally or otherwise.

"Even the best judge cannot deal with domestic affairs."

Or, "An incident on the street is just an incident; an incident at home is something else altogether."

Or, "An incident on the street is a straightforward incident, but an incident at home is usually related to eight other incidents. You revealed only one, and what am I to say about the others?"

Gao made sense, when Moses thought about it. The silversmith might not say anything, but Moses heard what he needed to hear after telling Gao what was gnawing at him. He felt so much better when there was someone to listen to him.

Gao's wife was frail and spent the better part of the year in a sickbed. Her father was Old Bai of Bai Village. Sometimes Moses gave her a ride back to her parents' home when he went to buy flour. She had epilepsy, an ordinary illness that manifested itself differently in her. For others afflicted with the malady, it acted up capriciously; in her case, however, episodes were related to her mood. She was fine when things were going well, but she would foam at the mouth and convulse on the floor if someone upset her or said something to make her unhappy. Each episode weakened her further. Her illness meant that Gao had to treat her gently and take pains to let her have her way in most matters, so she would not experience an episode. His wife was infertile, so they had no children. A childless woman was considered blameworthy in traditional China, but Gao never blamed her, to keep from causing an episode.

The relationship between Gao and his wife made Moses even more keenly aware of the sound logic behind Gao's reluctance to discuss domestic problems. His acquiescent attitude toward his wife reminded Moses of his own situation, which was a minor consolation. He had learned something from his fight with Xiangxiang, which had ended with a slap and a night alone in the warehouse. What he learned, however, was about himself, not about her. He could never win an argument with her, so he might as well take a page out of Gao's book and simply stop arguing. Since he was incapable of convincing her that he was right, why try to win her over with his argument? In a word, Moses learned a great deal about life from Gao and put that into practice by letting Xiangxiang have her way. Life became easier for both of them. It isn't always easy to let others have their way, but it is better to suffer alone than to give others the opportunity to make your life insufferable. That was another reason why Moses was so fond of Gao.

But Xiangxiang was mercurial, often catching Moses off guard. When first married, he disliked the business that she loved so much. A year later, he realized that she had begun to dislike it as well. They both had problems with the trade but for very different reasons. Moses did not mind working the dough and steaming the buns, and he enjoyed the flour-buying trips. He did not like selling the buns because of the need to talk. In short, there was something about the business that he liked and something he didn't.

Xiangxiang thought the business was not big enough. What she wanted was to run a diner, a business that required a hundred times more capital than selling steamed buns. She continued the business simply to save up enough for her future diner. Husband and wife drifted even further apart, for one was ambitious while the other was barely coping. When they got up to work in the morning, Moses focused on the task at hand, whether it was kneading the dough or steaming the buns, too tired to say anything. Xiangxiang, on the other hand, would stop at some point and begin talking about her diner. It would not be a tiny spot selling fried flatcakes or giblets soup; she wanted one that could host banquets. It would have ten rooms, with the capacity for eight tables, and she would offer all sorts of dishes, with chicken, duck, fish, or pork, all cooked to order. Though smaller than Hongshancheng on East Street, it would be more a restaurant than a diner. As he listened to her, he realized that she preferred the dining business not just because she liked selling food, but because it brought in money faster. She also liked the scene of regular customers, owner and waiters calling out orders, the sounds of meat and vegetables cooking in steamers, sizzles accompanied by flames leaping up from the wok, greasy smoke surging upward, and more. It was more than just the business itself that enamored her; she was also infatuated with the grandeur of running a restaurant. Moses figured that it was only a matter of time before she opened one. When she was in high spirits, she would ask him, "What do you think about a diner?"

He disliked the idea even more than a bun shop. She would clearly be the boss and he would be a waiter who was forced to talk to customers. A diner would have far more customers, and talking to them would exhaust him. Yet he put aside his personal preference and said what she wanted to hear.

"I like it."

One look and she saw through him.

"You don't mean it, I know." She frowned. "It's all right to do something wrong, since I can just say you're stupid. But what are you thinking when you don't mean what you say?"

He changed his tune when he saw she was about to lose her temper. "I don't like it then."

"So what *do* you like?"

"I've liked Luo Changli since I was young." He decided to be honest with her. "He was a famous funeral crier."

Despite her displeasure, she had to laugh about his lifelong admiration of a funeral crier.

A sad thing happened a few days after the funeral crier was mentioned; Zhan the priest passed away. Though in his seventies, he had been healthy enough to preach in Yanjin's countryside; his death was partially caused by the run-down temple that had been his residence. He should have gone to the new county magistrate, Old Dou, to ask for his church back, now that Shi had left. After receiving nothing but objections from two magistrates, he knew he should not try again, or he might have to leave Yanjin altogether. As a former soldier, Dou loved target shooting, so he banished the opera singers the moment he assumed duty and turned the church building into a training facility for a local militia. Zhan knew the folly of a scholar trying to reason with a soldier; that and his disillusionment with county magistrates convinced him to stay put in the temple.

It was hot on the eighteenth day of the seventh lunar month. The drafty temple should have been cool, but there was no breeze that day, so, like every other Yanjin resident, Zhan decided to sleep on the roof. After baking in a hot sun all day, it felt only slighter cooler than inside. He tossed and turned all night, bathed in sweat no matter what he did. A breeze came just before dawn, cooling him off, and he quickly fell asleep. But the breeze did something else. He awoke in the morning with a stuffy nose and a cough. He had planned to travel seventy li to Jia Village that day, so, as arranged, Little Zhao pedaled the bicycle over after breakfast. From the persistent cough, Zhao could tell that the priest had caught a cold. He looked up to see an ominous sky, with clouds in the northwest.

"Old man, it's going to rain, and you have a bad cough." Zhao never called Zhan sir, because he was the priest's assistant, not an acolyte. "We should stay in today."

Zhan thought that was a good idea, and he would have stayed in if he had been going anywhere else. But he wanted to hear the blind fortune-teller, Old Jia, play his three-string lute after he finished his work. So he looked into the sky and said, "I'm fine. It's overcast and there's no sun. It will be cool."

They got on the road, but had barely traveled ten li before they were caught in a rain squall that soaked them and turned the ground muddy. They had no choice but to turn back. As Zhao strained to pedal through the mud, the bicycle chain broke, and so they had to walk home, since it was impossible to fix it in the pouring rain. The distance could be covered in half an hour on a bicycle, but it took them two hours slogging through the rain. They both fell ill after they were back in town. Zhao caught a cold. Zhan already had a head cold, and now the chill brought on a high fever. He took several doses of herbal medicine from World-Saving Hall, but his condition worsened and he died at the age of seventy-three, five days after coming down with that cold. Racked by a burning fever over the last five days of his life, he did not manage to leave any last words. And that was the end of an Italian priest who had spent more than five decades in Yanjin. Moses was shocked to hear of the priest's death. Zhan had once been his mentor and, moreover, it was because of Zhan's suggestion that he'd ended up at the steamed bun shop. Moses was not entirely happy with his current life, but Zhan had meant well with his advice, talking to him not in the name of the Lord but as an elder for the first time. Moses recalled how Zhan had looked just like an aging father when the priest rapped the bowl of his pipe against the bed. The priest had often patronized his bun stand, and Moses continued to call him Shifu, despite the absence of their former relationship.

"Forget it, Shifu," Moses would say when Zhan handed him money.

"You cannot take my money if I have a meal at your house, but it's different now that you're running a business." Zhan was right. "I won't feel comfortable coming back if you won't take my money today."

Xiangxiang knew exactly how many buns they made each day. Moses would not have taken the priest's money if he had been in charge, but she was and she would yell at him if what he turned over did not match the number of buns sold that day. So he took the priest's money. It saddened him after the priest's death when he thought about charging his shifu for a few buns.

Sometimes Qiaoling tagged along when Moses set up shop, but only during the day, since she was afraid of the dark. Even in the daytime, she would whine about going home or ask Moses to put her in an empty basket when she was tired. She would sleep with the lid on. Everyone knew she was timid, and some would tease her.

"Hurry, run. There's a demon from Xiguan who loves to eat children's hearts."

She would burst out crying, sometimes even wetting herself.

Once someone picked her up and said, "Come with me, Qiaoling, I'm going to take you somewhere to sell you."

She would shriek as she ran for the basket. At such moments, Moses would get angry with the customer while trying to soothe the girl. She was afraid of everyone on the street, everyone but Zhan.

"How old are you, child?" Zhan asked her when he came to buy buns.

"I'm five years old."

"Time for baptism." The priest never forgot his mission.

Sometimes he would hand half of his bun to her. Qiaoling would not let anyone but the priest pick her up.

"You have to believe in the Lord when you grow up," Zhan said to the girl once.

"What's a lord?"

"When you believe in the Lord, you'll know who you are, where you came from, and where you're going." Zhan used the same old lines.

Everyone laughed at him. But five-year-old Qiaoling seemed to be considering his reply, which prompted Zhan to say emotionally to Moses "Maybe you are not meant to follow the Lord, but she is. She looks like a follower." Zhan continued, "What can God do if a sinner is not aware of his own sin? God leads you to salvation, while sin brings only damnation," he added tearfully, and the girl reached out to dry his tears.

Moses had heard the same things countless times when he was staying with Zhan, and he had never paid much attention. Now, after Zhan's death, Qiaoling reminded Moses of the priest, and he sighed emotionally. He had heard about Zhan's passing at noon the day after the priest died, while he was out selling buns. He asked Old Zhao the cobbler to watch his stand for him before rushing to the temple to pay his final respects. His eyes closed, Zhan was lying on a straw mat, attended by neither friends nor family. The Yanjin branch was under the jurisdiction of the Kaifeng Church, which kept cutting Zhan's funding because the Italian priest had only eight converts and had been engaged in a long-standing dispute with Old Lei over interpretations of the Bible. The Kaifeng Church sent only a condolence telegram to mourn Zhan's death. Moses had to laugh at the telegram, which was addressed to Zhan himself. The people in Kaifeng were unwilling to spend any money, and, besides, this was a perfect opportunity to cut ties with the Yanjin branch and let it die out on its own. People holding dissenting interpretations of the Bible were considered heretics, and that was likely not something the bishop Lei would concede.

Zhan's eight Yanjin converts came; even Little Zhao arrived, his head wrapped in a towel because of his cold. Old Lu from the bamboo shop, who had been a good friend of Zhan, was there also, though he did not believe in God. After a quick look at Zhan's personal effects, they saw there was not enough money to buy a coffin, so Lu handed Moses the money for him to buy a coffin from Old Yu on North Street. On hot summer days like this, the burial had to take place as soon as possible, so they took the coffin out of the town on the third day to have it interred. The eight converts said a few "Amens" when the coffin was lowered into the ground, fully aware that this marked the end of the Catholic Church in Yanjin—when the tree falls, the monkeys scatter—and they all sobbed. When the burial was over, Moses suddenly recalled Zhan's fondness for Jia's three-string lute, which was the main reason for his last trip. He would not have gone to preach at Jia Village and been felled by the rain squall if it hadn't been to listen to Jia play. They buried him to only the sounds of Amen and sobs. They should have invited Jia to play at the funeral; obviously, none of the eleven mourners, including Moses, had cared enough about Zhan and what the priest liked. But the man was in the ground now, so there was no point in fretting over it.

They returned to the temple. Since Zhan had no family in China, Old Lu took charge and ordered eleven bowls of mutton soup from Old Yang's Mutton Diner in Xiguan, plus 110 fried cakes. On their haunches in the temple, they had a meal together, a symbolic ending of the ceremony. As for the old bicycle Zhan left behind, it was about to fall apart and worth practically nothing, so Lu decided to give it to Zhao, who had given rides to the priest around Yanjin for the past eight years. When they were ready to leave, Moses took another look around and recalled how the priest would snort as he conducted Bible study. He stuck around a while longer after the others left. A roll of paper peeking out from under the straw mat caught Moses's attention. He picked it up and saw that it was a newly finished drawing of a church by Zhan. As a young man the priest had studied architecture with his uncle in Italy; he had done a terrific job drawing the church, with the various heights and widths clearly marked.

It was an eight-story Gothic structure with a center dome 40.6 meters in dia-meter and 60.8 meters from the ground. The bell tower was 160 meters high and the bell was 6 meters in diameter. A note indicated that the outer walls were made of marble, with seventy-two stained-glass windows. A cross above the door soared into the clouds. The church was made out to look imposing; next to it were drawings of the exquisite interior furnishings—the thorn wood cupboards and tables covered in gold inside and out, with gilded edges; wool curtains; awnings made of sheep and seal skin; a golden candelabra with six branches, each with three candleholders shaped like apricot flowers; a thorn wood altar; and a gold placard inscribed with "The Lord is holy."

It did not occur to Moses until now that Zhan lived in a dilapidated temple with his heart on the church the whole time, not the one seized by the vari-ous county magistrates but a much grander one. It was only a drawing, but it seemed to come alive when he took a closer look. He could almost see the seventy-two windows being pushed open, the bell tolling so loudly it nearly deafened him. A window seemed to open in his heart when he gazed at the windows of the church. He had learned nothing from the priest during Bible study; now the drawing made him feel that Zhan had to have been the best priest in the whole world. Granted, he had converted only eight Yanjin resi-dents, but faith was more important than numbers; the eight converts might not be the most pious, but at least Zhan believed in them. In a word, the priest had himself as the most ardent follower, even if he had failed to spread the gos-pel to others. Moses had not been a believer while Zhan was alive and had no intentions of following the Lord after the priest's death; he would follow Zhan, however. The light in his heart came from the priest, not God.

He turned the paper over after studying the drawing and saw two words written on the back in small, neat calligraphy, clearly also done by Zhan him-self: "Satan's Murmur." Moses felt a sharp pain in his heart, and yet he did not know what the phrase was supposed to mean. After mulling it over, he knew that it had nothing to do with the church, but with the thousands of people who did not believe in the Lord, and Zhan, who, Moses knew, had been help-lessly repelled by them all his life. It was his abhorrence of these people that instilled in Zhan the desire to build the church, in his mind at least. Moses felt something he had never sensed before; he could somehow relate to the priest's feeling, as he too was often beset by a kind of disgust.

With his heart in turmoil, he went home with Zhan's drawing and took it out to study it that night, when he couldn't sleep. This time he read the inscrip-tion on the back first before studying the church. At some point he thought he understood what the words meant, but then he was confused again, so he turned the paper over to examine the drawing. After a while, he started to see how the church was put together. Back home, a younger Moses had made objects like insects, shrimp, cats, and dogs out of bamboo strips. An idea occurred to him that he ought to follow Zhan's drawing and create a church out of bamboo strips. It would have to be scaled down tens or hundreds of times to make even a rough imitation. No one had taken the priest's ideas seriously, but Moses would treat the drawing of the church with care, not as a commemoration of Zhan, but for the newly opened window in his heart.

He began ten days later. There was no shortage of bamboo strips, for Lu's bamboo workshop had plenty of remnants, which Moses picked up on his way home in the evening. He would save money on material by splitting the bamboo pieces into smaller strips. In the past he got up before dawn to get the buns ready; now he got up late at night and sneaked into the woodshed, where he lit a lamp to study the drawing and begin constructing his church. It would surely take much more time and work to create an eight-story church than cats and dogs. He could make two or three bamboo cats or dogs in the time it took to eat lunch, but with the church, he didn't even have a foundation ready after five days. The construction itself wasn't all that time consuming; he spent most of his time and thought on the overall structure before the parts could be put together. Sometimes he stared at the drawing for a long time, adding only a few strips. Once he knew what to do with a section, it did not take much effort to weave the strips; he just had to take the time to plan ahead. Roosters would be crowing before he'd barely made any progress, and he had to put aside the church and run over to the kitchen to prepare the dough.

Qiaoling was intrigued by what he was doing; sometimes she came to watch him work at night when she got up to pee. Making the bamboo church at night was different from playing a role in the New Year's festival. The latter, a daytime event, interfered with the business, while the former only interfered with his sleep. Xiangxiang said nothing at first; once in a while, she was even curious enough to get out of bed, put something on, and go out to the woodshed to see what he was doing. She had thought he would stop after a few days of novelty, but he hadn't given up after a month. He still got up around ten each night to continue the construction, and he had only managed to finish one story, with seven to go, when she began to lose patience.

"You light a lamp to make this every night. What's the point?"

"I get my work done."

"What do you mean you get your work done?" She did not like his reply. "There's lots more to do. Why don't you go deal in scallions, since you have enough free time to fiddle with this?"

Now she was talking about something else altogether. When her ex-husband was alive, he had traveled to Taiyuan to buy scallions with two friends and sell them in Yanjin. The three rooms had been rebuilt with money from selling buns and from Jiang Hu's scallion trade. This was said in the heat of the moment, but when she gave it more thought, it seemed like a good idea for him to buy and sell scallions while she stayed home to make and sell buns. It would be a chance for him to learn a thing or two about the world and enlighten that blockheaded brain of his, so he would stop whiling away time like a loafer. Besides, it would bring in extra income. To be sure, it meant braving the weather, and it was much harder than staying home with the bun business; but it was, unquestionably, profitable. The sooner they saved up enough, the earlier they could open the diner. So she went to see Old Bu and Old Lai, asking them to take Moses along when they went out again. They agreed, mostly for the sake of Jiang Hu's family.

Moses was not happy when she told him. The hardships of travel bothered him; he did not like the idea of having to deal with people on the road. Moreover, he had just moved on to the second story of his church, and the construction was getting harder. The work would be delayed if he left now, not because of the time, but because of the many ideas in his head. He might not remember them all after the trip. She knew he hesitated because of the church.

"All you think about is the church. What about my diner?" She blew up. "Fine with me if you don't want to go. I'm going to burn down your church."

She got up and made for the woodshed, but he jumped up and stopped her. "All right, all right. I'll do it."

Moses put aside the construction and left with Bu and Lai on the tenth day of the ninth lunar month to travel to Taiyuan to buy scallions, a worthwhile venture under normal circumstances. But in Moses's case, it had resulted from his construction of Zhan's church, which had then led to Xiangxiang's complaint related to her planned diner. Moses had to laugh, despite his unhappiness, at the gulf between the cause and the effect of the scallion-buying trip.

He did not know Bu and Lai well. So it was not until they were on the road that he discovered that they picked on a newcomer, like Old Ta at the dye shop or the clerks at the county office. They ignored him the whole way, talking only to each other. That did not bother Moses. He, like Jiang Hu, was married to Xiangxiang, but the other two men were Hu's friends, not his; besides, he enjoyed a quiet journey without having to talk to them. But they ordered him around when they got to a diner; they sat at the table while Moses brought them tea or poured them water. When they spent the night at an inn, they lay down on the warmer side of the bed and made Moses sleep by the door, as cold autumn winds blew outside. He had to get up at midnight to feed the donkeys, while they stayed in bed. The two men argued with each other often, but were in total agreement when it came to getting Moses to run errands for them.

Over the years, Moses had tried various lines of work: making tofu, slaughtering pigs, changing water at a dye shop, splitting bamboo, delivering water to shops, tending a vegetable garden, and preparing dough for steamed buns. He was, however, new to the scallion-buying business, and strictly speaking, the two men were like his shifu. It did not seem out of line for them to act like a shifu; he had no trouble putting up with them.

On the evening of the third day out, they reached Qinyuan's county town in Shanxi. It was the very city where Jiang Hu had had the argument with a man from Shandong and had been stabbed to death three years prior. After finding an inn for the night, they fed the donkeys before going out to look for a place for dinner.

"Let's not go to the place where Jiang Hu was killed," Bu said. "It scares me every time I go by that diner."

"It's been three years, and I'm still impressed by his sense of loyalty," Lai said with a sigh, after casting Moses a glance. "The new doesn't arrive until the old is gone."

Moses knew they were praising Jiang Hu as a roundabout way of saying the new man, Moses Wu, could not compare. Having listened to enough tinged talk like that, he pretended not to have heard, since he couldn't argue with them. Besides, being new to the town, he focused his attention on the shops along the street. Someone called out from behind as they walked on.

"Hey, you three over there."

They turned and saw two men standing by a horse-drawn wagon on the roadside; they had a Shandong accent. Scallions were piled high on their wagon, but there was no horse. One was heavy-set; the other was skinny.

"You look like you're on your way to buy Taiyuan scallions," the skinny one said.

Moses kept his mouth shut, while Bu, unhappy to be stopped like that, grumbled, "We mind our own business. So what if we are?"

"Don't get me wrong," the heavy one said with a smile. "We're on our way back to Shandong from Taiyuan after buying scallions. Our hired hand fell ill on the road. He's been coughing up blood. We took him to see a local doctor, but the doctor could see we're from out of town and charged us an incredibly high fee for the medicine. We don't know our way around here, and we couldn't let the man die, so we paid the doctor what he wanted, but it's been three days and the man still hasn't recovered. We've spent all we have and still owe the doctor for the medicine. We've decided to sell this load of scallions to buy more medicine. We bought them for 3.6 fen a cattie but you can pay us 4 fen, which will save you a trip and a man his life."

It sounded like a good deal. Bu and Lai, who had been making the trip for years, knew it was a fair price. It would take two days to travel from Qinyuan to Taiyuan, making it a four-day round trip; they would save four days' travel and room and board for three men and their donkeys if they bought the scallions in Qinyuan. But Lai had his doubts.

"Are they really from Taiyuan? How do we know they're the real thing?"

"Go ahead, try them," the heavy one said.

"Where's your horse?" Bu also had his doubts.

"It's at the inn. We can't sell it. We wouldn't be able to get home without a horse to pull the wagon."

Lai went to check on the scallions. He checked the thickness before pulling one out from the bottom and chewing on it before nodding to Bai. "It's genuine, all right." He turned to the two men. "How many catties do you have here?"

"Six thousand exactly."

Bu gave Lai a look before saying, "No deal."

Knowing what Bu was up to, Lai took Moses by the arm and the three of them walked off.

"Fine with us," the heavy man said. "But you'll get the same price after you travel two more days." He added, "Why do we keep running into people who don't know what's good for them?"

Bu stopped in his tracks. "It's not that we don't know what's good for us. It's just that we do things our way."

"How's that?" the skinny man asked.

"As the saying goes, 'When you're in the marketplace, you have to sell even if the price is low.' We can't give you the price you want."

"We're only asking for an increase of less than half a fen after we've brought the scallions all the way from Taiyuan. That's not too much to ask, is it, Second Brother?"

"We'll pay the original price," Bu said.

"You people from Henan are just like the doctor here, aren't you? All you can think of is taking advantage of people."

"Forget it, then," Bu said as he dragged Lai and Moses away. The heavy man came up and stopped them.

"This is a life-and-death issue for us, Second Brother, and you'd be helping us out."

After several rounds of bargaining, each side made a concession and they struck a deal at 3.8 fen per cattie. The Shandong men went back to the inn and brought their horse over to transport the wagonload of scallions to the inn where Moses and the others were staying. They unloaded and weighed the scallions; it came to 5,920 catties, after being buffeted by wind and rain.

"We lost another eighty catties. We shouldn't keep doing this."

They departed, leaving Bu, Lai, and Moses to rejoice over the great deal. In addition to saving themselves four days' travel, they'd bought a load of dried-out Taiyuan scallions, and all they had to do when they got home was sprinkle water on them before the sale to gain back the weight. It was a terrific deal, no matter how they looked at it. Bu had done more than the others in cementing the deal, so he got to take 2,200 catties; Lai played a role, as well, and got to take 2,000, leaving 1,720 catties for Moses. He did not mind getting less, since he hadn't said a word in the bargaining process. They left the next morning in high spirits with their loaded donkey carts.

It was after midnight on their sixth day of travel when they returned to Yanjin. After bidding farewell to Bu and Lai, Moses took his cart back to the bun shop, where he quietly unlatched the door and tiptoed into the yard with the donkey to avoid waking Xiangxiang and Qiaoling. He also wanted to surprise Xiangxiang with the fact that he had managed to buy Taiyuan scallions without having to actually go there, a successful outcome on his first trip, no less. The yard, bathed in the moonlight, looked as if frosted over. He was about to unload the cart when he noticed that the light was on in the girl's room. He wondered why she wasn't sleeping with her mother. Could they have had a fight? Or were they sleeping together in the girl's room and had forgotten to blow out the lamp? Putting the scallions aside, he walked up to the girl's window and looked through a hole poked in the paper. Qiaoling was sleeping alone, lying on her back with arms and legs spread out and exposing her belly. She yelled out, turned, and went back to sleep. Moses shook his head and smiled, knowing that the girl had had a fight with her mother. He was about to unload the cart when he thought he heard someone talking in his and Xiangxiang's bedroom. She must be talking in her sleep, he said to himself, but a moment later he realized it was a man and a woman talking. The implication made his hair stand on end; forgetting the scallions, he walked in and went up to the bedroom door. Someone else was in there with his wife.

"Hurry and go home," he heard Xiangxiang say, "before the girl wakes up. It's almost daybreak, so I need to get up and prepare the dough."

That was followed by the rustling noise of them putting on their clothes.

"This is the last time," she said.

"He won't back for a few days, will he?" the man asked.

"Your wife would raise hell if she knew."

"I told her to go see her parents. She'll be there for three more days."

"Don't come tomorrow."

"It's been three, almost four years, and nothing has happened yet."

An explosion went off in Moses's head, not because he had just learned that his wife of more than a year had been sleeping with another man. What shocked him was the man. He knew that voice; it belonged to Old Gao, the silversmith next door. What was revealed in their conversation was even more shocking; obviously, they had been doing this for more than three years, and that had been hidden not only from him but from Jiang Hu, too. Both husbands were ignorant cuckolds! When Wu Xiangxiang sought to marry him, Moses had thought she needed a man in her life; now it turned out that he was being used as a smokescreen. And then there was the trip to Shanxi. He'd thought it was to buy scallions, part of the plan for her future diner; he had been making space for another man without knowing it. After she had often berated him, even hit him, he had decided to suffer silently and let her have her way. It became clear now that he was an easy mark, a worthless dupe. He had treated Gao as a friend, someone he sought out to discuss complex matters. Gao talked slowly, measuring his words logically and reasonably. Now it was clear to Moses that Gao was two-faced, never meaning what he said, and that he had been toying with Moses all along. They were talking inside again.

"We can't go on like this after we open the diner. You have to come up with something," said Xiangxiang.

"Don't worry. The woman next door isn't going to live much longer."

"But what about the worthless one?"

Moses knew that he was the worthless one.

"We can make good use of his pigheadedness." Gao was speaking in that measured tone of his again. "I gave you the idea to have him kill the Jiang brothers. Didn't he end up crushing them?"

"I can tell you want me to continue living with him like this. When Jiang Hu died, you said you were afraid your wife would die of anger. What will you do when she dies?"

"We'll talk about that when that happens. The simpleton will be easy to get rid of, don't you agree?"

Another explosion went off in Moses's head. He'd thought that Gao was trying to avoid trouble when he refused to talk about Wu family affairs; now he realized that Gao had an ulterior motive, which would have been all right if it weren't for the fact that not only had he refused to give him counsel, but was giving Xiangxiang all sorts of ideas. He had been the one, not Xiangxiang, who had gotten Moses to go to the cotton shop to kill the brothers. What else would the man not do, if he could instigate a murder? All along, Moses had thought that he and Xiangxiang fought all the time because they simply did not get along. Looking back now, he saw that while he thought he was arguing with her, in fact his opponent had been Gao. Who could say it hadn't been Gao's idea to open a diner? When Moses came home after selling buns all morning, he often saw Gao in their yard talking to Xiangxiang, just two neighbors chatting, and Moses did not pay any attention. They knew exactly what was going on; Moses was kept in the dark. Now, after they had enjoyed their time in bed, they were even passing judgment on him, calling him worthless. Moses recalled one of the three phrases Gao loved to use when analyzing matters: "You can do that, but you can't say it that way." And that was precisely what was happening. It could be done, but it defied reason. Confronted with this situation, Moses did not know what to do. A sudden nausea came upon him, making him shake all over, and he dropped to his haunches. He jumped to his feet only when Gao got dressed and opened the door. Gao was stunned. With an uncharacteristic shout, he sputtered, "Aren't you supposed to be away longer?"

He spoke as if it were Moses's fault for coming home early. Gao's shout alerted Xiangxiang and roused Moses from his dazed state. She froze when she ran out and saw Moses. After regaining his composure, Moses went wordlessly to the kitchen and came out with Jiang Hu's knife, the same one he had used the year before to scare the Jiang brothers. He had only feigned bravery that time, but not on this night, when he meant business. Gao and Wu recovered with a yelp and ran for their lives. Moses gave chase. After the wearying trip home, he was too tired and too shocked to be a match for two people running as fast as they could to get away from him. He lost them when they disappeared down an alley. He was panting so hard he had to squat down. The area was deserted, except for the sound of Ni San's clapper in the distance. After resting for a moment, Moses stood up, but not to keep chasing them. He had an idea.

He walked back to the bun shop and unloaded the scallions. Then he led the donkey and cart out of the yard and headed for Bai Village. It was barely light out when he reached it. He went straight to Gao's in-laws' door, where, with a sad look, he told Gao's wife that her husband had fallen ill and that she must return right away. She suspected nothing. Shaking from fear, she climbed onto the donkey cart without even packing a bag. From what he'd learned from Gao, Bai suffered from epileptic episodes when she was enraged, so he planned to take her to the county town before telling her what had happened between Gao and Xiangxiang. She would raise hell with her husband and with Moses's wife, while he could sit by and watch them fight it out. That would be much more satisfying than killing the adulterous pair, for that required only a plunge of the knife, while an altercation among the three of them could last days. Gao had said his wife would die sooner or later. But she was still alive, which worked to his advantage. The best scenario for him was for Gao's wife to die, which would put Gao and Xiangxiang on the spot, as they would have to deal with her death. If she died, adultery would escalate into something much more serious, and, instead of Moses, Gao and Xiangxiang would be the ones who pushed the woman to her death. Moses would love to see how they would react. Since it had reached this point, he might as well see just how bad it could get, not only to vent his anger, but also to avenge the other cuckold, a man Moses had never met. He felt he had grown up overnight; he also discovered a bright side to his heart, even though it was in fact ruthlessness. He did not think he was a vicious man, but if that is what he had become, it was Gao, a trusted friend, and Xiangxiang, his wife, who had taught him how to be that way. The pigheaded simpleton had finally learned what it meant to be resourceful.

But in the end he made a wrong calculation. It was the following noon when he brought Gao's wife back to the county town. The adulterers had packed up and run off together. Bai collapsed when she heard the news, foaming at the mouth as her body was racked by spasms before she passed out on the floor. Moses rushed her to World-Saving Hall on North Street.

14

Gao and Xiangxiang took what they could from their respective houses before running off together. Naturally, for Gao it was silver jewelry, some of which he had recently made to put on display. He also took some used silver goods that customers had brought in to be polished, cleaned, or remade into earrings, bracelets, rings, and hairpins. With Gao gone, his wife, Bai, was left to deal with customers, who cared more about their silver goods than about the eloping pair. They had to restrain themselves, however, owing to her illness. Gao became their target. He'd looked like a nice, trustworthy man, they said. Who could have guessed that he would steal another man's wife and other people's jewelry?

Xiangxiang had walked off with a jewelry box containing the money earned from selling steamed buns, capital for her future diner. The diner was out of the question now, of course. Xiangxiang and Gao had also taken money from their respective families, for they had no plans to return. Gao had not left a note for Bai, proof of how little he cared for his wife of a dozen years. Xiangxiang, on the other hand, had written Moses a few lines on a page torn from their account book.

No need to say anything; nothing would mean anything, anyway. I'll be gone when you get back. I took the money with me. You can have the shop and Qiaoling. It would be hard to take her along, and besides, she gets along with you better than with me.

Gao usually suffered for weeks after his wife had an episode. She would threaten to hang herself during a fit when she was unhappy with something he'd said. Her epilepsy did not bother him, but as he was afraid she might really kill herself, he always let her have her way. Now he was not around, and Moses was afraid she might take her own life. She did not, precisely because Gao was gone. Her fits had usually lasted two weeks or more, but this time she was over it in three days. The customers came back for their money once she had recovered; they were quite decent about it. She was the one who ranted.

"He wouldn't have run off with that slut if you hadn't left your silver jewelry with him. You want your money back, but what about my husband? Will you give him back to me?"

The customers could only laugh at her strange logic.

Moses stewed in anger for three days, but not because his scheme with Gao's wife had failed. If he hadn't gone to bring her back to town but had stuck around instead, they would not have been able to run off that easily; at least they would not have gotten off with all the money and valuables. He was unhappy mainly because they had left a mess for him to clean up. They were gone, leaving behind the green hat of a cuckold for him to wear. He might have been able to get something out of the affair if they had stuck around, but now that they had vanished into thin air, he had no idea what to do next. Logically, he should repeat his earlier feat and, knife in hand, search high and low for the pair, but he didn't. In the past, he might have. This incident served to show that he was a different person. He had planned to spare the couple and bring Bai back, having learned to "watch others fight so he could reap the spoils" or "kill his rival through proxy."

Now he was alone and needed to make a plan. Back when Xiangxiang was around, she was in charge, and he'd had to listen to her. He felt he had shed a burden now that she was gone. In a word, her presence in his life had been a huge headache. Why would he want to get the headache back after she'd run off? She had simplified matters by running off. Moses continued to mull over the situation. She was gone, but the bun shop stayed. As long as he had that, he would look for a Chen Xiangxiang or a Li Xiangxiang to replace Wu Xiangxiang. Who could say he wouldn't find another Xiangxiang to be a perfect match? With a Li Xiangxiang, he would no longer be Wu Xiangxiang's cuckold. Ultimately, he would be the bun shop owner. He would bring a woman into *his* family, thus rectifying the unusual arrangement between him and Xiangxiang; in a word, everything would be back to normal. Granted, it was a gigantic loss of face to have his wife run off with another man, so he had to hide his glee;

he put on a sad look and pretended to contemplate a lawsuit. Oddly enough, he did look troubled, not because Xiangxiang had left, but because he had to pretend to be unhappy.

The shop felt peaceful now that Xiangxiang was gone, with no one to tell him what to do or berate him for doing something wrong. It gave him a carefree feeling, a new sensation that actually put him slightly ill at ease. Qiaoling felt the same way. Her mother's running off with another man did not seem to affect her; she neither cried nor threw a tantrum. She ate and played as if nothing had happened. Her reaction reinforced Moses's resolve not to go after Xiangxiang. The girl moved in to sleep with Moses after her mother left. No longer afraid of the dark with Moses beside her, she did not need a night light, and they would chat awhile after he blew out the lamp. Xiangxiang never came up in their conversation, not once; they talked only about the present, never about the past.

For instance:

"Are you asleep, Qiaoling?"

"Why?"

"Remember I asked you to shut the chicken coop door? Did you do it?"

"Ai-ya! I forgot."

"Go close it."

"But it's dark out." She sounded anxious. "I don't want to go."

"A weasel would have made off with our chickens if we had waited for you to do it. I already shut it."

She laughed. "I promise I'll remember to shut it tomorrow."

Or:

"Are you asleep, Uncle?"

"Why?"

"Light the lamp."

"I just blew it out. Why are you being a pest?"

"I want to pee."

He laughed as he got up to light the lamp.

He had to quickly put on a sad look when someone came by during the day and stop the girl from playing or laughing. Qiaoling was quick to comprehend what was going on. The five-year-old girl learned to scheme with Moses; they both pretended to be wretched. He sensed himself changing into a different person, not because of faking his sorrow, but because of a sense of self during the phony act. He would not have known how to deceive in the past. On the other hand, he knew he could not keep it up forever, so he decided they would do it for ten days. After that, they would start over, with him making and selling buns. People could say what they wanted; he would focus only on what to do with his life. He had it all planned out: starting on the eleventh day, he would prepare the dough the night before and get up at daybreak to knead it. He would still steam seven steamers of buns. Qiaoling would tag along. All of a sudden, he was no longer afraid of the trade, now that Xiangxiang was gone. Talking to customers didn't seem so intimidating anymore. In the past, when Xiangxiang was around, he'd had to talk to them the way she wanted, but now he was free to say whatever *he* wanted, and when he wanted. After returning home in the afternoon, he would work on the church with Qiaoling. When the moment was right, he'd take a mutton leg to see Sun the matchmaker and ask him to find him a Chen Xiangxiang or a Li Xiangxiang. Old Cui, who had been his matchmaker, wasn't reliable, so Moses would not ask him this time.

He had it all planned, but it did not last ten days, for he was forced to go looking for Xiangxiang on the fifth day. Moses was turning flour into dough that morning, with the girl helping to peel scallions. There was also a piece of pork on the kitchen counter, another ingredient for the meat dumplings they were making. Old Jiang from Jiang's Cotton Shop came by. With practiced complicity, Moses and the girl quickly swept all the ingredients plus a large radish into the wok, replaced the lid, and put on a sad look the moment they heard him calling from outside. The shop had been the cause of much strife, from the enmity between Xiangxiang and the Jiang family to Moses's attempt to kill the Jiang brothers, so Moses thought Old Jiang wanted the shop back now that she had run off. It had been owned by the Jiang family, not the Wu family, so he would have to leave. That could be the purpose of Jiang's visit, but it was not the plan Moses had in mind. He reasoned that, since he had been married to Wu Xiangxiang, he was the rightful owner of the shop after she left. He would have had to resume his old trade of delivering water if she had chased him out of the house before she left, but she hadn't. Hence, he believed that the Wu family owned the shop, and he planned to use it to find himself another wife, no matter what the Jiang family said. Worst-case scenario would be for him to do battle again. He would fight to the end if it came to that. He had not felt that confident the time before, when he'd killed the Jiang family dog. But now, for the sake of keeping the shop, he was prepared to kill a person, if necessary.

To his great surprise, Old Jiang did not bring up the shop.

"She's gone, great nephew. So what do you have in mind?" the old man asked.

So he was here to talk about her, not the shop. Moses breathed a sigh of relief. He knew exactly what to say about her, and would have said it right away if this were in the past. But the new Moses sighed, with a grieving look.

"My mind is a jumbled mess, Uncle. I don't know what to do. What do you think I ought to do?"

"You have to do something when your wife runs off with another man."

"What do I do?"

"Old Gao got her to run off with him, so you have to go destroy his shop. Will you do that? If you won't, then her brothers will."

So that was what he had in mind. Moses had not expected that.

"We don't want his things. It's just that we'd be laughingstocks if we kept quiet and did nothing. We have to face people out there, and how are we going to hold our heads up if we don't seek revenge for the humiliation?"

So that was the reasoning behind it. Moses hadn't thought about that either.

"It's been four days, and we haven't seen any action from you. So the brothers said they would wait until tomorrow noon for you to do something. Don't blame the Jiang family for not giving you a way out if you still refuse to act by tomorrow noon."

Moses lowered his head to mull over the old man's words.

"And there's something else I want to say to you."

"What is it?" Moses looked up.

"I know what you're thinking." Old Jiang gestured with his cane. "You want to have the shop all to yourself. But you have to go look for her to do so, or you'll be laughed at."

Moses had known he would be laughed at, but he had his plan, so he decided not to respond.

"And there's something else," Jiang said.

"What is it?"

"You were right last time, when you said we were all grown-ups. So stop pretending you don't understand what's going on. We don't want the shop back, but not because we're afraid of you. We're keeping mum for Qiaoling's sake, so don't get any ideas."

That was yet another thing that Moses hadn't thought about. Wu Xiangxiang's father came that afternoon, shortly after Old Jiang left. Old Wu had been Moses's father-in-law, but not now, not after Xiangxiang had run off with another man. Old Wu was henpecked, just like Moses with Xiangxiang, but he put on father-in-law airs before Moses, despite a hint of defeat in his tone of voice.

"Qiaoling's Uncle, she's gone, so what are you going to do?"

It was about Xiangxiang running off again. Moses decided to respond in the usual way by looking downcast. Old Wu had recognized his status by calling him Qiaoling's Uncle, so Moses knew he had to follow the same protocol.

"Father." He couldn't call Wu anything else. "My mind is a jumbled mess. What do you think I ought to do?"

"Go look for her! You can't just leave it like that, without doing anything. How would it look?"

"I want to, but someone could die if I do. No one died that night because they left in a hurry. If I found her this time, someone would die."

Moses thought he would frighten the old man, but instead Wu just sighed and said, "That would take care of things, wouldn't it? We'll all lose face if you don't search for your wife. There's someone who won't stand by if you keep on like this, living in shame."

"Who's that?"

"My wife. She said she'd bring a knife and fight it out with you if you don't start looking for your wife tomorrow." He wasn't finished. "She sees what you have in mind. You plan to let her go and keep the shop to yourself, so you can get another woman."

"That idea never crossed my mind, Father." Moses was thrown into a minor panic.

"I've had four lousy days, so I sneaked out of the house to warn you. You know what she's like. She means what she says. Someone would surely die if she came with a knife, don't you think?"

Moses was flabbergasted. Their daughter was the one who had run off, but instead of going after her daughter herself, her mother targeted him, her son-in-law. The logic was beyond him. When Xiangxiang was around, she never thought twice about hitting him, and her shrewish mother, he knew, was ten times worse. He was not actually afraid of the woman, but if she came for him, that would surely lead to a different kind of trouble. He was the injured party in the first round of this fiasco, but he would be the culprit if there were a second round. Now that it had come to this, he had to go searching for his wife, in spite of what he wanted, even if he had to fake a search. But something stopped him.

"Of course, I'll go look for her, but what about Qiaoling?"

"Don't worry about her. She can stay with us."

The girl, who had stuck around to listen, glared at Old Wu and said in a voice that left no room for negotiation, "I won't do it."

Old Wu considered the girl's declaration and said, "How about going to your grandpa's place?"

Her grandpa's place meant Jiang's Cotton Shop on South Street. She replied in an equally uncompromising tone, "I'm not going to the cotton shop either."

"Now what do I do?" Moses spread his hands out at Old Wu. "The girl has nowhere to go if I'm away."

"I'll follow you wherever you go," she said to Moses.

He did not know how to respond to that.

The next day, the day the Jiang brothers would come to destroy Gao's jewelry shop, Moses locked up the bun shop and left with Qiaoling to search for Xiangxiang with a travel bag and some money. As it was to be a fake search, he only went as far as Xinxiang, a hundred li from Yanjin, where they found the cheapest lodging possible in Dongguan. They would spend ten days there before heading back to Yanjin, where they would tell people they'd been to Xinxiang, Ji County, Kaifeng, Zhengzhou, Anyang, and Luoyang, that they had searched high and low but had failed to find the adulterers. He would be able to answer to all parties and resume business at the bun shop. He even took Zhan's church drawing along, hoping to study the construction when he had nothing to do, so he could complete the construction upon returning to Yanjin.

The inn was next to a bus depot, with five rooms, each with a large bed that could accommodate a dozen travelers. Moses and Qiaoling started out in a room close to the front door and later moved to the innermost room when space opened up. Their new room was next to the stove, so the bed was warm throughout the night. They spent most of their time in the room and only walked around the immediate area if they ventured out. The depot was the farthest they would go, so the girl could look at the buses. She giggled when one of them blew its big nose before taking off with people inside.

The yard and the rooms of the small inn were clean enough. It was late in the year, so the big locust tree out in the yard littered the ground with yellow leaves each morning. The inn provided three meals a day, which required additional payment but was a convenience. They would tell the innkeeper what they wanted for the next meal, and the cook would have it ready. In the morning everyone had soupy rice with corn muffins, but they all had different items for lunch and dinner. Moses and the girl usually had a bowl of noodle soup with mutton at both meals, without adding anything else. Besides saving money, that would last them until the next meal, and the soup warmed their insides. Once, as they ate, Moses recalled the bowl of soup the barber Old Pei had bought him at Old Sun's diner years ago, when he was hiding in a haystack after losing a sheep because he had gone to watch Luo Changli at a funeral. Back then he had been Yang Baishun. Moses missed the barber and wondered how he was doing after all these years.

People came and went at the inn, most spending a night or two before getting on the road again. Old Pang, the cross-eyed innkeeper, was intrigued by Moses and the girl, who were staying longer than other guests but had nothing to do each day. The lodgers had to pay for their stay early each morning, which Moses did without fail, so Old Pang had no complaints. The inn had another long-term lodger, a rat poison peddler, Old You. A man in his thirties from Kaifeng, he had the face of a macaque and a raspy voice. He had been hawking his wares by the bus depot for a month, returning to spend the nights in Pang's inn. Xinxiang must have had quite a rat infestation if he could sell rat poison at the same spot for a month. Moses and Qiaoling quickly got to know him fairly well because they were all sleeping in the innermost room. During the day, when Moses took the girl to look at buses, they sometimes walked by You's stand to watch him sell rat poison. It came in individual packets wrapped in coarse paper, spread out on the ground. Qiaoling wasn't interested in the poison, but she loved seeing all the stiff, dried rats lined up by the poison packs. They were stuffed with straw and rags to prove that they'd died from ingesting You's poison. Once, she picked up a stick to poke at the rats and giggled when they remained motionless. A timid girl, she seemed to have gotten bolder after arriving in Xinxiang. A potential customer once walked up and kicked a dead rat on the ground.

"These are huge. Are they real?"

"These aren't the big ones. I keep those at home so people won't be scared."

Selling rat poison was a business with small profits that relied on the vendor's ability to hawk his wares. Old You had a raspy voice, but he could hail customers all day long with his sales pitch:

A year is added to the universe and fortune to us all
No one should have rats hidden deep in their hall
From Beijing to Nanjing
Everyone knows Old You's rat poison is the one to call

Or,

The Forbidden City is clamoring
Eight rats come gathering
The big ones squeal, the small ones screech
All mean to make sure Old You is not within reach
They want to kill Old You, why's that?
Because their aunts and sisters are lying out flat.

And so on.

Moses laughed when he heard him, as did Qiaoling. He knew he could never manage to do that; first, he could not come up with lines like that, and second, he would be mortified even if he could. Impressed by Old You's wit and talent, Moses could not get over the fact that a rat poison peddler with a raspy voice had to shout all day. At night the three of them ate dinner together. Moses and the girl had their usual noodle soup, while Old You preferred fried cakes stuffed with donkey meat, plus a bowl of cabbage soup with dried shrimp. The hot soup beaded his forehead with sweat. Sometimes he broke off a piece of a meat-filled pastry for the girl, who accepted the offer once they got to know him better.

"You shouldn't eat other people's food," Moses scolded her the first time it happened. "Where are your manners?"

"It's just a few bites," Old You said with a smile. "Children needn't bother with manners."

Old You was more than quick-witted; he was also a smooth talker. Being at least ten years older than Moses, he called him "Younger Brother," forcing Moses to address him as "Elder Brother." Old You smoked, but Moses did not. Before falling asleep at night, they relaxed on the heated bed, chatting while You smoked. Qiaoling would follow their conversation for a while, but would fall asleep before You finished two pipefuls. As he was from Kaifeng, he shared stories and anecdotes about places like the Xiangguo Temple, the Dragon Pavilion, Pan and Yang Lakes, Millennium City Park, Horse Market Street, and foods such as the famed Kaifeng soupy buns, Sha family's beef, Bai family's sheep hooves, Hu family's pot-stewed chicken, Tang family's stewed dog meat, and so on. He made Kaifeng out to be heaven on earth. Moses secretly laughed at the man's fanciful stories. Why would he leave Kaifeng to peddle poison in Xinxiang if his hometown was so wonderful? Sometimes they debated other topics, such as whether family members or outsiders were better, whether an impatient man was better than a slowpoke, whether it was better to be nice or mean to people. Absent sweeping generalizations, each of these was dealt with on an individual basis; the two men usually stuck to their own views. Old You would start out insisting on his opinion, but might relent if Moses seemed on the verge of losing his temper, and he would change his tone to one of agreement.

"You're right, too, Younger Brother."

He would then refrain from voicing his opinion as they moved on to another topic and would echo Moses no matter what the younger man said.

"You're quite right. Yes, indeed."

That was a talent he had honed by peddling wares away from home. He had to agree with his customers if he wanted to make a sale. For his part, Moses felt sheepish when the older man agreed with him. Once, when they were talking about selling rat poison, Moses complimented You's persuasive powers and pointed at his own mouth.

"This mouth of mine could never do that."

"You're wrong," You said with a sigh, to Moses's surprise. "Or you're mocking me."

"What do you mean?"

"I don't see an end to this life of flapping my lips to sell rat poison."

"What else would you like to do?"

"Get rich." He rapped the bowl of his pipe against the edge of the bed.

Who didn't want to get rich? But that usually involved dubious means and was thus inadvisable.

"Anyone who wants to get rich must first ignore his conscience. You don't look like you could do that."

Old You was caught off guard by the comment and took a moment to recover. "You're right," he said with a sigh.

Moses could tell that, like Old Pang the innkeeper, Old You was curious about the two of them staying at the inn with nothing to do. He never asked him about that, probably because they were chance acquaintances. But on this night, Moses and Qiaoling ordered noodle soup as usual. It tasted fine, but later, back in the room, the saltiness hit him. He decided to go back to the kitchen for some water. Old You, who had been out later than usual, was eating his dinner. Moses heard Pang and You talking about him when he reached the kitchen door. He stopped to eavesdrop.

"A man with a little girl staying here, doing nothing," Pang was saying. "What is he up to anyway?"

"I've been wondering about that myself," said Old You in his raspy voice.

"I've seen enough people in my line of business," Pang said. "The girl calls him Uncle, not Daddy. Could he be a kidnapper, waiting for a buyer for the child? Anything's possible these days. You never know."

They then moved on to other topics. Moses had to stop himself from storming in to raise hell. How was he going to explain the convoluted details and the reason behind his stay with the girl? What was the point of trying? They would spend their ten days before leaving, and he did not want to take idle talk seriously. Being mistaken for a kidnapper bothered him, though he found it funny as well. With a sigh, he went back to the room.

On days when the inn was empty Moses would sit under the locust tree, lost in thought. Qiaoling would sometimes go out alone.

"Where are you going?" Moses would call out. "You'll get lost."

"I'm just going to watch Old You sell rat poison at the bus depot."

The depot was nearby, and Moses was pleased to see the girl getting a little adventuresome. She had been timid about going outside at first, but now she was comfortable enough to leave on her own.

"All right. Go ahead."

She was not daring enough to go too far without Moses and usually spent only a few minutes outside the inn.

Time flew, and they had been there nine days. They would return to Yanjin on the tenth day. During their time in Xinxiang, Moses had put the fake search for Wu Xiangxiang out of his mind. Now that he would be going home the next day, he began to worry about what sort of lie he would spin for Old Wu, Wu's wife, Old Jiang, and anyone else who might ask about Gao and Xiangxiang, people such as Old Zhao the cobbler, Old Feng the harelip, Old Yu the coffin shop owner, and so on. How would he make his lie airtight? He had come only as far as Xinxiang, but planned to tell people in Yanjin that they'd gone to Ji County, Kaifeng, Zhengzhou, Anyang, and Luoyang. He had to make sure not to give himself away, especially with his lack of a smooth tongue, if someone asked about the streets and lanes in these cities. He did not want to become a victim of his own cleverness. He wished he could be as glib as Old You.

He would have to think about reopening the bun shop if his lie succeeded and the incident blew over. Wu Xiangxiang had run off with the profits from the shop, and he and the girl had spent quite a bit of money during their stay in Xinxiang. There probably would not be enough left to restart the business right away. He would like to ask Old Bai to put the flour on credit, but he never let anyone do that, so Moses would have to borrow from someone. But who? He could think of no one. If he could not get the shop business going again, his plan to get himself a Li Xiangxiang would fail.

Then his thoughts turned to the Jiang brothers' plan to destroy Old Gao's jewelry shop. He wondered if they had carried out their threat. If they had, what would it mean for him? He had thought that everything would be fine once he ended the fake search, but now it didn't seem that simple. He wondered where the rotten pair had gotten to in the two weeks since they'd run off. Beset by these uncertainties, he lay awake until midnight, when he got up to pack. The first thing he saw when he opened the bundle was Zhan's drawing. He had intended to study the sketch during his time away, but had forgotten all about it over the past nine days. He lay back down after finishing packing, but still could not sleep, while the girl and Old You were snoring away beside him. He got up, draped a jacket over his shoulders, and walked into the yard to stand under the tree for a moment. He left the inn, which was in the Dongguan eastern suburb, where the streets nearby were pitch black. The city, however, was lit up. Moses followed the road to the city, where he hoped to find a place with enough activity to serve as a distraction. Besides, he had only come as far as Xinxiang on his fake search and had spent most of his time in the inn, with no real sense of the city. So he thought he would take this opportunity to look around before going back. He would at least be able to tell people what Xinxiang was like if they asked. It would be a wasted trip if he couldn't even come up with reliable information about a single place.

He reached the city after what seemed like forever. The streets were lit up with electric lights, but there wasn't a single person in sight. Houses lined both sides of the street, but presented no clear picture of the city. So he walked on until he reached the western district of Xiguan and Xinxiang Station. It was past midnight, but the area was alive with crowds; the plaza was filled with stalls whose owners cried at the top of their lungs to draw customers for their tea, wontons, and spicy hot soup. After a brief stop, he walked onto an overpass, where he spotted a train from Beiping to Hankou entering the station. In his twenty-one years on earth, he had never seen a train before. At the time, China's trains ran on steam. Like an elongated dragon, the train whistled before blowing steam into the air, like the watery mist in his kitchen. It disappeared in the mist before stopping to disgorge passengers and take on new ones. Those people—where had they come from? And where were they going? Moses knew no one among all those passengers. He had family and friends, but was not close to most of them. Yet he felt an affinity with the sea of strangers who spoke a wide variety of dialects and wore anxious looks as they hurried aboard. They were all going somewhere to do something important to them, all but Moses Wu. He could not tell people what he was doing away from home—that he was conducting a fake search for a wife who had run off with another man. He felt an urge to get on the train and leave with these strangers, which would bring an end to his troubles. He'd go wherever they were going. But the train started moving. The crowd was gone in the blink of an eye and the platform was deserted. He felt like crying when he gazed at the big station clock; it was six in the morning. The eastern sky was lightening up as he turned to check; it was time to go back to the inn. He would go home with Qiaoling to Yanjin after breakfast. He left the train station and headed back to the inn.

It was light out when he got back. Qiaoling was not in the room; neither was Old You. Moses thought the girl must have been worried when she woke up to find Moses gone, and Old You could have taken her with him to sell rat poison. The bus depot would be the best place to find the girl, but Old You's spot was vacant when he got there. He asked an old man selling roasted chickens, only to be told that You had not shown up that day. The man actually asked Moses if You had fallen ill. Gripped by a sudden fear, Moses rushed back to the inn and went straight for the room. You's luggage and bundles were gone from their usual spot at the base of the wall, a clear sign to Moses that something had gone terribly wrong. He raced out to see Old Pang, who had just returned from his grocery shopping and had no idea what had happened. Panic-stricken, Moses cried out, bringing the cook out from the kitchen. The cook told Moses that he'd heard Qiaoling crying when he got up to make breakfast early that morning. She had been looking for Moses. Then the cook saw You take the girl by the hand and leave with her.

Moses was dumbstruck. Old You would not have taken his luggage if he'd gone with the girl to look for Moses. The missing luggage could only mean that he had kidnapped Qiaoling while Moses was away. Moses had thought Old You was joking that night when he said he would like to get rich; he had even said that Old You was too decent a man to do anything unsavory. In fact, beneath You's kind demeanor was an evil mind; he'd planned to get rich through the girl. Moses also recalled how the man had rarely contradicted him in their conversation; looking back now, he realized that someone who never disagrees with you usually harbors ill will toward you. There was another possibility, though. Old You might have mistaken him as a kidnapper, since Moses had been idle for nine days at the inn, and had outflanked him by kidnapping Qiaoling. The end result remained the same no matter what Old You had been thinking: Qiaoling was gone. Ignoring the innkeeper and his cook, Moses stormed out to look for them.

"None of you have paid up yet," the innkeeper shouted after Moses.

Too anxious to respond, he ran, passing the depot and looking down every street and lane. There was no sign of the man or the girl. So he went into the city, where, like a headless fly, he dashed here and there all morning until it occurred to him that his search in Xinxiang was pointless. Old You would not still be here after kidnapping Qiaoling, waiting for Moses to catch him. He was from Kaifeng, so that was where he would be going. Moses wondered how he had managed to trick the girl into going with him. Since she cried when she couldn't find Moses, Old You had lured her out of the inn by saying he would take her to find him. Then he'd probably told her that Moses had gone on to Kaifeng and that he would take her there. The shy five-year-old girl knew no one away from home but Old You, who had shared food with her, so she had to leave with him.

The more Moses thought about it, the more fearful he got; he ran back, not to the inn but to the depot to take the next bus to Kaifeng. When he got there, he learned that the buses for Kaifeng had already left and that all the afternoon buses were going to Anyang, Luoyang, or Zhengzhou. No more buses were going to Kaifeng that day. He turned and began running toward the distant city, which was 210 li away. He covered 120 li that afternoon. It was dark by the time he reached the Yellow River, and the ferryman had gone home for the day, leaving him no choice but to sit by the river and wait for daybreak. He had not been troubled by worries when he was on the road, but now, after sitting down to catch his breath, they flooded his mind. The girl had been with him the day before and now she was gone. It was his fault. Why had he decided to go for a walk in the middle of the night? Why had he needed something to distract him? Now see what had happened! Old troubles had been replaced by a new one. Compared with the disappearance of the girl, his old troubles amounted to nothing.

He abruptly recalled that in his hurry to go after Old You and the girl, he'd left his luggage at Old Pang's inn; but he couldn't turn back to get it now. Luckily, he'd had the foresight to sew his money inside his jacket. With these thoughts swirling in his head, he fell into an exhausted sleep. He dreamed about the girl. She was still around; Old You was just playing a prank on him. They were still at the inn, where Qiaoling was eating a piece of a flatcake. Moses walked up, snatched it out of her hand, and slapped her.

"You like that, don't you? Don't you know you'll be lost once you eat it?"

"Uncle." The girl started to cry.

His eyes snapped open. The sound in his ears was the rushing river, not the girl's weeping. Moses looked up to see the night sky studded with stars winking at him and bringing back memories, as he reflected on what he had experienced over the years, from making tofu, to slaughtering pigs, to refilling water tanks at the dye shop, to following the Lord and splitting bamboo, to delivering water on the street, to tending a vegetable garden at the county office, to marrying Wu Xiangxiang, and finally to Xiangxiang's affair with Gao. Every stage was filled with hardships, but all the hardships together paled in comparison with the disappearance of Qiaoling. A few years earlier, he had not understood most of what Zhan had said when the priest conducted his Bible study; the Lord had seemed unfathomably profound, impossible to predict, like playing chess with a master. He heaved a long sigh at the sky.

"What kind of chess move is this, God?" He began to cry.

Moses boarded the first ferry the next morning and crossed the Yellow River, where he took a bus to Kaifeng, arriving at noon. He had thought of going to the city to find work back when he had been at the end of his rope. Then he had run into an old schoolmate, Old Song, who had helped him find employment at Old Jiang's dye shop. He could never have imagined that barely three years later he would end up in Kaifeng, and not to get a job, but to look for a missing child.

New to the city, Moses had to rely on the anecdotal stories Old You had told him back at the inn; he went to all the places the man had mentioned: Xiangguo Temple, the Dragon Pavilion, Pan and Yang Lakes, Millennium Park, the horse market, and so on. He managed to make a round of all the places in one afternoon, but Old You and Qiaoling were nowhere to be found. When it turned dark, he began his search again at the night market. Shops were lit up along the major thoroughfare outside Xiangguo Temple, while small stands crammed both sides of the street, where soupy buns, pan-fried buns, hot and spicy soup, candied pears, wontons, and pig intestine soup were sold. The street was ablaze with carbide lamps at each stand. Moses went from stand to stand, searching carefully until the shops closed and the concessionaires had gone home, leaving nothing but a trash-littered street. A gust of wind sent waste paper fluttering into the air; the once-bustling area now looked utterly desolate. He was back to where he'd started, after searching from noon to late at night. He had spotted a few girls who looked like Qiaoling from behind, but all he received when he rushed up to turn the girls around were angry protests from parents. Hope was dwindling as it got later and the traffic on the street turned sparse. He had sat down on the steps outside a temple when hunger pangs reminded him that he had not eaten or drunk anything since beginning his frantic search for the girl. Wiping his eyes, he looked around; all the diners had closed, except for one at a street corner with its light still on. Moses dragged himself over to Old Tang's Stewed Noodles. The owner, a frightful-looking old man, was listening to a radio he was holding up to his ear. He had probably been too engrossed in the program to remember to shut the door, since his workers were gone. When he saw Moses come in, he said, "The fire at the stove is banked. I've got nothing for you."

"I know this is a lot of trouble, but please, Grandpa, I haven't eaten in two days. I won't make it through the night if I don't get something to eat."

The old man seemed surprised and, after a look at Moses, said, "I do have a bowl of leftover noodles, untouched by a diner. Would that work if I warmed it up for you?"

"Just what I needed, the hotter the better." Moses nodded.

Putting down the radio, the old man poked the embers in the stove to start the fire again before putting on a large ladle and adding water. He took a bowl of noodles out of a cupboard and poured the contents into the boiling water. Clearly made toward closing, the bowl had contained mostly leftovers. When the water came to a second boil, the old man thumped the bottom of a bamboo basket to empty bits of remaining mutton into the ladle, following up with soy sauce, vinegar, and salt. He scooped the noodles into a tureen, and when he saw there were too many noodles for a small bowl, he added some meaty broth and vegetables, doubling the contents to fill a regular-sized bowl.

With a grateful nod, Moses dug in and quickly finished everything, which, thanks to his hunger, was one of the best meals ever, and his first since the girl's disappearance. He was reminded of the noodles that had been their favorite back at the inn. Now with the girl gone, he ate the equivalent of two bowls, and was so mad at himself he slapped his own face before tears began to fall into the empty bowl. Alerted by the slap, the old man put down his radio and sat across from Moses.

"You've got something on your mind? You look grief-stricken."

The old man was the first person Moses could talk to openly in ten days, so he dried his tears and told him everything, except for the search for his wife. After hearing the twists and turns of his story, the old man said with a sigh, "You can never tell what people are thinking." He was obviously referring to Old You. "But Kaifeng is a big city, and it would be like finding a needle in the ocean. How are you going to do it?" He paused before treading gently: "In this case, it isn't just a search."

"What is it then?" Moses asked.

"It's a human life."

It had come to the point where the girl's life was at stake.

"We can only hope that he hasn't kidnapped her for profit. Maybe he wants a girl at home," the old man said.

Moses had to keep looking, no matter what. So he started anew the next morning and searched for five more days, walking down every street and lane. Kaifeng had been an unfamiliar place to him, but after five days he knew it as well as a tour guide. At some point he realized that he might be looking in the wrong place. Old You would have recalled telling Moses that he was from Kaifeng, so he would not have returned here, for fear that Moses would find them. It was precisely because he had kidnapped Qiaoling that he could not possibly come back here. He had to have gone somewhere else. Moses left Kaifeng and headed for Zhengzhou, where he spent five days before moving on to Xin-xiang. After five days of fruitless searching in Xinxiang, he had still failed to find Qiaoling, though he had made a trip back to the inn to retrieve his luggage. He left Xinxiang for Ji County, and from there to Anyang and Luoyang, looking over all the possible places they might have gone.

That went on for three months. He had used up all his money by the time he left Kaifeng, so he resumed his old occupations of delivering water and transporting goods for warehouses in every new place he visited. He would start his search again once he earned enough to get by. He had planned a fake search for Xiangxiang and Gao in Xinxiang several months before, intending to lie about looking in Ji County, Kaifeng, Zhengzhou, Luoyang, and Anyang. It came as a surprise to him that he had actually traveled to all these places in search of the girl. After failing to find Qiaoling in three months, he knew he could not return to Yanjin. He and Qiaoling were close, but he was only her stepfather; her true families were Old Wu and his wife in Wu Village and Old Jiang, his wife, and the two brothers at the cotton shop. They had never been close to the girl, and yet they would not likely let him off the hook when they learned of her disappearance. They would surely break his legs if they chose to spare his life.

Once again, feeling he had no place to go, Moses traveled aimlessly from Luoyang to Zhengzhou, where he found a porter's job at the train station. It was steady work and, with so many people coming and going, he could continue looking for the girl during breaks. Deep down he knew that Old You could have taken the girl far away and that his search was hopeless, but still he made a daily round of the plaza and the station waiting room when he wasn't needed as a porter. Now it was more to appease his conscience than to actually be reunited with Qiaoling.

Moses bought padded clothes when winter came. When he put them on, he saw how much weight he'd lost. One day he looked at himself in a bathroom mirror after searching the station waiting room. The large eyes staring back at him were sunken under a protruding brow line. He was shocked.

He spent more than two months at the Zhengzhou train station, including New Year's Day. He finished work as a porter at ten that night. Normally, the warehouse let him and others off at eight, but the station had added two cargo cars to a passenger train to Guangzhou in order to transport an urgent shipment of cotton yarn to Hankou. So the porters worked until ten that night, after which the others asked Moses to go for a drink with them. He smiled but did not go along; instead, he made his habitual rounds of the train station, a formulaic stroll by this time. He felt uneasy and could not sleep well if he did not do that each night. As he walked around, looking to his right and left, a woman's voice caught his attention.

"Come wash your face. Hot water here."

It sounded familiar, but he didn't pay much attention at first. The plaza was jammed with food stands, as well as stalls offering passengers hot water to wash their faces. On the steps outside the exit was a row of washbasins, each with a towel placed over the rim, next to a steel kettle wrapped in cotton padding. Water boiled inside the kettle. Behind each basin, a woman shouted: "Come wash your face. Hot water here."

Some of the passengers leaving the station crouched down to wash their faces to refresh their appearances and their spirits. It cost five fen to tidy up. Moses thought he must have misheard, so he ignored the shout amid the sounds from all the women and continued walking on. Then he spun around, and was dumbfounded by what he saw; one of the women behind the washbasins was none other than Wu Xiangxiang. To be sure, she no longer looked like the Wu Xiangxiang of six months before; she was thinner and her skin was darker with a hint of red from the harsh wind. She was haggard, her movements clumsy. Moses inched forward for a closer look before realizing that she was pregnant. He had been roaming the Zhengzhou train station all this time, but had failed to notice her selling water, which led him to believe that she must have drifted into Zhengzhou only recently. Looking around him, Moses spotted a man squatting at a corner shining shoes. It was Old Gao, the silversmith and owner of Qiwen Hall. His face covered in stubble, Gao was also much thinner.

In his search for Qiaoling over the past six months, Moses had completely forgotten about the adulterous pair. He would not have stayed near the Zhengzhou station if it hadn't been to look for the girl, and he could not have foreseen that, instead of finding the girl, he would run into them. He had to laugh over the strange combination of circumstances that had brought all three of them here, but the flames of anger were immediately rekindled. He would not have fallen into this state if it hadn't been for them. If not for their affair, he would not have had to go looking for them and in turn lose the girl, making it impossible for him to ever go home. He had hated only Old You for the girl's disappearance, but now he realized that the couple was so much more despicable.

Without a word to either of them, Moses turned and went back to the warehouse before emerging with Jiang Hu's knife. It had been a fake search when he left Yanjin with the girl, so the idea of killing them had never crossed his mind. The knife had been just for show. Now, in light of this chance encounter, with the girl gone and himself homeless, he knew he was no longer afraid of killing them. They were responsible for all that had happened to him recently. After killing them, he would run if he could; if not, and if he was arrested, he would willingly pay with his life. Three deaths would bring everything to an end.

A new throng of passengers was rushing out of the station when he returned; the noisy crowd around him posed a problem to his plan. Besides, one was selling water at the exit while the other one was shining shoes at a corner, which meant that one of them could get away when he managed to plunge the knife into the other. He had to take both of them down to purge the hatred in his heart. With that in mind, he went to wait by the bell tower. Sitting on his haunches, he could not stop thinking about them. Where had they been these past six months? Why had they ended up in Zhengzhou? They must have a place to stay. Once the crowd thinned out, he'd follow them to where they lived, or he'd wait until they were in a deserted spot. He'd let them live a few more hours, but a year from today would be the first anniversary of two deaths, or three, if he had to pay with his own life.

He waited two more hours, until midnight; only cargo trains came into the station—no more passenger trains. Except for the horns of cargo trains, it was quiet now, with so few people in the plaza. Gao had no more customers, Moses noticed, and he was putting his box over his shoulder before walking over to Xiangxiang by the exit. Moses got to his feet and felt the knife in his pocket. All the washbasins by the exit were gone, except for the one in front of Xiangxiang, who continued to wait for passengers. Gao walked up to her to say something, most likely to get her to pack up; she responded by pointing to the station. He put down his box to squat next to her, obviously waiting for the next train-load of passengers; that told Moses that they were unfamiliar with the train schedule. There would be no more passengers that night, and they needn't wait any longer. Moses saw Gao point into the distance and say something to her. Xiangxiang got to her feet and waddled over; it was a stand selling baked sweet potatoes. She said something to the old man at the stand, probably bargaining for a lower price, before handing him money for a sweet potato. It must have been hot out of the oven, for she was passing it back and forth between hands as she bit into it. She held it out for Gao when she got back to him; they snuggled up against each other as they ate. Still holding the potato in her hand, she fed him a piece at a time. He said something to her; she laughed and gave him a gentle slap before doubling over and spitting out the potato in her mouth.

A loud clap went off in Moses's head when he saw how the couple was enjoying the sweet potato, but not because he was furious over their intimacy. In all

220

the months he had lived with her, she had never shown any sign of intimacy like that. He'd thought it was because they simply did not get along, or that he was not a smooth talker, or that in her eyes he was worthless. Now he knew that those were not the issues; what made the difference was the man she was with. Back when they were married, they'd not had to worry about money from their small business selling steamed buns. Yet she complained about him all the time and berated him whenever she got a chance. With Gao, she obviously had to endure the hardships of a vagabond life, reduced to selling water and polishing shoes. But she didn't seem to complain or berate Gao; on the contrary, she followed his instruction to buy a potato and fed him as she ate. She had become a different person. Or, more accurately, she had a different man with her. She was childless after a year with Moses, but now she was pregnant after only six months with Gao. Killing him would not solve his problem, for it would not bring her closer to Moses or make her feel less attached to Gao.

Moses turned and went back to the warehouse. Before she committed adultery, the man must have said something to sway her. What exactly was it? Moses was unhappy that he could not figure that out, not then, and not until the day he died.

He packed up and left Zhengzhou the following morning, though not to avoid Xiangxiang and Gao; or maybe that was the reason. He had left home to look for them, and yet he wanted to avoid them now that he had found them. There was no reason for him to leave, even if he did not want to run into them again. Zhengzhou was a big city; he could let them have the train station and find another street corner to make a living. It was simple; Zhengzhou had become a site of sorrow. He felt bad when he thought of all the cities he had been to and lived in, not Zhengzhou alone—Yang Village, his birthplace, Yanjin county town, where he had spent a great deal of time, and several other places, such as Xinxiang, Kaifeng, Ji County, Luoyang, and Anyang. Every one of them made him sad.

Having given up on finding Qiaoling, he had to leave this sad place. He was reminded of something Old Zhan had said: Abraham left his land, his relatives, and his father's home, and went to a land that God showed him. But Moses was not Abraham; he would have no place to go when he left his land, his relatives, his father's home, and the places that made him sad. No one was there to show him the Promised Land. Once again, Moses Wu felt pangs of sorrow for being unable to go home, when he recalled Old Wang, his teacher at the private school. He decided he would go to Baoji to see Wang. For one thing, sorrow had also driven Wang out of Yanjin years before, even though

Wang's circumstance had been quite different. Wang had left Yanjin because of the death of his daughter, Dengzhan, which had puzzled Moses, until he himself lost Qiaoling. They had both lost a child, and though one had died and the other had been kidnapped, their feelings ought to be similar. Moses recalled how Wang had kept going until Baoji, the place where his heartache stopped. Everyone Moses knew was connected to matters that troubled or upset him, but not Wang, who had nothing to do with Moses's current life. He would not have to explain himself when he saw Wang. His mind made up, he went to the train station and bought a ticket for Baoji, where he would have a place to stay with someone he knew, leaving this sad place and cutting all ties with his past.

The New Year's holiday was over, but the train he was on was packed with travelers. Zhengzhou was a stop on the Beiping-Lanzhou line, so the crowded cars offered little space to stand, let alone sit. It would take two days and two nights to go from Zhengzhou to Baoji. With his bundle on his back, Moses pushed his way through the crowd, asking the seated passengers one by one where they would get off; he would stand by someone ready to get off and wait for the seat. After going through three cars, he had asked people who were going to Tongguan, Xi'an, Baoji, Tianshui, or worse, all the way to Lanzhou. He could not tell if they were indeed traveling that far or if they lied to him because they didn't want a stranger standing next to them. Finally, in the fourth car, he came upon a middle-aged man with a small, pear-like head who was gnawing on a piece of roasted chicken. Too absorbed in his food to think much when asked, the man tossed out a city, Lingbao, which was not his true destination. But Moses did not know that; all he could think of was he only had to wait a day for a seat, because Lingbao was still in Henan.

"I'll take your seat once you get off, Older Brother. Please don't give it to anyone else."

That caught the man's attention; he looked up at Moses and nodded reluctantly, knowing he could not change his destination now. Moses moved to stand next to the man, who turned out to be the talkative type. Probably also to get as much out of Moses as possible for the promised seat, the man asked with his mouth full, "Where are you from?"

Knowing he had to answer all the questions in order to keep the seat, Moses replied, "Yanjin."

He had second thoughts at once, since he'd been away from Yanjin for six months.

"Yanjin isn't on the rail line. So where are you going?"

"Baoji," Moses said. That was true.

"What are you going to do there?"

"See a relative."

As the "interrogation" proceeded, Moses recalled Old Zhan. That was precisely what the priest had said back then when he tried to convert the people in Yanjin. Once he found the Lord, Zhan had told him, he would know where he came from and where he was going. Moses had followed the Lord in order to get a job, and later abandoned his faith. It did not matter whether he believed or not; he had yet to solve the biggest problem in his life—where he was going. Funny that a total stranger on the train would ask him the same questions.

"What's your name?" The man did not let up.

That question nearly paralyzed Moses, who could not come up with an answer the way he had when the man had asked him where he came from and where he was going. Over the past six months, when he was wandering and searching, he met only strangers, and none of them had asked his name. He did not know what to say. He had gone through three name changes in his short twenty-one years of existence, from Yang Baishun to Moses Yang and then to Moses Wu. He was too flustered to know what to say. The man tore his face away from the roasted chicken and said impatiently to a seemingly dumbfounded Moses, "I asked your name. Is that such a tough question? Or are you a murderer on the run?"

"Ai!" Moses sighed. He had never killed anyone, that was for sure, but he had indeed committed several murders in his head—his father, his brother, Old Ma the carter, his wife, and Old Gao the silversmith. He was opening his mouth to explain when the train entered a tunnel after a blast of its horn, reminding him of Luo Changli, the funeral crier. Luo, who had sounded as grand as a train whistle at funerals, had been Moses's idol. It had been only seven or eight years since Moses had gone to watch him, but it now felt like half a lifetime ago. A few years back, he had thought about Luo every once in a while, but he'd slowly put him out of his mind, since so much was happening in his life and he had so many people to deal with. When he gave it more thought, Moses realized that Luo Changli was the main reason he was here on this train. He would have been home making tofu alongside his father if he hadn't had a preference for the "illusory" over the "concrete." Oddly enough, he had yet to exchange a single word with Luo. His emotions got the better of him and he did not feel like giving the man an explanation. Instead, he said, "I've never killed anyone, Older Brother. And you can call me Luo Changli."

PART II

———————

RETURNING TO YANJIN

1

When he turned thirty-five, Niu Aiguo knew that there were only three people he could count on if he ran into trouble. They were Feng Wenxiu, Du Qing-hai, and Chen Kuiyi. He could rely on them not because they would lend him money or help him out of a jam. Nothing of the sort. He simply liked the fact that he could run something by them when he could not get over or understand something or make up his mind about what to do. If he was beset by worries, he could go see them and feel he had shed a burden once he told them what was bothering him. If the worries were too vague or boundless to explain well, he would say nothing, and they would merely sit awhile, perhaps talking about something inconsequential until his mood lightened.

Feng Wenxiu and Niu Aiguo were elementary and middle school classmates. They should not have become good friends, because their fathers did not get along and refused to talk to each other. Aiguo's father, Niu Shudao, and Wenxiu's father, Feng Shilun, had once been close friends, which was why they traveled together before each new year to Changzhi to buy coal, not to sell, but to heat their houses. It took four days to make the round trip between Qinyuan and Changzhi. Being small in stature, Shudao could only pull two thousand catties, while the hulky Shilun could transport twenty-five hundred catties. The eastern side of Shanxi was lower than the western part. The cart was empty when they left, and the downhill trek made it possible for them to talk along the way. The return trip, however, was uphill, so they hunkered down and pulled hard to move the loaded carts, leaving them no chance to chat. When they stopped at a roadside diner for lunch or spent a night at an inn, they soaked hardtack they'd packed for the trip in a bowl of hot mutton soup, and would be bathed in sweat when they finished. The Niu family preferred steamed bread, while the Feng family liked fried flatbreads, so they shared their food. They were such good company, with lots to talk about, that the four-day journey never felt tiresome. Niu Shudao was two years older than Feng Shilun. When they met up in early winter, Shudao would usually say, "Let's go buy some coal again this year. What do you say, Younger Brother?"

"This year for sure, and next year, too, Older Brother."

So they set out again this year. As usual, they talked along the way out and silently pulled their carts on the way back, stopping for lunch and putting up at an inn at night. As they got on the road on the third day, wind gusts kicked up so much yellow sand they could hardly open their eyes. Luckily it was a tailwind, so they used bed sheets as makeshift sails, making it possible to travel ten li, not the usual five, in the time it took them to eat a meal. An adverse situation was turned into a boon. By early afternoon they were only eighty li from home, and Shudao got ambitious.

"Let's skip the inn tonight, Younger Brother. We can travel through the night and go all the way home."

"Great idea. We'll eat when we get home." Shilun was energized by the challenge.

After eating what they'd brought with them, they got on the road again. They were only fifty li away, night had fallen, and the axle on Shudao's cart snapped. Now they had to stop, but they were in the middle of nowhere. After propping the cart up with some wood, they sat down to wait for daybreak, when one of them would stay while the other one went into the nearest town to buy a new axle.

"It's a good thing there are two of us. If it was just one of us, there'd be nothing to stop people interested in stealing the load," Shudao said.

"I'm hungry, Older Brother, but I'm out of rations," Shilun said. "How about you?"

Shudao checked his sack. "I'm out, too."

It was only early winter, but the night was chilly, especially when the wind picked up. They'd known enough to bring blankets along, so they curled up to sleep after smoking a cigarette behind their carts away from the wind. Awakened by the chill around daybreak, Shilun got up to relieve himself and found, to his great surprise, Shudao secretly eating a piece of flatbread behind his own cart. Obviously, he'd still had food left but had lied about it, not wanting to share. By the time Shilun lay back down after relieving himself, he was stewing. He thought to himself: I stayed behind in the cold with you because your axle broke. Why didn't you share your food? It's not that I'm that hungry; it's just not something you do to a friend.

Shilun got up and pushed his cart off after Shudao went back to sleep. Shudao got up the following morning and saw that Shilun had gone on without him; he knew it was because of the hardtack. But he was still angry. He really hadn't had anything left in his sack when Shilun asked him about food; the last piece had rolled out of someplace when he was making his bed. He had no idea how or when it got there, but he knew he couldn't mention it, so he ate it without telling Shilun. That little bit of food was no reason to abandon a friend on the road, and the hardtack turned them into enemies who never spoke again.

It seemed ordained that the sons of bitter enemies should not be friends. In fact, they did not speak before they turned eleven, even though they were in the same class. They shared the hobby of raising rabbits, something both their fathers would not allow at home. Raising rabbits eventually brought Niu Aiguo and Feng Wenxiu together. Since they were not allowed to keep rabbits at home, they hid a pair of them in a disused brick kiln at the back of the village. One was male with dark fur, the other a female with white fur. Within six months they had produced nine bunnies with mottled fur. Every day after school the boys brought fresh grass to feed the rabbits, a task they enjoyed but must do behind their parents' backs. They even went so far as to avoid each other at school and to gather grass separately; they were only close when they met up to feed the rabbits. We recall that the Niu family preferred steamed bread and stuffed buns, while the Fengs preferred fried flatbreads. Naturally, Aiguo brought some buns for Wenxiu once in a while, and Wenxiu shared some of his flatbreads.

On the evening of the seventh day of the eighth lunar month, they each brought a basket of grass over to the kiln, only to find all eleven of the rabbits gone. They had either been eaten by weasels or dragged away by other predators, leaving a bloody, furry mess on the ground. The weasels must have wormed their way in because Wenxiu had left two bricks out of the opening the night before. Aiguo had said to close the opening completely, but Wenxiu had thought it would be all right to give the rabbits some fresh air. Aiguo did not blame his friend. They held their heads in their hands and wept.

There was a boy in their class named Li Kezhi, a gossip who spoke with a lisp. He was five feet eight at the age of eleven, a beefy boy no one would dare cross. His father worked in a coal mine in Changzhi, and Kezhi sometimes wore a headlamp to school to shine in the other boys' eyes. One gossipmonger in a class of fifty-six students was enough to wreak havoc. In the tenth month, Kezhi picked Niu Aiguo as the fodder for his rumor mill, though it was actually about Aiguo's older sister, Niu Aixiang, who sold soy sauce in the town co-op. Aixiang had been dating a mail carrier, Little Zhang, for two years. Zhang, who had a square face and a fair complexion, was not the talkative type; he normally just listened when he was with friends. But he laughed a lot, whether someone said something funny or not. He had visited the Niu house, riding over on his green postal bicycle, with Aixiang on the back, her arms wrapped around his waist. Once Zhang gave Aiguo a lighter, which he brought out to show his friend when they fed the rabbits. Aixiang had broken up with Zhang the month before, though not because they no longer liked one another. It turned out that, while going out with Aixiang, Zhang was also seeing a radio announcer, Xiaohong, at the county radio station. It was bad enough that he turned out to be a two-timer, but what really outraged Aixiang was her failure to detect his escapade during those two years. She actually blamed herself, not him, when she found out. He had seemed trustworthy because he didn't talk much and laughed a lot, and she was surprised to learn that a man like that could be so wicked deep down. So she broke up with him. That in itself was no big deal, and yet Li Kezhi spun it into the salacious tale that Aiguo's sister had slept with Zhang and had to have an abortion at the county hospital after he got her pregnant. After being ditched by Zhang, she tried to kill herself by drinking pesticide and was taken to the hospital again, where they managed to save her life. Niu Aiguo would not have minded if Kezhi had spread rumors about him or any other member of his family; just not his sister, whom he adored.

Niu Aiguo also had an older brother, Aijiang, and a younger brother, Aihe. As far back as he could remember, Aiguo knew that their father favored Aijiang, while their mother, Cao Qing'e, preferred Aihe. Aiguo himself was not their favorite. Wanting to be someone's favorite did not mean he craved more to eat or better clothes; rather, he wanted someone to speak up for him when he was picked on or to talk to when he was unhappy. Since neither parent favored him, he had no one to lean on or talk to except his sister, who was eight years older and protected him when she could. He had pretty much grown up around her.

On this day, Kezhi was spreading his rumor about Aixiang again on the athletic field. Aiguo pounced on him when he brought up the purported abortion and rammed the bigger boy to the ground. At eleven, Aiguo was half a foot shorter than Kezhi, who got to his feet, pushed Aiguo down on the ground, and slapped him a few times before taking off his pants to rub his buttocks against Aiguo's face. It must have felt awfully good, for he kept at it more than thirty times. Kezhi then turned on his headlamp. Aiguo began to cry when he could not struggle his way out of the boy's grip.

Suddenly there was a loud bang, and Kezhi slumped to the ground, having been hit in the head. The lamp was smashed and blood ran down the boy's face, while his pants were still bunched up around his knees. Wenxiu was panting, holding a yoke in his hand. Aiguo and Wenxiu ran out of the schoolyard, since they thought that Kezhi, his head covered in blood and his eyes wide open, was dead. Not daring to go home, they fled to the county town, where they hid for three days, scrounging for leftovers at diners or eating sugarcane they found in sewer drains during the day, and at night they crawled through a window at the county cotton collecting station warehouse to sleep on bags of cotton. Wenxiu's father grabbed him while they were walking down a street looking into shops on the third day. Li Kezhi did not die, after all. The Niu and Feng families each paid the Li family two hundred yuan. Aiguo and Wenxiu were beaten by their fathers when they returned home, but not because of the fight or because their parents had to pay. The fathers were upset because the boys should not have been friends. Wenxiu got the worst beating, for coming to the aid of his enemy's son.

The two boys graduated from high school when Aiguo was eighteen and Wenxiu was nineteen, but neither managed to get into college. Instead of going home to work at his father's sesame oil mill, Aiguo left to become a soldier, a choice he made after talking things over with his sister in town. She was still working at the co-op, but now selling sundry goods, not soy sauce. By then she was twenty-seven, still unmarried. She had remained single not because her heart was forever broken by the mail carrier; she had actually dated more than a dozen men, but had found none she could talk to. Contrary to Kezhi's rumor, she did not drink pesticide when she broke up with Little Zhang, but she did when it didn't work out with the ninth man she dated. She was taken to the hospital, where they pumped her stomach; she left the hospital alive, though her head rested on her shoulder and she belched frequently. An animated, fun-loving girl in her twenties, Aixiang had had long, thick braids that swung as she walked. By the time her brother Aiguo had graduated from high school, she had permed hair, which now looked more like a bird's nest, and she became so ill-tempered she flew into a rage at the slightest provocation. She was never upset to see Aiguo, though. Installing himself among the pots and pans, he told her his plan of joining the army.

"Where will you be?" she asked after a belch.

"Jiuquan, in Gansu."

"That's thousands of li from home," she said. "I know why you want to join the army. It isn't to become soldier; it's just that our family gets on your nerves. No, it isn't the family; it's our parents who annoy you. I felt the same about them when I was younger, because they only care for our brothers. But when you're older you'll know they are your parents, no matter what."

Aiguo did not respond. Aixiang belched again before adding, "You'll realize that they're the only parents we have. It wouldn't matter so much that they favor other children in the family if they would only stand up for us when we're in trouble. Even that doesn't bother me that much, actually. It's just that without their guidance, we don't know what to do or what's best for us." Her eyes grew moist.

"I want to be a soldier, but not because of them, Sis."

"What then?"

"They're recruiting soldiers to drive trucks. I want to learn how to drive."

"What good would that do you?"

"Once I know how to drive, I'll give you a ride to Beijing."

She laughed with her head cocked from her weak neck. Then she started to cry, as she took a watch from her wrist and slipped it on his.

Feng Wenxiu still did not know what to do when Aiguo made up his mind. So Aiguo tried to work on his friend.

"Come join the army with me. We'll drive together once we know how."

Wenxiu was color-blind, making him ineligible for the army, though even if he hadn't been, his father would not have agreed to let him, the only son, be so far away.

"It's not always bad when you're not your parents' favorite," Wenxiu said with a sigh. "And it's not always good when your parents care too much about you."

More than five hundred young men from Qinyuan joined the army that year. On the day they left town, they paraded in neat formation. It happened to occur on the day of the Lantern Festival; performers from the New Year's festival banged drums and gongs as they filed down the streets alongside the marching new recruits. Crowds thronged both sides of the streets, either to watch the performance troupe or to see the soldiers off. Dressed in identical uniforms, more than five hundred young men strode along to the command of "One-two, one-two," all in all, a spectacular sight. Niu Aiguo in his new army uniform had yet to learn how to march, and at some point, he found himself out of step. Flustered, he was trying to catch up when someone grabbed him from behind. He turned, and there was his best friend, Wenxiu. Aiguo looked at his own uniform and then at Wenxiu in his civilian clothes, and suddenly realized that they would not see each other for a long time.

"I'll write you when I get there."

"That's not why I came." Wenxiu was panting, his head bathed in sweat.

"Then what is it?"

"I've been waiting for you for some time. I want us to have our picture taken."

Aiguo looked up to see that they were just passing Old Jiang's Human Harmony Photo Studio on West Street. Impressed by his friend's careful planning, he asked the platoon leader for a short break. The leader looked at his wristwatch.

"Make it quick," he said. "You have five minutes. We have to board the trucks when we reach North Street."

Aiguo took his friend by the hand and ran into the photo studio. Wenxiu grabbed Aiguo's hand so tightly their palms were sweating when they had their picture taken together.

"We'll be best friends wherever you go."

Aiguo nodded and gave his friend's hand a tight squeeze. They walked out and ran to North Street, where the recruits were piling onto trucks. Wenxiu waved and ran alongside Aiguo's truck for a long time. Aiguo was taken to Huozhou, where they boarded a train, reaching Jiuquan in Gansu after three days of travel. He sat down to write Wenxiu a letter the moment he settled down. Two weeks later, Wenxiu's reply came, with the picture they had taken together—one in his new army uniform, the other in civilian clothes, neither of them smiling, eyes staring straight ahead.

Niu Aiguo spent five years as a soldier in Jiuquan. He and Feng Wenxiu kept up their correspondence for the first two years, after which the letters began coming less frequently. When Aiguo was discharged, Wenxiu, now a pork vendor on East Street, was married with two children. Aiguo rode a bike into town to see Wenxiu the day after he returned home. Nothing seemed to have come between them over the separation; they wrapped their arms around each other and related what had happened over the years. Wenxiu's wife came from a Ma family, the daughter of a meat shop manager on East Street. Wenxiu called her Old Ma, and Aiguo followed suit. A tall woman, she had large, bright eyes and a thick waist, which she blamed on childbirth, saying that her waist had been tiny enough to circle with two hands before she was married.

"He ruined my waist." She gave Wenxiu a pouting look before turning to Aiguo. "I regret marrying this bastard."

Wenxiu smiled without saying a word, the deep lines on his face visible.

The two of them resumed their relationship. Aiguo rode his bicycle, later a motorcycle, into town to see Wenxiu whenever he needed someone to talk to about what was bothering him. Wenxiu would give him a careful analysis as they talked it over. The same went for Wenxiu, who would come to Niu Village to see Aiguo in an electric three-wheeler he used to transport pork. They would always feel better after these talks. But Wenxiu was no longer the same man of five years before. His clear eyes had turned cloudy, which was not a problem. The change was in his drinking habit; he invariably got drunk and would change into a different person. A reasonable man when sober, Wenxiu would even disown his parents when he had too much to drink, and he liked to make phone calls. Aiguo realized that he could not talk to Wenxiu as freely as before, for a drunken Wenxiu might let slip the contents of an intimate conversation. Aiguo began to dread Wenxiu's phone calls, fearful he might get drunk and would not stop talking.

Du Qinghai, from Pingshan in Hebei, was Niu Aiguo's army buddy. His nickname was Budai, or "Cloth Sack." Qingai often told people that his hometown was by the Hutuo River. They were ostensibly stationed in Jiuquan, but in fact the base was more than a thousand kilometers north of Jiuquan, in the middle of the desert. Being in different companies, they did not meet in the course of their first two years. During a field training exercise in their third year, a division of seven thousand soldiers marched through the Gobi and spent the night in Jiji, a market town in Gansu's Jinta County. The town was too small to accommodate so many people, so the men pitched tents on the outskirts. Aiguo, from the fifth company of the second battalion of the third regiment, stood sentry at night, as did Qinghai, from the tenth company of the seventh battalion of the eighth regiment. One patrolled from east to west and the other from south to north, and they met at the entrance to Jiji. After exchanging passwords, one of them borrowed a light for a cigarette. With rifles strapped across their backs, they smoked and chatted for a while. Despite the different places of origin, they discovered they had a lot to say to each other, and the more they talked the more they had to say.

After two years in the army, Aiguo had made no close friends among the hundred or so men in his company, even though they spent nearly every waking hour together. Now he had found a bosom buddy on a chance encounter with Qinghai. They talked until reveille sounded at the camps, waking the soldiers into a blood red morning glow. Later they would tell people they became friends over a smoke.

Aiguo had signed up for the transportation section but did not get to drive a truck. Instead, he was sent to the kitchen to be a cook, while Qinghai, the infantryman, got to drive the company's truck. Their companies were stationed some fifty li apart, separated by the Ruoshui River and Mount Dahong, a branch of the Qilian Mountains. After their first meeting, Aiguo waded across the river and climbed the hill to see Qinghai every Sunday. The kitchen at Aiguo's company had a specialty, meat rolls; as a cook, he was able to take some of the rolls over to Qinghai. Every time Aiguo arrived, Qinghai used the pretext of transporting goods from town to take the truck to the Gobi, where they drove around and savored the meat rolls. When they finished eating, Qinghai taught Aiguo how to drive. So Aiguo learned how to drive despite not being in the transportation section. Whenever Qinghai went out on official business, he made a detour to come see Aiguo, even if it wasn't a Sunday.

"Make sure no one in your company knows about this," Aiguo said once. "This isn't a Sunday."

"I drove fast, so I have plenty of time."

Qinghai was of average build, with dark, glossy skin; he spoke slowly in a soft voice and smiled shyly before he finished, flashing a mouthful of white teeth. Aiguo had never been very articulate. Sometimes he didn't know how to begin a conversation and would turn one thing into another if he started out wrong; or one matter became two, or vice versa. But Qinghai spoke at a measured pace, was logical and precise, and always finished talking about one thing before moving on to the next. Everything was in proper order and neatly explained. Whenever Aiguo was troubled by something too tangled for him to analyze, or when he could not decide what to do or how to do it, he would save it until the weekend. By Sunday he would usually have several things to talk over with Qinghai. They would either drive around the desert or sit by the river as Aiguo brought up everything on his mind for Qinghai to comb through, like picking meat off a bone. Qinghai would do the same when he needed someone to talk to, but Aiguo could never clarify things for his friend.

"What do *you* think?" was about all Aiguo could say.

So Qinghai had to work things out on his own. He would ask Aiguo again after he gave the matter some thought.

"What do *you* think?" Aiguo would offer the same response.

So Qinghai had to work things out, until several "what do you think?" responses helped him clear whatever it was up. They would both feel much better.

They were discharged three years after they met, each returning to his hometown. Aiguo's Qinyuan was over a thousand li from Qinghai's Pingshan. When something came up, Aiguo could no longer cross a river and climb a hill to see Qinghai, who, likewise, would no longer hear "What do you think?" So they wrote to each other or phoned sometimes, but it was not the same as talking face-to-face. The distant help was no use to them if they had to make a timely decision on an urgent matter.

Five more years went by, and Aiguo was married with children. From one of Qinghai's letters, he learned that his friend was also married with children. Aiguo's wife, Pang Lina, was also a high school graduate who had failed to make college. Aiguo had met her through her sister, Pang Liqin, who had once worked in the same sundry goods section at the co-op as Aiguo's sister. Aixiang was thirty-two, still single, when Aiguo returned from the army; it was she who introduced Lina to her brother. Liqin's husband, Old Shang, was the manager at the spinning mill on North Street, and Lina worked there as a spinner. She was short and stocky, but her lean face gave her a pretty, pleasant look. She was a quiet girl who had once fallen for a high school classmate. The man had ditched her after he got into college. Aiguo was hesitant when he learned about Lina's romantic history.

"You ought to take a piss and look at yourself in it," Aixiang griped about her brother. "Who do you think you are? A demobilized soldier." She wasn't done yet. "You would have ditched her if you had passed the college exam."

That made Aiguo smile and put aside Lina's failed romance. Neither Aiguo nor Lina was given to talking, which, in everyone's view, made them a perfect match. They felt the same, after dating for two months, so they were married six months later. Life went by peacefully during the first two years; they had a daughter they called Baihui. But rifts began to show in their relationship after two years. It was nothing obvious; they just had nothing to say to each other. At first they thought it was because neither was the talkative type, but they came to realize that being taciturn was not the same as having nothing to say. The former meant they had could have something on their minds; the latter simply meant there was nothing there. Outsiders failed to see the differences, and their peaceful life reinforced the impression that they were a good match. Only they themselves knew, deep down, that the gulf between their hearts was widening by the day. Niu Village was fifteen li from the county town, where the spinning mill was located. In the first two years of their marriage, she came home to him twice a week, later once a week. At some point she began coming home every other week, and eventually not even once a month. Baihui hid from her mother whenever she came home.

Aiguo, who had learned to drive in the army, pooled some money with his brothers to buy a secondhand Liberation truck. He was often away hauling goods home or hauling dirt for Changzhi's highway construction department. Sometimes he was away for weeks, and husband and wife did not get together even once in two months. Their nights together when they were home at the same time had nothing to recommend them. Worst of all, he did not miss her after being away for two months.

Finally, one day he heard a rumor about her having something going with Little Jiang, the manager at the photo studio on West Street. He was the son of Old Jiang, who had taken a picture of Niu Aiguo and Feng Wenxiu ten years earlier, before Aiguo had left for the army. Little Jiang took over and changed the name from Human Harmony Photography to East Asia Wedding Photo Studio. One day, Aiguo went to the spinning mill to see Lina when he returned from a trip, but could not find her in either the factory or the dorm, though she already had gotten off work. He went straight to the photo studio, where, though the window, he saw her sitting there talking to Little Jiang. A woman of few words when he was around, she was having an animated conversation with Jiang, who must have said something funny to make her laugh. It was impossible to determine, from the way they talked, if something was going on between them, but at least Aiguo was sure that she had more to say to the studio owner than to her own husband. She had obviously found Jiang to be a better conversation partner than Aiguo. So it all depended on whom she was with, not whether she was born a talker or not.

Instead of going in to disturb them, he walked away to the crumbling wall outside the city and sat until sunset. That evening, he went to the mill again, but she still was not there, so he headed to the photo studio, where Little Jiang was taking a client's photo, without Lina around. The last place to check was Liqin's house, where, before walking in, he heard the two sisters talking.

"You ought to stop fooling around with Little Jiang. He's married, too. Besides, the whole town knows by now, and you don't want Niu Aiguo to hear about it."

Aiguo expected Lina to deny any untoward relationship with Jiang, so he was surprised to hear her say, "So what if he hears about it?"

"What if he beats you?"

"I want him to die from fright."

"What do you think you could do to frighten him to death?"

"I don't need anything else." Lina doubled over from giggling. "I'll have him under my thumb if I refuse him at night."

That was all the proof Aiguo needed to believe that his wife was indeed having an affair with Little Jiang, which didn't anger him as much as the way she talked about it with her sister.

He went back to Niu Village, where he spent a sleepless night and woke up feeling like killing the two of them. At least he had to demand a divorce, if he did spare their lives. But he couldn't make up his mind. He thought about going to see Feng Wenxiu, but decided against it; this was no ordinary matter, and what if Wenxiu got drunk and repeated it to someone else? Another friend, Du Qinghai, came to mind. Scrapping his original plan to drive to Changzhi's highway construction site the following day, he boarded a bus to Huozhou, where he switched to a train for Shi Village before getting on another bus to Pingshan County. From Pingshan he took a local bus to Du Village to see Qinghai after a two-day journey. It had been five years, and they could see they had both aged a bit. Qinghai was visibly moved by the unannounced visit, which also had an emotional impact on Aiguo; they even forgot to shake hands.

"How did you get here?" Qinghai rubbed his hands. "How in the world did you get here?"

Instead of finding work requiring his driving skill after he was demobilized, Qinghai had started a pig farm. His wife, a short woman with large eyes, was feeding the pigs with a slop bucket. She shook Aiguo's hand when she learned who he was. Qinghai had always been neat in the army, washing the gloves he wore to drive so often they had turned white. Now he was sloppily dressed and the area around his house was a filthy mess. A grubby little two-year-old was chasing after chickens in the yard. Aiguo also discovered that his friend was no longer chatty; his wife, however, was. She talked through lunch, while Qinghai buried his face in his food, mumbling his agreement every once in a while. She talked about their family affairs, which made little sense to Aiguo, and did the same during dinner, eliciting only an occasional response from her husband, who raised no objection no matter what she said. Later that night, Qinghai changed into clean clothes before leading Aiguo out to the Hutuo River. It was the fifteenth day of the month, so the moon was big and bright. Water flowed silently in the moonlight, which transported them back five years, to when they confided in one another in the Gobi Desert or by the Ruoshui River. Qinghai took out his cigarettes and they lit up. What they had on their minds was naturally different from that time. Aiguo gave his friend a detailed account of what had happened between him and Lina. Should he resort to murder or settle for a divorce? He wanted his friend to help him choose. Even with new worries and concerns, the structure of their conversation remained the same, with Aiguo talking and Qinghai analyzing. After Aiguo finished, Qinghai evaluated the situation for him, just as he'd done five years earlier.

"You're actually talking about something else entirely," Qinghai said.

"What do you mean?"

"You can't commit murder, nor can you get a divorce."

"How so?"

"You'd have done it already if you intended to kill someone, and you would not have come here to see me. So let's put murder aside and focus on divorce. That would solve your problem. Question is, can you find another woman afterward?"

"My father died while I was in the army and my brothers and I have yet to divide up the household property," Aiguo said after giving his friend's comment some thought. "My older brother is married with three children, and his wife is sickly. She sees a doctor every month, which, along with the medicine, costs at least two hundred yuan each time. My younger brother has a girlfriend, and he's waiting for us to build him a place so he can get married. It's all on me to earn enough from my trucking jobs to do that. "It might be easier to find a woman if I were still single. But now I'd be divorced with a child. It would be tough, especially with my brothers' situations."

"Right you are. It's not a matter of divorce or no divorce. You simply can't afford to, and I think that's what makes you hesitate."

Aiguo was quiet for a while before heaving a sigh. "Then what do I do?"

"With matters like this, you have to follow the popular saying, catch a thief with the loot and catch the adulterers in cahoots. If you don't catch the two of them together, you'd be better off treating it as gossip and not believe a word people say."

Aiguo silently smoked as he gazed at the flowing river. "There's something else, too, more serious than this. We have nothing to say to each other."

"All this would not have happened if you talked." Qinghai looked around before continuing. "I'll be honest with you, I have nothing to say to my wife either. Did you see the mess at my house? We're no longer soldiers standing sentry."

"How do I keep on, even if I could manage to live with her?"

"If you want to keep it going, then break the silence and say something to her." He added, "And of course don't find fault. Try to sweet talk her when you get home."

"What about that business at the photo studio?"

"You'll have to live with it for now. It will be a nonissue once she changes her mind." Qinghai clasped Aiguo's hands. "Remember the proverb 'Only a petty man bears a grudge'?"

Tears welled up in Aiguo's eyes as he rested his head on his friend's shoulder and fell asleep while looking at the flowing river.

Aiguo followed Qinghai's advice upon returning to Hebei; he did not kill anyone, nor did he ask for a divorce. He racked his brains for things to say when he was with Lina, starting with all things positive. Another three years went by before Aiguo realized that Qinghai had given much good advice back in the army, but the advice he had offered by the river was wrong from the outset.

Aiguo had another friend, Chen Kuiyi, whom he'd met while hauling dirt for the Changzhi highway project. A cook at the construction site, Kuiyi was tall and skinny; a large mole on his left cheek sprouted three black hairs. Originally from Henan's Hua County, he had gotten the job because of his brother-in-law, a foreman at the site. Like Aiguo, Kuiyi was not given to idle talk, which brought the two men together. With more than three hundred workers at the site, the kitchen was busy from dawn to dusk, and Kuiyi was always sweating. Aiguo came to the kitchen to see Kuiyi when he had finished hauling dirt. Kuiyi would keep busy steaming buns or stir-frying vegetables while Aiguo sat on a bench and chatted with him. When he was done cooking, he would find something to offer his friend—a newly cooked pig's ear or a pig's heart, which he had cut up. They would pour sesame oil over the dish and eat to their hearts' content, exchanging smiles when they wiped their mouths. Naturally, that did not happen every day; when there was nothing to eat, they just sat there and smoked after Kuiyi finished his work. If there was a pig's ear or heart to share, he went to the site to see if his friend could get away that day. When he spotted Aiguo among the workers, he signaled with his eyes.

"Something just came up," he would say to Aiguo before wiping his hands on his apron and walking off. Aiguo would finish as soon as he could before jumping off the truck and running over to the kitchen. By then Kuiyi would have prepared a plateful of sliced pig's ear or heart, sprinkled with scallion slivers and sesame oil. But it did not take long for their secret arrangement to be noticed by a coworker, Little Xie, from the Northeast. Xie was flagging truckers and workers when he saw Aiguo leave shortly after Kuiyi stopped by.

"What were you doing, Aiguo?" he asked several times.

"Nothing."

Once, when Kuiyi came to the site and signaled Aiguo, Xie trailed him back to the kitchen, where he saw the two men enjoying a plate of pig's ear and heart. Pretending that he had just happened upon them, Xie said, "Just that with nothing to drink?" Xie made for the bench, as if invited, but they ignored him. Aiguo got up and headed back to the site when they finished, as Kuiyi gave Xie an unfriendly glance and fitted a large steamer of buns over a wok.

"It's not mealtime yet."

Kuiyi was not stingy about sharing the food; he just wanted Xie to know it wasn't easy for two people to become friends. His friendship with Aiguo was built mostly on a similarity in temperament, which enabled them to carry on conversations on just about anything.

That aside, Aiguo could not count on Kuiyi if he had a problem, for his friend was worse than he was in sorting out issues. If Aiguo tended to turn one matter into two, it would not be impossible for Kuiyi to turn one into four. In fact, Kuiyi would come to Aiguo with his problems, and Aiguo would give him a sound analysis, earning such admiration that Kuiyi would bob his head in agreement. Whenever Aiguo needed someone to talk things over with, Kuiyi would helplessly wipe his hands on his apron, giving the same reply as Aiguo had with Du Qinghai in the army.

"What do *you* think?"

Aiguo would have to work things out on his own, so he combed through his troubles and learned how to solve his problems, after the final "What do *you* think?" from Kuiyi.

The construction foreman told the cooks to buy a slab of beef to celebrate the Dragon Boat Festival that year. The price of beef varied at the market, from 9.3 to 10.5 yuan per cattie. Chen Kuiyi returned with a slab of beef that had cost 10.5 yuan per cattie, the highest. The foreman, Kuiyi's brother-in-law, suspected that the beef was likely from the 9.3 yuan range. The slab weighed two hundred catties and, at 1.2 yuan extra for each cattie, it would profit Kuiyi to the tune of more than two hundred yuan. An argument ensued.

"Sure, there's beef that costs 9.3 yuan. There's even some for 6.8 yuan a cattie. It's water-logged." He continued, "Two hundred yuan is nothing. You borrowed a thousand from me back when you were in financial trouble."

Now he was talking about something else entirely.

"This isn't just about the beef," his brother-in-law said. "It's about cheating. Who knows what else has been going on?"

The retort so outraged Kuiyi that he slapped his own face and shouted, "Fuck you! Now I finally know what you're made of."

He untied his apron, packed up, and, surprisingly, boarded a bus back to Henan.

Aiguo was hauling dirt at the site when Kuiyi stormed off. He did not know about his friend's departure until lunchtime, when no food came out of the kitchen and the foreman gave everyone two packs of instant noodles. He ran into the kitchen, where the stove was cold and the slab of beef was lying on the floor, encircled by flies. Aiguo sighed, not because his friend had left without saying good-bye, but because he now had no one at the site to open up to anymore. The whole worksite seemed deserted all of a sudden.

Aiguo wrote to Kuiyi after he returned to Henan, even phoned him occasionally. He was reminded of his friend anytime some mentioned Henan. But he did not go to see him about his troubles, as he had when he'd traveled to Pingshan to seek out Du Qinghai.

2

Niu Aiguo's mother was Cao Qing'e. But her real surname was Jiang, not Cao; however, that is not entirely accurate either, for it should have been Wu. In fact, Wu was not her family name either; that should have been Yang. She had been kidnapped in Henan and sold to someone in Shanxi when she was five. Sixty years had passed, but she still recalled that her stepfather was Moses Wu and her mother Wu Xiangxiang, who had run off with another man. Her father had taken her along to search for her mother, and she had been lured away when they were put up in a shabby inn in Xinxiang. She could also recall what she had been called then: Qiaoling.

Qiaoling never forgot the three middlemen involved in her kidnapping and sale. The first was Old You, a rat poison peddler with a hoarse voice but a glib tongue. He sang doggerel to help hawk his wares and could make up a tune on the spot about an ordinary event. She had gotten to know him so well because she loved listening to him. They had stayed in the same inn, and You had sometimes shared his donkey-meat flatcakes with her. On that fateful day, he had gotten her up around daybreak to tell her that her father had gone to Kaifeng on an urgent matter and had told You to take her to see him there. Only five at the time, she had cried when she learned that her father had left without her, but she dressed and got on the road with You, thinking that her father must have picked up her mother's trail and gone after her.

Kaifeng was east of Xinxiang, but You did not head east. He took her west, reaching Jiyuan five days later. Qiaoling could not tell Jiyuan from Kaifeng; all she wanted was to see her father soon. She grew up quickly without him, going along with Old You in everything, which she hoped would facilitate the reunion. She wiped the sweat from his forehead when he squatted down to smoke and rest; she put food in his bowl and offered him water before he finished when they stopped for food. She acted as if she were ten years older.

Jiyuan is on the border between Henan and Shanxi. Old You ran into Old Sa, another human trafficker, in Jiyuan, where he sold Qiaoling for ten silver dollars. She did not realize what was going on until You turned her over to Sa. Once Qiaoling began to cry, Old You's heart softened.

"I guess I'll take her to Kaifeng and raise her as my own daughter," he said. "You have no idea what a wonderful kid she's been along the way. This isn't what I do for a living. I just had a momentary lapse of moral judgment."

"It's too late." Instead of taking the money, Sa just smiled at You.

"The money is still here. What do you mean too late?"

"I don't mean it's too late to go back on the deal," Sa said. "It's too late for you."

"How so?"

"You could have raised her as your own before the transaction. But now that you've done that and she knows about it, how are you going to keep her? She may be a sheep now, but she'll grow up to be a tiger. This is what the ancients meant when they coined the phrase 'raising a tiger to bring future troubles.' That stumbling block would stop her from treating you as family, no matter how good you are to her."

Old You had to agree that the man was right. Putting the money back in his pocket, he was turning to leave when the girl cried again. The sight saddened him so much that he too began to cry.

"This is no way to make a sale." Sa spat on the ground. "Since you're a fake cat, don't cry for the mouse's sake. You shouldn't be in this line of work if you don't have the stomach for it."

Qiaoling quickly learned how Sa was different from You. A veteran of human trafficking, he did not care how she felt and hit her when she cried. He even carried an awl with him and used it on her backside if she acted up, which frightened her no end. At night, before they fell asleep, he tied her to the bed to prevent her from running away, and he brandished his awl each day before getting on the road again.

"I'm your father, if anyone asks."

She called him Father in front of people, out of fear of the awl. Sa continued west, out of Henan, and arrived at Yuanqu County in Shanxi, where he sold her for twenty yuan to another man, Old Bian, a cross-eyed former fabric peddler from Shanxi. Bian had switched to human trafficking when he realized it was more profitable than selling cloth. Being relatively new to the trade, he was nicer than Sa and did not tie her up at night. After the transaction, however, he talked to others in the same trade, and they told him, after studying Qiaoling, that he had paid too much for the girl. It should have been his own fault for overpaying, but he blamed his failure in judgment on the girl. He stared daggers at her when he was irked by something she said. But she wasn't afraid of him, since he did not have an awl and did not hit her; his cross-eyed glare did not scare her. She could have run away at night when Bian was asleep, but she had been afraid of the dark since childhood, and, besides, they were in Shanxi, thousands of li from home, where she knew no one and could barely understand the local accent. She might fall into the hands of another human trafficker if she went out on her own, and could end up with another Old Sa, worse than her current situation with Bian. So she stayed put and let him take her north to Changzhi, where he tried to sell her on market days. He realized that Sa had tricked him after a few failed attempts. Qiaoling was small to begin with, and her dry, brownish hair made her look even smaller; he found it impossible to get a good price. One offered fifteen, another thirteen, one only ten. He could not get his investment back, and he walked off with her after dark, after another failed sale.

"I've overestimated your worth."

After two weeks, he still was unable to sell her, while at the same time he had to pay for room and board. He began to lose his composure, and the more anxious he was, the harder the sale. Soon it was late autumn. Yellow leaves blanketed Mount Nanyuan and the surrounding fields. Gusts of wind sent leaves falling to cover the road and the hill where fruit—pears, nectarines, chestnuts, and walnuts—was ripening and falling from trees. Wanting to economize on room and board, he bought only enough food for one person, starving himself and the girl. Qiaoling went out to pick the fruit and nuts on the ground. When she'd eaten her fill, she would chase the squirrels around the trees. Two more weeks went by, and she grew accustomed to the life of forever waiting to be sold. She giggled when a squirrel jumped onto a tree and bowed to her. Bian didn't mind her picking the fruit and nuts, but her apparent ability to enjoy life irked him.

"I'm here to sell you, not to give you a good time." He raised his hand. "I'll beat you if you dare laugh again."

Unfazed, she hopped away from him, laughing the whole time.

A few days later, she developed scabies. All the inns Bian chose for them were fleabags, where they had to sleep on straw under blankets used by countless travelers. It was hard to say where she'd picked up the infection. The scabies hurt so much she stopped laughing; instead, she cried, holding her head in her hands. Bian decided to take a look one day and saw that the sores were turning red, with pus seeming ready to burst from them. He was already having trouble selling her, and now with the scabies, she would be virtuously worthless.

"Damn you, deities and ancestors!" he erupted. "You have to saddle me with more trouble, don't you?" Then he crouched down. "Why don't you sell me instead?"

The funny sight of an irritated Bian made the girl, who didn't think the scabies were ugly, forget the soreness. She looked up and giggled.

A wealthy landowner named Wen lived in Xiangyuan County's Wen Village. He had a dozen workers on property that was slightly under twenty acres. One of them, goateed Old Cao the carter, was in his early forties. He hitched up three donkeys to a cart to pull five thousand catties of sesame seeds for sale in Changzhi. It was a sunny, windless day when he set out, but dark clouds gathered when he crossed into Tunliu County. Cao looked up and saw that it would very likely start to rain. Afraid that it would ruin his cargo, he whipped the donkeys for them to move faster; they traveled as fast as they could for eight li before he found an inn near Xiyuan River that would take him and the donkeys. By then the heavens had opened up, so he quickly got his cart in. A sheet of straw had kept the sesame dry, but he was drenched. Unhitching the donkeys, he asked the innkeeper to feed them while he walked into the kitchen after taking a look at the sky. He took off his coat and spread it out to dry over a heated brazier, releasing moist steam. Finally feeling better once he had warmed up, he spotted a man on the kang, with a child lying next to him. Cao put the dry coat back on before walking up to the bed. The child was a girl, her face red from a high fever; she was fast asleep, her nostrils flaring. Cao reached out to touch her forehead; it was so hot it burned his hand. He looked at the man, who was just sighing, a pipe in his hand.

"You staying here?" Cao asked.

The man cast a sideways glance at Cao and nodded.

"This has to be the worst, isn't it? Getting sick on the road. You have to take the girl to see a doctor, Older Brother. I don't think she'll just get over it."

"See a doctor?" The man gave Cao another glance. "With your money?"

"You're her father, not me." Cao was peeved by the rebuke. "I meant well, so why get angry at me?"

To Cao's surprise, the man held his head in his hands and began to sob, sending Cao into a minor fright. He must be terribly worried, Cao thought, or broke, and they were put up in the kitchen to save money. He tried to console the man, but the more he tried, the harder the man cried, until Cao was at his wit's end, when the man seemed to have cried himself out and looked up, revealing his crossed eyes to Cao. After he calmed down, the man told Cao he was a human trafficker and that the girl was not his daughter. New to the trade, he did not know the ins and outs of a sale and had spent twenty yuan on the girl; they had traveled through big towns and small villages for three weeks, but he had failed to sell her. The money he was offered could not cover the original purchase price, and, on top of that, he had to pay for room and board. Now the girl had scabies, which made a hard sale even harder. After that came a high fever. He was stuck, with no way out, which was why he looked down. Feeling so sorry for the man that he forgot he was a human trafficker, Cao tried to find a solution and sighed along with him when he could not think of anything.

"Why don't you take her, Older Brother?" The man grabbed Cao's hands.

Stunned by the odd offer, Cao quickly backed away.

"I have to sell sesame in Changzhi. Besides, I never thought of buying a girl."

"Just give me what you can. I won't bargain. Anything is better than having her die on me." Then, after a pause, he added, "I'll never be able to sell her if she dies."

Cao could only smile sympathetically, realizing that the man was decent enough. Cao's wife had not given him children, so the offer was appealing. But he said, "Buying a child isn't like buying a puppy. I can't agree to something so important just like that."

"Take pity on her, won't you?" the man said.

"This has nothing to do with pity. I have to go to Changzhi. Besides, I can't make such an important decision on my own. I'd have to talk it over with my wife."

That was all the man needed to press on. "Where are you from, Older Brother?"

"Wen Village in Xianghuan County."

By then it had cleared up outside. Cao paid for the donkey feed and got on the road again. To him, the matter was over once he left the inn. Imagine his surprise when, two days later, he returned to Wen Village to find the man and the sick child in his house. The girl was lying on the bed; the man was squatting on the doorsill, smoking a pipe. Cao was too flabbergasted to know what to do.

"So you're stuck on me, is that it?"

"Won't you warm a pot of liquor, Older Brother?" The man banged the bowl of his pipe on the door. "Sister-in-law wants the girl."

The sister-in-law was Cao's wife, of course; the surprises never ended. He was wondering how the man had talked his wife into taking the child, when she parted the door curtain and came out.

"I want the child," she said to her husband. "She looks good enough for thirteen yuan."

Cao noticed the new clothes on her, a sign that she was serious about the transaction. "But she's running a fever. We don't know if she'll live."

"The fever has broken," Cao's wife said.

Cao walked up to the bed to touch the girl's forehead. Indeed, no more fever. Sensing someone touching her forehead, the girl opened her eyes and sized Cao up. He did the same and saw she had almond-shaped eyes, a nose with an upturned tip, and a small mouth. Not a bad-looking girl. She had been burning up two days earlier at the inn, so how had her fever broken when they got to his house? Cao had to shake his head over the turn of events, but he would not relent.

"Did you look at her head? She's got scabies."

The man spoke up before Cao's wife could respond.

"These are different; they're new scabies and can be taken care of easily." He continued, "She's got small bones and tender flesh. She'll grow fast." He kept on. "She wouldn't be so cheap if she didn't have some minor problems."

He made a final push. "Why don't we settle the deal, Older Brother? I'm going back to sell cloth; no more of this."

Cao had to laugh at the man's resolve, despite his hesitation. In the Cao family, his wife had the final say, so he took out a key to open their money chest. They had only eight yuan, so he would have to borrow five more from his employer. Besides farming, the Wen family also owned a distillery for aged vinegar called Wen's Vinegar Distillery, where they produced about a hundred vats of vinegar each day. Every family in the area used their vinegar. Besides driving the cart, Cao sometimes helped out by turning the vinegar dregs at night when work piled up at the distillery.

Cao came to the backyard of the Wen house, where Old Wen and Old Zhou from Zhou Village were playing Chinese chess under a large locust tree. Living fifty li away, Zhou owned farmland and ran a liquor distillery called Peach Blossom Hamlet, as opposed to Apricot Blossom Hamlet, the most popular name in traditional literature. They made sweet and spicy liquor that supplied the families in neighboring counties for celebrations and funerals. Wen the vinegar maker and Zhou the liquor maker were best friends. During New Year's and on other holidays, Wen and Zhou visited each other and often met up on other days to chat and play chess.

When Cao walked in, Zhou was drinking tea, while Wen was looking at the board, clinking two chess pieces in his hand. Cao started to walk off, not wanting to broach the subject of a loan in front of the guest, but Wen looked up and called out to him.

"Do you need something?"

"It's nothing, Boss," Cao said after a brief hesitation.

"Go ahead, tell me. Mr. Zhou isn't a stranger."

"I'd like a loan."

"There's no holiday coming up. What do you need a loan for?"

Cao told the two men about buying the child.

"I really don't want the child, Boss, but that wife of mine won't listen to me." He paused. "You can dock my pay when you tally up my salary at the end of the year." He seemed compelled to add, "The little girl looked pitiful, with a head full of scabies."

Before Wen could respond, Zhou decided to jump in. A frequent guest at the Wen house, Zhou would normally go home the same day, but he spent the night on days when he stayed late. If he was staying, he would send his wagon and the driver on home and have Cao drive him back the next day. Zhou's wagon smelled like liquor, while Wen's cart reeked of vinegar. Every time Zhou got in, he would comment, "The smell alone tells me which cart I'm in."

They would chat along the way until they reached Zhou's place fifty li later. Since Zhou was a land and business owner, he was normally the one who took the lead in their conversation, usually asking about the Wen and Cao families. Zhou would ask a question and Cao would reply, which was why Zhou was familiar with Cao's family situation and felt comfortable to speak up before Wen.

"Let's put the child aside for now and think about Old Cao and his wife. They don't have anyone, and really they should buy the child. It's for the child's sake, the right thing to do. As the Buddhist saying goes, saving a life is better than building a seven-storied pagoda."

Cao did not know, until they had concluded the transaction, that his wife wanted the girl not for the child's sake nor for their own sake, and definitely not for their karma. She did it purely to spite her brother-in-law, Cao's younger brother, Cao Mantun. Old Cao, whose full name was Cao Mancang, had always been levelheaded, while Mantun was the opposite. Old Cao was a couple of inches taller than his brother. An impetuous, undersized boy, Mantun had been picked on by other kids in the village, and he turned into a bully at home. He pushed his parents and his older brother around, which was not manifested in taking food or toys away from his brother, but in insisting on having his way. Everyone had to listen to him. He had a habit of contradicting others' views and going against their decisions. Whenever he could not have his way, he threw a temper tantrum. That would prompt their parents to slap Mancang, not him.

"You're old enough and should know better. Why must you upset your younger brother like that?'

That baffled Old Cao, but he had to comply, no matter how unfair it was, and it became the norm even after they grew up and got married. They worked together, but Mantun took charge and made all the decisions. Old Cao was tall, so he married a tall woman; likewise, Mantun was short and married a short woman. Old Cao's tall wife was barren, while Mantun's stumpy wife had given him five in a row, three boys and two girls. Local custom dictated that the older brother, if childless, must adopt his young brother's oldest boy to take care of the barren couple and conduct the last rites, but also to inherit everything. Old Cao's wife did not want to adopt Mantun's oldest son. Mantun and his wife had children who were very much like them—short. At sixteen, the oldest son was no taller than a table and had thick legs and a big head, giving him the appearance of a pygmy. Old Cao's wife did not mind the boy's looks so much; what really annoyed her was how Mantun put down his older brother's family. He often said to Old Cao and his wife, "What are you waiting for? Just adopt my oldest boy and everything will be settled."

Old Cao did not have the courage to tell him he didn't want to, but his wife was not afraid of Mantun. At a time when women's infertility was considered a flaw, she refused to look at herself that way, and there was nothing anyone could do about it. She even got into fights with her husband over his inability to stand up to his younger brother. When Mantun pressured them to adopt his oldest son, she ignored him at first, until one day she decided to fight back.

"Let's drop it, shall we? You can keep your son. I'm not going to adopt him."

"Why not?" Mantun demanded.

"I'm not too old to have a baby."

"What if you are?" Mantun fumed.

"Then I'll get your brother a concubine."

That killed whatever hope Mantun had for his inheritance. She sounded confident, but no baby came after a few years, and she never brought up getting a concubine for her husband again. When the human trafficker showed up at her door, she decided to buy the little girl to raise as her own. She changed her name from Qiaoling to Gaixin—a "change of heart"—for her to think of her life differently. Instead of taking Gaixin to see a doctor about the scabies, Cao's wife took her to the Xiang River, where she washed her head. Pus was visible in the sores, so she squeezed the pus out before rinsing the spots with river water. Being tall meant she had powerful hands, hurting the girl so much she cried like a kitten. When it was over, the woman asked her, "Who's better, your real mother or me, Gaixin?"

"You."

"You're only five." The woman slapped her. "But you're already a liar."

The girl wailed and said, "I'm telling the truth. My mother ran off with another man, but you didn't."

Cackling like a hen, the woman laughed and plopped herself down on the riverbank. "Do you remember where you lived?"

"I do." Gaixin nodded. "Yanjin."

"So your mother ran off with another man. What about your father? Do you miss him?"

"My father is dead." The girl shook her head.

"Is there anyone you miss?"

"My stepfather."

"What's his name?"

"His name is Moses Wu."

The woman slapped her again.

"Don't ever think about Yanjin or your stepfather again. I'll squeeze your scabies whenever you do." She reached out for the girl's head, prompting Gaixin to cover her head and cry.

"I won't, Mother."

Old Cao's wife kept at her squeezing remedy and the girl's head healed and hair began to grow out after a month, to everyone's surprise.

Old Cao had objected to buying the girl, but not because he had his mind set on taking a concubine. He knew it was beyond the means of a carter to support two women, and even if he could, he knew that, given her nature, his wife would never be able to live with a second woman in the house. Buying a child simplified everything. He had thought that parents and a bought child could never be close, but he actually had a lot to say to the girl once they got to know each other. With a child in the house, it felt livelier. The girl was always on his mind now when he left with the cart.

Mantun was upset over the change, but not because he objected to the purchase, or because his older brother would not adopt his son, so he could inherit the property. He was piqued because his brother had not talked over such an important matter with him. Not being consulted was only the beginning. He concluded that his brother and sister-in-law were being spiteful when they decided not to talk it over with him first. He retaliated by ignoring his brother's family, even though they lived in the same compound. The two brothers no longer spoke when they ran into each other.

The end of the year approached. Everything was fine during the last month, but in the first lunar month, Mantun's six-year-old girl, Jinzhi, was afflicted with scrofula. It wasn't hard to cure; all they had to do was go to a Chinese herbal shop in the market and buy a plaster to cover the spot. She would get better in a few days. But Mantun did nothing, and the lump on her neck grew, from the size of a pea to the size of a date. One day, Jizhi was heard crying in the yard.

"My neck hurts so much, Father. Please go buy a plaster for me."

"No." He stomped his foot. "What's the point of having a girl, anyway? She'll have to be married off sooner or later."

Old Cao's family heard the complaint by her father and knew it was directed at them. Old Cao's wife vaulted out of the house with a club, ready to fight it out with her brother-in-law, if Old Cao hadn't stopped her.

"He's talking about his own daughter. What would you say to him, since he didn't mention Gaixin?"

Cao's wife considered his comment and spat on the ground.

Three more days went by, and the sore on the girl's neck grew to match the rim of a rice bowl. It hurt so much that she passed out several times. She looked at her father once when she woke up.

"My neck really hurts, Father. Please go buy a plaster for me. You'll find my New Year's lucky money in a hole on the wall in the shed."

"No." Mantun stomped his foot again. "You can die for all I care."

That night the girl did die; her bent neck drooped across her back as she breathed her last. All was quiet in Mantun's house until daybreak. He was heard wailing, but not over his own child.

"I'll never forget this, Cao Mancang."

He carried on until the following morning. Years later, Cao Qing'e would learn that her uncle, Mantun, had not intended for Jinzhi to die from the disease. That had been a show to torment everyone, and he would keep it up from the fifth till the tenth day. He had already gotten the name of a doctor for his daughter and had not expected her to die on the eighth. He had been crying not over the death of Jinzhi, but over the surprising turn of events, when a pretense became reality. In any case, the two brothers never spoke again.

That was one of Niu Aiguo's mother's favorite stories from her sixty years of life.

3

A salt peddler, Old Ding, and a farmer, Old Han, both lived in Niu Village in Qinyuan County. In addition to salt, Ding also sold soda ash, tea leaves, tobacco, needles, and thread. He did not own a salt field, so he bought salt and soda ash from shops in town to peddle in neighboring villages. A traveling peddler ought to be a good talker, but Ding hardly ever spoke. When potential customers in a village asked the prices of his goods, he simply gestured with his fingers.

"Can't you give me a better price, Old Ding?" someone once asked.

Ding shook his head wordlessly.

"You're supposed to haggle in business."

Ding ignored him. People in all the villages knew about Old Ding the eccentric salt peddler from Niu Village.

Old Han, as mentioned, was a farmer. He worked in the field, dealing with livestock and crops all day, which meant he ought not to be too talkative, and yet he must have uttered several thousand phrases each day. With no one to talk to while he was working, he stopped to chat with people on the street, even if he had nothing to say. He would talk up a storm while the other person could barely get a word in edgewise. So people in the village avoided him, which did not please him.

"Damn it, would it kill you to talk to me? Why are you all avoiding me?"

Ding and Han were good friends, despite being opposites where talking was concerned, for they shared a hobby. In late autumn, when wheat was planted after the previous crops were harvested, they went up the mountain to shoot rabbits. When he spotted a rabbit, Han always took careful aim. Ding, on the other hand, shot from the hip. The rabbit would duck into the trees in the time it took Han to aim, while Ding rarely missed his target. So when they came down the mountain three days later, Han would have a few rabbits hanging from the barrel of his rifle, whereas Ding would have bagged so many they weighed down the basket he'd taken along for that purpose. Ding would sometimes also shoot pheasants, river deer, and foxes.

Given such a dramatic difference in hunting styles, they should not have been out hunting together, if not for another shared hobby—singing Shanxi's Shangdang clapper opera. The taciturn Ding would turn into a different person once he started singing, his lips and tongue seemingly taking flight to produce well-articulated words and perfect notes, while he had a lively glow on his face. As they sang together, the two men could play friends, husbands and wives, or fathers and sons, in *Wu Family Hill, Breaking Out of Youzhou, White City Gate, Temple Murder,* or *Wife Murder.* Depending on their mood, they might sing a selection or an entire opera, which would make them forget all about hunting rabbits. At high points, Han would walk in circles, a rifle over his shoulder, and sing:

"Dear wife, I was away in the capital for half a year and returned to hear gossip. What were you doing out instead of staying home to take care of household affairs?"

Ding would act out a move of picking up a skirt to bow to Han.

"Dear husband, you have wrongly accused me. Please allow me to tell you everything in detail."

Han made the sounds of gongs and drums, followed by string music, while Ding pretended to shake the long, silky sleeves of a female role. Or Ding would drag out a protest:

"My son, you have misspoken. Come back."

Han would immediately spin around, still with his rifle.

"Father, you don't know all the details."

Ding then made all the requisite sounds for the segment as Han began to sing.

Their friendship also brought the two families closer. Ding had three boys and two girls, and Han had four daughters. Ding's youngest daughter, Yanzhi, was seven, while Han's youngest, Yanhong, was eight. The two girls often went out to cut grass together. One year in early fall, they went to the river as usual on the fifteenth day of the eighth lunar month. After an afternoon of work, they shouldered the grass and headed back before dark. They were walking through fields to reach the road when they spotted an object on the ground. It looked like a jacket or a sack. They both ran to it. Yanhong, being a year older, was faster on her feet and got there before her friend. She picked it up and saw that it was a cloth sack; it felt heavy. Tossing it into her basket, she carried it home and told her mother about it; she was rewarded with a slap.

"Couldn't you have picked up something else? A cloth sack? That's bad luck."

Yanhong burst out crying, while her mother opened the sack to find, to her astonishment, a mass of silver dollars. She emptied the sack and counted sixty-seven coins. When Han came home from the field at dinnertime, his wife called him into a room in back, where she showed him the sack and the money. He was dumbstruck by the sight of the shiny coins. He opened his mouth but nothing came out; he tried to say something again and failed a second time. A good talker had been rendered tongue-tied when confronted by this windfall.

The couple spent a restless night, making plans for the money: buy two more acres of land, add three rooms to the house, or buy more livestock. None of those would require that much money. Han got so worked up that he talked through the night. His wife summoned Yanhong the next morning.

"Say nothing about the sack. I'll strangle you if you breathe a word of this."

Yanhong was properly and tearfully frightened.

Ding came by when they were having breakfast. Han thought his friend was there to talk about their rabbit hunt, but Ding came straight to the point.

"I hear Yanhong found a sack yesterday."

Han knew the two girls had been together the day before, so he said, "Yes, and got a good beating from her mother. It was half-filled with dry animal droppings." Han feigned a sigh. "Finding a sack is bad luck, as they say. I wonder what misfortune will befall us now."

"Old Brother," said Ding, who was two years younger than Han. He smiled. "My daughter touched the sack, and she said it felt like coins inside."

Han knew he had to come clean. "It probably belongs to some shop owner. We're putting it aside to wait for the careless man to come claim it."

"What if no one comes to claim it?"

"We'll worry about that if and when that happens."

"We'll have to talk about it if no one comes."

"What do you mean?"

"Yanzhi found it with Yanhong."

"The sack is at my house now. So how can you say your daughter found it?"

"Yanzhi said they ran up to the sack together, but Yanhong, being a year older, snatched it away from my daughter."

"Then what's your plan, Old Ding?"

"We split it, fifty-fifty. Even if they picked it up together, Yanhong would have shared it with Yanzhi. As the saying goes, being there gives you a share."

"That's nonsense, Old Ding."

"I don't care about the money. I just want to make sure everything is done right."

"It's not going to work if that's what you have in mind."

"Then we'll have to do something else."

"Like what?"

"Go to the county office," Ding declared.

If the county office was involved, a found object would have to be confiscated. It was clear to Han what Ding was thinking; if he couldn't have a share, then neither could Han. They had been hunting rabbits and singing opera together for two decades, but only now did Han see how ruthless Ding could be. How could a quiet man be so caustic at such a critical moment? Han was thinking. Ding's tongue was sharper now than when he was singing an opera. Obviously, he had thought it through before showing up at his house; apparently their friendship had been built on shaky ground, and Ding was now showing his true colors. Han was not a greedy man and would be happy to share, within reason. This open confrontation meant that they would never be friends again, even if Han were to give him half the money.

"It was found, not stolen," he said spitefully, "so go ahead, see anyone you want."

"Very well, then." Ding matched his bravado. "It so happens that I need to buy some salt in town."

But before the county office was involved and Ding returned from his trip, the owner of the sack came looking for it that afternoon. It was none other than Old Cao, Old Wen's carter. He had taken a cartload of soybeans to Huozhou, where they would fetch a little more than in Xiangyuan. Huozhou was three hundred li away, a five-day round-trip journey. The loaded trip required three days; the return trip with an empty cart took only two. After selling the beans, he collected payment as well as money owed by the Huozhou grain supply station for wheat bought earlier in the summer. The grand total came to sixty-seven silver dollars. Fatigue set in on the trip home, and he dozed off from time to time, giving the donkeys their head. As they neared Niu Village, the cart jolted when it hit a pothole; his money sack fell to the ground and went unnoticed until he entered Xiangyuan. He broke out in a cold sweat and quickly backtracked, but, naturally, it was nowhere to be found. Left with no choice, he went village by village inquiring if anyone had found a sack. Starting the night before, by the next afternoon, he had gone through about a hundred villages, parched and hungry, as he'd had nothing to eat or drink. But in vain. Despairing of ever finding the sack when he reached Niu Village, he nonetheless felt obligated to ask around, simply to make himself feel better. To his surprise and delight, everyone, young and old, knew that someone in Old Han's family had found a sack. The villagers had found out about it when Old Ding raised a stink. So Cao showed up at Han's house. Knowing he could not hide the truth from Cao, Han was furious with Ding for causing trouble and ruining his chance to keep the money as he brought out the sack. The sight of the sack sent Cao crumpling to the floor; he emptied it and counted the money. Seeing that nothing was missing, he stood up and bowed to Han.

"I never thought I would get this back, Brother," he said. "If it had been me, I might not have given it back. But you did. I was prepared to hang myself if I couldn't find it. I could never pay my employer back the sixty-seven dollars. More than that, I wouldn't know what to say to my wife, and she'd hang herself, even if I didn't."

Cao studied Han's face before adding, "I can tell you're a farmer, Brother, but you're not greedy. It's not uncommon for people to pass up small change, but not sixty-seven silver dollars. You did not let that affect your judgment, Brother; you're a special man."

The praise embarrassed Han. Normally a good talker, he was tongue-tied at this moment.

"This is no small matter. If you don't think I'm unworthy, I would like to swear brotherhood with you."

The suggestion caught Han off guard. How could two total strangers become so close so quickly? Cao spotted a little girl in the yard, biting her fingers, a blank look on her face.

"Is that your daughter? She looks to be a year or two older than mine."

"She's the one who found your sack."

"Come with me," Cao said as he took Han by the arm.

"Where to?" Han was puzzled.

"To the market. We'll buy a chicken and kill it to swear our brotherhood, then we'll buy some new clothes for the girl."

A cloth sack thus started a lifelong friendship between Old Cao from Wen Village and Niu Village's Old Han.

"You can never tell what goes on inside a man," Han would sometimes say. "I lost a friend because of a cloth sack, but found another one, thanks to the same sack."

The first friend, obviously, was Old Ding; the second one was Old Cao. Xiangyuan was a hundred li from Qinyuan, and yet Cao crossed the mountains to visit Han three times a year over major holidays—the Dragon Boat Festival, the Mid-Autumn Festival, and New Year's. Han had thought the visits would last a year or two, but no, Cao kept coming. His sincerity prompted Han to return the visits. That lasted more than a decade, until Cao, who had been in his forties when he met Han, was nearly sixty.

One summer, the people of Niu Village built a new temple for Guangong, the God of War. On the day of the consecration ceremony, the village hired a troupe from Tang Village in Wuxiang County to perform Shangdang clapper opera. They planned a three-day performance, from the seventh to the ninth day of the sixth lunar month. A man named Niu Laodao was in charge of village affairs. Now in his seventies, he had been working in this capacity all his life, taking care of all matters, big and small. It had been his idea to build the temple in the first place. Compared with the neighboring villages, Niu Village was relatively new, not even a hundred years old, settled by members of Laodao's grandfather's generation. Having fled a famine area, they had picked the riverbank for their new home, later joined by people with different family names. The other villages, having much longer histories, made people in Niu Village feel inferior. All villages except theirs had a temple, which was the motivation behind Laodao's endeavor; he wanted to build a temple for the War God before he died. Laodao asked another man, seventy-year-old Jin Farong, Laodao's right-hand man in village affairs, to help. Hand in hand, the two old men went from door to door, asking everyone to pitch in to build the temple. Getting a temple built was a lot more complex than throwing up a chicken roost. Only Niu could have done it, for he had helped every family in the village whenever they needed it. Naturally, they responded positively to his requests, some offering money and others helping out with the work. When the construction was completed, they waited to welcome the statue of the God of War into his new home. Elated, Laodao decided to get even more ambitious.

"Why don't we have three days of opera after the consecration ceremony? That would spread the name of our Niu Village."

Carrying bamboo baskets, Laodao and Farong walked from door to door to collect money for the performance. After putting up money for the temple earlier, the village was less enthusiastic this time. Laodao knew how to be flexible, however, and he told them they could offer money or help out by lending tables and chairs or supplying wheat. The furniture would be used to erect the stage; the wheat would be ground and made into noodles to feed the performers. Finally, they had collected all the money and supplies they could; it came to 265 yuan. Laodao shouldered a sack for the money and, again with Farong, went to Wuxiang to hire a troupe run by Old Tang, originally from Yuxiang County. When he was away from home, in order to lend credibility to the authenticity of his Shangdang clapper opera, he told people that Shangdang was his hometown, even though his troupe was based in Wuxiang County.

"Where are you from, Old Tang?" someone would ask.

"Shangdang" was his invariable answer.

Niu Laodao mediated matters in both his and other villages, which was how he met the troupe owner. Laodao gave Tang all the details about the temple and settled on dates for the performance, before handing Tang the money. Tang's troupe charged a hundred yuan per day, which meant that Laodao ought to give him three hundred.

"I'm so sorry, Old Tang, but we're thirty-five yuan short," Laodao said.

"I wouldn't mind if it was one yuan or so, but thirty-five?" Tang looked at the money with displeasure. "I'm not sure I can do it."

"You know our village is small, and not much has ever happened there, so we have little to offer." Laodao continued, "Would you honor us with your performance, for the sake of two old men in their seventies traveling a hundred li to see you?"

The frown on Tang's face prompted Laodao to stand up and say, "How about I take off this jacket and give it to you?"

"That's not how we do things, sir." Tang shook his head, though he put the money away, a sign that he had accepted the job.

"I need to be frank with you now, Old Tang," Laodao persisted. "Even though the money is less than you expected, you must put on a first-rate show, adding whatever you find necessary."

"You don't have to worry about the performance. We will, for myself, if not for your sake. The Tang Opera Troupe will never do anything to damage its reputation. With less pay, it's up to you to make sure the performers are well fed. Singing is not easy; it requires energy."

"Don't you worry," Laodao said. "I guarantee there will be meat at every meal."

By the third day of the sixth lunar month, Niu Village was abuzz with activity. A stage was erected, decorative marquees were put up, and barn lanterns were hung by the temple. Peddlers selling fruits, snacks, and sundry goods had set up stalls in the village three days before. Old Han asked someone to relay an invitation to his friend, Old Cao, telling him to leave for Qinyuan on the fifth and arrive on the next day. They would enjoy the Shangdang opera together on the seventh. Cao wasn't sure he wanted to go. He preferred a quiet life and did not care for noisy opera. Besides, he was no longer young, and would rather not make the trip. If he had to go, however, he wanted his family to go along as traveling companions; but neither his wife nor his daughter felt like traveling that far. Their daughter, Gaixin, even said her feet had ached for three days after accompanying her father to Qinyuan for Han's fiftieth birthday. But Cao could not disappoint his friend, who was an opera fan and loved humming lines from the arias. So, early on the fifth, he got on the road alone.

Cao was barely out the door when he ran into Little Wen, the new manager of Wen's Vinegar Shop. Thirty-year-old Wen was the son of Cao's former employer, Old Wen, who had died eight years before. Everyone had called Old Wen "Boss," but the young man asked to be addressed as Manager. As soon as he took over, they noticed that he differed from his father in many respects. The old man had been steadfastly traditional, while Little Wen was keen on all things new. It was he who had bought Qinyuan's first cart with rubber wheels. It ran like the wind, drawing everyone's attention. Air brakes brought it to a complete stop every time. Old Cao was tentative at first. Since he was older, Little Wen called him Uncle.

"Faster, Uncle," he would say when he rode along.

It took Cao a year to get used to the increased speed.

Little Zhou, the new manager of Peach Blossom Distillery in Zhou Village, also bought a cart, at Little Wen's urging. He was the son of Old Zhou, the former owner of the distillery, who had died six years before.

"Where are you going, Uncle?" Wen asked when he spotted Cao in traveling clothes and carrying provisions.

"To an opera performance in Qinyuan County, Mr. Manager." Cao proceeded to tell Wen about the invitation. "I'm going for my friend's sake, not for the opera. It was no easy matter to get an invitation out here, a hundred li away."

"What kind of opera?" Wen asked.

"Shangdang clapper opera."

"Wait for me, Uncle. I'll go with you. I've been feeling bored lately." He added, "Like you, it's not for the opera. I just need to get away."

Wen's decision changed everything. Cao would have walked to Qinyuan, but now, with Wen tagging along, he'd take his three-donkey, rubber-wheeled cart. Traveling by foot would have taken a day and a half. His cart, with bells around the donkeys' necks ringing the whole way, crossed into Qinyuan County later that afternoon. When they passed a market on the way, Wen told Cao to stop so he could buy half a goat and a large basket of wild peaches from Apricot Blossom. He also bought two large jugs of liquor, preferring it to the liquor from his own distillery, which was not as smooth.

They reached Niu Village before sunset. With the manager of Wen's Vinegar Shop along to watch the opera, Cao gained a great deal of face, and so did his friend, Old Han. The rubber-wheeled cart, pulled by three shiny black donkeys, came to a nice stop, with a loud "puff" from its air brakes, right in front of Han's house. They unloaded the liquor, the goat, and the fruit, to Han's delight. Caught unprepared by the early arrival of Cao and Wen, he quickly had the yard swept and got a room ready, with new bedding on a new bed, especially for Wen. Niu Laodao came over that evening when he heard that the manager of Wen's Vinegar Shop was there for the opera. Being a regular consumer of Wen's vinegar, he complimented him on the product after the required greeting rituals were exchanged.

"You didn't have to come out here yourself." Wen stood up. "I'm just a vinegar merchant who doesn't deserve attention from a revered gentleman like yourself."

"No need to be so diffident, Mr. Manager," Laodao said. "There are vinegar merchants and there are vinegar merchants."

After telling them what to expect from the performances over the next three days, Laodao stood up. "Ours is a small village, with little to recommend it. Please don't laugh at us when you see something below your expectations."

Wen quickly got up to bow.

"Please come visit Xiangyuan when you're free, sir. Our local opera isn't bad."

Cao and Wen settled down in Han's house to wait for the performance to begin. Han killed a few chickens and a dog for the guests. Being talkative all his life, Han had to curtail his verbosity when he noticed Wen's serious manner and stern face; he even watched the younger man's expression to make sure he said nothing out of line. Still, he came across as a chatterbox, to which Wen responded with a smile, seemingly untroubled. On the seventh day of the sixth lunar month, the opera began in Niu Village as planned, drawing spectators from all over who thronged the area in front of the temple, now a scene of unprecedented festive activity. Niu Laodao, who had worked hard to make it all happen, fell ill from exhaustion and ran a fever. But he wrapped a blue cloth around his head and, helped by Farong, came out to take charge.

Tang's troupe performed two operas a day, one in the morning and one in the evening, taking the afternoon off to rest. The first day they put on *Peace Banquet at Sanguan* and *Qin Xianglian*, with *Famen Temple* and *Pi Xiuying Battles a Tiger* planned for the second day. *Tianbo Tower* and *Lovers' Lament* were scheduled for the third day. Unlike Wen and Han, Cao did not care much for opera and sat behind the others during the performance. He listened as Han explained the stories to Wen, who took out a handkerchief to dry his eyes when Han reached the sad parts, though he was not affected by the story he was telling. When the day was over, Cao had gotten a sense of what the operas were about, with newfound appreciation. What was presented on stage also occurred in real life, but the former seemed so much more enjoyable.

Wen took a nap during the afternoon break. When he got up, he washed his face before taking a stroll along the Xiang River. The river was high in the summer, nearly overflowing the banks as it raged eastward. Along the banks were more than two hundred large willow trees, each as thick as a man's waist. Wen walked on, with Cao and Han close behind.

"Your Mr. Wen is pretty easy-going," Han whispered to Cao.

"He's not much a talker, especially when something is in the air. He likes to mull things over."

"Mulling things over is important, and it shows he's subtle and shrewd, unlike me, always chattering away," Cao replied.

The third day's lunch was stewed dog meat, a dish that tends to heat people up. They also had a bit to drink, so soon the house felt stuffy and hot. Wen waved a fan to cool off, but could not stop sweating.

"Shall we move out back to eat by the river, Uncle?" he said.

"But wouldn't that seem unmannerly," Han said. "You're my guests, after all."

"We're all friends, so we can dispense with the formalities."

So they moved the table to a shady spot under a willow trees on the riverbank. With water flowing at their feet and a breeze blowing above them, they were much cooler. Drinking was enjoyable again. They ate, they drank, and they talked about the operas and about what went on in Wen and Niu Villages. They were still talking when the sun slanted westward and the river turned blood red from the sunset. Wen, now clearly intoxicated, looked around.

"This is a great place."

"Talk of a great place reminds me of something," Han said.

"What's that?" Cao asked.

"I want to be a matchmaker and find Gaixin a husband from here."

"Who do you have in mind?" Cao asked.

"Too bad I have four daughters. If I had a son, your daughter would have to marry into my family, but now I'll have to find someone else," Han said to Cao. "I'm not eager to be a matchmaker. It's just that you'd come more often if your daughter was here."

"I see." Cao laughed. "That sounds good, but it's a little too far for me."

Wen didn't think so. "Distance doesn't mean much if it's a good match," he said. "Even with all the people in the world," he continued, "it's hard to find someone you can talk to."

Han refilled the younger man's cup. "If that's what you think, Mr. Manager, then you'll have to be the go-between."

"Tell me which family you have in mind," Wen said with a smile.

"My dear friend Old Niu has a sesame mill. Gaixin would have a good life with that family. I think of them not because of their business. It's the son, a very reliable young man. Hard to find these days. Why don't I have Old Niu and his son over in a little while for you to check them out, Mr. Manager?"

"There's no hurry." Wen said with a laugh.

Cao and Wen treated the conversation as idle talk, but Han was serious. After the opera was over that night, he brought out some liquor and invited Old Niu and his son over to meet Cao and Wen. Niu Shudao looked to be seventeen or eighteen, somewhat short, with large eyes, and a bit shy. Wen asked him some questions, such as how many years of schooling he had and where he'd traveled to. Shudao answered every question studiously, and then walked off after wishing them a good time. Old Niu stayed behind to drink with his friend. The sesame mill owner could hold his liquor, as could Wen, who nonetheless got drunk quickly, since they'd been drinking all afternoon. A quiet, serious man, he was given to weeping and shaking his head when drunk, saying, "It's hard. It's really hard." He was a completely different person from his sober self. Fully aware of Wen's trait, Cao ignored him; Han and Niu, on the other hand, were shocked when a tearful Wen kept saying how hard it was. What was hard? they wondered.

When the performances were over, Cao and Wen headed back to Xiangyuan.

"What do you think of his idea, Mr. Manager?" Cao asked along the way.

"Which idea was that?" Wen was confused.

"The idea of Gaixin's marriage. My friend is serious about it, so I must be too. I'm afraid I'll have to give him an answer soon."

"I was pretty drunk that night." Wen recalled meeting the father and son. He sighed. "I missed quite a bit of the opera performances."

"Why was that?" Cao could not hide his surprise. Didn't Old Han treat you well enough?" "Or maybe Old Han annoyed you with all his chatter."

"Annoyance has nothing to do with how much one says." Wen shook his head.

"Or was the opera disappointing?"

"Old Tang's troupe put on a great performance."

"Then what is it?"

"I had a falling out with Little Zhou, the liquor distillery owner, before we left."

Now Cao knew why Wen had looked unhappy over the past few days. When he'd met Wen on his way to Niu Village, Wen had told him he needed to get away. At the time, Cao hadn't thought much about the comment, but now he realized that Wen really did need to get away. Also, Wen had bought liquor from Apricot Blossom Village, not from Zhou's Peach Blossom Village. Cao had thought Wen had done that to make Cao look good with his friend, but it was actually because Wen had had a falling out with Zhou.

"The Wen and Zhou families have been friends since your grandfather's time. You can't cut ties just like that. Was it over money?"

"That would have made things easy." Wen sighed. "It was because of nothing, just a single phrase."

"What is it?"

"I always thought he was smart, but it turns out he's not all that bright." Wen was evasive. "He's smart when dealing with trivial stuff and loses his sense of judgment over important matters."

"I can get someone to talk things out between the two of you if you'd like to save the friendship."

"Actually, it wasn't about a phrase or a matter. It's him. I never thought he could be so devious. He and I are different. We should not and could not be friends. Real friends are like you and Old Han." Wen heaved another sigh. "I've wasted years of my life."

Seeing how bad the younger man felt, Cao did not feel like pursuing the cause of the breakup. All he could do was to try to make his employer feel better.

"Well, if it's broken, there's nothing you can do about it. There are plenty of people out there, so you don't need a liquor distiller as your friend."

"I liked what I saw in Old Niu the sesame mill owner." Wen slapped his thigh. "It's hard to find an honest, straightforward person, someone you can get drunk with, someone you can be friends with."

A month later, a marriage proposal was formalized between Old Cao from Wen Village in Xiangyuan and Old Niu from Niu Village in Qinyuan. Gaixin, later to be known as Cao Qing'e, and Niu Shudao were married a year later.

That was another story Niu Aiguo's mother loved to tell about the sixty years of her marriage.

Sixty years later, Niu Shudao died. It was a windless, cool day when they buried him in the Niu family's private cemetery. Everyone stopped crying once the grave was covered with dirt, everyone but his wife, Cao Qing'e.

"Don't be sad. He's gone and will never come back," the others tried to console her.

"I'm not crying for that cursed turtle-spawn. I'm crying for my own sake, for ruining my life with him."

4

Cao Qing'e made a trip back to Yanjin the year after her marriage to Niu Shudao. She had spent the first five years of her life in Yanjin, then thirteen years in Xiangyuan, before moving at the age of eighteen to Qinyuan to live with her husband. No one she knew in Xiangyuan or Qinyuan had ever been to Yanjin. Back at Wen Village, Qing'e, or Gaixin at the time, often quarreled with her mother over Yanjin. She did not dare talk back before she turned thirteen, for her mother would hit her if she did. Old Cao's wife was a tall woman with powerful hands, so Gaixin never talked back when she was scolded, whether it was over Yanjin, or over her mistake of making the congee too thick or too thin, or cutting a shoe pattern incorrectly. No matter what Cao's wife said, Gaixin kept quiet, because she knew she would be hit if she didn't. By thirteen, however, she'd grown to be a big girl, about as tall as Cao's wife, which emboldened her to fight back when her mother gave her a tongue-lashing. Her mother stopped hitting her, though not out of fear or because Gaixin could overpower her; it was all because of one thing—the girl threatened to kill herself by jumping down a well. Frightened that she would actually carry through with it, Cao's wife stopped hitting her altogether. All they did was quarrel. At first, Gaixin was no match for her mother, but she had been to school, while her mother was illiterate, so at some point Gaixin began to win their arguments. When they squabbled, Old Cao just sat on his haunches smoking his pipe and not saying a word. When his wife lost an argument, she vented her anger on him.

"Didn't you see this ungrateful girl snap at me? Don't just stand there, do something!"

Cao would continue to smoke silently.

"When we bought her," his wife said, "I said she was five, old enough to remember everything, and that she'd be like a dog that will never be yours no matter how long you feed it. But you wouldn't listen. Now see what we've got?"

That was an unjust accusation. Cao was the one who had objected to buying the girl, while she had insisted on it. In their family, Cao's wife was in charge of everything, whether it was buying a girl or buying a lamp. But Cao kept quiet as he puffed away.

"What did I do in a previous life to deserve this?" her mother said. "Why are you ganging up on me? I should be the one to jump down the well."

With his wife raising a stink, Cao talked to the girl, not his wife. "Why are you always fighting? She's your mother, no matter what, so why must you argue with her?" He added, "Remember, argue only with people who will listen to reason. You won't get anywhere quarreling with her. So why do it? Arguing for argument's sake?"

Gaixin never talked back to Old Cao. When she was young, he rode her on his shoulders instead of carrying her in his arms or on his back when he went to feed the livestock in Wen's animal pen. Sometimes she fell asleep and peed on his neck. Being a carter meant he was often on the road. When he passed a market, he bought snacks, which he put in a basket and hung from a rafter for her to enjoy at her leisure. She liked to sleep late when she got older, and he was the one who had to get her up each morning.

"Time to get up, girl."

So when he asked her not to fight with her mother, she said, "I don't want to argue with her, but I don't want to be like you, under her thumb all my life."

Her frank response surprised him. He mulled it over for a while before heaving a sigh.

"You're right. When you fight with her, she leaves me alone." He patted her on the head. "That never occurred to me back when we got you."

Refusing to give in to one another, mother and daughter argued until nothing was off limits; they quarreled over matters at home and over their views on what happened out on the street. But they fought most frequently over a place—Yanjin. Gaixin, as we recall, was Qiaoling, who had left Yanjin at the age of five. She didn't remember much about the place, and what little she could recall was a blur, all but Moses Wu. When she was first sold to the Cao family, Cao's wife forbade her from thinking about Yanjin and Moses Wu, and threatened to beat her if she did. But it was only natural that the more she wasn't allowed to think about them, the more they occupied her mind. Yanjin was hazy and unworthy of her thoughts, so she thought about Moses. Gaixin, later called Cao Qing'e, still dreamed about being with him, even in her late teens. It was he who had lost her, but in her dreams, he was the one who was lost. In real life, she had been sold at the age of five, but in her dreams, she sold Moses, who cried when he was handed over to a human trafficker.

"Don't sell me, Qiaoling. I'll do anything you want when we get back."

She had been afraid of the dark and would not go out at night. In her dreams, Moses was the one who cried and said, "Don't sell me, Qiaoling. I'm afraid of the dark."

Or, "If you want to sell me, Qiaoling, put me in a sack and don't forget to close the opening."

Sometimes, when she awoke from a dream like that, she could see a crescent moon suspended between the branches of a date tree outside the window. After a while, however, his face began to blur in her mind. She tried hard to recall his features in the daytime but could only get a general impression, as his brows, eyes, nose, and mouth all turned into a blurry image. She hadn't expected that a person's face could become that hazy over time. Now Yanjin was a blur, and so was Moses. Her mother, who had never been to Yanjin, had many bad things to say about the place and about Moses. She was convinced that Gaixin argued with her purely because she wasn't her real daughter. Yanjin was the core of their problems. As a result, their quarrels always came around to Yanjin; it was the starting point and the final "destination" of all their spats. After berating the place for so long, Cao's wife became so well versed on Yanjin, like a frequent lodger at an inn where she knows where everything is and how to use it, she ran out of new complaints about the place. She was reduced to repeating her disparaging comments: it was a terrible place where the men were all stupid and the women shrews. Moses Wu would not have lost the child if he'd been smart, and Gaixin would be a nicer girl if Yanjin women weren't shrews.

"Are you sure you were kidnapped?" she once wondered aloud. "I wouldn't be surprised if you left because you couldn't stand to live there any longer. And was that so-called father of yours careless or did he leave you behind on purpose? You must have been an awful child if he'd let someone kidnap a five-year-old."

Gaixin, who remembered little of Yanjin, felt she knew the place like the back of her hand after her mother's tirades. Her Yanjin was different from her mother's version, though not because her mother's derision led her to conjure up a place with pretty mountains and flowing waters. Gaixin did not imagine Moses to be a smart man because her mother had called him an idiot; nor did he turn stupid when her mother thought he was smart. Simply put, her mother's criticism of Yanjin eventually solidified the importance of the place in Gaixin's mind. Sometimes her mother got so carried away in her attack on Yanjin that Cao would sigh and say, "It's surprising how a little girl is responsible for so many ills of a town." He turned to his wife. "Gaixin won't change her mind about us. As the saying goes, we remember those who raised us, not those who gave birth to us. Where do you think her home is? It's Xiangyuan, not Yanjin."

Gaixin did not share Old Cao's view. It was true that she'd spent only five years in Yanjin and thirteen in Xiangyuan. And yet, more than a decade in Xiangyuan paled in comparison to those five years in Yanjin. Xiangyuan was not her home; Yanjin was. Her sense of belonging might have been different in the beginning, but Yanjin was solidly her home now, after all the arguments with her mother. This Yanjin was not the place where she'd lived; it was a new Yanjin, the hometown in her heart. In the beginning, Cao's wife prohibited her from thinking about Yanjin and Moses; later, when their fights grew ugly, they became Gaixin's sore spot, her flaw. As a quarrel heated up, her mother would say, "Go home, then. Go back to Yanjin to be with that idiot father of yours!"

"All right, I will," Gaixin would say. "I can't wait to leave this place."

She did leave once at the age of fourteen. But she only knew the Yanjin in her mind, the spot where all the arguments were located, and had no idea where in the world the real Yanjin was. Being afraid of the dark, she ran off in the morning and returned to Wen Village before nightfall. Her father, Old Cao, was waiting for her at the village entrance.

"I knew my little girl would be back.

"Where did you think you could go without money?

"You won't miss your mother, but you'll miss me.

"I'd miss you till my heart broke if you were gone."

She crouched down and cried.

"If you really want to go back to Yanjin, I'll take you there in the winter, when there isn't so much work. You can meet your real father."

Cao meant her stepfather, Moses Wu, of course.

"Your birth mother ran off with another man nine years ago. I don't know if she has come back. You'd be able to see her if she did."

"I don't want to go back to Yanjin, Father," Gaixin said as she dried her eyes.

"Why?" Cao couldn't believe his ears. "Are you afraid your mother will hit you?"

The mother in this case was Cao's wife.

"Actually, I hate Yanjin, Father."

Cao mulled over her comment and its convoluted logic before heaving a sigh. He took her hand and went home as dusk deepened.

Gaixin, later Cao Qing'e, was married into Niu Village in Qinyuan when she was eighteen. She got into another fight with her mother over the marriage, after her mother had had an argument with Old Cao. When he and Little Wen, the manager of Wen's Vinegar Shop, returned from their trip to Niu Village, Cao mentioned the marriage proposal to his wife, who reacted angrily. She had never been to Qinyuan or Niu Village, but she was able to use her repertoire of tirades against Yanjin on these two places, not because she had anything against them, but because this was the first she'd heard about it. Essentially, it was about her authority at home and not the marriage proposal. If Cao had to discuss even the purchase of a lamp, how could he not say a word about such an important matter as their daughter's marriage? He rapped the bowl of his pipe against his knee as she raged against him.

"What am I doing now, if not talking it over with you?"

She had to drop that issue, so she focused instead on the distance, more than a hundred li from their home to the Niu Village.

"Have all the men in Xiangyuan died?" she rebuked. "Why Qinyuan? I went through all the trouble of raising her, and now you're going to let her fly off just when she can help me out around here. What was the point of buying her back then?"

Cao had had misgivings about the distance, but now he said, "That's my concern, too. It will take her two days to come home, with a night on the road." He added, "It wasn't my idea. Old Han played the matchmaker."

"What kind of disgusting friend do you have there?" She turned her anger on Han. "He knew it was a pit, but he told you to jump in anyway." Her complaint was redirected at Cao. "You're nearly sixty, and you still don't know how to choose a friend. Don't go back to Qinyuan ever again."

"Little Wen thought it was a good match, too."

"Who do you live with, Little Wen or me?" Her anger flared up again. "I know you're doing this on purpose. You're scheming with others to get at me so you can have another wife after I die of anger."

Now she was off onto something else, no longer focused on the marriage. Cao let her rant. Obviously, the marriage proposal was off. He decided he would find the right time to explain that to his friend in Qinyuan and to Little Wen, after which it would be as if they'd never mentioned it. He said no more. But to his surprise, Old Han, convinced that it was a done deal, brought Niu Shudao over three days later to meet the family, not suspecting that something had gone awry on Cao's end. Cao panicked when he saw the two men, worried that his wife would throw etiquette to the wind and berate his friend; that would be ugly. He needn't have been concerned; it took little effort by the silver-tongued Han to pacify Cao's wife shortly after he walked in the door.

"I offered this as an idea when my brother here was at the opera, Sister-in-law, but I know you're in charge at home, so I'm here to talk it over with you."

Cao's wife opened her mouth, but Han would not let her get a word in. "It was just an idle thought, without your input. It's entirely up to you whether it's a go or not."

She opened her mouth again, but Han cut in before she had a chance. "Seeing is believing. So I brought the boy with me."

She opened her mouth once more, and again Han was faster. "Your husband and Little Wen have met the boy, but what they think doesn't mean a thing. You'll be the judge and only you can see if he meets your expectations. Let's not talk about the marriage for now. Why don't you talk with him and teach him something?"

Being the talkative type, Han could not stop prattling and did not think much about what he was saying as he chattered away. Just about everything he said was empty talk, but to Cao's wife it felt like a potent settlement of all her concerns. Han had crossed the mountains to bring over the boy, who was now unloading sesame oil, fabric, sesame seeds, and a few cackling hens from a donkey cart. She cheered up immediately.

"You really shouldn't have. We're so glad you're here, and there was no need for you to bring anything."

Han and Niu Shudao spent three days with the Cao family, after which Cao's wife consented to the marriage, though not because Han was such a smooth talker or because she coveted the gifts Shudao had brought, but because the boy made a positive impression. Unlike Han, Shudao was not a chatterbox; he always thought before he spoke. He pondered what Cao's wife said and stood up to reply, "Auntie was right to say so." No matter what she said to him, he did exactly the same thing, thinking it over before standing to offer, "Auntie was right to say so."

Cao's wife was mightily pleased after a few rounds of "right to say so," not because Shudao agreed with her in everything, but because she had never seen anyone talk like the boy, who even stood up to answer her questions. During the three days, Old Han stayed in a room on the east side and the young man in one on the west side, where loud, clear sounds of Shudao reading from a book were heard early each morning. His arrival lent a new a tenor and aura to the Cao household, making it more like a farming family that stressed study. Cao's wife now had a favorable view of the marriage, of Old Han, and of Qinyuan County and Niu Village, which in turn brought Niu Shudao and Old Han, as well as Qinyuan and the two villages, again into Cao's good graces.

Little Wen came over when he heard about Han's visit. After spending three days in Wen Village, Han and Shudao left with their donkey cart for Qinyuan County. By then, Cao's wife had made up her mind to marry her daughter to Shudao, a decision that had Cao's blessing. Gaixin, later Cao Qing'e, did not approve. She had seen Niu Shudao when she was at Niu Village with her father, but they hadn't spoken. They didn't really have a chance to talk when he came to visit this time either, for he spent most of his time studying. In theory, his inclination for books should be considered a positive trait, but not to Gaixin, who simply did not like him. She hadn't cared for him when they first met and couldn't see any reason to change her mind now. In her mother's mind, the girl pretended not to like him to upset her; in other words, Qing'e had been fond of him until she'd seen her mother's favorable reaction. A marriage proposal was not an ironclad deal, and they could always find another prospect. But in this case, the more the girl resisted the marriage, the more determined her mother was to see it through. They had a big row.

"You marry him if you like him so much, but I won't," the girl said. "I'll marry anyone but him."

Now she was being spiteful, which, to Cao's wife, proved that she had been right about the girl's intention to annoy her. Instead of railing at the girl, she clapped her hands and screamed at her husband.

"You're the one who started it all. Now it's turned to shit, and you can deal with it." She continued, "I agreed to the marriage, so I'll hang myself if it doesn't work out."

That put Cao squarely in the middle of the mess.

Late that night, he got up to stir the vinegar dreg vats in Wen's distillery. When he walked into the yard, he saw that lights were still on in his daughter's room, so he put down his shovel and tapped on her door. She opened it to let him in. He squatted on the floor to smoke and signaled her to sit by him.

"He looks like a nice boy, so why don't you want to marry him?" Cao asked.

The girl was quiet, so he went on.

"Don't do it just to make your mother mad. You shouldn't ruin your chances just to spite her."

"I was doing that at first, but not now. I just don't like the way he looks."

"Why?"

"I don't think he's very smart. I stood outside his room to listen to him. He read the same passage every day. He got most of it wrong and added his own words."

"I could see he isn't too smart." Cao nodded. "But he looks guileless and reliable, which is precisely why I think you ought to marry him. Everyone likes a smart man, but for a husband, it's better to choose the guileless and reliable kind. Marriage is spending a lifetime together. I've been around for more than five decades, and I always lose out to clever people. Your mother, for instance. Didn't she pretend to be clever? Well, she ruined my life."

"I don't like him and I don't like Niu Village."

"You've only been there once. Little Wen at the vinegar shop has seen the world, and he likes it."

"Besides, it's too far from home."

Cao didn't know what to say. His wife had used distance as the reason for her objection.

"I get the feeling that I'm being sold again to a new place, Father. I'm afraid of the dark when I'm in a strange place."

"You're all grown up now, no longer a five-year-old." Cao sighed again. "As for the distance, I tell you, it has its advantage. You'll be away from your mother and her tirades. Old Han picked the family for you, so it can't be too bad. He's a good friend and wouldn't lie to me. What would he gain?"

She put her head on his shoulder and wept.

Cao Qing'e realized after she was married to Niu Shudao that Old Han had deceived her entire family. Neither the young man whom Cao and Wen met when they went to Qinyuan for the opera performance nor the one who later came to Xiangyuan to meet the Cao family was real. He was Niu Shudao, all right, but just not his real self. He had acted differently at their house. Han had taught him what to do during those three days, including standing up to reply with his stock phrase to Cao's wife. Han, the opera lover, had stolen the "right to say so" from the scripts, and he had also told him to get up early every morning to read out loud. By the time Qing'e married him, Shudao had shown his true self and turned into a different person, though not as stupid as she had thought. He wasn't dim, but he wasn't gentle or quiet either; nor did he like to study. He never again said "right to say so." He was, in fact, ill-behaved and unreasonable, and rude, whether at his house or elsewhere.

Qing'e's pretty face had caught Niu Shudao's fancy when she came with her father for Han's fiftieth birthday party. He had pestered his father into talking to Han so he could have her as his wife. Eventually worn down by his badgering, Niu went to see Han, who hesitated at first, because it didn't appear to be a good match to him, not to mention the distance between the two villages. But he could not say no to his good friend. Niu and Han had not been friends for long; Han had been close to Old Ding, with whom he'd gone rabbit hunting and sung opera. Han and Ding had had a falling out over a sack of money, after which Han drew closer to Niu, who wasn't into rabbit hunting or singing opera, but did share a hobby with Han, playing "squares," a kind of Chinese chess. After drawing grids on the ground to form fifty-six "eyes," or squares, the players used pieces of brick or grass stalks to barricade the opponent's pieces. It was like Japanese go, but not quite. Squares players tried to block the other person's piece, like a war game to control the world. The game was not the whole point for them, though. More important to the players was the competitiveness resulting from the fact that the wins and losses were about even, which made the game even more addictive. Besides, Han and Niu lived in the same village and saw each other every day, while Han and Cao only met up two or three times a year. In some ways, Niu played a more significant role in Han's life. A chatterbox by nature, Han also liked to take charge, so he began to change his mind after Niu's repeated pleas for his help. Taking Niu's side meant that lies were inevitable. In the end, Qing'e spent the first ten years of the five decades of her married life rectifying Shudao's personality flaws, but then she turned into her mother and Shudao turned into her father.

Qing'e had her first big row with Shudao after she was pregnant with Niu Aiguo's older brother, Niu Aijiang. The quarrel was insufficient to still her anger, so she ran off in the middle of the night. When Shudao got up the next morning and found her missing, he thought she had gone back to her parents.

"Let her be." He wasn't worried. "I'm not going to bring her back, or she'll get into the habit of running away."

He was still not worried after she'd been gone ten days, but Niu and Han were, and they forced Shudao to go bring her back from Wen Village. She wasn't there. He was shocked; so were Old Cao and his wife.

"Why didn't you stop her when she left?" Old Cao asked.

"She ran away at midnight, when I was asleep."

Cao stomped his foot, worried not about his daughter missing, but about her running off at night.

"How could you let her run away at night? She's afraid of the dark."

Cao's wife had fought with their daughter when she lived at home, but now, when the girl had gone missing, the mother pounced on Shudao with her fists.

"I spent thirteen years raising her. How could you let her go missing like that? Niu Shudao, give me back my daughter!"

Old Cao, who knew his daughter well, rapped the bowl of his pipe and said, "I know where she's gone."

"Where?" Shudao and his mother-in-law asked simultaneously.

"She must have gone to Yanjin."

Shudao had never been to Yanjin. "So will she be back?" he asked stupidly.

Old Cao was finally convinced that his son-in-law was dense, not stupid; he just didn't know what to do when something like this happened.

"It's hard to say if she'd return or not if she wasn't pregnant." Cao sighed. "But now that she is, she can't stay away forever." He sighed again. "She didn't run away when she could, and now she has when she couldn't. That's what so sad about it."

This was another anecdote Aiguo's mother frequently recounted.

5

When he was thirty-five, Aiguo's mother, Cao Qing'e, told him about running away from home at midnight in the fourth lunar month of the second year of her marriage to his father. Instead of going to Yanjin, she'd gone to Xiangyuan to see an old schoolmate, Zhao Hongmei, and spent two weeks away from home. She'd gone to see Hongmei not because she'd had a fight with her husband and had no place to go or because Yanjin was too far. In fact, the idea of going to Yanjin never crossed her mind. She went to Zhao's house to ask about her friend's cousin, a man named Hou Baoshan.

As a child, Aiguo had not been his mother's favorite. She'd favored his younger brother, Aihe, while his father preferred his older brother, Aijiang. Hence, Aiguo could not wait to leave home. He hadn't talked it over with his parents when he joined the army; instead, he'd gone into town to see his sister. But he drew closer to his mother when he turned thirty-five, after his father had died. When Qing'e had something on her mind, she chose to talk to Aiguo rather than his older brother, Aijiang, his younger brother, Aihe, or his sister, Aixiang. But Aiguo would not seek out his mother when he needed someone with whom he could share his troubles.

His mother usually just talked about what had happened fifty or sixty years before, and it had the tenor of idle talk now. For some reason, she reminisced more in the winter than in other seasons, and usually at night, when he sat across from her, with a lit brazier between them. After recounting an anecdote, she would laugh, then follow up with another anecdote and more laughter. Niu Aiguo did not laugh with her.

Years before, when Qing'e had gone to see Zhao Hongmei, she had not started out at night, but not because of her fear of the dark. She had very little to say to her husband after they were married. Not having much to say was easier during the day, for they could each be doing what they needed to do. But they had to talk at night when they went to bed, and that is when they argued. They would quarrel late into the night, when she would walk out and prowl the streets, too upset to be bothered by the darkness around her. As time went by, she got used to the dark and was no longer afraid. In all, they had more than eighty fights during the first year of their marriage. At the time, she was close to a female relative called Li Lanxiang. Once she said to Li, "I did get something good out of marrying Niu Shudao. I'm no longer afraid of the dark."

Qing'e and Shudao could fight all they wanted, but they still had nothing to say to each other after daybreak. Leaving the Niu house that night was the first time. After the argument, Shudao rolled over and went to sleep, while she decided to go to Xiangyuan to see Hongmei. After wrapping essential items in a bundle, she opened the door and walked out. She didn't get on the road right away, however, because she was hungry. Since she was pregnant with her first child, she needed twice as much food as before to stave off her hunger. She had never had to worry about her stomach when she fought with her husband in the past, but now even a slight exertion stirred up pangs of hunger. Putting down her bundle, she went to the kitchen, where she started a fire, mixed flour with water, and pinched off small pieces of dough to toss into a pot when the water boiled. When the pinch noodles were nearly ready, she mixed in an egg, added soy sauce, vinegar, and salt, and ladled it out. Then she leisurely enjoyed a bowl, after sprinkling chopped scallions and sesame oil. It was dawn when she finished, and, with a belch, she picked up her bundle and set out.

Qing'e had met Zhao Hongmei when they attended school in Fan Town in Xiangyuan County. It was a new school, which meant that age limit was not an issue, and all the students were older than average. Qing'e was sixteen, while Hongmei was seventeen when they were in the fifth grade. Hongmei was a top student, while Qing'e did poorly, so they had little to do with one another at school. But they often traveled together when they left home on Mondays for school and returned to their villages on Saturdays. The town was twenty li from Wen Village and twenty-five li from Zhao Village. Hongmei had to pass through Wen Village and climb a hill on her way home. Though a good student, Hongmei changed into a different person on the road and enjoyed talking about what happened between a man and a woman. She was the one who taught Qing'e about sex. Qing'e was surprised to learn that Hongmei, though only a year older, knew so much more than she did. By then, Qing'e had grown into a tall young woman but was still timid and afraid of the dark. Zhao was small, just a little over five feet at seventeen, but she was bold, and dark nights did not bother her. Sometimes it got dark before they reached home, so she would walk Qing'e home before heading to her own home. Or she would spend the night and share a bed with Qing'e before heading back early the next morning. On Monday mornings, she would have to leave before it was light to reach Wen Village, meet up with Qing'e, and walk with her into town.

When Qing'e was seventeen, the first East Is Red tractor showed up in town, driven by a young man called Hou Baoshan. In the spring and fall, Baoshan plowed the fields in neighboring villages. Tractors were different from oxen; oxen needed to rest at night after working the land during the day, while tractors could work day and night. Qing'e would wake up after a night's sleep and hear the tractor rumbling back from the fields. When the tractor driver plowed land in a particular village, the villagers took turns feeding him. He had his breakfast and dinner at one house, while lunch was brought to him in the field. Qing'e had been the one to deliver lunch to him when it was her family's turn.

Baoshan was a tall, lean young man with slender eyes and hair parted in the middle. He jumped down off the tractor, took off his white gloves, and sat on his haunches to eat his lunch. As she needed to collect the rice and water jars, the bowl and chopsticks, she watched him eat, and they began to talk. They were instantly closer when it turned out that he was Hongmei's cousin. Instead of gathering the utensils and jars to go home, she hitched a ride on his tractor to watch him plow the land when he had finished eating. Rows of soil opened up behind them like ocean waves, as they went from one end of the field to the other and back. She listened to him talk, amazed that he was the best conversation partner she'd ever met. He was good, not because he talked a lot and couldn't stop, but because, instead of cutting in, he always let her talk first before saying anything. She had to fight to get a word in when she quarreled with her mother, which was why she at first mistook him as the silent type. They talked about the tractor, the tractor station in town, the number of people working at the station, and what they did every day. When Qing'e brought up the topic of Zhao Hongmei, he answered all her questions, then smiled and stopped talking.

"You work day and night. Don't you ever get tired?" she asked.

"There isn't that much land in any of the villages, so I can rest after I finish." Baoshan continued, "Besides, I love tilling the land at night."

"Why is that?"

"The fields aren't much to look at it in the daylight. But they're nice at night, when I turn on the light. Would you like to try it one night?'

"Not me. I'm afraid of the dark."

"I could pick you up if you'd like to come out."

Taking his offer as a joke, she just smiled. Late that night, when she was already asleep, she heard someone gently tapping on the back wall. She got up, opened the door, and walked out to the back wall. It was Hou Baoshan, still wearing his white gloves.

"You look so quiet I didn't realize you could be so daring."

He took her hand and walked with her to the village outskirts, where they ran to the field. The tractor was waiting at the edge, its headlamp lighting up a broad area. They rode from one end of the field to the other and back. They seemed to be plowing the darkness, which opened up under the bright headlamp and receded to the sides. The darkness seemed to grow the more they tilled, but they vanquished it little by little. Her fear of the dark was allayed by the headlamp and by Baoshan, who sat next to her; she looked straight ahead without saying a word.

He left on his tractor three days later after tilling the land in Wen Village. She began having trouble sleeping after his departure, as the nights seemed to turn even darker, and she resumed her childhood habit of keeping a light on at night. Baoshan returned in the fall and worked the land in her village for four days. They ignored each other during the day, but at night he picked her up and they plowed the darkness together.

"This tractor of yours is no good," she said.

"Why is that?"

"It only runs in the fields."

"It can travel on streets, too."

"But too slow."

"What do you have in mind?"

"If it could go fast, you could take me someplace."

"Where?"

"It's quite far."

But she would not tell him where that far place was. They just rode from one end of the field to the other and back.

Old Han from Niu Village came with the marriage proposal the following summer. It rained the day after Han and Niu Shudao left Wen Village. Qing'e ran into town to the tractor station to see Baoshan, who was kept by the rain from going out to till the field. The tractor sat idle; Baoshan and other workers were playing poker. He had notes pasted all over his face, a sign that he was losing. He was surprised to see Qing'e run into the station, soaking wet; he peeled off the notes and ran over.

"What are you doing here?" He added, "Go into the kitchen to dry your clothes."

"No. I just have a question for you."

"You can ask me in the kitchen."

"No. We need a quiet place," she said and spun around to leave the station. They walked to the levee on the outskirts of town; he was also soaked.

"Can you take me away from here, Hou Baoshan?"

"Away from here? Where to?"

"I don't care, as long as we're away from Xiangyuan County." She glanced at him. "I'll marry you if you take me away."

Baoshan was too stunned to say a word. He scratched his head and tried to think. "I can't think of any place where we could make a home. You can marry me without leaving town. Besides, I couldn't drive a tractor if we ran away. There are only five of them in the whole county."

"Now I know that I am worth less than a tractor in your heart." She turned and ran off. Baoshan gave chase.

"What's your hurry?" he shouted. "We can talk this over."

She turned and spat out angry words.

"There's nothing to talk over. I hate a man with no guts."

Qing'e returned to Wen Village and married Niu Shudao six months later, and six months after that, she heard that Baoshan was also married. After her marriage to Shudao, to whom she had nothing to say, she often rued her rash reaction to Baoshan's hesitation over "running away." If she had stuck with him, they could have had a good life even if they hadn't run away. He would never fight, and he had a tractor that alleviated her fear of the dark. After marrying Shudao, she slowly overcame her fear of the dark, but it was not the same as being fearless with Baoshan.

On the night she and Shudao fought late into the night, she was suddenly reminded of Baoshan, so she packed a bundle and left for Xiangyun to see Zhao Hongmei. She wanted to know how Baoshan was doing. The journey took a day and a half, not to Zhao Village, however. By then Hongmei was married to a carpenter, Old Ji, who lived in Ji Village. Hongmei was surprised to see her.

"What are you doing here?"

"I want to ask you something."

That night, Hongmei sent her husband out to sleep in the cowshed so the two school friends could share a bed. With their arms around each other, they felt as if they were back in school, when Hongmei sometimes spent the night at Qing'e's house. They could not hold each other too tightly, however, because Qing'e was pregnant.

"What do you want to know?"

"I want to see Hou Baoshan and ask him to get a divorce."

"Before you ask him to do that, you probably should hear about how he's doing, and what his wife is like."

"I'll get a divorce if he will. That's all I need to hear from him."

"And what makes you think you can ask him that?"

"He touched me on the tractor."

"And you think that was a big deal?" Hongmei burst out laughing.

"It wasn't your average touch."

They fell silent for a moment before Qing'e spoke up again.

"It's not only about the divorce."

"What is it then?"

"If he would get a divorce, I'd get rid of the baby in my belly."

They were quiet again for a while until Qing'e said, "It's not only about the baby, either."

"What is it about?"

"I just want to kill someone. I even have a knife ready. Would you let me kill someone, Zhao Hongmei?"

Hongmei pulled Qing'e tightly into her arms.

"I also want to commit arson. I've loved setting fires since childhood. Would you let me set fire to something, Zhao Hongmei?"

Hongmei tightened her grip on her friend while Qing'e cried in her arms.

Pregnant Qing'e went to the tractor station in town the next morning to see Hou Baoshan. The station hadn't changed at all, still with the same yard and rooms. But Baoshan wasn't there; nor was his East Is Red tractor. Old Li and Old Zhao, who worked at the station, were sitting under the locust tree; they looked visibly older than two years before. Li told her that Baoshan had left to till land in Wei Village. She left town and went straight to Wei Village, where she was told that Baoshan had finished their land and gone on to Wu Village.

When she got there, people told her that he had come but hadn't stayed. He was just passing through their village on his way to Qi Village. That was where she went next. Finally, she heard the rumble of his tractor; she followed the noise to a hill behind the village and saw the East Is Red tractor. Baoshan was going from one end of the field to another and back. But there was someone else on the tractor—a woman, to be more precise. She was holding a baby who looked to be about six months old. As he drove the tractor, the woman was gnawing on sugar cane, spitting out the dried pulp. He jumped down off the tractor when it reached the end of the field. Qing'e could see he had put on weight and was seriously tanned. She heard the woman shout down from the tractor, "Hey, baby's father, take him and let him pee down there."

It was then that Qing'e noticed that the tractor was in much worse shape, and Baoshan was not wearing his white gloves anymore. Suddenly, she realized that this wasn't the Hou Baoshan she'd come looking for; the Baoshan she wanted to see had already died. Instead of going up to talk to him, she turned and left Qi Village; without stopping by Zhao Village to see her friend, she went to the county town in Xiangyuan, where she spent ten days at an inn before returning to Niu Village with her bundle. Niu Shudao and everyone else in his family thought she'd gone to Yanjin.

"Why didn't you tell me you were going to Yanjin?" Shudao said.

She ignored him. When she went to visit her parents during the Dragon Boat Festival, her father, who had also thought she'd gone to Yanjin, asked her about the place when they were alone after dinner.

"I didn't go to Yanjin," she told him.

"Where did you go?"

She held her tongue, and Old Cao did not press her, though he was convinced that was where she'd gone.

It would be another eighteen years before she did make a trip to Yanjin. Her father died in the autumn of that year, when Aijiang was seventeen, Aixiang was fifteen, Aiguo was seven, and Aihe was two. By then Qing'e had spent twenty years in Niu Village and had changed her husband's temperament so much that the couple no longer quarreled. Niu Shudao had turned into the now-deceased Old Cao, while Qing'e had turned into Old Cao's wife. Qing'e realized that she should not have tried to change her husband, for that meant changing herself as well. One of Niu Aiguo's childhood memories was of his father keeping to himself while his mother had a short fuse. She made all the family decisions, big and small, and his father usually sat quietly smoking. When she was angry, she beat the children—pinched them, actually. She

283

pinched their faces, arms, and thighs, or any part of their bodies she could get her hand on.

"Hold your tears. Don't cry," she warned as she pinched one of them.

Cao Qing'e was thirty-eight when she made her first trip back to Yanjin; it had nothing to do with the city, however, and had everything to do with her father's death at the age of seventy-five. Old Cao became a completely different person when he turned seventy. He had spent most of his life as a carter and a quiet man before the age of seventy; he rarely took the lead to make decisions, simply because he couldn't, for his wife was in charge of everything, and so they lived in what passed for harmony. As a child, she had often ridden on her father's shoulders and he, not her mother, was the one she went to when she needed someone to share what was on her mind.

Old Cao seemed a different man during the last five years of his life. His change was related to the changes in his wife. She had fought constantly with her husband and daughter. But when she turned seventy, she stopped arguing and, washing her hands of everything, refused to take charge any longer. She went along with whatever others said, as if nothing mattered to her. A woman who had bickered with others throughout her life suddenly clammed up in old age and smiled all the time. She was still tall; walking around with a cane, she looked kindly as she bent down to talk to people. When Qing'e's children went with their parents to Wen Village to visit their grandmother, they all agreed that she was a sweet old lady. Old Cao, on the other hand, had turned into his wife when she was young, a nagging, petty, ill-tempered, and bossy but incompetent man. When Qing'e came home with her children, Old Cao would glare angrily at the kids if they were ill behaved. A generous man when young, he became a miser in his seventies. When Qing'e was a little girl, Cao had bought her fried snacks and meat buns, but now he pulled a long face when any of her children refilled their rice bowl more than once, so they all said they went hungry when they visited Grandpa. Shudao usually smoked at the dining table. Once, when they visited the grandparents in the first lunar month, Old Cao refused to eat and put an angry look on his face. Qing'e thought her father was mad at the children for eating too much, but he called her aside afterward and said, "He smoked seven pipefuls of my tobacco at one meal."

She scolded her husband on the way home, after which she cried, not because he had smoked, but because she had noticed the changes in her father. She wasn't particularly sad when Old Cao died, nor did she miss him very much at first. Whatever good thoughts she had for him were used up during the last five years of his life. Yet she began to miss him terribly three months after his death; he showed up often in her dreams, when he was his old self, from his sixties down to when he'd just bought her, as Gaixin. She was sitting on his shoulders as they walked down the street, and he was smiling broadly, buying something for her to eat; he was on all fours as her horse; he stopped the sedan chair on her wedding day and refused to let her go, grabbing her hands tearfully.

"Who's going to look after me when you're gone, my little girl?"

Or, "Niu Shudao isn't reliable. You shouldn't marry him, my little girl."

In the dreams, she was the one who insisted on marrying Shudao, over her father's objection. Or she was marrying Hou Baoshan, not Niu Shudao, and had a fight with her father; Cao in her dreams would slap his own face when she refused to listen to him.

"It's my fault. I shouldn't have listened to Old Han."

She would take his hands and cry when he slapped himself.

"Let's talk it over, Father."

She then cried herself awake. One dream was different from all the others. In it, he was standing motionlessly against a wall, with his hands pressed against the surface.

"What's wrong, Father? Aren't you feeling well?"

He stared blankly, not saying a word.

"Look at you, Father. You missed a button there, and your shirt is bunched up."

She went up to unbutton his shirt, and then rebuttoned it for him when she found, to her horror, that his head was missing. Her headless father was still standing by the wall.

"Where's your head, Father?"

She woke up, drenched in a cold sweat, and could not go back to sleep. Over the next two weeks, she kept dreaming about her headless father, though not every night. Then the father in her dreams switched to Moses Wu, her stepfather when she was called Qiaoling. She dreamed about Moses before she turned eighteen. In fact, she dreamed about him so often that his face blurred, which in turn made her dream about him less frequently. Now, because of Old Cao, she began to dream about Moses again, but his face was still hazy or his head was missing, just like Old Cao. Both her fathers went headless: one dead, the other one with no news.

She abruptly decided to travel to Yanjin to see if her other father was also dead. She felt she had to find him, whether he was dead or alive. If he was still alive, she would take a look at his head and his face so she could put them back onto the body in her dreams. She got on the road the day after the idea oc-curred to her. As the one in charge at home, she did not tell her husband why she was going and what she planned to do in Yanjin. Shudao did not dare ask, except to say, "When will you be back?"

"Ten days or two weeks. Or I may not come back at all."

Shudao did not have the nerve to pursue further. She packed two bags, which she tied together to carry over her shoulder. Her oldest son, Aijiang, took her to Qinyuan County town on his bicycle, where she boarded a bus for Taiyuan. In Taiyuan, she switched to a train that took her to Shi Village, and boarded another train for Xinxiang. From there, she took another bus, reaching Yanjin after a four-day journey. A month later, she returned to Niu Village. Shudao had been worried when she was away for so long and breathed a sigh of relief when she returned. Lacking the courage to ask her anything, he simply said, "You went to Yanjin eighteen years ago. What does the place look like now?"

"It's a very nice place, of course. Otherwise, I wouldn't have gone there twice or spent so much time there. I found my family."

She looked about to cry.

After he turned thirty-five, Aiguo's mother started telling him what was on her mind. She told him she'd been to Yanjin once in her life and had spent only three days there. When she got there, she realized it was the same as all the places she'd yet to visit. The Yanjin in her childhood memories was completely differ-ent from the place she saw thirty-three years later. All the streets, East, West, North, and South, were different. Gone also was the yard to the west of West Street where her father, Moses Wu, and her mother, Wu Xiangxiang, had once made and steamed buns. More importantly, she failed to find her father, Moses Wu. Thirty-three years earlier, after she and Moses Wu were separated, neither of them had returned to Yanjin. For her it was because she'd been kidnapped and sold at the age of five. But why had Moses, who had been an adult and had not been sold, not gone back? After losing contact for thirty-three years, no one knew where he was or if he was still alive.

Qing'e remembered that her grandfather had lived on South Street and had owned Jiang's Cotton Shop back then. The shop was still there, but instead of human feet, now a machine with a diesel engine fluffed the cotton, making a clang-clang sound as it turned over and over. All the people she knew were dead, including her grandfather, and her uncles Jiang Long and Jiang Gou; she didn't know any of the surviving members of the Jiang family. It should have been a major incident when one of the children was sold, and the child's return should have been another major event. But what had happened thirty-three years earlier had become "hearsay" thirty-three years later. Those who were involved or knew about it were all gone or dead, leaving behind a group of people who had only heard about it; none of them cared about a kidnapping that had happened so long ago. Since no one was concerned about the kidnapped child thirty-three years earlier, they naturally didn't care when the missing child came back on her own thirty-three years later. To be sure, they all felt emotional about her return, but it amounted to nothing more than a trivial comment. So she left Yanjin three days later and went to Xinxiang to find the inn by the Dongguan Bus Depot where she had become separated from Moses. When she got there, she learned that the depot had been moved to Xiguan twenty years before, and in the site now stood a chemical fertilizer plant. It took up several hundred acres of land, where a dozen smokestacks puffed white smoke noisily and incessantly. There was no sight of the former inn. She left Xinxiang a day later.

"So you spent three days in Yanjin and one day in Xinxiang, but you didn't come home until a month later. How come?" Aiguo asked.

"I went to Kaifeng after that."

"What for?"

"I felt I'd returned to my childhood, even though I found a fertilizer plant instead, and I had this strong urge to see another man."

"Who was it?"

"Old You, the rat poison peddler who kidnapped me. He was from Kaifeng."

"Why did you want to see him?"

"He took me to Jiyuan, but he really didn't want to sell me." She added, "I just wanted to ask him a question, after all these years."

"What's the question?"

"What did he do with the ten silver dollars he got from selling me? Did he buy livestock or a piece of land, or did he start another small business?"

"What was the point of knowing about that after so many years?"

"I wanted to see him again, even if it was pointless to try. I wanted to see what he looked like. He was the cause of all these problems."

She continued her story. She'd taken a bus to Changyuan, from where she ferried across the Yellow River and boarded a second bus to Kaifeng. There she started her search, fully aware that she would not likely find him. His face had begun to fade in her memory; he wouldn't look the same as thirty-three years earlier, even if she could still recall what he'd looked like then. Yet she made the rounds of Horse Market Street, Xiangguo Temple, Pan and Yang Lakes, and the night market, walking down streets big and small, and searching every corner. She ran into hundreds and thousands of old men each day, but none of them looked like Old You. Even knowing full well that she could never find him, she spent more than three weeks in Kaifeng. By then, her search was no longer about Old You.

Her money was running low, and after ten days she could no longer afford to stay at an inn. So she spent her days looking for Old You and slept in the train station at night. One day she was bedded down on a bench in the waiting room at midnight, with one of her bags as a pillow and the other one under her feet, when she spotted her father. It wasn't Moses Wu, but Old Cao, from Wen Village. She wasn't at the train station any longer, but at the night market by the Xiangguo Temple. He was walking and she was chasing after him. He walked so fast she had trouble catching up, so she was sweating when she finally caught up.

"What are you doing in Kaifeng, Father?"

"To help you find Old You, of course." He fretted, his face a bright red. "I just saw him, but you stopped me when I was about to catch up with him. It's your fault."

Qing'e looked at her father, suddenly overjoyed by what she saw.

"Didn't you lose your head, Father? How did you get it back?"

He put a hand on his chest and said, "My head is back, but it feels terrible here." He grabbed at his heart.

"Did you lose your heart, Father?"

"No, I've got my heart here, but it hurts."

Qing'e was startled awake; it was just a dream. She opened her eyes to see strangers all around her in the waiting room; none of the faces in the bustling crowd were familiar. Throwing herself down on one of her bags, she began to cry, not because she had dreamed of Old Cao, but because he was suffering, even though he'd gotten his head back.

This was another anecdote she related to her son Aiguo.

She also told him she'd learned of something else from the trip to Yanjin— her birth father, Jiang Hu, had died in Qinyuan, Shanxi. What a surprise that she would grow up and be married to someone from the same city. Old Bu and Old Lai, who had bought and sold scallions with her father, had both died, so she could not find any information about her father's death, such as on which street and in which diner. Except that another father began to appear in her dreams; this one had a head but no face.

6

Niu Aiguo's visit to his friend Li Kezhi changed his attitude toward his wife, Pang Lina. As we recall, Niu had gone to Pingshan a few years earlier, where he sat by the Hutuo River to talk to his old army buddy Du Qinghai about his relationship with his wife. Since then, Aiguo had been following Qinghai's suggestion in dealing with Lina. He had decided against a divorce because it wouldn't work for him; she could be having an affair, but he had to live with it for now. He tried to bridge the gulf between them by taking the initiative to find topics they could share. He made sure only words of praise came out of his mouth, avoiding anything unpleasant; put differently, he focused on the positive when one thing could be brought up in two drastically different ways, turning criticism into praise. To talk to her meant they needed to see each other more often, so he rented a room in Nanguan to set up a home away from home in the county town, where he kept offering fine words to his wife, who did not have to wait until the weekend to go home. Whenever he returned from a trucking trip, he went directly to the county town, instead of going back to Niu Village. After a few years, however, finding things to say proved to be an arduous task, and nice words did not come easily. Or, to be more precise, it was hard to find things to say, and even harder to be positive all the time. Since they'd had little to say to each other, it always sounded forced whenever he brought up something to talk about, though it didn't matter much whether it was positive or negative, since they had trouble carrying on a conversation. If an exchange of unpleasant words was out of the question, then it was even harder to say nice things to each other. With their hearts so far apart, they had a different understanding of the same phrase; one could treat it as positive, while it didn't sound good to the other's ears. Besides, where in the world was he going to find so many nice things to say to her? He would get a headache trying to do that every day, not to mention the possibility that she might not appreciate it after he went to the trouble. Besides, he sounded phony even to himself after plying her with nice words, which sounded pleasing at first but got repetitive and annoying when he did it day after day. By then, whatever was said with good intentions turned irritating. Life had been smooth sailing when they had nothing to say to each other, but now his ceaselessly pleasant words grew tiresome to her. Sometimes he had something serious to discuss, but she would cover her ears, as she assumed that another round of fawning words was coming.

"Please, no more. Whenever you open your mouth, I feel like gagging."

Or, "You're so mean, Niu Aiguo. You take all the pleasure out of hearing nice words."

Aiguo finally realized that Qinghai's suggestion hadn't worked. When they sat by the river, they had been out of the army for ten years; more than a thousand li separated his home in Qinyan and Qinghai's in Pingshan, rendering Qinghai's idea ineffective. So Aiguo changed his approach and stopped trying to find things to say. Instead, he focused on action, doing the laundry, shining her shoes, and making her favorite fish dishes. New to cooking at first, he did a terrible job with fish, which was either overcooked and mushy, or underdone, or too salty or bland, or fetid smelling. After a month, however, he mastered the skill and produced tasty fish in various styles, whole fish braised or steamed in clear broth, fried fish fillets, or spicy steamed fish heads. Fish fillets had to be deep-fried twice to produce a crispy, brown skin, before adding copious amounts of cumin and sesame salt. Spicy steamed fish head required lots of green pepper and Chinese pepper. Once, when the fish was done, he washed his hands and changed into a suit before riding his bicycle to meet her at the factory.

"What are you doing here?" she asked when she saw him.

"I cooked a fish for dinner."

She smiled during dinner. Food worked better than words. After dinner that night, she was gentler toward him. One night she even put her arms around him and cried.

"It's been hard on you, I know."

He felt the same way, but it was different from what she said. He had to forget his own needs and feelings when he said or did something just for her.

Putting her before himself did not bother him, but he did not like the fact that everything he did was meant for her, not really a voluntary action carried out with no strings attached. Suddenly, he realized he'd lost his sense of self, which meant he had no ideas of his own. Who was he, then? Yet he did not care whom he had turned into; he knew his hardships and efforts over the years were not in vain when she held him and wept.

"As long as you come around with new thoughts and views."

He was referring to her association with Little Jiang at the East Asia Wedding Photo Studio. She immediately turned belligerent and pushed him away.

"I never had any other thoughts or views, so how am I supposed to come around?"

He never mentioned it again, and focused instead on making fish for her. What he had wanted was to hear her say that nothing had been going on between her and Jiang, and she didn't need to change. But with frequent trucking trips out of town, he could not stay home every day to make fish; he could only cook her fish when he was home, and go to pick her up at the factory in his suit. Slowly, everyone at the factory knew that Niu Aiguo had prepared fish whenever he showed up at the factory entrance.

One day, he delivered vegetables pickled in soy sauce to Linfen, over three hundred li from Qinyuan. Half the trip was on mountain roads with many hairpin turns, and choked with traffic. He left home before dawn and reached Linfen at night, when the city was lit up. After unloading the cargo at a warehouse, he wanted to turn around and go right back home. Old Li at the warehouse said he would like Aiguo to take a load of jute bags back to Qinyuan, but the workers had all gone home, and they had to wait until the next day. So Aiguo had to spend a night in Linfen, but it wouldn't be a bad deal, since the truck would be loaded on the way back. So he slept in the warehouse. Early the following morning, when the workers were loading the truck, he walked out and found a breakfast stall, where he ate a bowl of giblets soup and five fried flatbreads. The loading wasn't finished when he went back to the warehouse, so he walked out again and saw a fish market around the corner. He headed toward it, a large place that had seemed small when seen from the warehouse. It opened up before his eyes when he made the turn; the place was abuzz with action and bustling with shoppers and fishmongers. The massive market went on for more than two li from east to west, with stalls on each side of the path selling every kind of fish he could think of—silver carp, common carp, bighead carp, grass carp, ribbon fish, crucian carp, flounder, eel, loach, turtles, and so on. He stopped at a stall to pick out two bighead carps, with which he planned to make spicy steamed fish heads for Lina when he got home that night. The fishmonger, a skinny man who could not stop blinking, raised his thumb at Aiguo when he noticed that Aiguo had passed up all other stalls to buy from him.

"You've got good eyes, Older Brother. Would you like me to descale and gut the fish for you?"

"It's for tonight, so I need live ones."

"You don't sound local."

"I'm from Qinyuan."

"I've been there. Fine place."

The fishmonger weighed the fish on his steelyard. When that was done, he put the fish in a plastic bag, added water, and pumped in air before handing the bag to Aiguo. He even offered Aiguo a cigarette.

"Come visit Qinyuan sometime," Aiguo said.

With the cigarette in his mouth, he walked back to the warehouse with the fish. The bags were loaded by then, so he climbed into the cabin after waving goodbye to Old Li, started the engine, and drove toward Qinyuan. Twenty li later, he felt cramps in his abdomen, the sign of diarrhea; it must have been what he'd had for breakfast. Either the giblet soup was contaminated or something was wrong with the flatbreads. In any case, he had to hold off and keep going until he saw a roadside toilet. He stopped and ran in to relieve himself, which immediately made him feel better. Getting back on the truck, he started the engine and set off again. At some point, a casual glance at the bag hanging in the cab told him the fish weren't moving. He stopped the truck, opened the bag, and found two dead fish. It would have been all right, but the eyes were black, while newly dead fish should have white eyes. He touched them; the flesh was soft, as opposed to springy, which was typical of fresh fish. Now he knew that the fishmonger had weighed live fish, but had then put two dead ones from the day before in the bag. Likely he had decided to make the switch when he heard that Aiguo was from out of town. Aiguo recalled the skinny man who blinked incessantly, which, to Aiguo, was a telltale sign of the man's scheming tendency. He wasn't about to take that lying down, not because of the fish, but because of the man's deviousness. He turned around, even though he had already traveled thirty li. He drove back to Linfen and stopped at the fish market. With the plastic bag in hand, he went looking for the fishmonger; the skinny man was still there, hawking his wares at the top of his lungs. Live fish were leaping and jumping in a tank next to the man, who was surprised to see Aiguo return. Aiguo tossed the bag on the man's counter, and said, "What's this?"

The man blinked rapidly and glanced at the fish before turning to look at Aiguo.

"You're mistaken, Older Brother. These aren't mine."

Aigou would have been all right if the skinny man had admitted he was wrong, apologized, and given Aiguo two life fish; he would not have minded driving the sixty extra li. But the man refused to own up to something he'd done less than two hours earlier; instead, he blamed Aiguo, which enraged him.

"It's no big deal now, but it could be soon. So what do you say? Do we deal with it the nice way or the nasty way?"

"Nice or nasty, I don't care. There's nothing for me to deal with."

They got into a prolonged argument over the fish, drawing the attention of shoppers. Prevented from conducting business during the quarrel, the fishmonger spat at Aiguo, likely because he knew he was an outsider. "Have you lost your mind, trying to cheat me?"

Aiguo turned and walked back to his truck; he returned with a crank bar that was about four feet long and as thick as an egg, with a curved middle. The bar told the skinny man a fight was coming, so he picked up a scaling knife, backed up, and shouted, "Do you really plan to fight me? Do you?"

Aiguo kicked over the man's fish tank, and as the water flowed, dozens of fish leaped all over the ground. Aiguo raised the bar, but, instead of hitting the fishmonger, he brought it down on the leaping fish, smashing every one of them to a pulp. The skinny man waved his knife and screamed, "Someone's going to die today. I guarantee you!"

The other fishmongers crowded up to lend him a hand, one with a club, one a spear, and another with a long-handled fishing net. Aiguo waved his weapon, making the circle of men jump back. Someone shouted amid the clamor, "Big Brother is here. That'll do it!"

It was a swarthy man, at least five feet nine, with dense chest hair and a head of red hair. He came up, and the skinny man shouted as if to a savior, "That's him, Big Brother."

The man made his way through the crowd and wrapped his powerful arms around Aiguo. He tried to hit the man, who hit his arm and sent the bar flying. The fishmongers all cheered, while the man raised his bowl-sized fist to hit Aiguo. But he stopped, his fist suspended in midair, and blurted out: "What's your name?"

Aiguo looked up and found the man's face familiar, but couldn't recall who he was at that moment.

"Is that you, Niu Aiguo?"

Aiguo looked close and cried out in surprise.

"And you, you're Li Kezhi?"

Aiguo and Kezhi had been classmates in elementary school. Kezhi, who had been bigger than the other kids at the time, was the one who loved to gossip about everyone else and stir up trouble. Once he'd spread a rumor about Aiguo's older sister, Niu Aixiang, and the two boys had fought. Aiguo's best friend, Feng Wenxiu, had jumped in and cracked Kezhi's skull. Kezhi's father had been a coal miner in Changzhi, where he went with his father when the other kids went to middle school. That was the last they'd seen of each other. What a surprising coincidence that they should run into each other at a fish market two decades later. They sized each other up and laughed, the fight forgotten.

"It's really you. You loved to pick a fight even as a kid." Kezhi took Aiguo's hand and placed it on his own head.

"Touch it. Feel the scar."

"I didn't do it. It was Feng Wenxiu." Aiguo studied his friend's head. "You've aged." Then he added, "Why is your hair red?"

"It turned gray. I wanted to color it black, but the girl at the salon gave me the wrong color, so I beat up her boss."

They laughed again. The fishmongers dispersed when they saw the two men were old friends, leaving the skinny one to swallow the loss and pick up the fish paste on the floor, grumbling the whole time. Kezhi took Aiguo to a diner next to the fish market; he parted the door curtain and called out to the owner, "Go pick out a few fish and make us a chowder. We don't need anything else."

The diner owner quickly replied, "Right you are, Big Brother."

The owner was about to walk out when Aiguo stopped him.

"Anything but fish. Please bring us something else."

"What's wrong?" Kezhi asked.

"I gag at the sight of fish," Aiguo said. "I've had more than I can take."

"Why were you buying a fish if you've had enough?"

Aiguo laughed but didn't respond; instead, he said, "It's been two decades. I didn't expect you to become an overlord at a fish market."

"It's a long story," Kezhi said with a sigh.

As they drank, Kezhi told Aiguo what had happened since he parted ways with everyone at the middle school, how he went to the Changzhi coal mine, then to Linfen. Kezhi hadn't been a good student at his Changzhi high school, and he got into a fight with a classmate in his third year. He cracked the boy's skull with a bench, and the boy crumpled to the floor. Thinking the boy was dead, Kezhi ran away that night and arrived in Linfen, just as what had happened when Feng Wenxiu broke Kezhi's head years earlier. He had an aunt in Linfen who took him in because she didn't have children of her own. Later, when the boy did not die, Kezhi's father came to take him back home. He did not want to go, since he had never gotten along with his father, so he stayed with his aunt. The aunt treated him well, but the uncle, a steelworker at a machinery shop, was cranky and often complained about him, causing arguments between them. Later, when he failed to get into college, Kezhi sold mutton kebabs on the street; he moved out of his aunt's house when he got married and had children. Selling kebabs did not bring in enough to support the family, which was why he switched to the fish trade. After being a fishmonger for two years, he had the whole fish market under his thumb, thanks to his physical prowess, and soon he stopped selling fish altogether. He let out an emotional sigh when he finished his story.

"It looks like I control the fish market because of my physical strength, but in fact I'm just a shameless rogue."

Aiguo sighed as Li continued, "I don't spread rumors anymore."

Aiguo laughed. They talked about others in the class, such as Feng Wenxiu, Ma Mingqi, Li Shun, Yang Yongxiang, Gong Yimin, Cui Yuzhi, Dong Haihua, and so on. Two decades had gone by, and they had scattered in all directions to make a living. One of them, Wang Jiacheng, was dead, while another one, Hu Shuanglie, had lost his sanity.

"Our life is very much like grass that goes through a yearly cycle and dies."

"Our geography teacher, Mr. Jiao, died two years ago, shortly after the death of the language teacher, Mr. Wei," Aiguo said.

"I remember Jiao, a short man with a long face. I used to neigh like a horse whenever I saw him. Once, he cornered me against a wall and nearly pulled an ear off my head."

They were plunged into a sentimental reminiscence of the past. When they were finished talking about the people they used to know in school, Kezhi pointed to Aiguo and said, "I can tell you've got something on your mind."

"What do you mean?"

"Look at the crease between your brows. That's a sign of a mind engaged in something troubling."

Aiguo was half-drunk by then and, moved by Kezhi's confidence earlier, told his friend what was on his mind, which was his relationship with his wife: he had been able to talk to her when they were first married, but they had less and less to talk about as time went by. Then there was the possible affair between her and Little Jiang. He had wanted a divorce but hesitated, so he went to Pingshan to see his old army buddy Du Qinghai, who, after a discussion with Aiguo, concluded that he could not afford to be divorced. He went home and began looking for things to say, pleasant words. But that proved to be too hard, so he switched to doing the laundry and shining her shoes; he made her favorite fish dishes, which was why he'd bought fish in Linfen earlier that day. Kezhi banged the table when Aiguo finished.

"That was a lousy idea by your old army buddy."

"I don't think it's working."

"And it was a mistake to do the laundry, shine her shoes, and cook her fish."

"How so?"

"Why are you afraid of her just because the two of you have nothing to say?"

"But that's exactly the reason why I'm afraid of her."

"Wrong again. You have nothing to say, so you have nothing to lose. As they say, those with bare feet have no fear of those who wear shoes. Starting today, switch things around. Ignore her."

"What do I do if she wants a divorce?"

"Hang on to her and refuse to give her one. What can she do? She'll be backed into a corner."

The sudden enlightenment from his fishmonger friend woke Aiguo up to the reality that his relationship with Lina all these years was turned upside down. He hadn't realized that the fearful one could become fearless and vice versa.

"Those friends of yours are all worthless." Kezhi patted him on the shoulder. "Come see me anytime you're stuck with something."

Aiguo nodded. It was late in the afternoon when they finished lunch. Aiguo was going to buy more fish at the market, but Kezhi stopped him.

"Did you forget what I just told you? No more fish for her. Can't you buy fish in Linfen if you really want some?"

Aiguo shook his head and laughed. He gave up on buying fish and headed back to Qinyuan. It was dark when he got on a mountain road, about a hundred li later. Turning Kezhi's words over in his head, Aiguo began to feel it wouldn't work. His advice on how to deal with Lina did not differ much from his way of handling fish and the fish market, which looked tough but in fact could be summed up as "shamelessly unreasonable." That might work in a fish market, but how long could that attitude last in dealing with people? Besides, Aiguo wasn't so much fearful of Lina as afraid of leaving her, not because he had to be with her, but because he wouldn't have anyone if he left her. Or, worse yet, he would have nothing, not even his fear of her. If he left her, he would then have nothing to say and no one to say it to. That was what scared him. It was all on him, not her. It dawned on him that Li Kezhi's idea was shameless, but his own solution of doing the laundry, shining her shoes, and cooking fish wasn't all that different, and seemed as if he was waiting on her. In fact, Aiguo's approach could be even more shameless, on a larger scale than Kezhi's, which was less brazen. As the truck traveled along the twisting roads of Lüliang Mountain, its headlights moved up and down as they shone on the hills on both sides. Tears welled up in his eyes. It was daybreak when he got back to Qinyuan, where he went to the fish market and bought two bighead carps. He told Lina when he got home that he'd bought the fish in Linfen.

Lina got into trouble in October that year. She was caught in a Changzhi hotel room with Little Jiang. Niu Aiguo knew nothing about it. It was the October First national holiday, and she had been given five days off at the factory. She told Aiguo that she wanted to take a trip to Taiyuan with some friends from the factory, for she was dying of boredom after all this time in Qinyuan. She even asked him if he would like to go with them. In the past, when they took trips together, they were bored to tears, with little to say. Others went on trips with their spouses and talked about the scenery, but he and Lina looked at the sights with nothing to say. Besides, he had to truck fertilizer for the Qinyuan plant over the holiday period, so he told her to go without him. He could not have imagined that, instead of going to Taiyuan with coworkers, she had gone to Changzhi with Little Jiang. It was Jiang's wife who caught them in the Spring Sunshine Hotel. Zhao Xinting sold shoes in a department store in Qinyuan. A small, thin woman, she had single-fold eyes and never raised her voice at work. Aiguo had seen her before and thought she looked trustworthy. No one could have expected that she could be so cunning. Aiguo had not noticed anything unusual when Lina left secretly with Jiang, but Xinting had. A week earlier, Jiang had told his wife that he wanted to buy some wedding dresses and a digital camera in Beijing over the holiday. Xinting had no objection. The night before his departure, he was in bed while she did his packing. She unzipped a side pocket on his satchel and found two train tickets for Changzhi, not Beijing. He had lied to her. It was only a minor lie that day. But he had started lying to her a week before, and that was major. Something significant must have been going on if he needed to prepare so far in advance. She kept her anger in check and did not mention it. They had an eight-year-old boy they called Beibei, who was in elementary school. After Jiang left the next morning, Xinting took their son to stay with her friend, Li Qin, and boarded a train for Changzhi, after telling Qin she had to buy shoes in Taiyuan for the department store. She only knew that Jiang would be in Changzhi, a large city with many streets and alleys, so it would be nearly impossible to find him.

But she stuck to it, searching for three days, until one midnight, when she found his name on the registration book at Spring Sunshine Hotel, located in an alley on the edge of the city. Suddenly recalling that she'd had little to eat or drink for three days, she took a room in the same hotel, but instead of going straight there, she waited outside Jiang's room until dawn. She did not go up to knock on the door either. In the morning, when Jiang and Lina, both dressed neatly, opened the door to see a disheveled Xinting standing before them, they were frightened out of their wits. Xinting gave each a silent look and turned to walk away, trailed by Jiang, who shouted, "Come back. I'll explain."

She ignored him and went to the bus depot to buy a ticket for Qinyuan. When she got back in town, she went not to home, but to an agricultural product shop to buy a bottle of pesticide, Happy Fruits. With the bottle in tow, she went home and saw her son doing homework.

"Didn't you go to buy shoes in Taiyuan? Where are the shoes?" Beibei asked her.

"Weren't you at Li Qin's house? Why are you here alone?"

"I got into a fight with Feng Zhe."

Feng Zhe was Li Qin's son, who was a year older than Beibei. They went to the same school but were not in the same class.

"Go do your homework, Beibei. Mama is tired and needs some rest."

After the boy left, Xinting drained the bottle of Happy Fruits, and she did not wake up until three days later. She was in a bed in the emergency wing of the county hospital, with Little Jiang nearby. The pesticide would have killed her if she hadn't been sent to the hospital to have her stomach pumped. He was red in the face, rubbing his hands.

"You don't have to say anything. It's all my fault." He added, "I'm glad they saved you, so I won't have to drink pesticide too. Don't worry. I won't do it again. I'll come home every day to be with you and our son."

Xinting did not reply. When he went to the dining hall to get lunch, she struggled out of bed and, with her hand on the wall, left the hospital and went out into the streets. She stumbled her way through the streets for over an hour until she reached Niu Aiguo's house in Nanguan. Lina had been hiding out at her parents' house since being found out. Aiguo was home alone.

"Nothing would have mattered if I'd died, but since I didn't, I need to talk to you."

"What do you want to tell me?"

"I need to tell you what happened in Changzhi, or I'll die from keeping it inside."

She then told him how she had caught their respective spouses in the act.

"I waited outside their room in Spring Sunshine Hotel for half the night, and I heard everything. They did it three times, and after they were done, instead of going to sleep, they talked. One of them said, 'Let's go to sleep,' but the other one said, 'Let's talk about other things,' and the first one said, 'Why not?' He said more to her in half a night than to me in a year."

Xinting then began to wail at the top of her lungs. Aiguo had been in a daze since the discovery of his wife's affair. He had suspected as much, but had no proof, and besides, he had followed Du Qinghai's suggestion that he should believe in her innocence. But now everything was out in the open and he did not know what to do. He was dazed, not because of the affair itself, but because of the proof that he had been wrong all these years in saying nice things and making fish for her. He had no idea how to rectify the mistakes, nor did he know who to talk to. As Zhao Xinting cried her heart out, he asked stupidly, "What do you expect me to do by telling me this?"

"I'm not strong enough, but you're a man and you ought to go kill them."

Pang Lina returned three days later, looking visibly thinner. Sitting across from him, she said, "Let's talk."

"About what?"

"You know everything now, so let's get a divorce."

Aiguo was reminded of what Li Kezhi had said. Before the discovery of the affair, Aiguo had not wanted to adopt his friend's idea, but now the suggestion seemed both reasonable and workable.

"I won't do it," Aiguo said.

"Why not?" Lina hadn't expected that.

"We've been married for so long, and I'm responsible for you."

"In what way?" That was another surprise.

"Little Jiang did this, so he has to answer to you. Go tell him to divorce his wife and agree to marry you, and we can get a divorce."

"You don't have to worry about him."

"I do. I'm still your husband until we're divorced."

She bawled.

"I just went to see him and told him to get a divorce, but he doesn't have the guts. I got involved with him because I thought he was a real man. Turns out he's a coward, scared to death by a bottle of pesticide. I was so wrong."

She wept and talked, opening her heart for the first time since their marriage.

"You can't let him off the hook so easily," Aiguo said. "You have to keep up the pressure."

She suddenly saw through his intention. "You want this to be a fight between you and me, don't you, Niu Aiguo?" She cried again. "It's all that bastard Ma Xiaozhu's fault. He ruined my life."

Ma Xiaozhu had been her first love. They had been high school classmates, but he had dumped her when he left town to attend college in Beijing. Aiguo was surprised to hear the connection between the two incidents, but in the end it was all the same to him, however she twisted things.

"Let's get a divorce, Niu Aiguo. Please, I beg you. I don't want anything; you can have it all."

"No."

"I know you want to hold me back." She stopped crying and switched to an angry tone. "Go ahead if that's what you want to do. You're not afraid, and neither am I. We'll fight to the death."

"Keep going then, if you're not afraid."

"You're a vile man, Niu Aiguo." She got to her feet. "After all the years we've been together, I don't know who you are."

She turned and walked away, and Aiguo laughed, happily, carefree for the first time in years. She stopped coming home, and he put the matter aside, as he went about his daily routine of making trucking trips. Three days later, he took a load of chicken to Changzhi. He thought only about delivering the cargo on the way out, but when he got there he was reminded of the place where his wife had discovered Lina and Jiang together. It felt terrible. Every hotel sign that came into view was, in his mind, the one the lovers had stayed in; every store he saw was where they had window-shopped hand-in-hand. Recalling the details Zhao Xinting had given him about how she had caught them, he felt his heart was a jumbled mess. Every street seemed loathsome.

After unloading the chickens at the farmer's market, he had planned to go to the Changzhi Brewery to take a load of beer back to Qinyuan, but he couldn't now. Leaving the market with his truck empty, he tore out of Changzhi and returned to Qinyuan that evening. He parked the truck and, not bothering to eat, went out alone to ease his troubled mind. When he reached the ruined city wall, he spotted three figures strolling by the wall a ways away. He didn't pay much attention until he climbed onto the wall and looked down to see it was Little Jiang; his wife, Zhao Xinting; and their eight-year-old son. They were each holding one of the boy's hands, talking and laughing as they walked. Jiang was kicking a stone, sending it skittering ahead of them.

Aiguo froze at the sight, surprised that Xinting had recovered from the pesticide incident so quickly, and amazed at how the couple had repaired their relationship in less than a week. An outsider would never be able to tell that something terrible had occurred in their family only days before—someone had nearly died, and Xinting had even sought out Aiguo to kill her husband and his wife. Seen this way, the affair between Jiang and Lina had turned out to be a blessing to them; Xinting would not have taken the pesticide, and their family would not have undergone such a dramatic change and emerged from a near-disaster as a happy family. Everything was fine for them now, and only Aiguo was suffering. Pang Lina, if she had witnessed the scene, would be outraged, but Aiguo was the one who saw them, and it made his blood boil.

Getting off the city wall, he came to a diner in Nanguan, where he started drinking on an empty stomach and quickly got drunk. The inebriation intensified the depression, which in turn made him drink more, until midnight, when he was plagued not only by what had happened between him and Lina, but also by all that had happened over the past thirty-five years. Jumbled thoughts and unhappiness surged in his heart, like a stampede. He was dying to talk to someone. The first to come to mind was Li Kezhi the fishmonger, who, unfortunately, lived more than two hundred li away in Linfen; he couldn't reach him until the day after. His next option was Du Qinghai, his army buddy who lived in Pingshan, a three-day trip. With no one left to turn to, he walked out of the diner on unsteady feet, heading to East Street's butcher shop to see his old classmate Feng Wenxiu. In the past, he had avoided opening his heart to Wenxiu, who turned into a different person when drunk. But now Aiguo was the inebriated one and couldn't care less about Wenxiu's flaw. It took a wobbly Aiguo two hours to reach Wenxiu's shop. It was past midnight and the stars were out when he got there.

"Open up, Feng Wenxiu." Aiguo pounded on the door.

No one responded, so he pounded again, finally getting someone to turn on the light. It was Wenxiu.

"Who is it?"

"It's me. I need to talk to you."

Hearing Aiguo's voice, Wenxiu said, "Can't this wait till tomorrow?"

"No. I'll burst if I wait till then," Aiguo said and sat down outside the door, where he began sobbing. Alarmed, Wenxiu quickly opened the door, helped his friend inside, and made tea. Aiguo poured his heart out to Wenxiu, telling him everything that had happened; Wenxiu nodded, even though Aiguo stammered incoherently under the influence of alcohol, losing the thread here and there.

"I heard about that. I knew you'd been in a bad mood, so I didn't want to interfere." Wenxiu was sympathetic. "Since it's come to this, what are you going to do?"

"I feel like killing someone." Aiguo thumped his chest with a fierce glare. "That never crossed my mind until today, when I saw the Jiang family laughing like that. I have to kill someone. What do you think? Should I do it?"

"Sure, you should." Wenxiu rubbed his chin. "Little Jiang has gone too far."

"He's not who I want to kill." Aiguo shook his head.

"Then who?"

"That would be letting him off the hook too easily. I'm going to let him live, but kill his son, so he'll grieve for the rest of his life."

Wenxiu was flabbergasted to hear his friend's twisted scheme, which was dreadful but, in all fairness, was brought on by Jiang himself.

"I want to kill their son, not simply to torment Jiang."

"Then who?"

"Zhao Xinting. She told me to kill them a few days ago, and she's already back with her husband. The change was simply too quick."

Wenxiu got the drift and nodded, while Aiguo shouted, "I'm going to kill Pang Lina too. I've had everything bottled up inside all these years with her, and that's worse than what I feel about Jiang and Zhao. It isn't only about the affair."

Wenxiu nodded again. "What are you going to do after you kill them?"

"I'll die with them."

Luckily for them, Aiguo, not Wenxiu, was the drunken one on this night.

"What about your daughter? What would happen to Baihui with both parents gone?"

Aiguo wrapped his arms around his head. "That's what's eating me up inside."

It was, after all, a drunken outburst. When he sobered up the next morning, Aiguo did not kill anyone. Instead, he added a small kitchen to their rented house in Nanguan, not just to have more space, though they'd had to cook in the hallway, but also to set up a bed for him as he vacated his bedroom. He then brought his mother, Cao Qing'e, and his daughter back to live with him. The three started a new life together. Aiguo still refused to divorce Lina, who now was as good as dead in his mind; he wanted to wait to see what she would do in the end. As for Little Jiang, Zhao Xinting, and their son, Beibei, he would wait patiently for an opportunity to deal with them.

Something happened during the construction of the add-on kitchen. To feed the few carpenters and bricklayers he hired, Aiguo went to Wenxiu's shop to buy pork, a sale taken care of by Wenxiu himself. With so much on his mind, Aiguo forgot to pay. That evening, Wenxiu's wife came to collect the money. He counted out the money and paid up, but he had a bad taste in his mouth after she left. He had not intended not to pay. They had been classmates, close enough to share whatever was on their minds, so how could Wenxiu's wife come to collect money that same evening? Aiguo could not have known that she had not been sent by her husband, but had come on her own without telling him. Aiguo thought back to the free trucking trips he'd made to bring Wenxiu pigs and pork. How could he be so unrelenting when Aiguo bought a little pork from him? Aiguo wouldn't have minded if it had been a different time, but he was really peeved now, because his life was a mess after his wife had stirred up so much trouble. Your old classmate was bruised and battered, so couldn't you have temporarily forgotten the money owed for a little pork? It had been only a few days since he'd last been to see Wenxiu, but his friend had already changed into a different person.

That night, he had dinner with the workers, drank a bit too much, and related the unpleasant encounter to them. Aiguo had not been the talkative type, but he couldn't keep anything to himself after Lina's affair. The workers agreed that Wenxiu had not handled it well, and that was it, except for a bricklayer called Old Xiao, a close friend of Feng Wenxiu. After finishing up the day's work, he went straight to the butcher shop and repeated everything Aiguo had said. Wenxiu, who had been unaware of his wife's action, would have scolded his wife if he had known about it through a different channel. But he was miffed when he learned about it through Xiao, who had heard it from Aiguo. Sure, they were friends, but friendship doesn't mean free pork; he was running a business, not a soup kitchen. Ten catties of pork was no big deal, but what Aiguo had told people was infuriating; more outrageous was the fact that he went around telling people behind his back instead of bringing it up with him. Wenxiu and Xiao began to drink, and Wenxiu was soon drunk, which usually brought on a greater change in him than in Aiguo. He was now a different man, who had to vent any anger in his heart. He smashed a bottle as he yelled, "I can't believe that two decades of friendship isn't worth ten catties of pork."

Aiguo should have been the one to utter the lament, but, oddly, Wenxiu got to voice his complaint first. He dropped the issue of pork and moved on to something else.

"Serves him right. His wife slept with another man. He didn't know what to do as a cuckold. He has no balls. It didn't just happen yesterday. Everyone in town knew he'd been wearing the green hat of a cuckold for seven or eight years."

Wenxiu changed the subject and continued, "You think he looks like a decent man, don't you? Actually, he's quite nasty." He then confided to Xiao, "He told me three days ago he wanted to kill Little Jiang. Nothing wrong with that, but he said he wants to kill Jiang's son. He has only himself to blame if he can't control his wife, but instead he wants to kill someone else." Wenxiu spat on the floor. "Who is Niu Aiguo? A murderer, that's who he is."

He went to bed, forgetting what he'd said the night before by the time he opened up for business the next morning. All he could recall was his unhappiness with his friend. Old Xiao, on the other hand, was a gossipmonger who spread Wenxiu's drunken outburst, until everyone in town knew that Niu Aiguo wanted to kill two people, Little Jiang's son and Pang Lina. Wenxiu had said it when he was drunk, but the people who spread the word were sober, in very much the same way as Aiguo's confession under the influence was recounted when someone was not drunk. By the time all the gossip and rumors made the rounds through several mouths and got back to Aiguo, he did pick up a knife, ready to kill someone, though not Little Jiang's son and not his own wife, but Feng Wenxiu. He had confided in a good friend, who, to his surprise, had spun his words around and turned them into a knife pointing at him. Had he really said those things? Yes, he had. Was that really what he'd meant? Yes, but not entirely. It was now impossible to explain what exactly he'd meant, because everything—time, occasion, and people—had changed. What he had said was twisted out of shape. Niu Aiguo killed no one, but he was more vicious than a murderer, which was the most pernicious side of the rumor. Knife in hand, he walked out the door, but had barely taken a few steps before he crouched down. Could he really kill someone over ten catties of pork? No, he couldn't. He was all churned up inside, glummer than ever.

The kitchen had been planned for his mother and daughter, but he lost heart when the construction was completed, and the space was left empty. One day, he trucked a load of sesame to Xiangyuan, traveling over a hundred li from Qinyuan. It was noontime when he unloaded at Xiangyuan's granary, after which he went to a pickled vegetable factory in town for a load of goods and then headed out to return to Qinyuan. He was woolgathering as the truck zigzagged along the mountain road; he forgot that he hadn't had lunch. He dozed off around dusk, when Qinyuan came into view, and the truck veered off the road and hit a locust tree. He woke up to find a gaping wound on his head; he was bleeding badly as he scrambled down off the truck and saw a big dent on the hood, with liquid dripping to the ground. The vats were smashed and pickle juice was flowing freely down the bed of the truck. Without bothering to bandage his head, he was a sorry sight. Looking down at Qinyuan County, Niu Aiguo knew he had to leave the place or he would really murder someone.

7

Niu Aiguo met Cui Lifan in Hebei's Botou County. He had known high-strung people before, but none as portly as Lifan. Normally overweight people move slowly, with a leisurely approach toward life, while the skinny ones tend to act fast, which can foster impetuousness. But Lifan was heavyset *and* impatient. When someone that size gets anxious, he becomes irritable because his weight prevents him from carrying out what his heart desires. He often gets mad at himself before he has time to get mad at others. Lifan, who was from Cangzhou, Hebei, was beating up someone the first time Aiguo met him. He ran a tofu products plant on Xinhua Street, called Xueying Fish and Soy Products. After they got to know each other, Aiguo was puzzled why Lifan, a tofu maker, did not understand the point behind the saying that an impatient man never gets to eat hot tofu.

Aiguo was going from Shanxi to Leling in Shandong through Hebei. It was noon on the second day when the bus entered Botou, where it stopped by a roadside diner for the passengers to get some lunch or use the toilet. Aiguo, who was in a foul mood, did not feel like eating, so he left the diner and took a stroll along the highway. He came upon a large rapeseed field, blanketed with blooming flowers, turning one side of the highway a bright yellow. After enjoying the sight of flowers, he was about to turn back when he saw a tofu truck on the side of the road, its cargo leaking liquid. A fat man was beating up a skinny man beside the truck, slapping his face, which was getting puffy. Unable to take the beating, the skinny man kept backing up, dodging highway traffic as he did. Too clumsy to move easily between vehicles to catch the other man, the fat one panted and shouted, "Fuck you and your mother, Bai Wenbin."

He got even more irritated as he cursed, so he retrieved an iron bar from the cab and waved it threateningly. It was all too much for Niu Aiguo, who tried to stop the fight.

"Can't you two talk this over, Elder Brother? Don't hit him anymore, or you'll kill him." He added, "And if you don't, a car will."

When Aiguo asked what was going on, he learned that it was not a serious disagreement. The skinny man was the fat man's driver, and they were going from Cangzhou to deliver tofu to Dezhou. The truck had broken down at Botou, and the engine failed to start no matter what they tried. It was still early summer, but hot enough that the fat man was worrying about his tofu going bad. In fact, he was not as concerned about that as about losing his Dezhou customers to other tofu makers if he failed to deliver the goods. As he recounted the story, his ire rose up and he gave his driver another slap.

"I'm not hitting him because he's delayed our delivery. I told him last night to make sure the truck was ready for the trip. He said the truck was fine, and then went out drinking with friends. Now see what's happened? The truck broke down when we were barely on the road." He added, "This has happened too many times already."

"Hitting him isn't going to get the truck started," Aiguo said.

"It's not about the truck." The man was still breathing hard. "It's about him."

Aiguo said to himself that the man was to blame for hiring someone like that for a driver. He walked around the truck, opened the hood, and poked around. It was nothing serious, just a broken cable. Obviously, the man knew how to drive but not how to fix a truck. Aiguo told him to bring his tool kit; he found a wire and a pair of pliers to hook the wire to the cable, and then told the driver to start the engine. The truck came alive with a rumble, immediately cooling the fat man's temper. He handed Aiguo a cigarette.

"You must be a master mechanic, Elder Brother."

"Not really, but I've been driving a truck for two years." Aiguo wiped his hands with a rag and lit the cigarette.

"You don't sound local."

"No, I'm from Qinyuan, Shanxi. I'm going to Leling in Shandong."

Aiguo looked back at the diner and discovered that his bus had left while he was fixing the truck. The driver must have assumed that all his passengers were in the diner and hadn't bothered to count heads when they got back on after lunch. So he drove off without Aiguo, who looked down the road but did not spot his bus among all the other vehicles. He'd also left his rucksack on the bus. Luckily, it contained only a few changes of clothes, two pairs of shoes, and an umbrella; he'd kept his money with him. The man felt bad that Aiguo had missed his bus and lost his bag; someone had to be blamed for that, so he zeroed in on his driver and thumped him on the back of his head.

"It's your fault, you prick. See how you caused a delay in his important business?"

"It's no big deal." Aiguo pulled the fat man back. "I'm just going to Leling to see someone."

Touched by Aiguo's magnanimity, the fat man took his arm and said, "Come to Dezhou with me. I'll take you to Leling after I unload the tofu."

Aiguo had no better option, so the three men got in and drove the load of tofu to Dezhou. The fat man and Aiguo chatted along the way, while the skinny man drove silently with a doleful look. During the conversation, Aiguo learned that the fat man's name was Cui Lifan, and that the driver, Bai Wenbin, was the son of Lifan's sister. Aiguo recalled how back in Botou, Lifan had cursed his nephew by referring to the young man's mother, who would be Lifan's sister. Aiguo had to laugh over his curse. It got dark soon after they reached Dongguang County. Lifan told Wenbin to park by a diner outside the county limits, and the three went in for dinner. Lifan ordered a plate of raw cucumber infused with spices, stewed donkey sausage, two bottles of beer, and three noodle hot pots. Aiguo and Lifan were so engrossed in their conversation they didn't realize that Wenbin was gone until the meal was over. At first, they thought he must have gone to the toilet, but Lifan did not find him there; they went outside to call for him, but no reply came from the pitch darkness. He'd left in anger over the abuse he'd suffered. Lifan flew into a rage again.

"Fuck. He's done it again. He knows I can't drive." He continued, "He's got me in a jam in the past, but with you here today, I'm fine."

Left with no choice, Aiguo got into the driver's seat and started the engine. They continued their journey to Dezhou.

"Are you going to Leling to visit family or maybe collect a debt?" Lifan asked.

"Neither." Aiguo kept his eyes on the road. "I'm going to look up a friend I haven't seen in years." He added, "I'm also going to see if I can find work there."

"You don't have to go to Leling for that." Lifan slapped him on the shoulder.

"What do you mean?"

"Why not come to Cangzhou and be my driver. That would work out nicely for both of us. I'll pay you well."

Aiguo was going to Leling to see Zeng Zhiyuan, an old army buddy, not to find a job but to put some distance between him and the heartbreak he'd suffered in Qinyuan. But he would need a job when he got there. Zhiyuan was a date wholesaler, and Aiguo had thought he could work with him. Now, with Lifan's offer, he had second thoughts about selling dates, a business that required talking to people all the time. Here he would be alone, driving a truck and not having to talk a lot. He knew plenty about driving a truck and nothing about selling dates. Leling or Cangzhou: it made no difference to him. They were both just places to stay. He was tempted, but he said, "But my friend and I have already settled. Besides, your nephew is your driver. Wouldn't I be taking his job away?"

Lifan spat out the window and said, "You won't be taking his job away. He did that to himself. Relatives are more trouble than they're worth. It's better to work with anyone but them. I won't deal with him ever again if you agree to come, but if you don't, then I'll have to slap him around again when I get back."

Now Lifan was conflating two matters, and Aiguo had to laugh. Lifan saw that Aiguo was not entirely opposed to the suggestion, and he gave him another shoulder slap.

"Be smart. Cangzhou is bigger than Leling."

A strange turn of circumstances had Aiguo going to Cangzhou, not Leling, after he helped Lifan deliver the tofu that night.

When Aiguo's heart was broken in Qinyuan and he'd made up his mind to leave, Leling had not been his first choice. Not knowing where to go before he left town, he first went back to Niu Village. Over the years, he and Lina had been busy with their own jobs, leaving their daughter, Baihui, in the care of Aiguo's mother, Cao Qing'e. Before leaving town, Aiguo thought he ought to tell his mother, so they sat down to eat and talk, while his daughter played on the floor. After he turned thirty-five, his mother began sharing details of what had happened half a century earlier. Aiguo had not taken his mother into his confidence, not in the past and not now. Lina's affair was the reason he was leaving Qinyuan, the place where his heart was broken, but he did not tell his mother about that or about his disillusionment in Qinyuan. Having no place to go after leaving, he decided to lie and say he was going to drive for construction sites in Beijing.

Cao Qing'e already knew about Lina's affair and her son's despondent state of mind, but since he did not bring it up, she did not either, which he took as a sign that now, in her sixties, she had finally become a true mother to him. She had favored his younger brother when they were young. To him, maternal favoritism was wrong, and he'd borne a grudge for years. When he told her about going to Beijing, instead of talking about the nation's capital, she talked about herself. After turning sixty-five, half of the teeth on her right side had gone bad and ached constantly, forcing her to chew only on the left. She got into the habit of cocking her head to the left, sort of like his sister, who had suffered a neck problem after ingesting pesticide. With her head tilted to the side, she said, "Now that I'm seventy, I've finally come to understand one thing. You can pick just about anything in the world, except for life itself."

Aiguo looked at his mother without replying.

"I also understand something else. In life we focus on the future, not the past."

He knew she was trying to make him feel better, but he said nothing in response. He wept later on the road when he thought about what she had said, not really about the words but about the way she'd cocked her head when offering her roundabout consolation. As he left Niu Village, Aiguo went through all the people he could possibly go to see and came up with only two. One was Du Qinghai, his old army friend; the other was Li Kezhi, the fishmonger in Linfen. Putting them side-by-side, he considered his prospects. He hadn't seen Kezhi in years, outside of that chance encounter in Linfen's fish market, while Qinghai was an old friend; the latter seemed to be the better option. He heaved a sigh as he realized that, with all the people in the world, he had only two he could count on when he had no place to go.

He boarded a bus in Qinyuan. Three days later, he reached Qinghai's village, where they had a heart-to-heart talk by the Hutuo River. He had not been enthused to see Qinghai this time, not because of any enmity or because Qinghai had given him a bad suggestion, but because he was unable to calm his jumbled mind. In fact, he felt more unsettled than when he'd first left Qinyuan. He was seeing an old friend, and yet his mind was besieged by too many thoughts, worse than in Qinyuan, a sign that he'd come to the wrong place.

He spent the night on the bank of the Hutuo River; he scooped up water to quench his thirst at midnight and drank his fill. Then he retraced his steps the following morning, with the intention of going to see Li Kezhi, taking a bus to Pingshan, then to Shi Village, followed by a train to Linfen, a trip of two and a half days. He was still feeling restless, even worse than when he'd reached Qinghai's village, which told him that Linfen wasn't for him either. Suddenly, he recalled his army buddy Zeng Zhiyuan, in Leling, Shandong. Together they had gathered food for pigs on Qilian Mountain, and he was someone he had no trouble talking to. They had exchanged phone numbers before they were demobilized.

He really had no one else to go to, so at the Linfen station, he placed a phone call to Zhiyuan. Aiguo had expected his friend to have changed his number by then, but he decided to give it a try. The number had changed, but the recording told him that all he needed was to add two eights before dialing. He did, and Zhiyuan, who picked up the phone, sounded more excited than Aiguo. He said he was selling dates when Aiguo asked what he'd been up to since they got out of the army. Before Aiguo could bring up his plan, Zhiyuan said, "Come to Leling. I want to talk to you about something."

"What's it about?"

"It's too complicated to explain over the phone. We need to talk face-to-face."

Aiguo laughed. He had been the one who needed to see Zhiyuan, but it turned out that Zhiyuan wanted to see him about something.

"When would you like me to come?"

"How about now? The sooner the better."

Aiguo laughed again. Zhiyuan had been known as a slowpoke back in the army, so who could have predicted how completely he would change in ten years? Aiguo went to buy a train ticket after he hung up and headed back to Shi Village from Linfen. From there he boarded a bus for Yanshan, where he would transfer to Leling. But before he reached Yanshan, his bus stopped at Botou and he met Cui Lifan the tofu maker, which led to his unplanned stay in Cangzhou. He chose Cangzhou over Leling not simply because he was better suited to be trucker than a date seller, but because a sudden calmness came over him when he entered the town. Qinyuan was over a thousand li from Botou, but to him it might as well have been another world. Pingshan, where Du Qinghai lived, was also about a thousand li from Qinyuan, but it did not help with his emotional turmoil. When he thought about the changes in his mental state, he realized that he should not seek out friends when he was agitated; in fact, he would feel better with people he barely knew, which was why he chose Cui Lifan over Zeng Zhiyuan. When they got to Cangzhou, he called Zhiyuan to say he was tied up and would have to delay going to Leling.

"Where are you calling from?" Zhiyuan asked.

"I'm still in Qinyuan." Aiguo decided to lie.

"It's already been four or five days, and you haven't left yet?" Zhiyuan sounded disappointed. "We're old buddies, but I guess I can't count on you at critical moments."

Aiguo heard the complaint, but had no idea what his friend meant by "critical moments." He hemmed and hawed. "I'll definitely come see you once I'm done here."

The promise was not a lie. He did plan to go once he found time after settling down in Cangzhou. He would go, not just to see an old friend, but to find out what those "critical moments" were all about.

Summer came to an end, replaced by fall, and soon it was winter, by which time Aiguo had been in Cangzhou for six months. Earlier, when he had stopped at Botou, he had left his rucksack on the bus, along with his clothes. He had replaced them with new fall and winter clothes. In Cangzhou, he had discovered that Hebei people in general prefer strong flavors in their food, which had the advantage of saving money. He made two friends during the six-month period. One, naturally, was Cui Lifan, who ran Xueying Fish and Soy Products. Lifan's operation was on the small side, with only a few workshops and about a dozen workers, who made tofu, thick and thin dried bean curd, shredded bean curd, and vegetarian chicken out of soy. Lifan had always wanted to make fermented bean curd and stinky tofu, because they were more profitable than other products he sold. But he would need a large quantity of vats and jars, and an expansion of his facility. Moreover, those two products needed culture preparation and fermentation, a process that usually lasted two months, a much longer duration than it took to make the other products. So he talked about it but never got around to going ahead.

The tofu business had been in the Cui family for several generations; Lifan had inherited it from his father, who had gotten it from his father. It had once been called Xueying Fish, which back then made fermented bean curd and stinky tofu, in addition to regular soy products. At the time, stinky tofu had a different name, *qingfang,* or green squares. According to Cui Lifan, the green squares from the Cui family plant were mouthwatering, sweet despite their foul smell. In addition to salt and red peppers, they added a secret sauce passed down from earlier generations. The tofu from Lifan's plant was white and full flavored; it was also hard as a brick, so it did not break when dropped and maintained a chewy texture. In Lifan's words, all tofu makers bought their soybeans from similar suppliers; what made one better than the others was the brine, which was why his tofu had such a fine reputation in Cangzhou. That made it possible to sell his products not only there, but in neighboring counties as well, like Botou, Nanpi, Dongguang, Jin County, and Hejian, and even as far as Dezhou in Shandong.

Aiguo heard that both Lifan's father and grandfather had been patient men who took things slowly; but Lifan was impetuous and rash, so unlike his predecessors. Once Aiguo knew Lifan better, he realized that the tofu maker had a good heart despite his temper, and, in fact, only two things roiled him. First, he lost his composure when someone went back on his word, like his nephew, Bai Wenbin, who had told Lifan the truck was ready when asked, and then it had broken down soon after they were on the road. Second, he was inflexible in his understanding of how things worked. Once a matter is settled, he would get angry if people changed their mind. He would be fine if he and you reached an agreement after a discussion about something; he would also accept an outcome if you made a mistake after discarding an earlier plan and adopted a new one. He often said about himself that he lost his temper only on account of the rationale behind something. Aiguo laughed when he heard his friend's self-portrayal, for he also needed a clear understanding of things, a trait that had caused him considerable grief over his thirty-five years. They were brought closer together because of this shared attribute.

When Aiguo first came to Cangzhou, the tofu maker's temper worried him that he might have to leave soon. He would stay as long as possible and could always go to Leling if it was time to leave. But Lifan never got angry at Aiguo, once he realized that he too was someone who listened to reason. Moreover, Lifan, who was five years older than Aiguo, often sought Aiguo's opinion if he could not make up his mind about something, so his new friend settled in at Xueying Fish and Soy Products, where he drove the truck to Cangzhou and the surrounding counties, even to Dezhou. His favorite town was Hejian, where he got to enjoy his favorite dish, nicknamed "toad swallowing honey," fried flatbreads stuffed with donkey meat.

Another friend Aiguo made was Li Kun, who owned a roadside diner in Yangzhuang, which Aiguo passed on his trips to Dezhou. It was the same diner where, six months earlier, he had intervened when Lifan was slapping Wenbin and had left his rucksack on the bus. The diner was called Old Li's Gourmet Food Court, though in fact it occupied a mere three rooms with seven or eight tables, offering home cooking, including Kung Pao chicken and shredded pork with garlic sauce. Aiguo ate at Li's diner either on his way to Dezhou or on his return trip to Cangzhou. Over the first three months, he and Li never exchanged a word, because Aiguo, always in a hurry, left as soon as he was finished. In addition to his gourmet food court, Li, a man with a medium build and a moustache, was a partner in a fur business that took him away from the diner from time to time.

One of Aiguo's regular trips to Dezhou took all day, owing to heavy traffic and roadwork, forcing him to spend the night in Dezhou, where the weather took a bad turn that evening. Snow was falling when he headed back to Cangzhou the next morning; it was fairly warm at first but got colder and colder as a thick layer of snow accumulated. There were few vehicles on the road; the surface turned slippery and his wheels skidded so badly he had to slow down. By late afternoon the sky had darkened, and the snowfall was heavier; with a northern headwind, he saw snowflakes swirling in the head-light beams. Visibility was down to a few feet. He kept at it until he reached Yangzhuang, where, afraid that the truck would skid into a roadside ditch, he decided to halt his journey and drive to Old Li's diner, where he would wait for the snowfall to stop or at least die down before getting back on the road. The diner was empty because of the heavy snow; the owner, Li Kun, a fur coat draped over his shoulders, stood at the door to watch the falling snow. Aiguo parked his truck, got out, and patted his clothes while walking in. A young woman behind the counter, head down, was working on the accounts; in her mid-twenties, with almond-shaped eyes, a high nose bridge, and curved lips, she was full-figured, with ample breasts. Aiguo assumed she was Li Kun's daughter or a daughter-in-law, so he did not pay her any attention. Cold and hungry, he ordered a bowl of hot-and-sour soup and a pan-fried flatbread stuffed with pork and cabbage. He smoked as he waited for his food. When he finished his cigarette, he looked up and saw the waiter walking up with a plate of sliced meat from a pig's head, spicy beef tendons, cured fish, and a large hot pot of stewed donkey entrails and assorted mushrooms.

"I didn't order all this," Aiguo said.

Li Kun came out of the kitchen before the waiter could respond and set a bottle of Hengshui Aged Liquor on the table.

"The snow is getting heavier, and you can't go home today. So drink up."

Li Kun stopped him before Aiguo could protest.

"My treat. Let's enjoy ourselves on this snowy day."

"I can't eat for free." Aiguo rubbed his hands.

"I'm often on the road for the fur trade, so I know how it feels to be away from home."

Li Kun and Aiguo started in on the bottle. The woman came over and sat beside Li Kun when she was done with the accounts, which told Aiguo that she was actually the man's wife. Thinking she was too young to have much capacity for alcohol, he was surprised to see that she was as good a drinker as the men. In their conversation, Li Kun asked Aiguo his name, where he was from, and why he was in Cangzhou, to which Aiguo responded one by one. He then told his host that he had wanted to go to Leling, not Cangzhou, but had ended up in Cangzhou after stopping a man from beating another man. Li Kun and his wife laughed and then shared the story of their business—not the diner, but the fur trade. Before long, one of them said the wrong thing and the couple began to argue, starting with the business and moving on to their domestic affairs. Unfamiliar with the fur trade and the Li family business, Aiguo did not know just what they were arguing about, but was amused that they were quarrelling in front of him. Knowing the wisdom in staying clear of people's domestic strife, he kept his head down and continued to drink. He could not help thinking about the couple's difference in age; Li Kun, who was in his fifties, had married a woman in her twenties. No wonder they didn't see eye to eye. Aiguo was reminded of Old Su, who ran a bathhouse on North Street in Qinyuan. A widower, he had married a twenty-five-year-old woman when he was fifty-two. They got along so well they walked out of the bathhouse holding hands.

Aiguo had always abhorred quarrels, for his parents had argued almost daily when he was a boy. Later, when he married Lina, they had not fought much, but that did not mean they got along; not having much to say to one another prevented friction. He had tried to find nice things to say to her, and yet she had carried on her affair anyway, until her infidelity was discovered, nearly causing Aiguo to commit murder. Listening to Li Kun and his wife bicker actually gave him a warm, fuzzy feeling.

The snowfall showed no sign of letting up after dinner, so Aiguo was put up in one of the guest rooms. He could still hear them arguing before he fell asleep; he shook his head and smiled. The sky cleared up the next morning, so he drove back to Cangzhou. From then on, he stopped at Li's Gourmet Food Court on his way either to Dezhou or back to Cangzhou. It was no longer just about food; he knew the people and the place, which was comforting. Cangzhou was an unfamiliar place to him, while here in Yangzhuang he knew someone, so he always looked forward to seeing Li Kun and his wife. After they got to know each other better, Li Kun sometimes asked Aiguo to bring him provisions—beer, cigarettes, pork, and other commodities from Cangzhou or Dezhou. Aiguo obliged him, of course.

Soon winter was over and spring returned. One day, when Aiguo was on another tofu delivery trip to Dezhou, the truck's radiator broke on his way back. He raised the hood and tried to fix it but couldn't, and he wound up hurting his hand. After logging more than three hundred thousand kilometers, Lifan's truck was clearly near the end of its useful life. Aiguo wrapped his hand in a rag. Since the radiator could not be repaired, all he could do was fill it with water and go as far as possible before stopping to add water again. He made it to Old Li's Gourmet Food Court, where he stopped to add water. The hole was so big the water went right through it. Afraid he might burn up the engine, he decided to stop, so he wiped his hands again and entered the diner. Li Kun was away on fur trade business. His wife was behind the counter working on the books; diners who were passing through town sat at several tables. By then, Aiguo had learned that Li Kun's wife was named Zhang Chuhong and that she was from Zhangjiakou, not Botou. The couple had met when Li Kun went to Zhangjiakou to buy furs; he divorced his first wife to marry Chuhong. She was a few years younger than Aiguo, who was, in turn, younger than Li Kun, so Aiguo called her Saozi, or older brother's wife. She doubled over laughing each time he addressed her that way, making him laugh sheepishly along with her.

"My radiator is broken, Saozi. I'd like to leave the truck here and take a bus back to Cangzhou," he said as he walked in the door. "I'll be back tomorrow, with a new one."

"All right," she said, without looking up.

He walked out to wait for a bus. It was around six o'clock, and there should have been a bus for Cangzhou, but he waited until eight and no bus came. It must have left early; if not, it could have broken down somewhere along the way. He had no choice but to go back to the diner. He saw through the window that the place was packed with clamoring customers. Wanting no part of the commotion, he found a stool and sat by a locust tree to smoke. It was the fifteenth day of the month, and a large moon was inching its way into the sky. A breeze turned the leaves into dancing shadows on the ground. Looking up at the bright moon, he experienced pangs of homesickness, as it had been nearly a year since he'd left Qinyuan. He missed only his daughter and mother, not the place or the house. Since arriving in Cangzhou, he had sent money home every month, usually three-fourths of his pay, leaving the rest for himself. He also called home once every two weeks. Back in Niu Village, Cao Qing'e had shared her thoughts with him and had sometimes talked late into the night to tell him things that had happened fifty or sixty years before. But mother and son had little to say after switching to phone calls. Apparently, talking on the phone was different from chatting face-to-face. He asked her the same questions each time.

"How are you and Baihui doing, Mother?"

"We're fine. How about you?"

"I'm fine too."

And then they hung up. He had told her he was going to Beijing before he left; over the phone he said he was in Cangzhou, because he could make more money here than in Beijing. He never asked about Pang Lina, nor did his mother mention her. Nearly a year had gone by, and he had no idea what she was up to. Once, in a dream, he was among many people lining up to get in a door. He was shoving and pushing those around him when he spotted Lina in the distance. He had forgotten about her affair, or maybe they were still together. In any case, he called out to her, "Hurry. Come quickly or you'll be late."

Lina pushed her way through the crowd, but it wasn't her; it was Little Jiang of East Asian Wedding Photo Studio on West Street in Qinyuan. Aiguo's heart swelled with old resentment and new anger; he plunged a scaling knife into Jiang's heart. At this point, he awoke to find himself drenched in a cold sweat. Looking at the moon now, he recalled the dream and had to shake his head with a mournful sigh. Clearly, not only had he not gotten over the affair, but its effects had actually become more entrenched in his mind.

The diners were leaving in groups, so he walked inside. Chuhong was surprised to see him back.

"I thought you left."

He told her why he hadn't, and she laughed.

"I haven't eaten yet, so why don't you join me for a drink?"

She told the cook to make some food for them before locking up the counter drawer when she finished with the books. It was ten o'clock by the time she sat down to drink with Aiguo. The cook and waiter, who were both from the next village, went home when all the customers were gone. Aiguo and Chuhong were the only two left. In the past, Li Kun had always been home when Aiguo stopped at the diner, so the three of them drank together. This was a new experience, one that made them feel awkward at first. But as they drank, they began to talk, starting with their respective hometowns. Chuhong talked about the donkeys and Dajingmen Pass at Zhangjiakou, while Aiguo told her about Yongji's green persimmons and Linyi's pomegranates, followed by stories about their best friends. Chuhong mentioned a middle school friend, Xu Manyu, back in Zhangjiakou, a confidante with whom she had shared everything for ten years or more. Her parents had opposed her marriage to Li Kun, and her mother all but turned on the gas in the house to kill herself. She made up her mind to marry Li Kun after talking it over with Manyu, who had a hair salon in Zhangjiakou; business was good, but Manyu was not satisfied, so she'd gone to Beijing for more opportunities, and the two had lost contact.

"Who's your best friend?" she asked when she finished her story.

"Li Kun," Aiguo said after giving the question some thought.

"I thought you were an honest man, but it turns out you're quite devious."

He smiled and mentally went through all his good friends. His best friend was not Li Kun, nor Cui Lifan, nor Feng Wenxiu in Qinyuan, with whom he'd had a falling out before leaving town, nor Li Kezhi in Linfen, nor Zeng Zhi-yuan in Leling. In the end, he had to pick Du Qinghai in Pingshan, but he had become a different man, no longer the comrade-in-arms Aiguo could count on. He'd given him a lousy suggestion when they'd met again several years after leaving the army. Aiguo and Chuhong had downed half a bottle and were both getting tipsy. Chuhong began to cry. She told him about her and Li Kun. They'd had so much to say to each other when they first met, which was why she had defied her parents and insisted on marrying him, a man in his fifties, leaving her hometown to live in Botou. Her talks with Manyu had not really made a big difference in her decision. Chuhong had not expected that they would be left with little to say after only two years, and everything had changed. Moved by her tale, Aiguo then told her about what had happened with Pang Lina. It was a long story and more complex than the life between her and Li Kun. But the night was long and they had nothing better to do. He got so worked up he revealed everything, from beginning to end, leaving nothing out. He would not have come all the way to Cangzhou if not for Lina. He cried, too, when he finished. It felt good to finally get it all out. He had never before revealed any of this to anyone, and by the time he finished, he was in tears. They were both crying, and that embarrassed them. Chuhong decided to change the subject.

"I wasn't this heavy back home in Zhangjiakou. I put on the weight after I got here."

"How slim were you?" Aiguo asked.

She got up, walked into a room in the back, and brought out a photo to show him. Indeed, Chuhong was slim, but still with ample breasts.

"Do you know why I'm drinking with you today?" she asked him.

"It just sort of happened, I guess."

"No. Today is my birthday."

Aiguo stood up and said, "Happy Birthday, Saozi."

She reached out to rub his head. The normally timid Aiguo, now emboldened by too much liquor, laid down the photo and wrapped his arms around her, surprising even himself. He had thought she would push him away, and if she had, he would have treated it as a lark. But she didn't; she stayed in his arms and let him rub her back. He then led her into the inner room, fully expecting her to struggle, but she didn't. When they were in the room, he pushed her down on the bed, took off her clothes and his own, and unhooked her bra to fondle her breasts. She pushed him aside and got up at that moment; he thought she was going to get dressed. Instead, she walked naked to bring over warm water in an enamel mug and washed his privates. When she was done, she wiped him dry and bent over to put her mouth around him. Aiguo nearly fell to pieces, for it was nearly a year since he'd been with a woman. They went at it for three hours. She cried out so loudly that the sound reverberated around the room, while he was covered in sweat, as if he'd been hosed down. The moon felt as hot as the sun as it shone down on the bed. Aiguo discovered what a real woman was like for the first time. In the past, when he had made love with Lina, she'd always kept her eyes shut and did not make a sound. Chuhong moaned with her eyes wide open; the louder she moaned, the wider her eyes opened, and the wider her eyes grew, the louder she screamed. He opened his eyes. He could not help but think that there was a predestined connection between the diner and him. He had left his rucksack on a bus outside the diner, and this was what he'd received in return.

It was nearly dawn when they were finally done. Aiguo sobered up; the sweat had dried on his body and a sudden fear gripped him. He felt bad about his friend, Li Kun. Chuhong tried to assuage his guilt feelings when she noticed the look on his face.

"He has his own fun when he's on a business trip."

"How do you know?"

"He got something nasty down there once, and so I stay away."

That was another surprise. Now he knew why she'd washed him and why the couple was constantly fighting. Obviously, that was the core issue in their arguments, which appeared to be about other things. He also realized that she was more daring than he, which only scared him even more. What had happened the night before would have been quickly forgotten if Chuhong and her husband had a good marriage, but with that particular problem between them, he felt as if he'd poked at a wasps' nest. He wasn't afraid of being stung; he just couldn't stand the fact that he'd added a metaphorical wasps' nest to the one created by Lina. When he returned to Cangzhou the next day, he made up his mind to not have a repeat with Chuhong. Recalling his truck back at the diner, he returned with a new radiator later in the afternoon, but he did not dare walk into the diner. Rather, he hid in the field by the highway, where, instead of the usual rapeseed, the farmers had planted corn this year. He crouched down to smoke until midnight, littering the field with cigarette butts. Then, sneaking out on tiptoes, he quietly went back to the diner, raised the hood of his truck, and, holding a flashlight in his mouth, started to replace the broken radiator. The job took two hours, but he didn't make a sound the whole time. Obviously, nothing is impossible when you put your mind to it, he learned.

He got into the cab, started the engine, and roared away, like a car thief. Over the next two weeks, he stayed clear of Botou, taking a long detour to avoid Old Li's Gourmet Food Court, on his way to and from Dezhou. Yet avoiding the place only made him think about her more, no matter where he was; she was always on his mind, whether he was in Cangzhou, Nanpi, Dongguang, Jin County, Hejian, or Dezhou. He thought about her when he was driving and when he wasn't in his truck. He missed the dense hair between her legs, like lush grass, and the little pool of green water in the grass. The grassy patch and water were not the only things about her he could not forget; everything about her body, inside and outside, from top to bottom, was always on his mind. And it wasn't just her body; he visualized the way she walked and talked, as well as her voice. This was the first time in his life he missed anyone that much. After two weeks, he could hold out no longer and returned to the diner. Li Kun was away again and they were alone that night.

"I thought you were brave. I guess I was wrong."

He didn't reply.

"So why are you here again?" she asked.

He put his hand between her legs and took her into the other room. Two weeks of absence made them go wild, like dry kindling meeting a raging fire. In the past, Aiguo had stopped by Li's diner every time he drove to Dezhou from Cangzhou and back, but now that changed. Sometimes, when he delivered tofu to places other than Dezhou, such as Nanpi, Dongguang, or Jin County, he traveled the additional distance to stop at Old Li's Gourmet Food Court. Sometimes Li Kun was home and sometimes he wasn't. If he was around, Aiguo kept up the pretense of calling his wife Saozi, and she would double over laughing. The laughter was the same to Li Kun, but not to them. If Li Kun was away, Aiguo would spend the night with Chuhong, not just for sex, though; they had a lot to say to each other, but it was more than that. They liked the intimacy of sex, as well as the feeling of being with each other. Sometimes they would do it three times in one night, after which they would stay awake to talk in each other's arms. He could tell her everything, including things he could not say to anyone else. Words came to him so easily when he was with her, especially words that often escaped him during conversations with others. He talked unlike any other man, for they had their own style of conversing. They talked about happy things as well as those that upset them. With other people, they felt upbeat talking about happy events, but exasperated when they brought up depressing matters; in contrast, they talked cheerfully with each other even about cheerless matters.

For instance, Pang Lina had been a sore spot that caused heartache when Aiguo mentioned her, but she was now reduced to a simple subject matter from his past. With Zhang Chuhong in his life, Aiguo's attitude toward Lina underwent a change. They also spoke about Chuhong's boyfriends before she met Li Kun, about her first time with a man, about whether it had hurt and if she had bled. She kept nothing from him, and then asked him how many women he'd had; she wrapped her arms around him when he told her she was his second, after Pang Lina. Sometimes, after talking awhile, they would think they ought to go to sleep, but one of them would say, "Let's talk about something else."

"Why not?"

At moments like that, Aiguo had a sudden uneasy feeling that he had become Little Jiang, while Zhang Chuhong was Pang Lina. The exchange was the same as the one Jiang and Lina had had in bed when Jiang's wife, Zhao Xinting, was waiting outside their room in the Spring Sunshine Hotel.

Once, when they were in bed talking, Chuhong said, "I want to be with you more than with anyone else, Laogong. Take me away from here." She called him Laogong, slang for husband.

"Where to?" He was stunned.

"Anywhere. I don't care, as long as we can be away from here."

Aiguo had come to Hebei to escape his miseries, and now Zhang Chuhong wanted to leave Hebei, which told him that something different was going on. He would have been fearful if this had happened a month earlier, but not now, for he was a changed man, no longer afraid of the changes in his life. Little Jiang had been frightened when his wife discovered his affair with Lina, so he'd backed off and avoided her. Aiguo did not turn into Little Jiang. At the time, he was unaware that he had changed over the past month.

"We can leave after I go back to Cangzhou and work something out."

"I'll tell you something if you're brave enough to take me with you." She tightened her arms around him.

"What is it?"

"I'll tell you later."

Aiguo returned to Cangzhou and started thinking about places they could go. After reviewing his options, he came up with three. One, they could go to Shandong to see Zeng Zhiyuan in Leling; two, they could go to Du Qinghai in Pingshan; three, they could seek out Li Kezhi in Linfen. Each seemed feasible at first, but none turned out to be workable after thinking it through. They could all work if he went alone, but not if Chuhong was with him. It dawned on him that he had few places to go. He was wondering what to do when Cui Lifan said something that gave him an inspiration. Li Kun had not detected anything going on between his wife and his friend, but Lifan, the tofu maker, could tell that Aiguo was acting differently. One day, he went along to collect payment when Aiguo delivered tofu to Dongguang. Aiguo was driving, as usual, with Lifan in the passenger seat. Aiguo was quiet, his mind busily searching for a place to flee with Chuhong. Lifan studied his face.

"I can tell something has been bothering you."

"What do you mean?" Aiguo asked.

"Your face was sallow when you first came to Cangzhou, but it later gained a glow. And now you look washed out again."

Lifan was right about Aiguo's worries, so he said nothing. Lifan continued, "You were quiet, and then you talked a lot, but now you're quiet again."

Aiguo was in a jam and needed someone to talk to, and he considered Lifan a good friend, since they both enjoyed analyzing matters. Moreover, Lifan had never met Chuhong or her husband. Since Lifan had asked, these factors combined to make Aiguo decide to open up to Lifan. He told him everything. When he got to the part about her request and his indecision, Lifan gave him a loud slap, to Aiguo's surprise.

"You're in big trouble."

"What do you mean?"

"By big trouble, I don't mean your affair, but your plan to run off with her."

"What do you mean?"

"Running off is the easy part. The question is, are you going to have some fun with her or do you plan to marry her?"

"We weren't serious at first, but now it's different. I want to marry her; she's the only person I can talk to."

"And that's where your troubles begin. I won't stop you if you plan to dump her after having some fun. But if you married her, could you take her back to your hometown?"

Aiguo had told Lifan about Lina. Lifan was right again.

"It's still a mess back there." Aiguo shook his head. "I'm not divorced yet, so I couldn't do that. It would just be asking for trouble."

"Then where would you go with her?"

"I've been thinking about that for days, but haven't come up with a good place."

"That's it, then." Lifan clapped his hands. "If you're going to drift around, I can tell you right now that you two are doomed. Think about it. Her husband has a diner and a fur trade, so he can afford to support her. But you, you're a truck driver. It's easy to take care of yourself when you're out there, but two people would be hard. Can you manage it?"

Aiguo did not know what to say.

"You two have a lot to say because she's being supported by her husband, and all you need to do is talk. But when you have to provide for her, you'll have to worry about living in the real world, and you'll be talking about nothing but real life things."

Lifan's words were a wake-up call. It became clear to Aiguo why he had been so indecisive over the past few days; he could not make up his mind, not about where to go, but about what to do once they got there.

"And that wouldn't be the end of your troubles," Lifan added.

"What do you mean?"

"Your indecision. You either leave with her now or cut off all ties with her."

"How so?"

"The truth usually comes out when the point is reached where a couple must flee. No one knows when it snows at midnight, but people know when it rains. Someone will be killed if you don't make up your mind soon. Her husband is local, but you're not. Do you think you can get off easily when he finds out?"

Aiguo broke out in a cold sweat from the fear his friend instilled in him. He had nearly committed murder when he'd first learned about Lina's affair. He had even thought of killing Jiang's son, but he'd let them live in the end, not because they didn't deserve to die, but because he had a daughter. Zhang Chuhong and Li Kun had no children. When Li Kun found out about them, neither Chuhong nor he would mean anything to him, and he could well decide to kill one or both of them. Aiguo was awake all night after they returned to Cangzhou, which was, understandably, different from staying awake with Chuhong. After turning the matter over in his head for some time, he decided against running off; he would cut off all ties with her. So he did not see her for a week and started taking round-about detours again to avoid Botou on his delivery trips. But their relationship had reached a point where it was no longer solely up to him whether or not to sever ties. She called him after he'd been absent for a week.

"I've got everything ready, so why aren't you here?"

"I haven't decided where to go yet." Niu was evasive.

His tone of voice told her he'd had a change of heart.

"Your words were barely out of your mouth before you changed your mind."

"No, that's not true." Niu was afraid to tell the truth.

"Let's go to Hainan."

"We don't know anyone there."

323

She blew up. "Do you honestly think we could go someplace where we know people?" She started crying, but quickly turned belligerent. "I'm telling Li Kun if you're not here in three days."

Her ultimatum terrified him. He would have packed up and left Cangzhou right away but for his guilt feelings and the worry that she would find him despicable. It did not overly concern him that she might despise him, since he would never see her again; the problem was the loss of self-worth he'd feel for the rest of his life. He was caught in a real bind and could not find a way out until his mother came to his rescue. His older brother, Aijiang, called him from Niu Village to tell him that their mother was seriously ill and he should hurry back home. His initial reaction to the news was not concern over his sick mother, but relief that he had found an excuse to leave Cangzhou. After hanging up, he went to see Cui and told him about the call. Cui did not believe him at first, treating Niu's imminent departure as his way to avoid Zhang.

"You don't have to leave. Just stop seeing her."

By then Aiguo's concern had shifted to his sick mother. With no time to give Cui further explanation, he packed up his stuff before racing to the bus depot. He left Cangzhou.

8

Niu Aiguo's mother died on the fourth day after his return to Qinyuan. In his memory, Cao Qing'e had never been seriously ill, so it came as a surprise that she was bedridden this time. She was laid up for a month, but would not allow her children to notify Aiguo. A month later, the three of them decided to call him when they realized that she probably would not get better. By the time Aiguo raced home, she was already in the county hospital. She could still talk before being hospitalized, but once there, she was too ill to say a word, effectively turning into a mute, after a lifetime of chattering. Aiguo's older brother, Aijiang, told him that their mother had talked all night before her hospitalization.

"What did she say?"

"Just gibberish. We were too worried about her to pay much attention."

As she lay in the hospital bed, Aiguo to her left, Aijiang to her right, and Aixiang at the foot of the bed, Aihe, the youngest, stood against the wall, gouging the surface with his fingers. With tubes in her nose and arms, Cao Qing'e was racked by a high fever that put her in a sort of coma. She had not been able to get much down over the past month, so she was now skin and bones. With their mother losing her ability to talk, the four siblings went quiet also, not because they felt awkward talking while their mother was rendered a virtual mute, nor because they were worried about her. They simply did not know what to say to one another.

The doctor had told them that she'd had lung cancer for three or four years, based on the results of his examination. She'd not said a word about it over those years, so naturally her children had no inkling of what went on inside her. The doctor also told them that she could have had surgery back then, but now the cancer cells had spread to her spine and central nervous system, affecting her ability to talk. At her age, an operation would do no good, so they could only keep her going with medication. At lunchtime, Aihe stayed behind, while the other three went out to get something to eat at a diner next to the hospital. The noontime broadcast of a Shanxi opera on the town's loudspeaker was carried in the air, the music undulating to the scale of the wind.

"In all these years, she never said a word about it," Aijiang said. "She was always pinching us when we were kids, but now we know she loved us all along."

During the year of Aiguo's absence, his sister had picked up smoking. She lit a cigarette as she looked at him.

"Remember I told you she's our mother, after all, before you joined the army?"

"Why didn't she tell us?" Aijiang fumed, seized by a sudden anger. "If she had, she could have had surgery. But now, nothing can be done, and we can only worry about her. Why did she do that?"

Aiguo would have agreed with them if this had been a few years earlier, but now he thought they were both wrong. Their mother might have kept quiet about her illness for three or four years because she loved them too much to cause them worry, but it could also have been because she was disappointed in all of them. Her four grown-up children each had problems. The oldest, Aijiang, had a sickly wife who required daily medication. Aixiang was in her forties but still single. Aihe was into the first year of his marriage to an irritable woman with a sharp tongue, a carbon copy of his own mother in her younger days. She dominated everything they did. The last sibling, Aiguo, was in more serious trouble than any of them; he had not gotten along with his wife through the six years of their marriage, and then she'd had an affair, forcing him to leave Qinyuan for Cangzhou. With all her children having so much to deal with, no wonder Cao Qing'e decided to keep her illness to herself. None of the children was having it easy in life, so she had no one to talk to even if she had wanted to.

Possibly she did not tell them because she didn't know what to do with them, after the disappointment they had caused her. She shared what was on her mind only with Aiguo after he turned thirty-five, but she talked about events from fifty or sixty years earlier, not about the present. In the past, he had thought she hadn't talked about the present because there wasn't much to say; now he realized that she wouldn't have anyway, not even when she wasn't feeling well. When she recounted her past to him, he had treated it merely as a chat around the fire, but now it dawned on him that she was already ill. She simply stopped talking, in a way, once she had told him everything from all those years before. In fact, they had already found little to say when he called her from Cangzhou, which he had attributed to the difference between talking face-to-face and speaking over the phone. When he returned and learned that she had been laid up for a month, but would not let his siblings tell him, he assumed that the other three had taken the refusal as a sign of her preference for Aiguo. Now it seemed obvious that she did love him, but that she was even more affected by the sense of disappointment and powerlessness he'd caused her. He was also hit by a sudden realization that she had told only him, of all her children, about her past, not because she felt more comfortable talking to him, but because he had been in more trouble than the other three; it had been her way of giving him solace. In the previous year, when he'd gone to see her before leaving Qinyuan, the place of his heartache over Lina's affair, his mother had known everything about what had happened to him, but she hadn't let on. Like her, Aiguo did not reveal to his siblings what had been on their mother's mind.

The diner's owner, a fat old man, was used to illness and patients. From the three worry-laden faces at Aiguo's table, he could tell that someone in their family was seriously ill. A chatterbox himself, he tried to comfort them when he brought the food.

"You won't feel so sad once you understand everything."

Aiguo would have agreed with the man in the past, but now he couldn't. He would have fewer worries if he did not understand everything and actually felt worse when he did. They had ordered mutton soup and fried flatbreads. Aijiang and Aixiang took a few bites before putting down their chopsticks. Aiguo, in contrast, had not had a real meal over the past three days as he hurried home from Qinyuan. The local specialty tasted so good he gobbled up five fried cakes and drained a big bowl of mutton soup. He was bathed in sweat when he finished. Suddenly, he recalled his mother lying unconscious in a hospital bed, going without eating for a month, while he enjoyed the food so much he'd all but inhaled his food. Holding the empty bowl in his hands, he felt tears fill his eyes, prompting the fat owner to offer more consoling words when he came to clear the table.

"Everything has to come to an end. You'll feel better if you take the long view."

That did not sound right to Aiguo. He would actually feel better if he just focused on the present and would fret if he looked too far into the future.

Ignoring the man, Aiguo blurted out to his siblings, "Mother isn't foolish. She did the right thing."

They were confused, and so was the old man.

Cao Qing'e regained consciousness that evening. She opened her eyes, looked around, and opened her mouth, but nothing came out. She tried again but still couldn't make a sound. Her children came up while her mouth was gaping wide, but none of them could decipher what she tried to say. Getting increasingly anxious, she drew a square in the air with her hands, her face turning red from the urgency; she gestured in the air, but they were still at a loss. Aixiang took out paper and pen, and her mother nodded. She padded the paper with a magazine for her mother to write two words in a shaking hand: *Go home*.

The children looked at one another. How could she go home in her current state? Going home would just be waiting to die. They thought it must be her feverish brain talking.

"It's all right, Mother. The doctor told us you'll get better," Aiguo said.

Qing'e shook her head to indicate she'd meant something else.

"Are you concerned about money? Don't worry. We'll take care of it," Aijiang said.

She shook her head again.

"Are you worried about us? We'll takes turns staying with you, and we'll be fine." Aixiang said.

She was still shaking her head.

"We did everything your way when you were well, but now you're sick and you have to listen to us." Aihe decided to be blunt.

Knowing she couldn't get them to understand what she meant, she gave up trying to communicate and turned to face the wall. Soon she lost consciousness again. That night was Aiguo's turn to stay at the hospital. He watched his mother sleep; before long, he laid his head down on the edge of the bed and fell asleep, exhausted from the three-day travel to rush home. He felt he was elsewhere and his mother was in fine health; they weren't in the present, but back a dozen or so years before, when he had been in the army. In his late teens, he had few worries and his face had a red glow, devoid of wrinkles. He was in bed when the bugle sounded, an emergency muster for the whole company. It started out with a company muster, followed by a battalion muster, then regiment, division, and finally corps, with tens of thousands of soldiers mustering in a desolate Gobi Desert, where they started marching. The soldiers were in full combat gear, each carrying a rifle fitted with a bayonet; they marched in unison, making a loud rustling sound, as they shouted out cadence. The line was so long that both ends seemed to have disappeared; it looked like a straight line from front to back and from right to left. The sun came out to shine on the bayonets, creating bright crisscrossed rays. They kicked up so much dust that half the sky was blotted out. He had no idea who they were marching for, but could sense that they were invincible, a huge number of soldiers in the prime of their youth marching forward with their rifles and of one mind. His friend Du Qinghai was beside him. Aiguo wondered how Qinghai, from a different company, could be marching with him. He smiled at Qinghai and Qinghai returned the smile, but out of the blue, Qinghai's bayonet tilted and lanced Aiguo's arm; he woke up with a yelp to find himself in a hospital room. He was beset by nostalgic sentiments. A short dozen years had gone by just like that, and he was getting old; it wasn't him, actually, but his heart that had aged.

The light was dim in the room. A wind started up around midnight and blew in through the open window, sending the single bulb swaying above his head. He realized that his mother had woken up again and was pinching his arm. So it hadn't been a bayonet in his dream, but his mother's pinch. Qing'e had had a bad temper when the children were young and, instead of beating them, she would pinch them whenever she was in a foul mood. She didn't care where she pinched.

Aiguo thought his mother had pinched him because she was in pain, until he saw her gaping mouth. She wanted to say something, obviously.

"What do you want to say?"

Suddenly recalling that she couldn't talk any more, he brought her pen and paper. With her shaking hand, she wrote two characters: *Bai-hui.*

Aiguo's seven-year-old daughter, Baihui, had never been close to Aiguo or her mother, Lina; she liked her grandmother best, since Qing'e had raised her. The girl loved beans. When the family had congee, Aiguo and Lina would give her the beans left at the bottom of their bowls, but she wouldn't eat them. She would only take beans from her grandmother's bowl. Qing'e began teaching her to read when she turned four, writing down Chinese characters on a small blackboard for her. After a few years, Baihui knew several hundred characters. Grandmother and granddaughter quarreled often, however, and, when exasperated, Qing'e would yell at the girl, "Stop arguing with me, Baihui, or I'll pinch you."

Or, "I've argued with people all my life, so I could outtalk you even with half my mouth shut."

Showing no sign of fear, Baihui would giggle.

When Cao Qing'e began to recount events from the past to Aiguo after he turned thirty-five, Baihui usually ran around the brazier, and, when she was tired, instead of going to her father, she would fall asleep in her grandmother's lap, arms around her neck. Aiguo and Lina, who had both been busy, felt reassured with Qing'e taking care of their daughter, and Aiguo had no idea that his mother was already sick back then. Now, looking at the girl's name on the paper, Aiguo finally understood why his mother had written "go home" the previous afternoon. Qing'e was concerned about the little girl.

"Big Sister-in-law is taking care of Baihui. Don't worry about her."

Qing'e shook her head; that wasn't what she wanted to say.

"Would you like her to come here?" Aiguo then asked.

She nodded.

"I'll bring her over first thing tomorrow morning."

Early the next morning, Aiguo had his younger brother bring Baihui to the hospital, but Qing'e was unconscious when the girl arrived. Aihe went off to tend to other business after delivering the girl. When Qing'e awoke and saw Baihui, she took the girl's hand and pointed to her own mouth before pointing to the girl's and looking over at Aiguo. Obviously, he thought, his mother wanted Baihui over not because she worried about the girl, but because she wanted Baihui to speak for her. Qing'e gestured for pen and paper, which Aiguo handed to her. Her hand was so weak that her handwriting was mere squiggles. She was sweating after struggling to scribble "mother," and then "death."

"Do you know what grandma meant?" Aiguo asked his daughter.

The girl shook her head, so agitating Qing'e that her face turned red. Aiguo assumed that his mother was talking about herself dying, so he said, "Your illness isn't serious. You'll be fine soon."

His mother shook her head; he was wrong again.

"Do you want me to tell Papa what you told me?" Baihui suddenly got what her grandmother wanted, and Qing'e nodded.

"What did Grandma tell you?" Aiguo asked his daughter.

"Lots and lots of things. She talked to me every night."

Aiguo realized that his mother had started talking to his daughter after he left for Cangzhou, probably because she had no one but Baihui, a little girl, to talk to.

"Do you want me to tell Papa about your mother's death, Grandma?"

Qing'e nodded rigorously as tears welled up in her eyes. Cao Qing'e's mother had been the wife of Old Cao, a carter in Wen Village in Xianyuan County. It had been twenty years since her death. Qing'e had told Aiguo all

330

about what happened fifty or sixty years earlier, but with the girl, she focused on events from twenty years before. Qing'e's father, Old Cao, a man of few words, had always treated others with courtesy, and Qing'e had been close to him ever since childhood. After her marriage, she still shared what was on her mind only with him, not with her mother. But after he turned seventy, Old Cao became a nag, petty and ill tempered, and he wanted to make all the decisions, but had trouble carrying things out. Qing'e was not particularly sad when he died, and did not miss him at first. He had exhausted her fond feelings for him during the last five years of his life.

Her mother, Old Cao's wife, had been a chatterbox as a young woman. She had a bad temper and, as the head of the household all her life, was forever quarreling with her husband, and with her daughter for half her life. But after turning seventy, she abruptly stopped arguing with people, let go of her household dominance, and refused to make a decision. She agreed with whatever others said and went along with their suggestions, as if nothing concerned her. A woman who had squabbled with so many for most of her life now wore a pleasant smile. Still tall in old age, she cut a warm and caring figure as she leaned against her cane and bent down to carry on a conversation. After Old Cao's death, Qing'e traveled from Niu Village to see her in Wen Village, and the two women, who had fought all the time, could now actually sit down to talk and talk. They had so much to say to each other, precisely because they could not have talked without getting into a fight in the past. On each visit, they would talk late into the night, whether Qing'e stayed for three days, or five days, or even ten days. The topics of their talks covered everything, including her mother's life as a young girl, Qing'e's children, things in their respective households, and more. Qing'e recalled little of what they talked about, only that they talked. Sometimes they got sleepy and should have gone to bed, but Old Cao's wife would say, "Let's talk about other things."

Qing'e would say, "Why not?"

Or she would say, "Let's talk some more, Mother."

"Yes, let's do that."

After three, five, or ten days, Qing'e had to return to Niu Village. Mother and daughter would get up before daybreak to cook and have breakfast together; then they would pack some food for the road and her mother would walk her all the way to the bus depot in town. They would continue talking as they walked; sometimes they stopped and sat down by the road to talk more before setting off again and stopping to sit down for more talk. It would be noon by the time they reached town. They would eat the food they had brought with them and sit beneath the locust tree by the depot to talk. Qing'e would let the first bus go, and the second. Once, Cao's wife said to her daughter, "I thought Xiangyuan was too far a place for you to marry into, but now I feel it's a good thing it's far."

"Why is that?"

"I can walk all the way here with you, because it's far," Cao's wife said. "I think of all these things to say to you because we don't get to see each other often."

Qing'e did not board until the last bus of the day was leaving. When she looked down through the window, she saw that the depot was empty of passengers; her mother, the only one left, was leaning against her cane, mouth open. Qing'e wept despite herself.

A month before Cao's wife died, her legs swelled up so much she was confined to her bed. Qing'e traveled from Niu Village in Qinyuan to Wen Village in Xiangyuan to be with her mother for the last month of the old woman's life. She lay in bed while her daughter sat next to her, and they talked for a whole month, saying enough to last a lifetime. They were still chatting the day before she died. At one point, Cao's wife lost consciousness, so Qing'e called out, "Come back, Mother. I haven't finished."

Her mother awoke and they resumed their conversation, until she lost consciousness again. Qing'e called out again. That happened five times. When Cao's wife woke up the last time, she said, "Don't call me back the next time I go, Girl. My body feels heavy, and I haven't been able to walk for a month. But earlier in my dream, I walked and walked and got to a river, where my legs suddenly felt light. There were flowers and grass by the river. And I said to myself, I haven't washed my face for a long time, so I ought to get down to wash it with the river water. You called out to me just before I could wash my face, and I ended up back here, back to this sick bed. Don't call me back next time, Girl. I can't take it anymore, so don't think I'm cruel or that I have no more to say to you."

So Qing'e did not call out to her mother when the old woman lost consciousness again.

Unable to comprehend the significance of her grandmother's story, Baihui looked at Aiguo when she finished relating the account. Aiguo did not understand either, at first, so he looked over at his bed-ridden mother. Seeing the incomprehension on her son's face, Qing'e shook her head, so worked up that her face turned red again; she banged on the bed with a shaky hand and pointed to the door with the other. Suddenly Aiguo knew exactly what she wanted.

"Let's get you out of here, Mother. We'll go home now."

She finally nodded, though by then she was sweating. At that moment, Aiguo felt that he was not as close to her as she had been to her mother. But none of his siblings was as close to their mother as he was; they were upset when they returned to the hospital that afternoon and learned about Aiguo's decision to take their mother home.

"Can you call yourself human if you refuse to have Mother stay for treatment?" Aijiang said.

"You're not feeling well, Mother, so stop worrying about us," Aixiang said.

"Don't listen to Mother," Aihe said to Aiguo. "And we're not going to listen to you."

That infuriated Qing'e. Aiguo could not explain to his siblings what was going on with their mother, not because it was complicated, but because it would take too long to clarify the complex, convoluted even, reasons behind her wish. How would he begin? Would he tell them that their mother, besides worrying about them, was actually disappointed in their circumstances and powerless to change them, then follow up with the story their mother told Baihui, who had then recounted it to him? When their mother could still talk, she chose to talk to Aiguo, not the three of them, and later, she talked only to Baihui. She might have sensed that it was pointless to say anything to them. And now Aiguo felt the same way; it was useless to explain things to his siblings.

"Mother can't talk anymore. Why don't we just listen to her this one last time?" Aiguo said. "You can hold me responsible if anything happens. At worst, she'll die, and you can blame that on me, all right?"

That effectively shut them up. The tubes were removed that afternoon, and they took her back to Niu Village. She was upbeat when they got home, but soon lost consciousness again and did not awake until early the next morning. In addition to the loss of speech, she was having trouble moving around. Aiguo knew his mother had realized that her time was up and she wanted to die at home. But she looked around as if searching for something. It dawned on him that, besides dying at home, there was something his mother wanted. He thought she might be looking for a person, so he told his siblings to wake up everyone. All of them, including Niu Aijiang's wife and child, Niu Aihe's wife and child, as well as Baihui, all crowded around Qing'e's bed.

"We're all here, Mother. Would you like to say something to us?"

He had forgotten that she could no longer speak and figured she just wanted to look at them all. But she shook her head. That was not what she wanted. It was clear to her that none of them knew what she had in mind. Aiguo brought over pen and paper, but she was too weak to hold the pen now, as she strained but failed to raise her arm. Aiguo held her hand and, guided by what little strength she had, moved it to the head of the bed to knock on it. None of them, not even Baihui, could guess why she was doing that. Qing'e was left to stew in her agitation until she lost consciousness; she was out for a day but regained her ability to talk when she awoke, to everyone's astonishment. They crowded around her, but she ran out of time. She called out "Heavens," followed by "Father," and breathed her last. After she died, her children placed her in a coffin and, while tidying up her bed, found a flashlight in her bedding.

"Now I know why Grandma was knocking on her bed," Baihui spoke up.

"Why?" Aiguo asked.

"She told me she had been afraid of the dark as a child. So she must have wanted to take a flashlight with her."

That made sense to Aiguo, who agreed that she must have wanted to light up the road ahead in the afterworld. She had called out "Father" likely because she wanted it to help her find him. She had raised four children, but her seven-year-old granddaughter, Baihui, was the only one who finally deduced what was on her mind. Aiguo ran out, bought two flashlights and a dozen batteries, and put them all inside the coffin.

Silence fell upon the house after her death. Aiguo could think of nothing to do; nor did he remember to cry. That night, when he and Baihui slept on the bed Qing'e had shared with her granddaughter, he had too much on his mind to sleep. Most of her teeth on the right side had gone bad years before, but until her death it had never occurred to him to get her fitted with dentures. He touched his own teeth before sitting up to smoke, but he could not find a match or a lighter. He thought he'd seen a lighter somewhere but could not find it anywhere. He searched the outer room first, and then the back room, where he opened a desk drawer. No lighter or matches, but he found a letter from Yanjin. On the yellowed envelope was the name of the recipient, Cao Qing'e. Its postmark showed it had been sent eight years before. The letter had been written by someone named Jiang Surong. It said that Moses Wu's grandson had come to Yanjin recently to see Cao Qing'e and asked if she could come to Yanjin to talk to him. The writer added that Moses Wu had died ten years earlier, after fleeing to Xianyang, Shaanxi. He would not allow anyone in his family to return to Yanjin while he was alive, so his grandson did not make his first visit until a decade after his death. Having heard his mother's childhood stories, Aiguo had always thought she never got in touch with Moses Wu. Now he realized that everything had changed eight years earlier, when she made contact with Wu's family. Aiguo and his siblings had been preoccupied with their own lives when the letter arrived, so no one had noticed anything. What puzzled him was why his mother hadn't made the trip. Nor had she said a word about it to anyone. Then he had another sudden realization: his mother rapped on the head of her bed before she died not for a flashlight, as Baihui guessed, but about this particular letter. The wood was to direct them to the wooden desk. She had insisted on coming home from the hospital for one purpose: to find the letter. Such a simple matter should have been easily explained, but in her case it had taken a long-winded detour, and he had to negotiate a circuitous route to finally understand the last thing she said. She'd called out "Father"; it was not Old Cao she meant, but Moses Wu, from whom she'd been separated all those years. But he had been dead for nearly two decades, so why did she want the letter at that moment? Aiguo read it again. Jiang Surong had written his home number at the bottom. Clearly, Aiguo surmised, his mother wanted the letter so she could have someone call Jiang and ask him to come to Qinyuan so she could say something to him or ask something that she had refused to ask eight years before. With that realization, he picked up the phone, but put it down before dialing. What was the point of having Jiang over now that his mother was dead? He had not felt like crying on the day she died, but now he did, ruing his inability to understand his mother's last words.

A mourning shed was put up early the next morning for family and friends to come pay their respects. Her four children and all the close Niu family descendants put on hempen mourning garb and knelt by the coffin. Beneath the photo of her, four meat dishes, four vegetable plates, and four dishes of dried fruits were laid out. Groups of mourners filed in. With each group's arrival, spirit paper was burned, sending thick columns of smoke into the air; with each group's arrival, Aiguo and others had to prostrate themselves before the coffin and wail. They knew who the mourners were at first, but lost track after crying so much that their heads began to throb. They cried until they were hoarse. At noon on the third day, one of the visitors bowed before the coffin and then, instead of leaving, came into the shed and tapped Aiguo on the shoulder. It was Li Kezhi, his old classmate, the Linfen fishmonger. Some of Aiguo's school friends had come to offer their condolences, but they all lived close by. He had not expected Kezhi to travel all the way from Linfen. He stood up and grasped his friend's hands.

"I didn't make a special trip. I was here on business and heard about it."

Aiguo held Kezhi's hands tightly.

"I have something to say to you."

Aiguo led him out of the mourning shed and into the main room, where they sat on the bed Aiguo shared with his daughter. He expected his friend to offer condolences and was surprised to hear Kezhi say, "I know you're grieving over your mother's death, but can we talk about something else?"

"She's gone and won't be back, no matter how much I cry. So go ahead," Aiguo said hoarsely.

"I went to see Feng Wenxiu and learned that you two had had a falling out."

Aiguo and Wenxiu had clashed over some pork the year before, after Lina's affair. Wenxiu had used what Aiguo had said when drunk against him, telling people that his friend was a murderer. At the time, Aiguo had even thought of killing Wenxiu. Now a year had gone by, and the incident was fading in Aiguo's mind, but it hadn't gone away.

"I don't want to talk about him."

"But he felt bad for you when he heard of your mother's death. He knew it would be awkward to pay his respects, so he asked me to bring you this as a token of his sympathy."

Kezhi took out two hundred yuan. Aiguo now wondered if his mother's death could be a good pretext to resolve the issue between Wenxiu and him.

"Feng said your mother was like an aunt to him, even after you two stopped talking. Those are two different matters."

Aiguo had wanted to say he never wanted to see Wenxiu ever again, but what Kezhi told him made his nose ache, and he took the money.

"But that's not what I want to talk to you about."

"Then what do you want to talk about?"

"I shouldn't be here saying this, but I've been asked to."

"What is it?"

"Lina came to Linfen to see me a few days ago and asked me to talk to you. She had an affair and your relationship with her cannot be repaired, so you will never be back together. This has dragged on for a year, so why not go through with the divorce? She won't hold you back, and neither should you do that to her."

Aiguo was speechless, not because Lina wanted a divorce, which she had asked for right after her affair had been found out, but because she had actually gone to Linfen to see Li Kezhi and ask him to intercede on her behalf. Lina had come to pay her respects when she heard that Cao Qing'e had died. She'd come in the morning and left that afternoon. At lunchtime, they had walked past each other without exchanging a word, though Aiguo had noticed her new hairstyle. Her ponytail had been replaced by a permanent wave; she'd had a full figure, but lost a lot of weight when her affair was found out. A year later she had gained back the weight, with a healthy glow to her face, and it dawned on him that first she must have gone to see Feng Wenxiu, who would have told her to go see Kezhi, believing that Aiguo would take Kezhi's advice. There had been a time before Aiguo learned of the affair, when he had listened to his friend's advice to ignore her, with the adage that those with bare feet need not fear those who wear shoes. But now Kezhi was back to get him to change his mind about Lina. Aiguo might have gone along with it if it had been anyone but Kezhi raising the issue. He might even have been willing to hear him out if he had brought it up in passing. But he refused to back down now that Kezhi and Lina had talked it over before Kezhi came to see him. He would have considered the possibility of a divorce if not for her glowing face.

"Sure. I have no problem with that. She can go to court and file for divorce."

"She doesn't want to waste the effort if you won't go through with it. You're the injured party, after all." Kezhi continued, "This ought to be settled, don't you think?"

Aiguo did not want to say more about the divorce, so he returned with a question of his own: "Don't you remember what you said to me back in Linfen? You told me not to let her off the hook. Now you turn around and tell me to get a divorce. Aren't you slapping your own face?"

Kezhi sighed. "Let's put the divorce aside for now then. What are you going to do about Baihui?"

"What do I have to do?" Aiguo was puzzled.

"Back when Auntie was still alive, she took care of Baihui, but now she's gone. Lina thinks it's hard for a man to bring up a daughter, so she'd like to take Baihui with her."

Aiguo was slowly realizing that his wife was calculating each move. He would have been amenable to talking about who should care for Baihui before his mother died, but now with her gone, there was no room for discussion, not simply because it served to punish Lina, but also because Baihui had been his mother's mouthpiece when Qing'e could no longer talk, even though the girl had not made the correct guesses. Still, she had told the girl many things, and he wanted to know what they were. Cao Qing'e had told her son things from half a century before, but with Baihui she had focused on events of the past twenty years. Feeling that what she told him was mere idle talk, Aiguo had barely listened to what she said; she'd told him what was on her mind, but he had never shared his thoughts with her. Now that she was gone, everything she'd said took on greater importance, not merely because it came from his mother, but also because he was incensed over Lina's scheme to exploit his mother's death and take Baihui away from him. He might not have been so adamantly opposed to a discussion if she had brought it up earlier, but he could not relent now, not when Lina mentioned it right after his mother had died.

"I can't let her have Baihui. She was an unfaithful wife. How would it make the girl feel to be with a mother like that?'

"Auntie is gone now, so how are you going to raise the girl when you're always on the road?"

"I'll stop doing that, starting today," Aiguo said. "I'm going to stay in Qinyuan, and I'll take Baihui along if I have to go on a trip."

"Now you're cutting off your nose to spite your face."

Suddenly suspicious, Aiguo gazed into his friend's eyes.

"You've been working on this really hard. What's in it for you?"

Kezhi smacked his lips and decided to come clean.

"Actually, it wasn't Pang Lina who came to see me. It was her sister's husband."

Lina's brother-in-law, Old Shang, was a buyer for a cotton mill on North Street in Qinyuan.

"I want to get out of the fish business in Linfen and come back to Qinyuan as a buyer for the mill."

The motivation behind Kezhi's advice became clear. At least he was honest enough to tell the truth. Being friends meant being frank with each other, but this was not something one would do to a friend. Aiguo also realized that Kezhi had come to offer his condolences not because he happened to be in town; he had made a special trip to come see him. Aiguo would have been receptive to the suggestion if he hadn't seen through his ruse, but now that Aiguo had a clear sense of how everything had come about, he was outraged.

"We've been friends for years, so let's just drop it now, Kezhi. You don't know what might happen if you don't."

Kezhi had not anticipated that the conversation would end like that, so he flicked his hands with an unhappy smile.

"Look at you. It's been only a year since we last saw each other, and now you and I have switched personalities."

9

Niu Aixiang was married three months after her mother's death. As a young woman, Aixiang had sold soy sauce and sundry goods in town but left for the city when she found life too boring there. Eight years before, she had rented a booth in a department store to sell stockings and socks. She'd also sold panty-hose, cigarette lighters, flashlights, key chains, nail clippers, cell phone cases, thermos cups, and so on. Zhao Xinting, the wife of Little Jiang, who ran East Asia Wedding Photo Studio, also had a booth in the same department store selling shoes. Xinting's booth was on the first floor, while Aixiang's was on the second floor. Aixiang and Xinting had chatted when they ran into each other before anyone knew of the affair between Lina and Jiang. They stopped talking afterward. A failed romance twenty years before had ended with Aixiang in-gesting pesticide, which left her with a weak neck and a belching problem. The year before, she had taken up smoking, which, strangely enough, had cured her of belching after all these years. Her neck remained slightly angled, so she made sure to walk straight, though that produced a bit of a waddle.

Her husband, Song Jiefang, was a guard at a distillery on East Street. He had been widowed the year before and, at fifty-six, was fourteen years older than her, not a huge age difference. But he had been married before and had grandchildren from his two married sons, so he appeared to be much older. A one-time soldier in Sichuan, he had been a guard at the distillery since being demobilized thirty years before. He was on the slim side but had a square face and a large mouth. He did not talk much, not because he was taciturn, but because he wasn't articulate enough to always get across what he meant. So he tried not to speak whenever that was possible, remaining mum nine out of ten times something came up and doing whatever logic dictated. The one time out of ten he didn't was usually because there were several possibilities, and he had to speak up once he made his decision. He would struggle for words until his face turned red, but still nothing came out. When he managed to say something, it usually started with "How shall I begin?"

Or, "I know what I want to say . . ."

His first wife had sold baked wheat cakes in Beiguan. She'd also sold steamed buns, twisted buns, meat buns, and steamed buns stuffed with pork. A heavyset woman, she'd been a good talker, with a glib tongue, or what the locals called a catfish mouth. Like many overweight people, she was loud when she talked, had a hot temper, and tended to argue a point to death. Jiefang had to relinquish all decision-making at home, which, in other men's cases, would breed resentment; but it was precisely what he needed and wanted, for he would not have to say anything. His wife took charge of all things, be it major events like building a house or their sons getting married, or trivial matters such as what size of a vat to buy for pickling duck eggs. If she could not make up her mind, she would ask Jiefang, who would be flustered.

"How shall I begin?"

Or, "What do you think?"

She would then mull the thing over and analyze it by herself, then ask him again.

"What do you think?" he would say.

So she carried on with her analysis but got angry after several rounds of "what do you think," even though she had everything figured out by then.

"What evil deed have I done in a previous life to deserve a worthless husband like you?"

Or, "I spend my whole life with myself, not with you."

Jiefang would usually respond with a smile and not say anything, just do what had to be done. Not given to chatter, he loved to hum tunes at work. He had expected to live carefree like that forever, but his world underwent drastic changes once his sons were married; likewise, his wife had thought she would be in charge of the family the rest of her days, but their sons married women who were good talkers, more like her, not Jiefang. When the three talkers discussed an issue, none of them would ask the others "what do you think"; instead, they would say, "I think we ought to do this or that." Within a year, the first son's wife refused to talk to the second son's wife, and neither daughter-in-law would speak to Jiefang's wife. After being in charge of the family since her marriage, she could not voice her views, and no one listened to her, which so upset her that she fell ill.

With her laid up, the daughters-in-law decided to take over the wheat cake business, and they eventually got into a scuffle over the shack. The second daughter-in-law broke the nose of the first daughter-in-law, while her opponent bit off half of her ear. They fought all the way home from Beiguan, where their husbands joined the fray. Before they were done, their mother hanged herself in the bedroom; her tongue was hanging out of her mouth when Jiefang found her. She was still alive when they brought her down from the rafter, but she breathed her last after they sent her to the emergency room. Jiefang opened his large mouth wide and wailed after his wife died, but he returned to his post at the distillery when the funeral was over; he never hummed again, however.

"Don't take it so hard, Old Song," someone said. "She ran your life all these years, and now that she's gone, you're a free man."

Jiefang tried but failed to come up with a reply, except to sigh and say, "How do I begin?"

Niu Aiguo had known Song Jiefang before he married Aiguo's sister. After his mother's death, he stopped making trucking trips and stayed in Qinyuan to care for Baihui. The girl had reached school age, so he took her into the county town to attend school. They rented a house in Nanguan. Aiguo fixed up his old truck to take her to school before going to the train station to wait for any odd trucking job that came his way. He worked only in the day, not at night, for he needed to pick his daughter up at school in the evening. When they got home, he made dinner and then tucked her in. Baihui even said he was a better cook than his mother, especially his fish dishes. Sometimes he transported liquor for the distillery on East Street, where he ran into Jiefang. At the time, Jiefang was just Jiefang the guard, and he never imagined that one day he would become his brother-in-law.

Niu Aixiang and Song Jiefang were brought together by Hu Meili, a seamstress on South Street and one of Aixiang's friends from middle school. Meili was a cousin of Jiefang, who met Aixiang at Meili's house. Jiefang arrived first and Meili said to him, "When you meet her today, Older Brother, please stop saying, 'How do I begin' and 'I know what I want to say.'"

Jiefang blushed. "I know what I want to say."

When Aixiang came, Jiefang jumped to his feet before she could say a word and, in soldier fashion, clicked his feet together and said, head held high, "My name is Song Jiefang, I'm fifty-six years old, and I'm a guard at the distillery on East Street. My parents have passed away and I have two sons. They're both married, each with a daughter. That's all I have to say. Now it's your turn."

Aixiang and Meili doubled over laughing after a momentary silence. Aixiang laughed so hard she cried. Later, she told him that she hadn't had such a hearty laugh in decades. They decided to get married two months later, to Aiguo's surprise. Tomb Sweeping Festival occurred five days before the wedding. Aixiang and Aiguo went home together to sweep their mother's grave but said little on the way. When they got back to Niu Village, no one said anything either on the day they went back with their brothers, Aijiang and Aihe. Later that evening, after dinner, instead of saying anything to Aijiang or Aihe, she called Aiguo over to the Qin River behind their house and told him about her marriage. They sat on the willow-lined riverbank as the water quietly flowed by their feet and a crescent moon hung in the western sky. His mother had once told Aiguo that her marriage to their father, Niu Shudao, had been arranged by Old Han, a friend of her father, Old Cao, and Little Wen, the owner of a distillery in Wen Villa, by this very river. Aiguo, having been favored by neither his father nor his mother as a child, had had no one to love him but his sister, Aixiang, who was eight years older. She had virtually raised him. Later, when he was older, he went to her, not their parents, if he needed someone to talk to. That was the case when he was considering joining the army. As they grew older, they were busy with their own lives and could spend little time together. Now she was getting married. She seemed to have become a different person; or she had returned to her old self, wanting to share what was on her mind with him.

"I'm getting married but I feel unsettled."

Aiguo said nothing, so she continued. "I have no one to talk to now that both Papa and Mama are gone."

Aiguo still said nothing, so she went on. "I really don't want to marry him."

"Is he too old for you?"

"At my age, can I be choosy and favor a younger man?" She sighed.

"Isn't he clever enough, no good with words?"

"That's not it."

"Or don't you like his face, so square and ugly?"

He knew she loathed men with a square face, since her first love, Little Zhang the mail carrier, had one. Jiefang had rough skin *and* a square face.

"I don't mind men with square faces anymore." She shook her head. "I'm getting old," she said with deep emotion.

He took a close look at her. She was indeed showing signs of aging: crow's feet around her eyes and slack skin. She had been alone for so many years. Though still middle-aged, she did look like an older woman. She always straightened her neck in front of others, but not with him; the sight of her head angled toward her shoulder saddened him. He had been so engrossed in his own chaotic life that he rarely spent a moment thinking about her.

"No, you're not old, Big Sis," he said. "You're quite pretty."

"To tell you the truth, I'm getting married not for marriage's sake." She took his hand. "I just want to find someone to talk to. I'm forty-two now and I feel bottled up being alone all day long. I don't care if everyone in the county town knows about Old Song's age and his personality. I am, however, afraid that you'll all laugh at me."

"No matter how bad, it could never be worse than my situation, Sis. I've been a cuckold for seven, almost eight years. Do you find me laughable, Sis?"

Aixiang shook her head. Aiguo was, in fact, uneasy about his sister marrying Song Jiefang, though not for the same reason as she. He was not concerned that others might laugh at her, nor was he worried about Jiefang. It was Jiefang's daughters-in-law who bothered him. They had probably caused the death of Jiefang's first wife, which made him nervous about his sister's life after marriage. She might suffer at their hands. But instead of bringing up these thoughts, he simply said, "Go ahead and marry him, Sis. We'll never laugh at you."

"I could kill that mail carrier from twenty years ago. He ruined my life."

Saddened by the memory, she rested her head on Aiguo's shoulder. That sounded similar to him. Then he recalled how, two years earlier, when the affair between Pang Lina and Little Jiang came to light, she had spat out a similar grievance about Ma Xiaozhu. Before marrying Aiguo, Lina had dated Xiaozhu, who had dropped her when he went to college in Beijing. Aiguo had been too furious to pay any attention to her outburst, and now he had nothing to say when he heard something similar from his own sister. As they looked across the river at the inky mountains, with more mountains behind them, she fell asleep with her head on his shoulder.

What had worried Aiguo did not happen in her marriage to Song Jiefang. After causing their mother-in-law's death, his daughters-in-law left her alone, not because the three women got along well or that she was mean to them, but because Aixiang cut off ties with them before they had a thing to do with each other. With them, it was never "How do I begin," "What do you think," or "I think"; she simply did not talk to them. She forced Jiefang to renounce all interactions with his sons' families the day after the wedding, dumbfounding her new husband.

"Father and sons no longer have anything to do with each other for no obvious reason? How do I begin?"

"What do you mean, no obvious reason? Their wives are murderers," she said.

Jiefang understood what she was getting at, but was still hesitant.

"But shouldn't we wait for an excuse?"

"You can wait, but I can't. Either you stop talking to them or you go live with them and we'll file for divorce."

"We've been married only one day—" Jiefang felt like laughing despite his emotional state. "So we stop talking to them immediately after we're married, is that it? People won't blame me; they'll say it's your fault."

"I don't care if I get a bad reputation. Not seeing them is a minor problem. The big problem will be if something bad happens later."

Jiefang realized that he'd married a shrewd woman, even shrewder than his first wife, who had talked things over with him before she made up her mind, even though she always had the final say. At least they had gone through the motions of talking it over, unlike now with Aixiang, who made decisions unilaterally, without a word to him, and then told him to carry out what she had decided. He was having trouble getting over the shock, while the hesitant look on his face made Aixiang, a woman of her word, take out the marriage certificate, put on her jacket, and drag him toward the door to go to court. Jiefang threw up his hands.

"This, this, how do I begin?"

He had to stop seeing his sons' families because of his fear of divorce. In fact, he did not cut all ties, though he had agreed to do so; he just went behind her back, while she turned a blind eye, feigning ignorance. Aixiang had absolutely nothing to do with his sons and their families. Aiguo realized he had a shrewd sister when he heard that; she was much more decisive than he where important matters were concerned. She went straight to the root of a problem and nipped it in the bud. Had he acted like her, he would have been in better shape now. From the first day of their marriage, Aixiang ordered her husband about as if he were a little boy. A hard-working woman when she was young, she stopped doing just about everything after her marriage. He was responsible for all household matters—doing the laundry, shining her shoes, and cooking. She smashed her bowl if the food was not to her liking. That was similar to several years before, when Aiguo had tried to please Lina by cooking fish for her. The only difference between Jiefang and Aiguo was that Aiguo had no choice, while Jiefang was happy to do it. Merely a month into the marriage, Aixiang started putting on weight, her skin was softer, and even her neck did not look crooked. Jiefang always checked the look on her face when they were home alone; she looked at the wall, not his face, when she talked to him.

Once, Aixiang, Jiefang, and Aiguo went back to Niu Village together. Aiguo rode a bicycle, as did Jiefang, with Aixiang on the back. The weather was fine when they left town, but a drizzle started halfway there. Jiefang and Aixiang were wearing jackets, but Aiguo had on only a vest over a long-sleeve shirt. He shivered in the cold.

"Take off your jacket, Old Song, and give it to Aiguo."

Without hesitation or objection, Jiefang stopped the bike and took off his jacket. Aiguo refused to take it, though he was touched, not just because Jiefang had shed his jacket for him but because the man's face showed no resentment when he did. Later, when Aiguo went back to the distillery to transport liquor, Song Jiefang seemed like a different man. Sometimes they would sit down for a drink and share thoughts. Once, when the topic of their respective unhappiness in life came up, Aiguo told Jiefang his biggest disappointment was not having a good wife, while Jiefang said his was guarding the gate of a distillery for three decades.

"Isn't it a good job?" Aiguo asked in surprise. "You sit here all day enjoying peace and quiet."

"Actually, I don't care much for peace and quiet." Jiefang shook his head.

Aiguo could not have guessed that Jiefang preferred action.

"What would you have liked to do then?"

"Mail carrier, traveling a hundred li a day on a motorcycle. I'd say, 'Niu Aiguo, bring your seal for an urgent telegram.'"

Aiguo laughed, charmed by the man. Coincidentally, Aixiang's first boyfriend, Little Zhang, had been a mail carrier, also with a square face. Gradually, not only Aiguo but also his daughter, Baihui, grew fond of Jiefang. In the past, Aiguo had had to race back in the afternoon from one of his trips to pick up Baihui at six. Now, with Jiefang, he would phone his brother-in-law if it was getting late and ask him to pick up his daughter. One day, his truck broke down on his way home. He looked at his watch; it was five o'clock, so he called Jiefang. The truck was repaired shortly after he hung up, so he made it back to town at six and went straight to Baihui's school. The girl had twisted her ankle that day jumping rope. From a distance, Aiguo saw Jiefang carrying Baihui on his back, the two of them talking and laughing as they headed home. He smiled at the sight. As time went by, Baihui had little to say to her father, or to her aunt, for she had found a conversation partner in Aixiang's husband.

On weekends, she went to see Jiefang at the distillery after finishing her homework. With grown-ups, Jiefang was tongue-tied and could only mutter things like, "How do I begin?" and "I know it in my heart," but he turned into a much better talker with Baihui. He told the girl about the world outside Qinyuan. Besides his army life in Sichuan more than three decades before, he recounted places he'd visited after returning home to Qinyuan. He'd been to Taiyuan, Xi'an, Shanghai, and Beijing. In fact, he'd never been anywhere but Sichuan. He'd learned the names of major cities by watching television and, using the street layout in Qinyuan as a model, re-created thoroughfares and lanes in these cities. He was then able to give a plausible account of any of them, looking nonchalant when finished. Baihui, who addressed him as Old Uncle, asked him once, "You've been all over Taiyuan, Old Uncle. What's it like?"

"Nothing special. There are people everywhere. Boring."

"What's Xi'an like, Old Uncle?"

"It's not much different from Taiyuan, not very interesting."

"What about Beijing, Old Uncle?"

"They're all the same," Jiefang said, "but still better than Qinyuan, no matter how boring they are." He added, "When you grow up, Baihui, you go to Shanghai and run a ferry boat on the Huangpu River. I'll visit you."

Aiguo once said to his sister, "I don't think you're very nice to Jiefang, Sis. He's actually a decent man."

"In what ways?"

"There isn't a mean bone in his body."

"But doesn't that make him somewhat dim?" Aixiang asked. "I was looking for someone I could talk to, but a whole day can go by and I have hardly a word to say to him." She added, "I laughed each time I saw him before we were married. Since then I haven't laughed once."

Sometime later, Jiefang said to Aiguo, "I got a good deal by marrying your sister, Younger Brother."

"She has a bad temper, but nothing gets past her."

"I don't mean her."

"Who then?"

"I mean Baihui. I was usually tongue-tied in the past, but I've become a pretty good talker since meeting Baihui."

On a sweltering day in the eighth month of that year, Lina ran off with another man. Not Little Jiang of East Asia Wedding Photo Studio on West Street, but her own brother-in-law, Old Shang, the buyer at the cotton mill on North Street. She had quit her job as a weaver and become a storekeeper at the cotton warehouse, with Shang's help. Everyone knew she had had something going with Little Jiang, but no one was aware that she had also been seeing her sister's husband, not Niu Aiguo and not Pang Liqin, Lina's sister. They did not know if she had already been seeing Shang while carrying on with Jiang, or if she had hooked up with her brother-in-law after breaking it off with Jiang. Now Aiguo knew why, shortly after Cao Qing'e died, Shang had gone all the way to Linfen to see Li Kezhi and had asked Li to come to Niu Village to talk Aiguo into divorcing Lina. It also became clear to him why Lina, who had lost weight after her first affair had been found out, had gained back the weight and a red glow on her face. Aiguo was surprised by this affair with Shang, but it did not hurt him as much as the previous affair. They weren't legally divorced, so it was still his wife who had run off with another man. It wasn't her fault but his that they remained married; she had asked for a divorce, but he had refused. He hadn't agreed because he wanted to punish her, but now he knew that he had failed to achieve his purpose and had been the cause of her running off a second time. It did not bother Aiguo so much, since he no longer thought of her as his wife. Her sister, Pang Liqin, was the one who nearly went mad. Liqin and Aixiang had once worked in the same department store; they had been Lina and Aiguo's matchmakers. Instead of blaming her own sister and her husband for the affair, she came to see Aiguo, steaming in outrage. She plunked herself down on a sofa after walking into his door and wailed.

"It's all your fault. You can't even keep your wife in line. How could she do this to me? My own sister!" she stopped crying long enough to say.

"How could he do this? Sleep with his wife's sister! Sleeping together wasn't enough for them. They had to run off!" More crying followed.

"No wonder they were always talking and laughing when I was away, but shut up when I walked in."

More wailing.

"People told me they did it in the warehouse at the cotton mill. They even left blood stains!"

Now she turned her wrath on Aiguo.

"Are you blind? Why didn't you notice anything?"

When Lina had run off with Little Jiang, Jiang's wife, Zhao Xinting, had come to see Aiguo, asking him to kill the adulterers and making him laugh through his tears. Now that she had run off with Old Shang, Shang's wife came to him, also making him laugh despite his irritation. He had not been the one who'd let her run off. They'd had no contact in spite of their status as husband and wife, so how was he supposed to keep an eye on her? Aiguo thought he had been innocent when Lina ran off with Jiang earlier, but this time he might have to take responsibility for her running off with her sister's husband. If he had not been to Cangzhou and had a fling with Zhang Chuhong at Old Li's Gourmet Food Court, he would have simply condemned the couple, but now, after his own experience with a married woman, he could understand why Lina and Old Shang must have had a lot to say to each other, which was why they'd decided to leave Qinyuan for a new place. Aiguo had agreed when Zhang Chuhong had asked him to take her away from Cangzhou, but had backed out, fleeing to Qinyuan when his mother had fallen ill. He had not given Chuhong a call since then. Both Little Jiang and Aiguo had let down the women with whom they had been having affairs at critical moments, but not Old Shang, who'd had the guts to abandon his family and leave a familiar place to be with the woman he loved. Instead of raging over Shang's action, Aiguo felt only admiration. But how was he supposed to explain all this to Liqin? She would probably fly into a bigger rage if he even tried.

"Give me back my husband, Niu Aiguo." She banged on the table. "Give me back my sister."

"How do I do that?"

"Go look for them."

Aiguo felt like laughing again despite the situation. Liqin was still hoping to find them even under such circumstances, but Aiguo wasn't interested in looking for them. After running off twice, Lina had ended her relationship with him. It was like a wound that hurt when he took the scab off the first time, but would heal during the second scabbing. He would agree on the spot if she came to ask for a divorce, but in the end, it was Lina, not Aiguo, who brought their relationship to an end. Whoever ended it had to shoulder greater responsibility, so he felt he was lucky. She had been so extreme in her action that he had been relieved of a big burden; it hadn't ended between them formally, but in his heart it was over. From now on, he would continue his current lifestyle, with Baihui, Aixiang, and Jiefang.

"You can't look for them on matters like this," Aiguo said to Liqin. "Someone could die."

"I don't care if anyone dies, as long as I can vent my anger."

But he couldn't go looking for the couple just so she could vent her spleen, or worse yet, commit murder for her to gain vindication. But the question of whether or not the couple should be found wasn't his decision alone. Besides

Liqin, even his sister and brother-in-law thought he ought to go find them. So after Liqin came to him during the day, his sister and her husband came that night.

"It's out in the open now, and you can't sit around and do nothing," Aixiang said. "You have to go look for them."

"What's the point of looking for a whore like that?" Aiguo replied.

She lit a cigarette and took a drag before continuing.

"You can't look at it that way. It's not for their sake that you go find them."

"Then for whose sake?"

"There needs to be an accounting."

"To whom?"

Jiefang, who was getting more worked up than his wife, gestured.

"It's no big deal for a woman to run off, but she did it with the wrong person. All of Qinyuan is roiled now that a woman has run off with her sister's husband."

It hadn't occurred to Aiguo to think about that. Aixiang sighed and said, "You must go find them. It wouldn't have mattered if you were divorced. But you have to do something when your legally wedded wife runs off with another man. None of us can continue to live in Qinyuan if you don't make a move."

Obviously, he had to go look for them, even if it was just for show. He would have agreed to a divorce long ago if he had known it would come to this. Aiguo was reminded of what his mother had told him about her father, Moses Wu. Years ago, when Qing'e was still called Qiaoling, her mother, Wu Xiangxiang, had run off with Old Gao the silversmith, and Moses had taken Qiaoling along to look for them, a fake search. Aiguo could not have imagined that he would become Moses seventy years later. They were two men on fake searches—one was Cao Qing'e's father, the other her son. Perked up by Aiguo's decision to go, Jiefang rolled up his sleeves and said, "Don't worry. I'll go with you if necessary."

"Two is better," Aixiang said with approval. "You can talk it over on the road if you run into problems."

Aiguo did not want Jiefang to go with him to look for Lina and Old Shang. He knew his brother-in-law well; Jiefang was bored with his job of guarding the distillery and could not wait for some action. This was a perfect opportunity for him to go on a trip; however, he was a genuinely decent man, so he would take the search seriously, while Aiguo would not, and they would not be in agreement on the road. He didn't mind not having someone to talk to; with Jiefang around, he would not be able to fake the search.

"I ought to take Baihui along if I'm going to look for them. She is, after all, Baihui's mother."

Aiguo knew that Baihui had never been close to her mother, which meant that he and the girl could be in agreement about the search. With his wife running off like that, he wasn't sad, but he couldn't deny that it hurt. With Baihui around, he would have someone to talk to. It was just like seventy years earlier, when Moses Wu had left with Qiaoling and embarked on a fake search for Wu Xiangxiang. It was summer break, so it would not interfere with the girl's studies. Jiefang could not object to Aiguo's decision to take his daughter along, so he swallowed and shut up. He had more to say to the girl than to anyone else in the world, so it came as a surprise that Baihui would take his place and go with Aiguo at a moment like this. With the decision made, the three of them started packing for the father and daughter, after which they had a discussion about the possible places to find the pair. They went through Lina's and Old Shang's relatives outside Qinyuan. After checking around, they had a change of heart and agreed that she would not go to her relatives, who were also her sister's, and Shang's relatives all knew his wife. As a buyer for the cotton mill, they surmised, Shang must have a lot of out-of-town friends, so they started going through the places he'd frequented on buying trips. Those were mostly in Shanxi, such as Changzhi, Linfen, Taiyuan, Yuncheng, and Datong; Shi Family and Baoding in Hebei province; Weinan and Tongchuan in Shaanxi province; and Luoyang and Sanmenxia in Henan province; as well as the farthest spot, Guangzhou. In the end, they decided that Aiguo should go to these places. It was midnight when they settled on the travel plan; Aixiang and Jiefang went to Liqin to get the phone numbers of Shang's out-of-town friends, while Aiguo went to bed. Before dawn, however, Baihui ran a fever, and it did not break; in fact, it got worse after daybreak. When Aixiang and Jiefang hurried over with the phone numbers, Aiguo pointed to the girl in bed.

"I'll have to wait until she gets better."

"Time is of the essence with a search like this, or they could go even farther away. You have to try to catch them before they leave Shanxi."

"What about Baihui?"

"You can count on Old Song. He'll take care of her for you."

With the girl having fallen ill, Jiefang had hoped to take Baihui's place as Aiguo's travel companion, but he didn't dare bring it up when Aixiang told him to stay home to care for the girl. With everything settled, Aiguo had run out of excuses not to leave, so he picked up his bag and got on the road on a fake search for Pang Lina and Old Shang.

10

To conduct a pretend search, Niu Aiguo knew he had to come up with a place where he could hole up for two to three weeks before returning to Qinyuan, when he could tell people that he'd gone to Changzhi, Linfen, Taiyuan, Yuncheng, and Datong in Shanxi; Shi Village and Baoding in Hebei; Weinan and Tongchuan in Shaanxi; and Luoyang and Sanmenxia in Henan; even going as far as Guangzhou. He was not responsible for their departure, and as long as he tried but failed to find them, he would be blameless. He could now account for himself to Pang Liqin, to his sister, to his brother-in-law, to his daughter, and to the whole town.

But he still could not come up with a place to go while he was on the bus to Huozhou. He could go anywhere other than Changzhi, Linfen, Taiyuan, Yuncheng, or Datong; Shi Village or Baoding; Weinan, Tongchuan, Luoyang, or Sanmenxia; and, of course, Guangzhou. He had to avoid these places so as not to run into the couple by accident. He could stay with a friend for a while, or he could forget his friends and stay in a small inn near Huozhou for two or three weeks before returning to Qinyuan, where he would tell people he'd looked everywhere for them. It still bothered him that his wife had run off twice, especially now that he was on the road. He would probably go crazy if he shut himself up in an inn for two or three weeks. It would be better to stay with a friend, to whom he could pour his heart out; he could forget his troubles if they talked about anything other than his wife. Only a few years before, he'd had quite a few places he could go, but now he had fewer options. Li Kezhi was nearest, but they'd had a falling out after Aiguo refused to take Kezhi's advice to divorce Lina when Kezhi came to Aiguo's mother's funeral. Linfen was definitely not an option. Cui Lifan, the Cangzhou tofu maker, was farther away, but too close to Botou, where Zhang Chuhong lived. Aiguo had fled from there only a few months earlier, so no Cangzhou either. There was also Du Qinghai, his army buddy in Pingshan, but he'd gone there after Lina's first affair. He'd been so agitated that when he reached the entrance to Qinghai's village, instead of going to see his friend, he'd spent a night sitting by the Hutuo River. With that experience behind him, how could he be sure he wouldn't feel even more agitated this time? So that was out. Zeng Zhiyuan the date merchant in Leling, another army buddy, was the only one left. Aiguo had planned to visit Zhiyuan but had changed his mind in Cangzhou, where he'd spent a year; he'd thought he would find time to see Zhiyuan after he settled down in Cangzhou, but had failed to do so when he was tripped up by his relationship with Zhang Chuhong. No matter how bad he felt about that, he would be ill advised to go see Zhiyuan now, given the way he'd treated his friend. But since he had run out of options, when his bus stopped at Huozhou, he called Zhiyuan to sound him out. If Zhiyuan extended another invitation, Aiguo would go spend some time there; but he would have to make other plans if Zhiyuan appeared no longer interested in his visit. The call went through, but it was Zhiyuan's wife who picked up the phone; she told Aiguo that her husband had gone on a date-selling trip. When Aiguo asked when he would be back, she wasn't sure, saying it could be a few days, a couple of weeks, even a month. Aiguo called Zhiyuan's cell phone and reached him this time in Qiqihar. He did not sound aloof; in fact, he sounded as warm as the previous time, telling Aiguo that his plan had been to go to Tangshan, but business opportunities kept arising as he met more and more people, so he decided to go to Qiqihar.

"Where are you now?" he asked Aiguo.

"I'm at home."

Zhiyuan did not seem as eager to see him as he'd been in their previous call.

"I was eager to talk something over with you, but it's too late now. I'll give you a call when I return to Shandong. Come see me in Leling when you're free."

It did not sound to Aiguo that Zeng would be back home any time soon, nor was he interested in inviting him over. Obviously, Leling was out. After he hung up, Aiguo wondered why Zhiyuan had been so eager to see him the first time and what exactly he had wanted to discuss with him. Once again, he was stuck, with no place to go, when he suddenly recalled Chen Kuiyi, the cook at the highway construction site in Changzhi. Kuiyi had been from Hua County in

Henan. They had become friends over their shared aversion to chatter. Kuiyi had come to Aiguo when he needed someone to talk to and Aiguo had gone to him in similar situations. An inarticulate man with others, Aiguo had been a pretty good talker with Kuiyi. He could analyze the man's problem, peeling away issues like picking meat off a bone. But all Kuiyi could do for Aiguo was ask, "What do you think?" They would go on like that for a while until Aiguo saw through the problem. The same thing had occurred with Du Qinghai in the army, though the roles were reversed.

Kuiyi would go to the construction site to get Aiguo when he had pig's ears and hearts in the kitchen; he would say, "Something's come up," and Aiguo would follow him to the kitchen, where they would share a plate of pig's ears and hearts. Later, Kuiyi had an argument with his nephew, the site foreman, over the price of a slab of beef. He was so outraged by being accused of skimming that he quit and left Changzhi for his hometown. He and Aiguo had called each other a few times after that. Once Kuiyi told him that as a cook at Hua County's Huazhou Restaurant he made much more than he had at the Changzhi site. As the saying goes, there is always a place for a man, if not here, then there. Aiguo was happy that the argument had been a blessing in disguise. They'd lost contact after getting tied up with their own affairs. Aiguo had pretty much forgotten about Kuiyi until this minute. Why not give him a call? he thought. He could spend some time with him if it wasn't a problem for Kuiyi. But he couldn't recall his friend's phone number. He looked through his address book, but there was no number for him; obviously, he had committed it to memory five years earlier and hadn't felt the need to write it down, never expecting he wouldn't be able to recall it five years later. Having run out of options, he decided to look up Kuiyi without contacting him first, even though he did not know if he was still where he'd been back then. He could get lucky, but if not, it would at least count as a search. He needed to be on the road instead of roaming aimlessly all over the place. So he boarded a train for Shi Village, where he transferred to another train to Anyang before taking a bus to Hua County, a trip of two and a half days.

The bus pulled in at night, when the streets were all lit up. Emerging from the bus depot, he was greeted by crowds all speaking the different but familiar Henan dialect. With his bag slung over his shoulder, he asked around about the Huazhou Restaurant, and learned that it was only a couple of blocks from the bus depot. He expected the restaurant to be a diner, for these days businesses often adopted grand-sounding names. When he turned the corner, he found himself in front of a high rise with a neon sign at the top proclaiming the Huazhou Hotel. It was a hotel and restaurant, not a road-side eatery. Being a hotel cook would surely bring in much more than working at a highway construction site. Aiguo was happy for his friend. What made him even happier was how much calmer his distressed mind felt now that he was in Hua County. The place felt welcoming. After Lina's first affair, Aiguo had gone to Pingshan to see his army buddy Du Qinghai before heading back to Linfen to be with his schoolmate Li Kezhi. His mind had been in a constant state of agitation in both places. So he'd gone to Botou, where calmness came over him, and he decided to stay. But neither place had a welcoming feel about it. Now, in the wake of Lina's second affair, he felt welcomed. It was a wise decision to look up Chen Kuiyi, he thought. He was disappointed, however, when he walked into the hotel and asked the woman at the reception desk about his friend. The receptionist told him that none of the cooks were named Chen Kuiyi. He thought the receptionist did not want to help because he was from out of town, so he persisted.

"Chen Kuiyi is a friend of mine. He told me over the phone that he was a cook at the Huazhou Restaurant. I've traveled a thousand li from Shanxi, miss, so won't you help me out?"

She laughed at how worked up he was. "You Shanxi people are sure impatient. Of course I'd help you if he was here, but we don't have a cook by that name."

Noting the doubting look on Aiguo's face, she picked up the phone and called out the head chef from the kitchen. A stumpy, heavyset man in a paper toque, he spoke to Aiguo in Cantonese. He scratched his head when Aiguo told him Kuiyi's name, saying he'd been at the hotel for eight years and had never known a cook with that name. Aiguo was finally convinced that he had come to the wrong place. Kuiyi must have given him a different place or he had mis-remembered it. As he walked out of the hotel, he was suddenly reminded that Kuiyi had once told him he was from Chen Village. The Huazhou Hotel turned out to be the wrong place, but Aiguo was sure that Kuiyi had been from Chen Village. So he decided to go there, where he would learn of Kuiyi's whereabouts.

With his bag over his shoulder, Aiguo asked an old man selling roast chicken at a roadside stand where Chen Village was. The man said it was located next to the Yellow River in the easternmost corner of Hua County, more than a hundred li from the county town. As he thanked the man, Aiguo knew he could not make it to Chen Village that day and would have to spend the night there and set out the next day. The Huazhou Hotel was beyond his means, so he checked out a few inns along the street, some more expensive than others.

The expensive ones cost fifty to sixty, even seventy to eighty yuan a night, while the cheaper "inns for carters" went for fifteen or twenty. He was continuing on with his inquiry when he saw a bathhouse with a neon sign—Jade Pool Bath City. It sounded fancy but turned out to be a simple bathhouse. He walked in and asked about the cost, which was five yuan for a bath and another five for a night's stay. He could spend the night after a hot bath. A wave of hot air typical of such a place and the smell of human bodies assailed his nose the moment he stepped into the bathing area. He parted a curtain and entered the men's section, which was divided into an inner and an outer room. The inner one had a large pool, while the outer was filled with dozens of plank beds. Several men were standing by the beds, some taking off their clothes for a bath, while others were getting dressed after their baths. There were also naked men sleeping on beds, some snoring loudly. Steam and the sound of people talking could be heard from the inner room, but he could not see any of the bathers. After finding a bed by the wall, Aiguo took off his clothes, locked his bag and clothes in a storage box at the head of the bed, and, stark naked, walked over to the pool, key in hand. A skinny, naked man came toward him, shuffling along in slippers. Aiguo saw the towels draped over the man's shoulder and knew he was one of the back scrubbers. They passed each other as the man emerged from the steamy mists.

Aiguo jumped into the water, which was so hot he shuddered. It occurred to him that the skinny man looked familiar. He quickly got out of the water and, dripping water, raced to the outer room, where the man was getting dressed. It was none other than Chen Kuiyi, who had three black hairs on a large mole on the left side of his face. Aiguo rushed toward him.

"What are you doing here, Old Chen?"

The man froze at the sight of Aiguo; partially dressed, he sized Aiguo up and down before crying out in surprise.

"Hey, it's you, Niu Aiguo!"

The two men, one naked, one bare-chested, hugged and thumped each other on the back.

"What are *you* doing here?" Kuiyi asked.

"What are you doing *here*?" Aiguo asked. "Didn't you tell me you were a cook at the Huazhou Hotel? How did you end up as a back scrubber in this place?"

"I was hired by the hotel, but I actually never liked cooking." Kuiyi looked embarrassed. "So I didn't go." He added, "I hadn't had any options when we met in Changzhi, so I took up the position of a cook."

"You like scrubbing backs?"

"No, I don't, but I like soaking in hot water, and scrubbing backs lets me soak in the pool every day."

Now Aiguo knew that Kuiyi had lied about being a cook at Huazhou Hotel, but he let that go because he knew that saving face was important to his friend.

"Scrubbing backs is good, and it keeps you warm in the winter."

"Why are you here?" Kuiyi changed the subject. "I didn't expect to see you again in this lifetime."

Aiguo did not want to tell a friend with whom he'd just been reunited the true reason behind his visit. "I was just passing through Hua County. I was actually thinking about going to Chen Village to see you tomorrow."

"Wonderful! I'm so glad you're here. I can't talk now; there's something I need to do first. Tomorrow, we'll spend a few days talking our hearts out. I don't have close friends here, and I've been dying for someone to talk to."

"What do you have to do now? Can I help?"

"I have to go back to Chen Village. My two sons got into a fight. You see, they're both married and their wives don't get along. I'm going to go home and give them both a good beating." He paused. "Do you want to come with me or would you rather wait for me here?"

Aiguo would have liked to go with Kuiyi but knew he should stay away if he had to deal with a family dispute.

"I'll wait here. I heard that Chen Village is over a hundred li away. How are you going to get home so late at night?"

"I ride a motor scooter now." Kuiyi smiled.

After getting dressed, Kuiyi was about to walk out when a fat old man walked in with bamboo tallies to collect money from the bathers and those who planned to spend the night. He placed a tally on the bed for those who paid up. Aiguo was about to take his money out, but Kuiyi stopped him.

"He's my friend, from Shanxi," he said.

The man rolled his eyes. "I don't care whose friend he is, or where he's from. He has to pay if he wants to take a bath and spend the night."

Kuiyi drew closer to the man. "Fuck you! He's not paying. What are you going to do about it, huh?"

Aiguo pulled him back.

"Don't ruin your friendship over ten yuan."

"He's doing this because of me, not you." Kuiyi spat on the floor.

Aiguo could have paid, and everything would have blown over, but he knew he couldn't do that now that Kuiyi had said that he was the old man's target. The man glared at Kuiyi and turned to collect money from others.

"Is he the manager?" Aiguo asked.

"Does he look like a manager to you?" Kuiyi said. "He's the manager's uncle. He takes care of the beds, but he thinks he's better than everyone else. Ignore him."

Kuiyi raced out when he finished, leaving Aiguo to shake his head with a smile. He had thought it would be easy to find Chen Kuiyi in Hua County, but not that easy. He went back into the pool and rubbed three days' worth of dirt from his body. After scrubbing and rinsing himself off, he went to the other room and sat on his bed, breathing hard for a moment before calming down enough to lie down under a blanket. Exhausted from all the travel, he fell asleep. In his dream, he was still in Qinyuan; he climbed the ruined city wall and was surprised to see Pang Lina when he got to the top. He had thought she'd left with Old Shang. It turned out she was right here, on the ruined city wall in Qinyuan. He'd thought she'd had another affair, but she hadn't, not with Old Shang, nor several years earlier with Little Jiang. She was her old self. They'd had little to say to one another during their married life, but in the dream, Lina, who held his hand, started to talk about the past. In real life, they had messed up their life together in different ways, but everything has its cause and effect and it all seemed to make sense. As they talked, he had a sudden new understanding that they could lead a different life. At some point, they stopped talking and wept in each other's arms. Then it wasn't Lina but Little Jiang and Old Shang standing on the wall with him. They started arguing over Lina, and a fight broke out. At some point, Lina was back on the scene, crouching to the side, crying with her hands over her face, like Lady Meng Jiang, who cried over her husband's death at the Great Wall. During the scuffle, Little Jiang took out a knife and plunged it into the belly of Aiguo, not Old Shang. With a yowl, Aiguo woke up in a sweat, to see that he was in a bathhouse in Hua County. Lina had run off with another man in real life; how had she become a different woman in his dream? They had been talking about their past and weeping in each other's arms.

When he'd first set out on the fake search, he'd known that, despite his non-chalance, he still cared deeply about the affair, which was why he hadn't wanted to stay near any of those possible cities and had chosen to come see Chen Kuiyi. What occurred in his dream told him that he had cared all along, but not the way he cared in his dream. As he experienced deep emotions, he felt something on his belly, and he was woken up not by the stab of a knife but by a hand tapping him. He opened his eyes to see the old man standing before his bed, obviously back for his payment. It dawned on him that his friend had no standing at this bathhouse; he was in fact faring worse than back at the Chang-zhi highway construction site, where at least he was in charge of pig's ears and hearts. Aiguo had no intention of getting into an argument over ten yuan, so he opened his locker, took the money from his pocket, and handed it to the old man, who took it and laid a tally on his bed.

"Don't spend a night if you can't afford it," he mumbled.

He would have had every right to complain if Aiguo had not paid, but he was still grumbling even after taking Aiguo's money. Angered, Aiguo sat up to argue with him but cautioned himself to avoid an altercation when he was alone in a strange town. Besides, he would make it hard for his friend to do his job if he had a squabble with a coworker. So he lay back down, pretending not to have heard the old man. But he tossed and turned, unable to go back to sleep, not because of the unpleasantness with the old man over ten yuan, but because of the dream, which brought back a jumble of thoughts. So much had happened over the years, including his mother's death and his fling with Zhang Chuhong at Old Li's Gourmet Food Court. Everything entered his mind, one thing after another, eventually prompting him to sit up and smoke two cigarettes with his arms around his knees, though that did nothing to drive away unpleasant thoughts. He looked up at one point and saw himself in the mirror on the wall; he was surprised to see that he was turning gray, even though he was only thirty-five. Somehow that minor shock made him sense that he was hungry, and he recalled that he had skipped dinner; he'd been too busy looking for Chen Kuiyi and a place to spend a night to get something to eat. He got up, dressed, and walked out of the bathhouse to find a diner. It was nearly midnight, and the shops along the street were closed; the streets were deserted, devoid of pedestrians, with only an occasional truck or two. The nights were cool at this time of year, and he shivered when a wind blew over. With no plan, he walked down the street, eventually spotting an open food stall under a lamppost, which saved the vendor the trouble of getting electric lights. The middle-aged vendor was adding water to his pot, while a middle-aged woman was making wontons next to him. They looked like husband and wife. Aiguo walked up to see their offerings—wontons, dumplings, and noodles with stewed mutton; he asked the price of each and learned that he'd paid less for the first two and more for the third elsewhere. A large bowl of noodles was three yuan, but two-fifty at other diners, but here they charged only two yuan for a small bowl, plus a free supply of shredded pickled vegetables. Aiguo sat down and ordered a large bowl of noodles with stewed mutton, then took out a cigarette. As he waited, a tractor trailer roared in from the outskirts and came to a screeching halt at the stall. Bags of chemical fertilizer were piled high in the truck's bed, pesticide in the trailer. The tires on both the truck and the trailer were nearly flat, a clear indication that they were overloaded. Three men jumped down off the cab. One was in his fifties, one in his thirties, and the last one in his twenties. Aiguo knew, as soon as they started talking, that the one in his thirties was in charge, for he asked the prices and decided what they would eat. The other two simply went along. The crew-cut man in charge asked, "How much is a bowl of dumplings, Boss?"

"Three-fifty."

"How many are there?"

"Thirty."

"Give us two bowls."

"Two bowls for three people? Who's not eating?" the woman asked.

"We're all going to eat." Crew-cut banged the table. "Can't you divide the sixty dumplings into three bowls?"

"Sure, I can do that." The man laughed. "But I've never seen anyone eat like this."

"Well, it'll be a first for you then."

Aiguo didn't pay them much attention. His noodles arrived. He peeled a few cloves of garlic and started in on the noodles. They were good, but the soup was too salty for his taste, so he asked the woman to add a ladleful of broth. It tasted just right after he added some vinegar. The noodles warmed him up enough that his forehead was sweaty and his appetite returned. He ordered four flatbreads. The truckers' dumplings were ready by the time Aiguo finished two of them. As they ate their dumplings, the lead man asked, "How much are the mutton noodles, Boss?"

"Two-fifty for a large bowl; two for a small one."

"Give us three small ones, but put them in large bowls and add some chopped scallions and noodle soup."

Aiguo could tell the man knew what he was doing. They could eat their fill without spending too much, and the extra soup warmed them up.

"You three must be from Yanjin," the vendor said with a smile.

"How did you know?" Crewcut said.

"Yanjin people are pesky."

In Henan, "pesky" referred to troublemakers, which Aiguo understood. The Yanjin men laughed, as did Aiguo, who recalled that his mother had been born in Yanjin. So he turned and asked the woman, "How far is Yanjin from here?"

"About a hundred li, the next county over."

Aiguo had come to Henan to pretend to search for Pang Lina and Old Shang, but had ended up in Hua County because he happened to recall an old friend, Chen Kuiyi. He hadn't realized that Hua County was so close to Yanjin. By accident, a fake search for his wife had nearly led him to his mother's hometown. Then another thought occurred to him; before his mother died, she had lost her ability to talk, so she'd strained to rap on her bed in search of a letter. At the time, they had not understood why she was doing that, so she had failed to find the letter, which Aiguo had discovered by chance. After reading the letter, he knew why his mother had been looking for it; she probably wanted someone to phone someone named Jiang Surong in Yanjin and ask her to come to Qinyuan before her death. She might have had something to say or a question to ask. Aiguo had been calm before these thoughts occurred to him, but now that they had resurfaced, he put down his bowl of noodles, got up, walked around the table, and went to sit by the three truckers.

"Where do you live in Yanjin?"

The older and the younger men both remained quiet, while the man in his thirties glanced at Aiguo and replied after detecting no ill will from him.

"On North Street in the county town. Why?"

Aiguo moved his stool up. "Do you know a woman named Jiang Surong?"

The man shook his head and looked at the other two, who considered the inquiry and also shook their heads.

"Which street does she live on? What does she do?" the older man asked.

"I don't know which street, but I know she's in the cotton-fluffing business."

"No one does that anymore." The older man laughed.

"There are thousands of people in Yanjin. We couldn't possibly know every one of them," the younger man joined in.

The truckers finished their meal. Obviously in a hurry to get back on the road, Crew-cut paid up and waved to the other two. They climbed into the cab and the truck sped away.

If he hadn't come out that night for dinner, Niu Aiguo would have stayed in Hua County for two or three weeks before returning to Qinyuan. But after learning that Yanjin was not far away, he boarded a bus for there early the next morning. He had never felt any connection to Yanjin before but seemed tightly bound up with the place after recalling the letter his mother had struggled to find before her death. At first he hadn't thought there was any point in calling Jiang Surong, since his mother was gone. Now, especially because his mother was dead, he wanted to find the woman and ask her if she knew why

360

his mother had wanted to see her and what questions she might have meant to ask. He could not ask her anymore, so maybe he would find answers from Jiang Surong, the woman his mother had wanted to see. Moses Wu's offspring had made contact with Jiang Surong eight years earlier, so Aiguo hoped to find out more about Moses when he got to Yanjin. It had been two decades since Moses Wu's death, but he might have said something before dying. According to the letter of eight years before, Moses Wu's grandson had traveled from Xianyang to Yanjin to see Cao Qing'e, who had done nothing about it until just before her death, when it had obviously become very important to her. Aiguo would not have recalled all this if he hadn't run into the Yanjin truckers, but now that he had, he was determined to get to the bottom of things. At first, he thought he would be doing it for his mother's sake, but soon he realized it was for himself, as if he had a mysterious connection with Moses Wu from seventy years before. For one thing, Moses Wu had been one of his mother's fathers; for another, he and Moses shared similarities in their life experience, though they were seventy years apart, at least in their fake search for a woman. Why hadn't Moses Wu ever returned to Yanjin after losing Qiaoling, Aiguo's mother, Cao Qing'e, in the process? It would do them no good if Aiguo found out why, since they were both deceased, but it might help untie the knot in his heart to have all the answers. Every lock has a key, but he did not expect the key to his problems to be hidden in something from seventy years earlier. Now he could see why a calmness had come over him, and why Hua County had felt welcoming. He had thought that was because it was an agreeable place, but it turned out that it was because of its proximity to Yanjin. This would be his first trip to Yanjin, despite its close connection to him. Before leaving Jade Pool Bath City, Aiguo left a note for Chen Kuiyi. He didn't tell Kuiyi he was going to Yanjin, not to hide the trip from his friend, but because the reasons behind his journey were too involved to explain in a simple note. He only wrote:

Old Chen,
Something urgent came up back home in Shanxi, so I have to leave. I'm glad to have seen you again. I'll return and we can talk. Take care of yourself.
Niu Aiguo

When he finished, instead of giving the note to people working at the bathhouse, as he knew that Kuiyi did not get along with at least some of his coworkers, he left it with a woman tending a cigarette stand outside the bathhouse. Her look of reluctance prompted him to buy a pack of cigarettes, after which he headed for the depot to catch a bus for Yanjin.

He had no idea how big Yanjin was until he got there; it was much bigger than either Hua County or Qinyuan. In the middle of the town was a pagoda, beyond whose ground was the Jin River, which flowed majestically down the center of town. People swarmed around the bridge over the river, carrying goods on poles over their shoulders, pushing carts, and selling vegetables, meat, fruits, or odds and ends. The town was equipped with loudspeakers that played Henan operas, operas from ballads, and two-string operas. Besides the common Henan tunes, he also heard opera from Wuxi and Shanxi, an indication that Yanjin was frequented by people from all over. With a county town of this size, it would not be easy to find someone with a name but no known address. He started in the morning and by noon had gone from East Street to West Street and then North Street to South Street, but he wasn't anywhere near finding Jiang Surong. He was convinced that the Yanjin truckers were telling the truth when they told him they had no idea who she was. Jiang Surong had included her address and phone number in the letter to Aiguo's mother from eight years earlier, and Aiguo had held on to it, first in Niu Village and later in the rental house in Nanguan. He thought of calling his sister's husband in Qinyuan and asking him to retrieve the letter from his Nanguan house in order to tell him the address and phone number. But fearful that he might let slip his fake search for Pang Lina and Old Shang, he decided against the idea and continued to ask around. Finally, his determination paid off, when he reached a man selling stewed rabbit legs at Beiguan Train Station. The man, also surnamed Jiang, was in fact a member of the extended Jiang family, and, with directions from him, Aiguo located Jiang Surong near a theater on South Street.

Jiang Surong turned out to be a woman in her late thirties whose grandfather was Jiang Long. Back when Aiguo's mother was alive, she had told him a lot about Yanjin and the Jiang family, which gave him a general idea of what the place and her family were like. But everything turned out to be quite different from his mental image when he got to Yanjin and met Jiang Surong. She wasn't even born when Cao Qing'e came to Yanjin and the Jiang family had been fluffing cotton, a trade they later gave up. The dozen or so people in Jiang Long and Jiang Gou's generation had grown into several dozen, and they were engaged in all kinds of work. Jiang Surong, for instance, owned a sundry shop selling cigarettes, liquor, soy sauce, vinegar, pickled vegetables, instant noodles, soft drinks, and mineral water, with a freezer by the door carrying popsicles and ice cream. It even had a name, Surong Retail Shop. Before getting the address from one of the Jiang relatives, Aiguo had made three trips back and forth on South Street, but had missed the name on the sign. After getting Aiguo's name but not the reason behind his visit, Jiang Surong was on her guard, for she thought at first he must have come to see her about some difficult matter in Henan, to borrow money or something. He was able to put her mind at ease by telling her he wanted to know more about the past. She sighed mournfully when she heard of the passing of Cao Qing'e.

"I wish I'd had a chance to meet this grand aunt of mine."

Incredibly, however, she knew nothing about Moses Wu's grandson's visit to Yanjin, or the letter she had written, asking Qing'e to return to Yanjin.

"Didn't you write the letter, Cousin?"

"No, I didn't. I have absolutely no idea what the man wanted to say. You see, I'm not a patient woman, and I don't like writing letters. Luo Anjiang wrote it for me."

She told Aiguo that Moses Wu had changed his name to Luo Changli seventy years earlier, after fleeing to Xianyang, which was why his grandson was called Luo Anjiang. When Luo Anjiang wrote the letter, he did not think he could explain the twists and turns of his grandfather's life clearly, so he put down Moses Wu as his grandfather's name. Aiguo wondered why Moses Wu had changed his name and what might have happened, but he did not have time for seventy-year-old details. He wanted to know first about eight years earlier.

"What did Luo Anjiang tell you when he was here?"

"I don't remember much except that he wanted to meet your mother. His family name must have been Yang, so he should have gone to Yang Village after coming to Yanjin, but he didn't. He came here instead because he wanted to find your mother."

"How long did he stay here? Did he talk to anyone?" Aiguo asked.

"It looked like he was weighed down by something, because he barely touched his food and didn't talk to anyone. He went back to Shaanxi two weeks later, when he received no reply from your mother."

"If he wanted to meet her so badly, why didn't he go directly to Shanxi after getting our address from you?"

"That's what I said. In fact, I could tell the day after he arrived that he wasn't sure if he really wanted to meet her. He'd meet her if she came, but he would never go to Shanxi." Jiang Surong added, "I don't know what he was worried about."

It didn't matter what Luo Anjiang's misgivings were; Aiguo had traveled from Hua County to Yanjin for nothing, like trying to scoop water with a bamboo basket, as the locals would say. Jiang Surong had a younger brother, Jiang Luoma, who was in his early twenties and drove people around in a three-wheeler. He happened to stop by his sister's shop for some water when Aiguo and his sister were talking. He asked her who the stranger was; he was curious about Aiguo's trek to Yanjin over something from eight years earlier, once he learned who Aiguo was. He stuck around to listen in on their conversation. His curiosity increased when he realized that Aiguo had not come all the way only to learn what had happened eight years before, but also for some seventy-year-old matters. He was gripped by the story, while his sister was getting bored. Aiguo stopped asking questions when he saw that Jiang Surong had little to add. That afternoon, her brother gave Aiguo a tour of the Yanjin County town in his three-wheeler. A chatterbox himself, he told Aiguo what had taken place seventy years earlier as he pointed out various sights. When they got to a spot on West Street, he told Aiguo that was the house where Moses Wu and Wu Xiangxiang had made steamed buns. It was now a plant that made pickled vegetables. Then they came to a roundabout on North Street, which, according to Jiang Luoma, had been the church site of the Italian priest, Old Zhan; it was now occupied by Golden Basin Foot Bathhouse. By the tobacco factory under the bridge on East Street, there had once been a well, the one Moses Wu had come to as a water carrier. When they returned to South Street, Luoma pointed to the theater by his sister's shop and told Aiguo that it had been the spot where Moses Wu had cowed the Jiang brothers. The stoneroller still stood to the side of the theater entrance. He had gotten all this information from family members; he was the only one left in Yanjin to have any knowledge of that past. Unfamiliar with either present-day Yanjin or the Yanjin of seventy years before, Aiguo had little inkling of the sequence of events related to him.

"You came all the way from Shanxi to Yanjin, not just to ask about what had happened seventy years ago, is that right?" Jiang Luoma asked.

Aiguo was taken aback and asked, "What do you think I'm here for?"

"I've been wondering about that all afternoon. You could be looking for some object if it were about the present, but what could a steamed bun vendor have left behind seventy years ago?"

"It would have been so much easier if it were an object."

How was he going to tell Jiang Luoma about the torturous path of his journey, from the death of his mother to Lina's second affair and his fake search for her and Old Shang, to his trip to Hua County to see Chen Kuiyi and the encounter with the three truckers from Yanjin, and eventually his visit to Yanjin in search of stories from seventy years earlier? In fact, it would only get more tangled if he even tried. All he could say was "Let's say it was an object. I didn't find it."

That answer animated Jiang Luoma, who said, "Will you go to Yang Village?"

That was where Moses Wu, or Luo Changli, had been born and raised, so he should pay a visit, but Moses Wu never returned there after fleeing to Xianyang and changing his name to Luo Changli. Nor had he ever returned to Yanjin. Luo Anjiang had not gone there when he came to see Yanjin, so it didn't make much sense for Aiguo to go there.

"No, I'm not going to Yang Village. I'm going to Xianyang to see Luo Anjiang."

Jiang Luoma had not expected that.

"You're more stubborn than me, Older Brother. I've never met anyone quite like you."

The next day, Aiguo asked Jiang Surong for Luo Anjiang's address in Xianyang. Eight years earlier, Luo Anjiang had been hesitant about going to Shaanxi, but Aiguo was decisive about his trip to Xianyang. Luo Anjiang's hesitation only intensified Aiguo's determination to go see him, not just to see him, but also to find out if Luo Changli, or Moses Wu, had left any last words seventy years before. Moses Wu had gone to Shaanxi from Henan seven decades earlier, and now, seven decades later, Niu Aiguo was making the same trip. A quick calculation told him that Moses Wu had been twenty-one when he left for Shaanxi, while he himself was well into his thirties as he embarked on a similar journey. He had left Qinyuan to conduct a fake search for his wife and her lover, but after traveling all this time, he was now going to Shaanxi on a real search for Moses Wu. Seven decades earlier, Moses Wu had also left Yanjin on a fake search for his wife and lover. No one could have predicted that in seven decades, one man on a fake search would be on a real quest for another man who had feigned such a search. He felt like laughing over the absurdity of events.

Jiang Surong was surprised to hear his travel plans, but she did not try to stop him.

Niu Aiguo boarded a bus to a place called Xinxiang, where he took a train bound for Lanzhou. He could not find a seat on the jam-packed train and had to stand in the aisle for a day and a night. Someone stole his wallet out of his pants' pocket, when he dozed off on his feet. He still had the train ticket, however, in his shirt pocket, luckily not in his wallet. The train arrived in Xianyang in the afternoon of the following day. With the ticket and his bag, he walked out of the station, imagining how inconvenient it would be if he were to meet Luo Anjiang for the first time when he was penniless; besides, Anjiang might get the wrong idea about his visit. He silently cursed the loathsome pickpocket; by itself, losing his money was no big deal, but it could delay his important business. He went to the train station warehouse and earned eight hundred yuan carrying loads for five days. Normally a porter could only make about four hundred yuan for five days' work, but Niu worked day and night to make that much, until he lost count of how many loads he'd carried. Money in hand, he walked out of the warehouse early on the sixth day and went to the train station plaza, where he bought some water from a stand. After drinking the water, the fatigue from five exhausting days caught up with him. It was still early, with few passengers around, so he lay down on one of the bench seats for travelers, using his bag as a pillow, with the idea of taking a nap. He was asleep the moment he stretched out. It was still early morning when he awoke, and the sun had yet to rise, giving him the impression that he'd just taken a nap. But the woman selling water told him he'd slept for a whole day. She hadn't paid him much attention, she said, when he was sleeping the day before. But she returned that morning to see him still sleeping and thought he might be sick. He woke up on his own just as she was about to wake him. He had awakened only because of an urgent need to use the toilet, not because he'd had enough sleep. Then he noticed sweat stains on his arms; he must have sweated during his sleep, and the sweat had dried before he sweated again. With an embarrassed smile, he told the woman he was fine, he just needed a good sleep. He went first to the toilet and emptied his bladder before going into the station to wash his arms, wipe his chest, and clean his face; he felt refreshed. After breakfast at a stand in an alley, he followed the address he'd written down in Yanjin to find Luo Anjiang's house at 128 Shuiyu Temple Lane, Deli Street, Xianyang. He did not think he would have much trouble locating the place, not with the exact address in hand. He got there, but only to be told that Luo had died eight years earlier, and was survived by a wife and two children.

His wife, He Yufen, was a thin, frail woman in her forties with a fair complexion. Their older child, a young man in his late teens, was away working, while the younger one, a ten- or eleven-year-old girl, was in primary school. Yufen was astonished when he told her the reason for his visit, but she was patient and accommodating. Starting with her accounts of Moses Wu, that is, Luo Changli, and ending with her husband, she spent two hours telling him about what had happened over the past seventy years. She did not look annoyed when retelling the past; perhaps she'd had no one to talk to after her husband's death. She was so unlike Jiang Surong, who had grown impatient in the midst of her own narration. Yufen spoke at a measured pace, and she stopped to glance at Aiguo when she finished one part of the story, smiling to mark the end.

Moses Wu had sold flatbreads in Xianyang, she told him. He'd also sold sesame flatbreads, baked wheaten cakes, a Henan specialty, and meat from cow's and sheep's heads. He'd worn a white cap all day, like a member of the Hui people. She heard that he had gone to Baoji to look for someone before coming to Xianyang. Not finding the person there, he had returned to Xianyang, where he'd married and had three boys and a girl, who later gave him more than a dozen grandchildren. After marrying Luo Anjiang, Yufen knew that Luo Changli had not had much to say to his own wife, or with his sons or their wives. With the grandchildren, he also had little to say to any of them, except for Luo Anjiang, causing everyone in the family to complain that he played favorites. Her mother-in-law had told her that Luo Changli had said that Luo Anjiang resembled someone else the moment he was born. The grandfather began talking to the boy when he turned five; they slept in the same bed and could talk late into the night. After he was married, Luo Anjiang chose Grandpa Luo Changli over Yufen to talk to. It had been twenty years since Luo Changli died. When Luo Anjiang discovered he had stomach cancer, he insisted on going to Yanjin in Henan, saying he was concerned about something Grandpa Changli had said. He'd put it out of his mind until he was ill and realized that he had little time left; he wanted to find Qiaoling, the daughter Grandpa had lost, before he died. He would naturally give up if he couldn't find her, but if he could, he would tell her in person what her father had said. The effort alone would put his mind at ease, whether he found her or not.

No one in the Luo family would agree to the trip since he was so ill, but three days before the Autumn Festival, he sneaked out when no one was paying attention and went to the train station to buy a ticket for Henan. He then spent two weeks in Yanjin without finding Qiaoling, so he returned and died three months later. Yufen had not expected Qiaoling's son, Niu Aiguo, to come looking for him eight years later. She gave him another look when this part of the story came to an end, but didn't smile this time; instead, she sighed emotionally with her hands over her face. Aiguo was reminded of what Jiang Surong had said about Luo Anjiang, who, during his two weeks in Yanjin, had looked heavy-hearted and barely ate anything. Now Aiguo knew that not only had he been downcast, but he had also been suffering physical pain. Obviously, he had also been the type who kept everything hidden, which had likely escaped Aiguo's mother eight years before. If she had known that he was seriously ill, she might have made the trip to Yanjin. He had to wonder why his mother had chosen not to meet him and, if he really wanted to meet her, why he had not gone to Qinyuan. They did not meet when they could have. She then felt a sudden urge to meet Luo Anjiang just before she died, just as he had done when he was near the end of his life. She had no idea he had been dead for eight years. They chose not to meet probably because they did not want to deal with the past, but then why had they changed their minds before dying? Aiguo was confounded by the intricacy of the human mind.

"Do you know what Grandpa said to Older Brother?"

The Grandpa, of course, was Moses Wu, or Luo Changli, and the Older Brother was Luo Anjiang.

"He and I had little to say to each other." She shook her head. "So he rarely revealed what was on his mind to me."

"Then who did he talk to?"

"Not to his children either. He has a cousin named Luo Xiaopeng. They spent a lot of time together."

"Is he home?"

"He took my son to work in Guangdong. That way uncle and nephew could look after each other."

"Do you have their phone number?"

"The life of a migrant worker is tough. They move around a lot, staying in Zhuhai for a while before moving to Shantou, then Dongguan. With no fixed address, there's no contact number."

Apparently, he would have to locate Luo Xiaopeng somewhere in Guangdong if he wanted to find out what Luo Changli had said. It became clear to him that trying to learn something that was seventy years old would not be easy. He wasn't sure if he should go to Guangdong, not because it would be hard to find Luo Xiaopeng or because he had neither the time nor the money, but because Luo Changli's having much to say to his grandson was entirely different from his grandson's having much to say to his cousin. They would have spoken about many things, precisely because they could talk easily. How would he know if Luo Anjiang had mentioned to his cousin what their grandfather had said to him? Even if he had, it had to do with Luo Changli and Qing'e, not with Luo Xiaopeng, who might or might not have remembered.

When she was done with her story, Yufen took Aiguo into the main room to look at pictures of Moses Wu and of her husband. One of the framed pictures on the wall was a family photo, in which Luo Changli, or Moses Wu, was a tall, thin, old man with a pointed head and a goatee. He sat in the middle, looking straight ahead. His grandfather was a total stranger, of course, since they had never met. Luo Anjiang stood to the side, looking stern, staring straight ahead, like Moses. Before seeing the picture, Aiguo had imagined his newfound cousin to have big eyes, not the small, squinty eyes in the photo. Earlier, when Yufen told him that Moses Wu had said that Anjiang looked like someone else shortly after he was born, Aiguo thought Luo Changli must have been referring to Aiguo's mother, Cao Qing'e, or Qiaoling, which explained the close relationship between him and the grandson. But Luo Anjiang did not look like Aiguo's mother at all, so obviously Moses Wu meant someone else. Who could it be? Aiguo could not figure that out. Yufen then took him into another room, where she took out a sheet of paper and said that Moses Wu had treasured the sheet of paper. He had passed it on to Luo Anjiang, who had also treasured it and kept it in the chest. He would not let anyone see it. It was yellowed and worm-eaten in spots. Aiguo opened it and saw it was the drawing of a grand house, apparently a church, with a cross on its dome, as well as a large clock. It was an impressive drawing but, without knowing anything of its origin or purpose, he did not know what to make of it, despite its exactitude to a real church. He turned the sheet over and saw two lines of writing; the first line was in tiny calligraphy, "Satan's murmur," the second one in fountain pen ink, "I'll set a fire, if not murder." The handwriting was different, obviously by different hands, and blurry in places. His heart skipped a beat when he read the lines, but with the owner gone, he would never know who wrote them or under what circumstances they were written, let alone what they meant. Yet he gave it a try and studied for a while without getting any sense out of them, except that they both seemed harsh, a mental state not unfamiliar to him. With a sigh, he folded the paper and handed it to Yufen, who put it back into the chest.

They continued talking after dinner.

"You've traveled from Shanxi to Yanjin, then from Yanjin to Xianyang. You didn't make the trip just to know more about the past, did you?"

She appeared to be a mild-mannered woman and easy to talk to. They had just met, and did not know each other well, making her the perfect person to unburden to. Besides, he had been traveling alone, with no one to talk to, and was bursting with words. He told her everything, from his mother's hospitalization and her death to Lina's second affair, which meant he had to talk about her first affair and his sojourn in Cangzhou, as well as his fake search this time and his journey to Hua Country, Yanjin, and then Xianyang. It felt good to talk. He sighed when he was finally done.

"I know I'm using this search for my mother's past as a diversion from my own problems."

She too sighed. "I don't think you should continue, if that's what you're thinking."

"How so?"

"You won't feel any better even if you find what you're looking for."

"What do you mean?"

"I can tell that what's bothering you is more serious than your search."

His heart raced, for she was right about what had been weighing him down, something he had not been able to grasp. They talked until midnight and then went to sleep in separate rooms. After washing his feet, Niu lay down on the bed and tossed and turned, still unable to sleep when the clock in the main room struck three o'clock. He could hear Yufen and her daughter snoring in the next room. He got up and draped a jacket over his shoulders before walking out into the yard, where there was a locust tree. He moved a stool over to sit under the tree, head down, engrossed in his own thoughts. At some point, he jerked his head up to see a half moon hanging right above him. It was very bright. A gust of wind rustled the leaves, creating shadows that swayed over his head. It reminded him of eight months before, when he had seen a similar moon at Old Li's Gourmet Food Court. The moon back then had been much bigger than this one. He had been on his return journey after delivering tofu to Dezhou from Cangzhou. The radiator on the truck had broken, so he'd left his truck at Old Li's diner. There was also a locust tree in the yard. It was the same night he and Zhang Chuhong had started their affair, after which they'd gotten closer and had more to say to one another. They could talk all night without feeling tired, sleepy, or hungry. One day sometime later, she'd wrapped her arms around him in bed and asked him to take her away, away from Botou. Not his usual self that night, he'd changed into another man and agreed on the spot. She'd tightened her arms around him when she heard his answer.

"I have something to say to you, now that you've agreed."

"What is it?"

"Not now. I'll tell you later."

Later, he'd used his mother's illness as an excuse to flee back home, after a conversation with Cui Lifan, the owner of Xueying Fish and Soy Products, for he was afraid that someone might be killed, that he couldn't get away with her. Seven months had gone by since that night. He hadn't had the nerve to recall the affair over the past seven months. Now the scene before his eyes brought it back, and he was hit by the feeling that what she had not said to him carried the same weight as what Moses Wu had wanted to say to Qiaoling. He might not be able to heal his troubled heart, even if he could go to Guangdong to find out what Moses had wanted to say to Qiaoling, while what Zhang Chuhong had not said could help unlock his heart.

He would have gone to Guangdong to find out what Moses had wanted to say to Qiaoling if he hadn't recalled his past with Chuhong, but not anymore.

Now he wanted to go see her. He had been too much of a coward to keep his promise to her seven months earlier. On this night, he seemed to gain courage, after his journey from Qinyuan to Hua County to Yanjin to Xianyang. He had backed out on the relationship with her, but something else made him braver seven months later. An emboldened Niu Aiguo was like Old Shang, who had dared to run off with Pang Lina.

The next morning, he went to a shop at the lane entrance and used the phone to call Old Li's Gourmet Food Court. The call went through, but the man who picked it up had a gruff voice; it wasn't Li Kun. Aiguo thought it might be the cook, Fatso the Third, so he asked, "Is Zhang Chuhong in?"

"No."

"Is she out grocery shopping or out of town for a few days?"

"She's been gone six months."

Shocked by the reply, Aiguo ventured another question.

"How about Li Kun?"

"Not here."

"Where is he?"

"No idea."

Something did not sound right to Aiguo, so he asked, "Is this Old Li's Gourmet Food Court?"

"It was, but not anymore."

"What is it now?"

"Old Ma's Auto Repair Shop."

He hung up. Something important must have happened. He decided he could not stop now, so he dialed Chuhong's cell phone, a number he had memorized but avoided using over the past seven months, afraid that she would come after him. Apprehension bolstered his courage, and he went ahead and dialed the number, his heart beating fast the whole time. He listened to a recording that said the number was no longer in service, intensifying his concern, now that he could not find either of them and did not know what had happened. He went back to Luo Anjiang's house to say good-bye to Yufen before heading to Botou. Surprised to hear that he would leave so soon, she asked him where he was going. Instead of telling her he was going to Botou, he said he would go back home to Qinyuan. She was relieved to hear his reply.

"I know you didn't sleep well last night. You probably miss your daughter."

Aiguo nodded and began to pack his things.

"I don't have anything to give you, except for parting advice."

"Which is?"

"Life is to be lived forward, not backward. I wouldn't be here today if I hadn't kept that in mind."

It was the same phrase his mother used. He nodded again and, after saying good-bye, went to the Xianyang station for a train to Shi Village, from where he boarded a bus to Botou and got off on the evening of the third day at what had been Old Li's Gourmet Food Court. It had been a clean little courtyard but now housed an auto repair shop, where the ground was stained with grease and littered with used parts. The enticing aroma of food, which had wafted in the air, had been replaced by the pungent smell of gasoline and engine oil. The owner of Old Ma's Auto Repair Shop was, naturally, called Old Ma, a fat, fortyish man with a square head. He bared his arms and had a tattoo of a panda on his shaved chest. Other men normally picked dragons or tigers or leopards for their tattoos; Aiguo found a bamboo-eating panda on a man's chest funny. Old Ma kept a little monkey in the yard, where Ma's mechanics were fixing vehicles when Aiguo arrived. Ma was using a whip to make the monkey do somersaults under the locust tree. It made Ma look even fatter. Not knowing Old Ma's relationship with Li Kun, Aiguo decided to hide the real purpose of his visit. Instead, he told Ma that he'd worked at Old Li's Gourmet Food Court seven months earlier and had come for owed wages. Old Ma cast him a glance before responding, with his eyes on the monkey.

"I can tell you're lying right off."

The moment Old Ma opened his mouth, Aiguo knew that he was from the Northeast and that his gruff voice was the one on the phone.

"Why?"

"You can say a lot of bad things about Old Li, but it's off the mark when you say he owed you wages."

Aiguo knew he'd made a mistake, for he was aware back when he and Li Kun were friends that Li Kun was a generous man. It had been snowing heavily when they first met, and Aiguo had been forced to stop at the diner; they had not known each other, but Li Kun had treated him to food and liquor. So Aiguo quickly corrected himself.

"I was in a hurry to leave and he didn't have enough cash on hand. I happened to be passing through today, so I stopped by to see him."

Ignoring Aiguo, Ma went back to training the monkey. Instead of having the monkey perform somersaults, he put a metal ring on a stool to make the animal jump through. The monkey was pretty good at somersaults, but not jumping hoops; it ran to the stool from three meters away at high speed but lost its nerve when it leaped into the air. Afraid to jump through the ring, it came to an abrupt stop in front of the stool, falling to the ground from its momentum. Ma was angry. Off to the side, a mechanic was soldering a welding rod against the outside of a vehicle, creating blue sparks with a sizzle. Ma pointed at the sparks and said to the monkey, "There's no point in being afraid. You think a metal ring is hard? Wait until you have to jump through a ring of fire."

The monkey apparently understood what Ma said, for it curled up under the tree and shook. It did not look like Ma would stop the training anytime soon, so Aiguo took a step forward.

"Can I have a word with you, Older Brother?"

Ma gave him another glance. He thought Aiguo wanted a job, so he sized him up.

"You have to work if you want to stay. Know anything about auto repair?"

Aiguo knew that Ma had misunderstood what he wanted, but he did not want to bring up his questions right away, afraid that Ma might ignore him again. Going along with Ma's line of thought, Aiguo said, "I drove one of those a few years."

Ma glared at Aiguo.

"You're lying again. Why would you be peeling onions at a diner if you knew how to drive?"

Aiguo pointed at the vehicles in the distance.

"Pick one out, and I'll show you."

It sounded like a challenge to Old Ma, who tied the monkey to the tree and pointed at a heap with no doors.

"Come with me to get some tires."

So the heap was Ma's ride. Aiguo could tell by now that the man with a panda tattoo on his chest was a no-nonsense man. Left with no choice, he tossed his bag into the back, started the engine, and drove Ma into town to buy tires. By the time they came back with over a dozen tires, the two men were fast friends. After Old Li's Gourmet Food Court had been turned into Old Ma's Auto Repair Shop, another roadside diner had sprung up next to Ma's place, called Jiuxian River Restaurant. It could be called a restaurant, but it wasn't all that different from Old Li's place, with three rooms and seven or eight tables and offering the same simple Kung Pao chicken and shredded pork with garlic. There was no river nearby, so it was anyone's guess where the name came from. It was dinnertime, so Aiguo treated Ma to a meal. Fat as he was, Ma had no capacity for alcohol and was drunk after a few glasses; once he had too much to drink, he turned into a different man, a bit like Feng Wenxiu, the butcher on East Street in Qinyuan. With the fierce eyes of a wasp and the rough voice of a jackal, Ma had a mean look but was forthcoming and friendly now that they had spent time together. Before Aiguo even started with his inquiry, Old Ma poured his heart out to him across the table. Originally from Huludao in Liaoning, Ma had been in the grain business and had run a bathhouse before opening an auto repair shop in his hometown. Something happened in Huludao and he was badly hurt, but he did not go into details about what that was. He was slurring his words by then, so Aiguo got the impression that there had been five incidents altogether. Someone had done him wrong in four of them, and the last one was his fault. So in the end, he'd come to Botou when Huludao disappointed him.

"I couldn't stay in Huludao any longer." Ma banged on the table. "So why couldn't I come to Hebei?" He drew close to Aiguo. "I don't bother anyone; I just train my monkey. Anything wrong with that?"

Aiguo nodded and did not change the subject until Ma took a break to light a cigarette.

"I can tell you're from the Northeast. Did you open the shop here because you're a friend of my old boss, Li Kun?"

"I met him. I sensed he was a decent man, when we negotiated the price for the spot. I didn't know him well; we met through a mutual friend."

Ma's reply put Aiguo's mind at ease.

"I thought the diner was doing well, so why he did he close it?"

"Something happened in his family." Ma seemed to be staring at him.

"What happened?"

"Old Li and his wife got divorced."

"Why?"

"She'd had an affair. I heard that Old Li hadn't known about it until one day, when they had a fight over something else, and in the heat of the moment, she told him."

Aiguo's heart skipped a beat; he must have been the third party. Zhang Chuhong had told her husband about their relationship, probably because she wanted to burn her bridges and she'd made up her mind to leave Old Li.

"She had no feelings for Old Li, but he cared about her too much. So they had a bit of a problem. I heard someone nearly got killed during the divorce."

Aiguo broke out in a cold sweat out of fright. He finished a cigarette and composed himself. "So they got divorced and she left," he said. "How would that affect his business?"

"You don't understand." Ma flicked his hand. "Old Li might have been hurt, just like me, feeling bad about Huludao and coming to Hebei."

"Where did he go?"

"I have no idea. Someone said he went to Inner Mongolia; someone else said Shandong."

"Where's his wife?"

"I heard she went to Beijing to be a streetwalker," Ma said emotionally. "You can tell how bad their marriage was if she'd rather walk the streets than be his wife."

Aiguo was speechless. It might have been him or something else that had led Chuhong and Li Kun to get a divorce, but no matter what, he was implicated. Seven months earlier, when he'd left Chuhong and fled back to Qinyuan, he'd been worried that since she had his address in Shanxi, she might decide to burn her bridges and look him up. But instead of going to see him, she'd burned her bridges in a different way and gotten a divorce. She hadn't called him over the past seven months either, which proved how disappointed she was. What he had learned only made him more eager to see her, and he did not care what she was doing; and he was no longer interested in knowing what she'd planned to say to him seven months earlier. He might have wanted to know before coming to Botou, but now he realized that whatever it was would no longer be meaningful, even if she told him, not after so much time had passed and their situations had changed. He wanted to find Chuhong now, not because of some unsaid words, but because of something he had to tell her. When he fled and let her down, he had been afraid that someone might die, but now it would be worth it if someone were to die because of what he wanted to say to her. Yet even that would not be possible now. Li Kun and Zhang Chuhong had gone their separate ways, which rendered pointless all the important matters of the past. He would have trouble finding her, precisely because none of that mattered anymore. Her cell phone was no longer in service, and she had a new number. When someone changed her cell phone number, it could only mean that she wanted to sever ties with her past. Old Ma said she'd gone to Beijing six months earlier, but Aiguo was not sure if that was true. Even if she had, it was hard to say whether she was still in the capital now or if she had left for some other place. Even if she was still in Beijing, the city was so big that he would not know where or how to find her. Aiguo recalled that she had mentioned some of her friends back when they were together. She was from Zhangjiakou, with a close friend named Xu Manyu, who had run a beauty shop before leaving for Beijing. He wondered if Chuhong had gone to Beijing to find her. She had told him that they hadn't had any contact in two or three years. He recalled that there was another friend, a schoolmate named Jiao Shuqing, who was a ticket seller at the Zhangjiakou

Train Station. He had a brainstorm; a train traveled all over, but a train station never moved, so he could go there to look her up. The people at the train station would know where she'd gone even if she'd left the job. When he found Shuqing, he would know whether she had kept in touch with Chuhong; even if they hadn't, Shuqing would be able to help him find Chuhong's family home. Then through her family he was sure he would eventually find her whereabouts and phone number.

He decided to leave for Zhangjiakou the next morning. With that in mind, he did a quick calculation; he had been on the road for more than three weeks since leaving Qinyuan, traveling from west to east, from north to south, from south to west, from west to east, and from south to north. His only concern was his daughter. The girl would be going back to school in a couple of days.

Before he set out for Zhangjiakou the next morning, he phoned his brother-in-law, Song Jiefang, at the distillery. He asked Jiefang to get the girl back in school, after telling him he could not return to Qinyuan just yet.

"Where are you?" Jiefang shouted into the phone.

"Far away. In Guangzhou."

"You haven't found Pan Lina and Old Shang, have you? Why don't you come home?"

"No. I have to keep looking."